THE CINNAMON ROLL ALPHAS

Tempting Fate

a **second-chance** romance

SARA WHITNEY

Tempting Fate: Special Edition

Copyright © 2022 Sara Whitney

Published by LoveSpark Press

This book is a work of fiction. Names, characters, places, and incidents are either products of the author's imagination or used fictitiously. Any resemblance to actual events, locales, or persons, living or dead, is entirely coincidental.

All rights reserved. No part of this publication can be reproduced or transmitted in any form or by any means, electronic or mechanical, without permission in writing from the author or publisher.

Copyediting: Victory Editing
Illustration: Elen Bushe
Cover Design: Noh Designs

Ebook ISBN: 978-1-953565-08-2
Print ISBN: 978-1-953565-09-9
Print Special Edition ISBN: 978-1-953565-16-7

First Edition: March 2022

v. 1.6

To Erin and Natalie.
Sandwiches can!

Second chances can be twice as hot

Faith Fox grew up rich, but she turned her back on the family fortune after her parents drove away the only boy she ever loved. And she's never regretted that decision—not even when her struggling non-profit runs out of funds and she has to rely on a corporate donation to keep it afloat. There's just one small problem: she's intimately acquainted with the man in charge of the money, and he's *definitely* holding a grudge.

Leo Morales' new job comes with all the power and influence he could ask for, but he hasn't forgotten the way Faith and her parents humiliated him when he had nothing. Unfortunately, the grant he oversees requires him to work side by side with the woman he's spent years trying to forget.

At first, Faith and Leo fight like hell to keep their reluctant collaboration strictly professional, but when a storm strands them in a tiny tent in the woods, the situation gets personal fast.

One sleeping bag. Two exes. Enough pent-up desire to power a whole town. But can their fragile new beginning survive once they're out of the woods and back to reality?

Keep in touch!

Scan to follow Sara

Newsletter, **free books,** social media, and more!

CONTENTS

Chapter 1	1
Chapter 2	12
Chapter 3	21
Fourteen Years Ago	31
Chapter 4	33
Chapter 5	42
Chapter 6	52
Chapter 7	63
Chapter 8	74
Chapter 9	85
Thirteen Years Ago	95
Chapter 10	99
Chapter 11	111
Chapter 12	122
Chapter 13	133
Chapter 14	143
Twelve Years Ago	154
Chapter 15	159
Chapter 16	171
Chapter 17	184
Chapter 18	197
Chapter 19	208
Chapter 20	220
Chapter 21	230
Chapter 22	242
Chapter 23	251
Chapter 24	260
Chapter 25	271
Chapter 26	283
Chapter 27	293

Chapter 28	303
Chapter 29	315
Chapter 30	326
Chapter 31	336
Epilogue	347
Acknowledgments	351
Also by Sara Whitney	353
Praise for Sara Whitney	355
About the Author	357

ONE

Faith Fox pushed open the restroom door and let the *tap tap tap* of her shoes carry her to the sink. She braced her hands on the marble countertop and peered in the mirror.

"Fancy meeting you here," she murmured. Her reflection didn't look amused.

Only twenty minutes of conversation with her parents and Faith felt flushed and ruffled, but she didn't dare splash water on her cheeks for fear she'd disturb her carefully applied makeup.

Instead, she tugged her jacket down, hoping it covered the top of her skirt. She'd scavenged her only tweed suit from the back of the closet, and it was snugger than the last time she'd been forced into dinner with her family. She prayed the button on her waistband would hold.

Faith ran her hands over the severe bun that had tamed her hair, checking again that the streaks of electric blue were hidden thanks to her strategic straightening, twisting, and pinning. There was no need to cause conniption fits among the gentlepeople dining at the country club tonight; just knowing the color was there made her brave enough.

Pressing the backs of her fingers to her cheeks, she tried to smile reassuringly at her reflection. "You got this. You'll eat some salad and drop one tiny question and say good night. It's ninety more minutes in hell, tops."

Having failed to pacify her reflection, Faith slunk out of the ladies' room, limping a bit courtesy of the blister forming on her pinky toe. Damn high heels. She paused in the lobby to take the weight off her aching foot, studying the restaurant's forest-green walls and gilt-framed hunting scenes as she did.

Faith hated gilt frames. And hunting scenes. And forest green.

Desperate for an excuse not to return to her table and the unthinkable task she had to undertake, she glanced to her left where the mannequin-faced hostess was having a tense conversation with a customer who was obviously spoiling for a fight.

The man wore dark pants and a wrinkled button-down shirt, and he couldn't have looked more out of place at the Beaucoeur Country Club restaurant. Beyond his rumpled appearance, there was something almost dangerous about the barely leashed stillness of his tall frame. He was coiled and ready to spring. Faith drifted closer, observing the clenching and unclenching of his fist where it pressed against his leg.

"And there's no way you can bend the rules?" he growled.

"I'm sorry, sir. No exceptions," said the cool blond hostess, ending their argument by holding up a blue blazer.

The man snarled and turned his back on the hostess, giving Faith her first glimpse of his face. At first all she saw were wild black curls and an untamed beard.

Then she saw his eyes.

"Leo?" she choked out. Those eyes snapped up to hers, and just like that, the years fell away and her shock shifted to a wild bolt of joy. It was Leo Morales. *Her* Leo. Bigger now, broader than he'd been. But it was *Leo*.

His scowl dissolved, and the corners of his lips curved upward as he stepped toward her. She started moving too, until they were standing in front of each other.

"Hi." She was suddenly breathless.

"Faith." He rasped out her name and his head was tilting down, and she was lifting her chin and waiting for the press of his lips on her mouth like it was the most natural thing in the world. Like it hadn't been twelve years. Like he hadn't broken her heart the last time she'd seen him. Just like she'd broken his.

"*Ahem*." The hostess cleared her throat and waved the blazer, shattering the strange moment.

The synapses in Faith's brain kicked back into gear, and she blurted out, "What are you doing here?"

He straightened abruptly, the warmth draining from his eyes. "Amazing who they'll let in these days, isn't it?"

She pulled back in dismay. "No, I didn't mean it like—"

"Of course you didn't." Leo cocked his head, his narrowed, glittering eyes undercutting the casual gesture. "I'm sure foxy little Faith meets guys like me for dinner here all the time."

Faith sucked in a breath but wasn't able to hide the tremor that ran through her body. The glow of seeing him again receded under the weight of the disdain rolling off him. How was he still so angry?

Leo glanced to the right and waved at two older men in suits who'd just entered the restaurant. "Great catching up with you, duchess. Let's get together soon, maybe talk tennis? Share stock tips?"

Turning on his heel, he snatched the garment from the hostess, shrugged it on in one smooth movement, and turned to greet the rest of his party.

Faith stood frozen, alarmed to feel tears dancing along the underside of her lashes. The hostess caught her eye and raised a perfectly arched brow in curiosity. She sneered back and turned her spine into a steel girder, willing her racing heart to stop slamming against her sternum. Leo was still angry with her? Fine. That road ran both ways. It might have faded over the years, but she still carried that hurt with her too. Also guilt, but dwelling on that wasn't going to help anything right now. Nothing to be done but get through dinner, head home, and run a bath so hot it would scald this whole night from her memory.

Still, what a colossal joke, Leo crossing her path today of all days.

Cursing under her breath, she minced across the dining room in her too-tight suit, wondering if his eyes were tracking her progress under the soft restaurant lights. She hoped not for several reasons—not the least of which was what a catastrophe a meeting between Leo and her parents would be. And God, her toes throbbed.

"Good, you're back." Her father didn't even wait for her to slide into her seat and return her napkin to her lap before slicing into the thick slab of prime rib that had been delivered while she was away from the table.

Faith and her mother exchanged a rare moment of mother/daughter unity and rolled their eyes together over the unabashed display of carnivorism.

Faith picked up her fork, speared a bite of salmon, and yanked the Band-Aid off. "Mom, Dad, can I ask you a favor?"

Her parents' eyes flew to her in unison, and now she really *was* flushed. Damn Leo for rattling her so much that she'd just vomited out the question that she was there to ask. So much for trying to finesse it.

No. No more thinking about Leo. She just had to get through this humiliating parental episode.

"I beg your pardon?" Her father's round face hung slack as he stared at her.

Faith bit her lip before barreling ahead, offering her parents the brightest smile and perkiest voice she could manage. After all, this was why she'd agreed to dinner, dressed in a suit, and troweled on the makeup. She wasn't going to let anything knock her off her game. "I'm just having some housing difficulties and need a temporary place to live."

Her mother's preternaturally smooth forehead didn't so much as crease as the corners of her mouth turned down. "Someplace temporary? Why on earth?"

"Typical renter problems!" Faith's forced cheer was making all her pronouncements sound far too chipper, but the tone alone wasn't enough of an answer for the duo raising their eyebrows at her over their wineglasses. Her nerves started to leak through, causing her to burble more of the story than she'd intended. "My landlord sold the house, and the new owner decided to do some major renovations and jack up the rent once my lease is up next month. That doesn't leave me with much time to find a new rental, and I'm kind of limited in my options."

"I'm not understanding where the favor comes in." Franklin Fox blinked at her behind his rimless glasses, no doubt processing the shock at his independent daughter making any kind of request.

You and me both, pal. Faith was equally surprised that she was even considering this. Still, what choice did she have?

"It turns out I don't have *quite* enough for first and last month's rent at the places I walked through." She kept her chin up and her voice strong. "You know I haven't asked you for anything since high school graduation, so I was thinking—"

Her father scoffed and sliced off another bite of prime rib. "What, that job of yours doesn't keep you afloat?"

It took every ounce of her willpower not to shrink into the high-backed wooden chair at the disdain in his voice. "Ah. Well."

That halted the progress of her father's fork entirely, and he turned to her mother. "I'm sure we're misunderstanding our daughter, Betsy. Because it sounds like she's saying that she's wasting her time at some do-gooder outfit that doesn't even *pay her* properly."

Franklin's voice rose at the end of the sentence, and Betsy cast her eyes around her as if to gauge which of their friends might have overheard his outburst. Faith's irritation overrode her nerves, and even though it was the absolute last thing she should do, she opened her mouth to defend her job.

"Beaucoeur BUILD isn't some..." But she bit back that dead-end argument. It hadn't worked once in the past seven years. Instead, she exhaled on a count of five. *Kind.*

Calm. Collected. Her therapist's suggested mantra to get herself through difficult conversations was getting a workout tonight. "I'm in charge. I pay myself. And if I needed to reinvest some of my salary to keep it running—"

"Ridiculous," her father snapped. "I want to know where in your college studies you learned that you give away your work for free."

Faith laced her fingers together tightly in her lap to hide her frustration. She'd launched the tutoring center to help the underserved students in the Beaucoeur public schools rather than joining the family business as her father had always expected. And although her nonprofit had helped countless kids succeed in grade school and high school and even get into college, arguing the point with her father yet again wouldn't win this argument.

"I just need some help while I wait on some funding to come in," she muttered, already regretting everything. Maybe she could stay with Thea for a bit.

But by now her mother had recovered from her initial surprise, and her aquiline nose practically twitched in excitement. "How long a wait?"

Trust Mom to figure it out first. Her dad might think he was head of the household, but Betsy always had been faster at the uptake.

"Not long," she said, not fighting the sag this time and letting defeat wash over her as the weight of her imploding life pressed down on her chest. "I'm applying for a grant that'll carry me through the next two years."

"Mmm." Her father's skeptical tone rankled.

Feeling like the teenager she'd been the last time she asked her parents for anything, she sighed. "I just... *Please.* I've already had to lay off two people, and I can't afford to lose any more. I need one tiny little favor."

Sure. It might be tiny to Franklin and Betsy, but to Faith, it was the difference between success and watching her dreams get crushed in a trash compactor.

"We're not reinstating your trust fund. Absolutely not." Franklin practically bellowed his pronouncement, then viciously sawed a hunk off his meat. "You made your choices, and you'll live with them."

"I don't want that!" She might have regretted the loss of the money over the years, but she'd rather dismantle BUILD brick by brick than tell her parents that. She loathed what she was about to do, but she was out of choices. "I was wondering about Fox Industries' corporate apartments. Could I stay in an empty one for a few weeks? Two months, tops."

Neither parent said a thing, so Faith kept going, the words running together in her haste to sell this plan. "I'll keep it clean. I'll... I'll clean any of the others that are vacant as well. Dust. Water the plants. Whatever you need."

Franklin and Betsy exchanged glances, after which her mother rested her slim hand on her father's wrist. At the gesture, Faith felt the first spark of hope. Her dad was the stubborn one, but her mom was the maker of plans and manipulator of moods.

Betsy gave Franklin a small nod and then turned to her. "No, Faithy."

"What?" Faith had to have misheard her. Even Franklin looked surprised at her mother's firm tone.

"I said no to the corporate apartment. Those are for Fox Industries employees, and you are not, as you know."

The ambient restaurant noises faded to the background as Faith's vision turned hazy. She'd swallowed her pride and come crawling to her parents after all these years, and now they were refusing a favor that would cost them *nothing*?

"Unbelievable," she hissed. "You're seriously saying no to this one little thing because I didn't join the family insurance juggernaut?"

"Everyone stay polite!" Betsy singsonged through a tight smile. "People are staring."

Faith didn't have to glance around to know that was true. A scene at the country club would be conversation for the rest of the year.

"What we *will* do," her mother continued in an aggressively calm voice, "is let you move back home."

"Move home," she repeated faintly. "With you."

Her mother lifted a thick cloth napkin to her lips and give her flawless nude lipstick a gentle pat. "It's the perfect solution."

Faith collapsed into her seat like a puppet with cut strings while Franklin absorbed the news immediately.

"What an excellent idea! So that's settled." He beamed at his wife and then tucked back into the slab of meat on his plate.

Faith's brain churned as Betsy turned her attention to her own meal.

"But I..." She struggled to come up with an objection to this lifeline. A lifeline that might end up strangling her, sure, but a lifeline nevertheless.

"You can move in anytime and stay as long as you like," her mother said. "We haven't changed a thing in your bedroom."

Her bedroom. That nightmare of princess pink, waiting to swaddle her in its eyelets and ruffles and never let her go.

Ignoring every rule of dining etiquette, Faith leaned

her elbows on the table and dropped her head into her hands. She was genuinely screwed in the housing department unless she wanted to move into that studio with the creepy super who'd been a little too excited about having his own key to her place. At least she had the perfect grant to apply for. Her program was likely the kind of community-development project they were looking for, and it was the only thing keeping her moving forward these days. The grant would save BUILD.

Still, to move in with her parents at twenty-nine, when she'd kept them at a frostily polite distance for the past decade? Her stomach lurched at the humiliation, but what choice did she have?

Her father barked out, "Oh, for God's sake, Faith, it won't be forever. And we'll be traveling quite a bit for the next few months, so that's even less time that you'll have to endure us."

His brusque voice indicated he considered this a done deal, and to Faith's horror, she realized he was probably right. What other choice did she have? Her bank account was empty, the school year was imminent, and her new landlord was practically putting drop cloths down around her furniture.

Faith gave a strangled scream the likes of which had likely never graced the walls of this stately dining establishment, then pulled herself together just as quickly. "Thank you so much. I'll be out of your hair as soon as BUILD is secure again." She stabbed a lettuce leaf, grumbling, "Just don't expect me to join you for family dinners."

"Certainly not. I'm not Emily Gilmore," Betsy agreed. At Faith's astounded expression, she raised one thin blond eyebrow. "What, you think I haven't seen *Gilmore Girls*? Oh, Faith, we have so much to catch up on!"

Her mother raised her wineglass in a salute, clearly delighted at the thought of having her daughter back under her thumb, and Faith's anemic chuckle in reply was interrupted by the tiny pop of the button on her skirt, choosing that moment to exit the conversation by exploding off the waistband.

TWO

Leo Morales spooned ice cream into his mouth and tried to forget all about this shit show of a night.

The fight over the blazer. The awkward dinner with his new bosses. And Faith Fox.

Faith fucking Fox.

He dropped the plastic spoon into the bowl. His sundae was good, but it wasn't *that* good.

Faith fucking Fox in her country-club suit with her country-club family watching him have a humiliating fight over that country-club blazer. And he'd almost kissed her.

Worse, he was eating his ice cream in the one place that made it impossible to stop thinking about her. The picnic table behind the Dairy Bar had been their spot. They'd spent countless summer afternoons sprawled across the sun-warmed wood, making out and dreaming up lazy, wildly improbable plans about their future.

Leo had avoided it on the rare occasions that he'd been back in Beaucoeur over the years. But tonight, after choking down food that tasted like sawdust, he'd needed some sweetness on his tongue, and this was the only destination he could think of.

Unfortunately, the hot fudge in his cup was overpowered by the long-ago memory of Faith's mouth, cold from ice cream and sweeter than anything he'd ever tasted. The hot bolt of longing for those days was so intense that it took him a long moment to recognize that the sound he was hearing was his phone vibrating against the wood of the table.

He glanced down and heaved an affectionate sigh before bringing it to his ear.

"Hola, Mami."

"Mijo! Are you in town? You didn't call!"

"I am." He pivoted on the splintery bench so he was sitting with his back against the table. Beaucoeur in June was warm but not too humid yet, and he sucked in a lungful of his hometown air, allowing himself to relax for the first time in forty-eight hours.

"Sorry. I was running late and had to go straight to the restaurant."

"It's okay. How was the flight? How was the dinner? When are you coming over?"

He set the ice cream bowl down next to him and stretched out his legs, seeking relief for muscles that were still twitchy from the cramped plane. Under ideal circumstances, flying from Manaus to São Paulo to Miami to Chicago to Beaucoeur was a full day, but when you added in countless flight delays thanks to a tropical storm and three—three!—mechanical issues, he'd been traveling for a little over two days by the time he made it to the country-club lobby.

"Dinner was good." Dinner was awkward as hell. "I can't wait to see everybody, but I need to get settled at my new place tonight." And hopefully sleep for a full day before he rejoined the warm embrace of his family.

His mother clicked her tongue. "It's silly for you to rent. You can stay with me, or one of your sisters would have room."

A burst of applause punctuated her words. Like every Puerto Rican of her generation in Leo's family, Luisa Morales was on the phone with the television blaring—a game show, based on the racket—while the radio was also on and pumping out music, which meant his father was likely listening as he puttered around the kitchen. Leo couldn't have asked for a better, more loving childhood, but was it any wonder he'd escaped to the serenity of the rainforest the instant he was able to?

"I appreciate that, but work set me up. My boss gave me the keys tonight." He didn't have any details beyond the address and the fact that it was furnished and the rent was affordable, but it didn't matter. Pretty much anything would feel luxurious compared to his old digs.

"The boss, how was he? Was he nice?"

His new boss was not nice. He'd spent the evening with prissy disapproval stamped all over his fleshy face while he lectured Leo about the dignity of his new position and eyeballed Leo's untamed Boricua hair.

He'd already been anxious about the dinner—about taking the job in the first place even—and then every fucked-up step of his travel over the past few days had ended with him running so late that he hadn't had a chance to clean up or change. Not that he'd had anything to change *into*, what with his luggage being lost somewhere between Brazil and Illinois. He should've just asked to push the dinner back, but he hadn't realized until too late how close he'd be cutting it between his arrival and the dinner. Calculating fucking travel times had tripped him up again.

And of *course* he'd needed a jacket at that nightmare restaurant. He'd known that, just like he'd been painfully aware as he stood in the lobby that he looked exactly like what he was: a man who'd been digging holes in a jungle the day before he hopped a plane to start a whole new career that he wasn't at all prepared for.

Just like he hadn't been prepared for *her*.

Seeing Faith had knocked him sideways. Once he'd realized who the thick-bodied blonde in the lobby was, it had all hit him in a rush: the urge to kiss her, to take her someplace private where they could catch up on the past dozen years. He wanted to tell her about the career he'd chosen, the work he'd fallen in love with, the new job he was equal parts proud of and terrified about. And he wanted to hear everything that had happened to her since they'd last spoken.

Then, just as quickly, he'd remembered *why* they'd stopped speaking. Her shock at discovering her broke, brown-skinned ex-boyfriend standing in a country-club lobby had helped.

"Mijo?" His mother's voice pulled him back into the conversation. "Your boss?"

Right. She'd asked him a question. "My boss seems like he'll be..."

He lifted his gaze, and every thought in his head evaporated at the sight of the phantom from his teenage years come to torment him. Had the strength of his memories conjured her somehow?

"Mami, tengo que colgar," he said hastily, eyes not budging from the figure in front of him. "I love you. Hablamos mañana."

He hung up the phone and stared. It wasn't a phantom after all but the adult version of his high school fantasy, frozen in midstep and holding a twist cone. Faith looked different and the same after all this time. Familiar and foreign at once. This wasn't the willowy high schooler he'd loved. This wasn't even the meticulously coiffed country-club member he'd tried to cut down earlier tonight.

She was in flip-flops, and she'd unbuttoned her ugly pink jacket to reveal a tight black tank top underneath. She definitely didn't have all those curves the last time he'd been in a position to examine them. In fact, she'd filled out everywhere since high school; in place of her angles, she was soft all over. Abundant.

And then there was her hair. God, he couldn't tear his eyes away. It was the same platinum blond it had been when he'd spent hours tunneling his fingers through it, and it still fell long and straight past her shoulder blades. But now two bright blue streaks framed her face and reflected the color of her eyes.

Eyes that were sparking with fury.

"Oh perfect," she spat out. "Just... *ugh*. Just scoot over."

She stomped up to the table and glared until he shifted to give her room to sit next to him. *There* was the brash girl he remembered. If he had to guess, she was as embarrassed as he was to be caught visiting their old make-out spot, and just as she had in the past, she was covering her discomfort with attitude.

She flopped down, positioning herself so no part of her touched any part of him, and licked her cone once before speaking. "Let's not talk. I'm just here to drown my sorrows in lactose, and then I'll go."

He grunted and dragged his gaze away from her pink mouth. Every stupid part of him wanted to keep her at his side a little longer even though it killed him to think about how she was swirling her tongue through that ice cream while pointedly not looking at him.

In high school, she'd always ordered a small twist while he'd cycled through pretty much every treat on the menu, sometimes in the same night. He'd been constantly ravenous as a teenager, and the only treats he'd stayed away from were the strawberry flavors because Faith was allergic and he didn't want his tongue to be the reason her throat swelled up.

The branches of the weeping willow behind them ruffled in the breeze as they sat together in silence. Had she moved back to Beaucoeur after college? The one time he'd looked for her on social media, her privacy was buttoned up tight, so he had no idea what she did now or where she did it. If she lived in Beaucoeur, did she come to the Dairy Bar often? Did she think of him when she did?

The circular pools of illumination from the parking lot lights fell across the table, so he both heard and saw her sigh.

"It's been so long, Leo." Her voice was soft, her anger gone. She kept her eyes on her cone.

"I know, Dutch."

Dutch, short for duchess. The old endearment had slipped out at the restaurant. Now he'd used the nickname that had sprung from it, and the hitch in Faith's breath told him she'd noticed.

His night wasn't improving, in other words.

He picked up his bowl, but the ice cream and fudge had melted into a soup, so he set it on the table behind him while he grappled with the burst of elation he felt to be sitting next to her again. Next to *Faith*. After all this time.

He really ought to get up and leave. For fuck's sake, she was the cause of the worst humiliation he'd ever suffered. Instead, he did something stupid.

"This is new." He lifted his hand to point out one of the blue streaks, his fingers a breath away from touching her hair. He wondered if it was as silky as he remembered.

Faith leaned back so her gaze could move across his face. "So is this." Her expression unreadable, she shifted the cone to her left hand and extended the fingers of her right, ghosting them over his beard. "The last time I saw you, I think you only had to shave once a week."

Explanations crawled up his throat: How he'd spent his twenties getting dirt under his nails for a tiny nonprofit dedicated to reforestation and environmental education in South America. How he'd traded that life for a *Fortune* 100 company that allowed him to move back to his hometown but might not let him make the difference he wanted to make in the world. How he was terrified that they'd discover he was a fraud and chase him back to the poor side of town where he came from. Where he maybe never should've left.

But he'd learned his lesson about showing his vulnerable underbelly to Faith, so he just ran a palm over the mass of hair on his jaw, silently vowing to shave at the first possible opportunity. The movement pushed his cuffed shirtsleeve up, and Faith's eyes focused on his inner forearm. She inhaled softly, and they both looked down at the tattoo sketched in minimal black strokes of a fox sitting alert on its haunches, head tilted slightly to the side. Faith moved her hand, and this time her fingers made contact with his skin, stroking down and then up the fox's body.

"You never added any color," she said. Then in a thicker voice, "You never covered it up."

Leo forced himself to pull his arm away from the electricity of her touch. "Never thought about it much either way," he lied, keeping his expression flat while his brain helpfully dredged up every miserable day he'd plodded through after their breakup.

She seemed to sense his shifting mood and looked down at the ice cream that now dripped down her hand. She picked up his bowl, dropped the remnants of her cone into it, and swiped her fingers down the front of her expensive skirt.

And that was the reminder Leo needed. Never again with this girl. People like the Foxes used couture as napkins. They used people like him as napkins. The mystery of what Faith Fox was doing with a tweed suit and flip flops and wild blue hair? He wasn't going to solve it. He didn't *want* to solve it. He just needed to make damn sure they both remembered that.

So he did something unforgivable.

Letting his eyes drift shut, he leaned toward her and inhaled against her neck. She tensed but didn't pull back, and every drop of his blood thrummed from being this close to her again.

"You smell the same." His voice was husky and dark, far darker than he intended. How could it not be with her skin warm against his?

She huffed out a shaky breath. "Yeah?"

"Yeah." He cupped her cheek, turning her head so her lips were a breath away from his. Then he hardened his heart and struck. "Money. You still smell like daddy's money."

She was off the table before he was able to clear her achingly familiar scent from his nostrils, the harsh shadows of the pole light turning her eyes into twin black holes. Her chest rose on a sharp inhale, but when she spoke, her voice was steady and flat.

"Go fuck yourself, Leo." Then she walked away with an unhurried stride, leaving self-loathing to curdle in his gut alongside the ice cream.

THREE

"Come on, come on, come on." Faith glared at the pinwheel of death as it spun and spun on her six-year-old MacBook. "You can do it, baby."

"That the last of it?"

Her head snapped up to see Aiden, her best friend's boyfriend, standing in the doorway, easily hefting a huge box that she knew damn well was packed full of books.

She flicked her eyes around the four bare walls of her kitchen before zeroing back on the screen like a laser. "Probably. The new super can keep whatever's left at this point."

Her belongings didn't matter right now, not when the grant that would keep BUILD running was slipping through her fingers. She'd submitted every required document almost a month ago, just after that horrible dinner with her parents and that even worse run-in with Leo that had been so painful she'd absolutely refused to let herself dwell on it. She thought she'd done all the required work well in advance of today's noon deadline, but an autogenerated email had landed in her inbox that morning warning her of unreadable PDFs in her application.

Unfortunately she'd been busy hauling her belongings out of her former home and hadn't seen it until twenty minutes ago. Cue panic, shrieking, tears, and what might be a minor heart attack as she raced to her laptop to figure out what files needed to be resaved and uploaded again. Thank God her friends had been willing to keep juggling boxes while she hyperventilated at the kitchen countertop.

"Why are you so sloooooow?" She moaned, flexing the fingers of both hands, then clenching them into fists. Her old-ass laptop was trying to turn her prematurely gray as it whirred and thought and froze and whirred some more. All that drama to process the second-to-last document she needed to resubmit.

"Success!" She lifted a fist in triumph when the Received message flashed on her screen. One more to go. She'd get this off, then pack up the computer stuff and start dealing with her parents to—

The lights in her empty apartment snapped off.

"What?" Her eyes jumped to her screen where the I'm thinking pinwheel had been replaced by the dreaded No internet connection dinosaur. *"What?"*

Thea came charging into the room. "Are you okay?"

"No!" She shrieked and buried her hands in her already disheveled hair. "This grant application's due in *eight minutes*, and I don't have any internet."

Make that seven minutes. The time on the laptop read 11:53 a.m.

"Looks like you don't have any power either." Aiden had followed Thea back into the house and flicked the nearest light switch several times. "Did you set your electricity to be disconnected today?"

"Yeah, I told them anytime after noon..." She looked frantically around, as if the answer lay somewhere within these bare walls.

Thea's mouth dropped open. "It's not noon yet! You have—"

"Seven minutes. I know." She swallowed back a sob. "But I doubt I can get it turned back on in time."

She'd been so close. *So close.*

"I'll start knocking on neighbors' doors to see if they'll share their Wi-Fi password," Thea announced.

"Thank you." Faith yanked the elastic out of her hair and rebundled it on top of her head, as if a tighter bun might cause the internet to magically restore itself.

Aiden pulled his phone from his pocket. "I've got a hotspot I use for job sites. That might be faster."

"Thank you." She sniffled, clicking on the Wi-Fi icon to see if any neighbors had a non-password-protected network. Her one chance to keep the doors open, and now she had roughly 250 seconds to steal someone else's internet to make it happen.

"It's up," Aiden said. "You should see it as an option."

She refreshed the list of options. "AdonisAir?" Even as her entire future crumbled around her, she could appreciate how much he must hate that.

But he just gave a soft smile. "Thea named it."

"Gag," she said flatly as she chose the network. "It's asking for your login."

He came around the kitchen island to join her. "Is it? That's weird."

Her fingers gripped the edge of the counter so tightly

that her knuckles turned white. "Yeah, super weird. Just... just enter it please?"

He shook his head. "Sorry. I'll have to look it up. I never remember passwords." He fished his phone back out and started tapping again as Thea bustled through the door.

"Nobody's answering their door. Either they're all at work or this is the unfriendliest neighborhood I've ever been in."

"Both." Faith spoke past the fear clogging her throat. It was 11:57 now. "How are we doing, Aiden?"

"I'm looking," he said. "Ah, here we go. Ready?"

He gestured to her keyboard, and she all but shouted, "Yes!"

He rattled off a string of alphanumeric characters that made it sound like he was having a stroke, and Faith typed them all with trembling fingers. Eleven fifty-eight.

She hit the Enter key, and an error message popped up. "Oh God, I entered it wrong."

Thea's murmured "Shit" did nothing to steady her nerves as Aiden patiently went through the password again, this time emphasizing which were uppercase and which were lowercase. It worked on the second try, and Faith gave a little sob.

"Okay. Here we go." She refreshed the page and confirmed that the main application and the funding breakdown were uploaded, as were the letters of support from community stakeholders. All that was left to upload was her personal statement. She clicked the button, selected her document, and held her breath as the pinwheel made its appearance again. "Come on, come *on*."

The spinning stopped, and a confirmation page

popped up. She exhaled hard, her head falling forward in relief.

But wait. That wasn't a confirmation page. It was an error message.

"It's 12:01," she said woodenly. "I missed the deadline."

The room fell silent until Thea tentatively asked, "What are you going to do?"

Faith straightened, wiped her tears with the hem of her T-shirt, and closed the laptop with a snap.

"I'm going to fix it."

THE ELEVATOR DOORS SLID OPEN, and Faith pressed her sweaty palms against her thighs before stepping onto the busy floor.

She could do this. She'd already talked her way past security and secured a visitor's badge that permitted her to be on floor eighteen of the Digham corporate headquarters. They probably shouldn't have let somebody with this much unholy fire in their eyes onto the premises, but at a young age she'd learned the art of acting like you had every right to do what you intended to do, and those lessons died hard. Now she just had to convince one more person to do her a tiny favor, and she'd be set.

Did she regret not trying to make herself look a touch more presentable before storming Big Dig HQ? Sure. But what was the point? She was full-on mid-July moving-day gross, so pausing for a cute french braid and some mascara wasn't going to make much of a difference either way. Time to get this handled.

She stepped off the elevator and surveyed the enormous cubicle farm in the middle of the open floor, flanked on both sides by rows of glass-walled offices.

"Can I help you?" A sixty-something man holding a cup of coffee appeared at her elbow, unsubtly taking in the stretch of legs exposed by her beat-up running shorts. Faith recognized that look. It was the one that said her shorts were too short, although she knew damn well that if she were a size 2, the look in his eyes would be completely different.

Joke was on him though; she gave exactly zero fucks what he thought about her exposing her plus-size self to the fluorescents of his office building. She also knew how to handle this type of guy. She'd grown up around a million just like him, all with the same smug entitlement oozing from every pore of their doughy faces.

She cocked a hip and gave him Angelina-at-the-Oscars attitude. "I'm looking for the Digham Foundation offices. Could you point the way?"

The posture adjustment combined with a tone that suggested she was telling, not asking, did the trick. The man straightened slightly, self-importance in his tight smile. "You're in luck. I'm the president of the foundation. What can I do for you?"

Shit. If this was the guy she'd have to suck up to, she really should have changed back into the pink tweed. Not that she was going to let him see her sweat. Well, sweat any more than she already had today. God, a shower would be amazing right now.

Focus, Faith.

She graced him with a small smile. It's what Angie would do. "Fantastic. I need to speak with someone about a grant."

His judgmental little eyes swept over her again before

he turned and stalked off, leaving Faith to scurry after him.

"You found the right man," he said as they speed-walked past the maze of cubicles in the center of the office. "I've been in charge of Digham's charitable giving for going on thirty years now."

"Thirty years! That's impressive." This guy obviously wanted to talk about his big important job, and Faith picked up the pace so they were walking side by side and she could fawn appropriately. She'd apparently taken the correct approach because he nodded crisply.

"I have a grant manager who oversees the foundation employees in the field in Mexico, India, and China, along with a liaison in Washington, D.C. Plus there's our engagement manager and our administrative assistant."

"And the person who handles the grants for projects here in Beaucoeur, right?" she asked.

That was the only person she cared about at the moment, but somehow it was the wrong thing to say. The anticipation on his face vanished, and he scowled. "Yes. Him too."

His already pinched voice got even more nasally, and Faith dialed her perkiness up to eleven to try to get him back on her side. "That's, what, eight people? You must stay busy."

He raised a hand in greeting at one of the cubicle dwellers they power-walked past. "I'm just back from New York this morning, actually. I'm the recording secretary for the National Counsel of Corporate Foundations. Lin-Manuel Miranda was the guest of honor at our annual meeting."

"Oh wow." Faith didn't have to fake being impressed that time. "Did you get to meet him?"

The man stopped walking so quickly she almost tripped over him.

"I sat next to him at dinner." He straightened a snowy shirt cuff and lifted his chin to stare into the middle distance. "He was *magnificent*."

"I bet," she murmured. So the guy was a name-dropper. She could work with that. "Is meeting celebrities pretty common in the foundation world, Mister.... I'm sorry, I didn't catch your name." She smiled up at him, and his eyes did another disapproving sweep down her body before he answered.

"Carlisle Lockhart."

Of course that was his name, and of course having an actual conversation with her hadn't wiped the disgust off his face. But he smoothly shifted into motion again, and she dutifully followed.

"For a company as large as Digham, yes. We often have featured guests at the foundation's annual gala."

"That must be amazing for your employees, Mr. Lockhart." Time to bend this back around to what she needed. "And you said the community grant manager's new? He must be excited to mingle with celebrities."

She'd fully slipped into her corporate pandering mode. Guys like this usually ate it up, but he just puckered up his mouth like he'd sucked on a lemon. "Doubtful. He's extremely focused on more... local issues."

Local issues seemed like exactly what the community grant guy should be doing, but Faith knew better than to argue. Fingers crossed the person she was here to talk to would be less of a prick.

When they arrived at the door to a suite that housed the foundation offices, Faith turned to Carlisle with her brightest smile. "Thank you so much for telling me a little about your work, Mr. Lockhart. You're doing such important things here!"

This time she channeled her mother, who never met a king of capitalism she couldn't charm. Then again her mother didn't usually have to do said charming in a faded Chicago Cubs T-shirt. But Carlisle Lockhart at least had the good manners to hold open the door for her rather than letting it slam in her face, so she straightened her shorts to keep them from drifting into wedgie territory and followed him into the suite. Behind one of those closed doors was the person who had the power to save her or sink her.

"Darla," he said to the steely-eyed, silvery-haired woman at the reception desk in the center of the waiting area, "this young woman has some questions. Can you get her sorted?"

That handled, Carlisle offered her one last oily smile, then disappeared into the corner office, leaving Faith alone with Darla, who was at least more welcoming than her boss.

"Hi," Faith said. "I need to speak with someone about the community grant."

Darla's pink-lipsticked mouth turned down sympathetically. "I'm so sorry. The deadline was noon today."

"I know." Faith shifted her purse up her shoulder and tried to sound just-us-girls conspiratorial. "That's actually why I'm here. I had tech problems with my submission, and I was hoping to speak with the person in charge."

The admin's eyes strayed to the closed door on her far left. "He's in his office at the moment, but I don't know if that's—"

"Please?" Faith shifted the purse again. Her bulky old

laptop weighed a *ton*. "I'm sure if I just explain, he'd be willing to work with me."

The sky-high lift of Darla's eyebrows spoke volumes as she picked up her phone to place a call. "Mr. Morales, I have someone here to see you." Her eyes cut to Faith's outfit. "Yes, I will." She hung up. "Have a seat. He'll be right out."

She gestured at the small sofa to the side of her desk, and Faith sank onto it, grateful to set her bag down. But she only had a few moments to go over her strategy before the office door Darla had indicated flew open and the unseen inhabitant barked, "Come in."

The abrupt tone startled her to her feet, and she glanced at Darla.

"Good luck," the other woman said with a small chuckle that put absolutely none of Faith's nerves at ease.

As she took a step forward, a few thoughts hit her at once.

Carlisle Lockhart's new employee. Leo's unexpected appearance in Beaucoeur. That growly voice. Mr. Morales.

Surely not. *Surely not*.

She turned to Darla to whisper, "What's Mr. Morales's first name?" just as a figure filled the doorway in her peripheral vision. She turned her head slowly, and when the broad-shouldered man came into view, her worst, wildest suspicions were confirmed.

Leo. In a suit and looking unbearably good—other than the horror on his face as he stared at her.

"You've got to be fucking kidding me," he gritted out.

Welp. There was absolutely no way she'd be getting an extension on that deadline now.

FOURTEEN YEARS AGO

Faith always got a burger at lunch. It was her lone act of defiance in an otherwise obedient life. Her mom was always nagging her to watch her calories, so at lunch she ordered a hamburger, cut it into precise quarters, ate one, and threw the rest away.

Then one afternoon, someone new was sitting at the lunch table with Thea and the guy she was seeing.

"Faithy, this is Leo. He and Sam are buddies."

Faith smiled at the boy sitting across from her. He frowned back, looking ready to bolt from the table. But his hungry eyes tracked her movements as she dissected her burger with two neat slices. While she, Thea, and Sam had trays full of food, the table in front of Leo was empty.

"Are you not eating?" Faith asked. Thea and Sam were arguing about weekend plans, leaving her to make conversation with this stranger who seemed to be all bones and thick black hair.

His wary eyes bounced up from her food to take in her face. "Nah. Forgot my lunch money." His gaze immediately dropped back to her plate.

"Here." She slid her allotted burger quarter onto a napkin and pushed the plate with the other three-quarters in front of him. "I was going to throw this out anyway."

Faith heard him swallow hard. He glared down at the plate for a beat, then pushed it back to her. "I don't want your garbage food."

Faith scoffed. "It's not *garbage food*. I only want a little bit of it. Forgive me for trying to keep it from going to waste."

She snatched the plate back, but he wasn't looking at her. He was looking at the burger again, where ketchup now oozed down the side of one of the quarters. She watched his Adam's apple bob as he swallowed again.

Her anger vanished, and she adopted a softer tone.

"Seriously. You'd be doing me a favor if you'd finish it for me. I always feel bad tossing it."

He looked at her for a long moment with those dark eyes.

"Okay. Thanks." He reached for the plate, and by the time Faith had finished her quarter, his plate was empty.

Two weeks later, Thea and Sam had broken up. But by then, Leo and Faith were inseparable, in the cafeteria and beyond. By then, she'd realized that nobody was *that* forgetful about their lunch money. The truth was, Leo didn't have any cash for lunch, so she started buying two burgers and an extra chocolate milk every day. Feeding him. Loving him.

Hoping he'd stay.

FOUR

Over the years, Leo'd had more stressful on-the-job experiences than he could count. It had started with rude fast-food customers when he was in high school and reached dizzying heights at various points as he was leading tree-planting excursions throughout South America where it was a toss-up whether language breakdowns, equipment failure, or lack of electricity would be the thing stopping work that day. But nothing had prepared him for the never-ending adrenaline parade that hit him every time he bumped into Faith.

"What are you *doing* here?"

He practically bellowed the words, then felt like a complete asshole when she deflated in front of him.

"Are you... are you the community grant... guy?" She glanced over her shoulder at Darla, as if the other woman might save her. And didn't that just make him feel worse? Faith had been a lot of things when he'd known her, but she was never timid.

"Yes." His struggling brain refused to make sense of her sudden appearance in the middle of his new life. Why would she want to talk with him about the grant? Maybe she was here to give money. She was the only child of the Fox dynasty, after all.

He crossed his arms and leaned against the doorway. "We don't accept contributions. All foundation money comes from Digham's earnings and are earmarked—"

"I'm not here to donate." She brushed a runaway strand of moonlight hair behind her ear. "I need an extension on the grant deadline."

He laughed. He couldn't help it. It just slipped out. "*You're* applying for a grant?"

Her lips flattened. "Yes."

"No." He said it fast and final. Anything to get her out of this office.

She blinked. "No? Just like that?"

"Just like that."

Their gazes locked, and neither of them spoke. Then her eyes narrowed.

"Are you this much of a dick to everyone who walks through your door?"

At that, Darla gave a muffled cough, and Leo bit back a growl. This was bad enough without an audience.

"Get in here." He gestured impatiently into his office, and Faith dragged her feet as she moved forward, pressing against the doorframe as she sidled past, like she was scared to brush against him. Smart, actually. He wasn't sure how he'd react either.

"I'll hold your calls," Darla said sweetly as he kicked the door shut behind him, trapping them inside his office. Together.

He was standing far too close to her, so close that he could hear her tiny inhale. For a moment it looked like she was going to run. Just turn on her heel and bolt out the door. But after a beat she lifted her chin, clearly not wanting to give him the satisfaction of taking a single step back.

"I'm hoping you can help me," she finally said. He recognized her tone as the performatively friendly one she used to use with teachers and authority figures, the one that made people fall all over themselves to help that nice Fox girl.

And that's when it occurred to him: *he* was the authority figure now. This job he desperately wanted to succeed at had made him the only person who could give Faith something she needed. The very idea of that role-reversal pulled the corners of his mouth up. Faith Fox, in his power.

He was going to enjoy this.

Faith must've seen something she didn't like in his face, because she glanced over her shoulder at the closed door. "Is there any chance there's another person working on the grant that I could talk to?"

He just smiled more broadly and dragged his eyes down her body and then back up.

"I'm it, Faith. What do you want? And why are you here in your gym clothes?"

She flushed, her cheeks glowing red, and it sent his blood rushing south. Seeing her undone had always worked for him, and she was all kinds of undone now. As a bonus, her outfit gave him an eyeful of every new curve and dimple on her plush body.

"None of your business," she snapped. But her fingers gripped the bottom of her shorts and gave them a tiny tug like she was trying to pull them lower on her thighs, which made him realize he was acting like a creep. That reminder snapped him back into the headspace he'd need for this encounter.

"Oh, I think it is my business." He turned and settled into the expensive leather chair behind his desk. The sensation was foreign after years of setting up his workspace at a folding table and chair in a tent.

"Not the..." She gave a strangled shriek and stomped toward him, slamming her bag down on the floor at her feet and glaring at him. "You don't get to talk about my clothes."

"Apologies, duchess." He rested one elbow on the arm of his chair and gestured at her. "If anyone knows how to dress to visit Digham HQ, it would be a member of the Fox family. I never should've questioned you."

She rolled her eyes, and the explosion of warmth in his chest at seeing the familiar expression on her gorgeous face was wholly unwelcome. Warm feelings didn't have a place when it came to her, not if he wanted to stay indifferent. And indifference was what he needed right now.

"I'm here to ask for an extension on the grant application. A tiny one."

"An extension?"

"Tiny." She held up her thumb and index finger, squinting at him through the gap. "A few of the files I uploaded last month were corrupted. And I didn't get the notification until just before noon today. I got them all reuploaded except for the final document."

"Unfortunate," he said mildly, giving her nothing to work with. It felt good watching her squirm. Just a bit of payback for making him feel so small all those years ago as he read what she'd written about him when she thought he'd never see it.

"Please, Leo. I submitted my personal statement sixty

seconds too late." Her bravado crumpled, and she blinked her big blue eyes at him. Her lower lip even quivered slightly. As performances went, it was tremendous.

But he shook his head. "No. Rules are rules." His lip curled as he remembered his last interaction with her father. "And I'm sure we've already got plenty of applications that bring something of value to the table. Applications that actually *need* the grant money."

He shrugged dismissively, and she got his meaning loud and clear. "God, just say it."

He tilted his head to study her. "Okay. If you want to get all charitable, why not just ask mumsie and pop-pop to write you a check and be done with it?"

His verbal jab brought her spark back. Good. A defeated Faith was no fun to spar with.

"First, never call my parents that again." She jabbed a finger in his direction, voice hard as steel. "Second, not that it's your business, but I haven't taken a cent from them since the day we graduated from high school."

"Poor Dutch." He let his skepticism bleed through. "No more annual Audi upgrades?"

"Nope," she snapped. "The car I drive still has our sex stains on the upholstery."

"Jesus." He straightened, his blood heating at the memories that conjured.

She kept rolling, leaning across the desk to get in his face. "If you must know, I cut my parents out of my life after what my dad did to you."

Leo's smile didn't reach his eyes. "Ah, but it wasn't just him, was it?"

"Correct." She pushed away from him, crossing her arms defensively over her chest. "I wrote the essay. And he showed it to you to get you to break up with me."

"Which I did," he said in as bored a voice as he could muster, ignoring the way his pulse was pounding in his ears.

"Yes. I recall." She sucked in a deep breath. "So I put myself through college on scholarships and loans, and I'm still paying them off with my crappy salary." She rubbed a hand tiredly across her forehead, a hint of defeat creeping into her posture. "And even though I haven't even paid myself that crappy salary for the past few months because the state funding dried up, the last thing I want to do is ask them for money, not even to keep Beaucoeur BUILD open."

As shocked as he was to hear that Faith had walked away from her fortune because of everything that had happened, he was even more surprised to hear the name of her organization.

"*You're* Beaucoeur BUILD?"

"I am." She planted her hands on her hips, drawing herself up to her full height. "And you'd be an idiot not to give my application full consideration. Now *apologize*."

Her ferocity stopped him in his tracks. "Listen, I didn't know about the money thing—"

"Not that!" she shrieked.

He tossed his hands in the air, utterly baffled by what she was after. "For what then?"

"For... for..." A blush crept over her cheeks, almost as if she was thinking something dirty. Curiosity coursed through him. What was she picturing that made her drag her tongue across her lower lip like that? Before he could ask, she shook her head sharply and pivoted back to the subject at hand. "I take it you know about BUILD?"

He nodded, grateful to be on slightly safer ground. "A bit. It's highly regarded, from what I understand."

She leaned a hip against the edge of his desk, a calculated look on her face. "Pretend I'm not me for a second. Would something like that have helped you in high school? A no-cost tutoring center with specialized programs based on student needs?"

His brows snapped together as she deftly poked at that old wound. Faith had been the first person to realize that his problems with math ran deeper than simply needing to study more. The truth was, a program like that would've made a huge difference to him in high school. But he'd be damned if he'd admit that to her.

She read the answer on his face. "Of course it would've helped," she said softly. "Would you have actually used it though?"

He scoffed. That would've been asking for help, which had been only slightly preferable to death for him back then.

She made a flourish with her left hand as if she'd just won her argument. "So you see why I need resources. It's hard to reach stubborn boys like you."

He sank back in his chair. "Yeah. I see your point." He tipped his head back to study the ceiling. Beaucoeur BUILD was really, really good. His supervisor Savannah often pointed to it as a model for the tremendous benefit a well-designed local nonprofit could provide. The reality of the situation, though, was awful.

"I can't do this." To his horror, his voice cracked as he said it, but Faith just smiled encouragingly.

"An extension? Sure you can."

She didn't understand his hesitation.

"It's not that. I can make an exception if I want." His eyes met hers, pinning her in place. "It's just... It's you. And it's me."

"Yeah. I get it." She pressed her lips together. "But Leo, so many kids need this program."

Kids like you. She didn't say it, but it's what she meant. And what a kick-in-the-nuts reminder that was of the circumstances that had led them to this moment.

"Still so dedicated to helping the less fortunate," he murmured.

She flinched, and he knew they were both remembering the spectacular end of their relationship. The girl he loved had used her college admissions essay to write about how she'd saved him from his learning disability. Dysculia. A term he'd never even heard until he'd read it in her words. She'd blamed his poverty, his subpar grade school, even a healthy streak of toxic masculinity that kept him from asking for help in his classes. But *she'd* noticed and *she'd* helped, and then she'd written all about it to secure herself a spot at Northwestern.

And in the years since, she'd gone on to create an organization that had helped hundreds of kids in Beaucoeur. He admired the work she was doing, was grateful for it even. But at the same time, part of him still fucking hated her for treating him like her own little charity case.

She fidgeted, palpable guilt rolling off her, but when she spoke, her voice was steady. "I'm so sorry for writing that, Leo. I've regretted it for years."

He waved off her words. The damage they'd done to each other back then couldn't be undone with an apology. But he did have a job to do, and it was in his power to make sure BUILD would be considered for the grant money. If he did, it would be to help those kids, not Faith.

He flexed his jaw. "Email me what you're missing. I'll add it to your application."

"Really?" she breathed, her tense shoulders relaxing.

His hand flew up, palm out. "I'm just the grant manager. The board of directors has the final say on recipients."

He clung to that reminder as she fished her laptop out of her bag and set it on the edge of his desk, flashing him a smile so full of sunshine that the warmth traveled all the way down his spine. But he forced himself to ignore it, adopting the stony expression that worked wonders to keep wayward volunteers in line on job sites. She got the hint, her eyes snapping down to her laptop screen.

"Sorry. Um. What's your email?"

He rattled it off, already doubting the wisdom of this whole situation. Too late though; her computer whooshed as it sent, and his dinged as it received. She was the one who broke the silence.

"Thank you so much," she began. "I can't tell you—"

"Save it." His tone was back to just shy of hostile, but he had to get her out of his office. This was too much. Too dangerous. "I'll make sure your application goes into the pile, but that's it. We're not friends, Faith. We're not anything. You need to remember that."

Her chin snapped back, and it was a beat before she spoke again.

"Like I ever forgot." She shoved her laptop into her bag. "Thanks for this anyway."

With that, she walked out.

FIVE

"I still can't believe it. What kind of monster is fine with me starving to death?"

Faith slammed the laundry basket onto the bed with a huff, and Thea scooted back against the headboard to make room for the explosion of clean clothes about to come. "You're not going to starve to death."

"Well, Leo doesn't know that," Faith grumbled.

"You're right. He doesn't know anything about you anymore." Thea recrossed her legs and settled the bowl of popcorn back in her lap. "And besides, you said the board of whatevers are the ones who decided."

When she'd received the rejection email that afternoon, she'd called Thea for emotional support. And Thea, who was sleeping with the boss, left Murdoch Construction early to come console her with popcorn and company.

Not that Faith was a ball of sunshine to be around right now. She scooped up an armful of bras and underwear and dumped them into the top dresser drawer, then slumped against it, her back to Thea. It gave her a moment to collect herself. Leo was a stranger to her now, and he'd turned down her grant application. Well, his board did. So now what?

She didn't have an answer to that question, and that realization had her struggling to pull breath into her lungs.

Kind. Calm. Collected.

She exhaled slowly to her mantra, and by the time she turned back around, she'd forced a smile onto her face.

"Yes, well. Their loss."

She was aiming for breezy, but she just sounded flattened, which was how she'd felt since she'd gotten the email two hours ago. At least it hadn't been from Leo; the brief message that had crushed the remaining chance for the survival of BUILD had been from Carlisle, the self-important old dude who'd been so openly judgmental of her at Digham HQ.

"It is," Thea declared, tossing a piece of popcorn at her that she dodged.

If she squinted a little, she could almost pretend she and her bestie were gossiping about their evil calculus teacher and who hadn't been asked to prom yet. But no, they were two grown-ass ladies talking about grown-ass lady problems. They were just doing it in a room that fourteen-year-old Faith had entirely covered in pink ombré.

In the three weeks since she'd gotten the shock of her life at the Digham Foundation offices, she'd pinned every last hope on the grant coming through. So much for a Big Dig rescue.

"Leo Morales working at Digham. Never in a million years."

It was like Thea could read her mind—no surprise

given their twenty-year-long friendship. Her friend shoved the popcorn bowl in Faith's direction, and she leaned forward and swiped a handful, chewing glumly.

"He was in a *suit*."

Thea shook her head in disbelief. "How'd he look?"

Incredible. Not that Faith would say that out loud, not even to her best friend. Instead, she settled on, "Different." That was true at least. But even the visual delight that was Leo in a slim-cut suit, with a close shave and his hair falling in a neat wave, couldn't distract her from the anxiety threatening to drown her, and she shoved the laundry basket to the floor and flopped backward on the bed.

"Maybe it's for the best." Faith groaned and rolled to her stomach, pressing her face into the mattress.

"It really did sound like a terrible idea," Thea agreed easily. "Too much emotional damage."

"Right," Faith murmured, although Thea's assessment didn't sit quite right with her. She didn't *want* it to be that way. Didn't *want* the thought of working with someone who'd been so important to her once upon a time to be so upsetting. But there they were.

In truth, no amount of money was worth the humiliation of standing in front of her first love while he regarded her with loathing in his eyes. Yet again she relived the moment when she'd been frozen in the center of his office as his gaze traveled over her from head to toe, as hot and dark as she remembered from years ago. She was vain enough to want to die because he'd seen her looking so disastrous, especially when he looked the very opposite. He'd matured from a good-looking teenager into a gorgeous adult. How entirely evil of him.

And there she was, a total winner who was squatting

at her parents' house with no other prospects in sight and no way to keep her business operational.

Time to figure out her next move. She rolled off the bed and yanked a T-shirt from the basket on the floor, angrily folding it into a neat square and setting it on the mattress. Her college-years stint at the Gap had prepared her for that at least. Maybe the store at the Beaucoeur mall was hiring.

It took three more folded shirts before she was able to speak aloud the thought that had been dogging her all day.

"I should just ask them to reinstate my trust fund."

Thea dramatically dropped the bowl onto the bed, but they'd made enough of a dent in the popcorn level that none spilled out. "You'd do that?"

She grabbed another shirt and angrily applied herself to making creases. She would've been given full control of her trust account when she turned twenty-one, but after the Leo thing, she'd been furious with her parents and too young and impulsive to consider the long-term consequences. So she'd signed paperwork disclaiming the money, and the funds had returned to her parents' estate. She'd been almost entirely at peace with the choice until the BUILD funds dried up.

"I was so stupid." She said it more to herself than to Thea, and she meant that for more than just the money. Yes, she'd been rash to walk away from the money, but she'd also been thoughtless with Leo and inflexible with her parents and overall too quick to pull down the walls of her own life. "I'm going to have to ask them for money even though I know they'll say no. No way is my dad backing down."

What other choice did she have? The state funding

wasn't coming back, the Beaucoeur school district had cut off the grant program because of budget issues, and she clearly hadn't sacrificed enough goats to get a federal grant. It's not like she could charge the kids.

Thea frowned. "Maybe Aiden could—"

She leaned forward and rested her hand on her friend's knee. "Thank you, but I'm not asking your boyfriend's construction company if they want to sponsor a tutoring center."

"He would though."

Thea's smile was so radiant that Faith didn't even have the heart to roll her eyes over the happy-couple smugness. "I'm sure he'd find a way to do it if you asked."

While Thea basked in her private little cocoon of relationship bliss, Faith made her way through her T-shirts, calculating expenses as she folded. The amount she needed to meet payroll, conduct student outreach, upgrade the technology, keep paying rent on the office... Even if she hadn't insisted that her parents dissolve her trust fund, there wouldn't have been enough in there to keep BUILD running on a long-term basis anyway. She needed a partnership with renewable funds.

Hell, even asking them for a small loan to keep a few full-time tutors and buy the tablets they needed might be a stretch given how un-liquid her parents always said their finances were. But if she gave up the lease on their office and worked out of public spaces—the library, unused classrooms in a few of the school buildings—she might be able to make it work for the upcoming school year. Of course, she had no idea how she'd ever be able to pay the loan back, and it likely meant living at her parents' even longer. So much for the independence she'd been so proud of since she'd told her dad to go to hell the day of her graduation party.

"You're buzzing."

Thea's words pulled her attention away from the ancient Beaucoeur High School shirt she had in a death grip. "What?"

She nudged her phone toward her. "Your phone."

Faith dropped the shirt, struggling to contain the nerves that twisted through her stomach. The number had a Beaucoeur area code, so it could be anyone from another staff member calling to quit to her landlord refusing to return her security deposit. Her phone brought nothing but bad news these days. She snatched it off the pink quilt and took a steadying breath before tapping the Answer button.

"Hello?" She was going for confident and breezy, but the voice that emerged was little more than a wheeze.

A pause, then, "Faith?"

She recognized the rasp of Leo's voice immediately. Her knees turned to water, and she immediately sat down on the bed. At least she tried to. What actually happened was that she missed her target by several inches, and her ass clipped the mattress and knocked her off-balance, sending her sprawling to the floor.

"Hello?"

His voice sounded tinny as it traveled from her phone's speaker on the carpet near where she lay like a starfish, staring at the bright white of her childhood ceiling.

"You okay?" Thea hissed, peering anxiously at her from the safety of the queen-sized bed. Faith waved her away and groped for the phone, not even bothering to pull herself into a sitting position. Flat on her back felt like the proper way to have whatever conversation was in store for her.

"Hi. Leo?" There. She sounded like a respectable adult, mostly.

"Uh, everything okay there?"

A wild laugh lodged in her throat. She was weighing the benefits of homelessness versus begging for a loan, and she'd had to fish a pair of her dad's boxer shorts out of her clean laundry that morning.

"Everything's peachy. Just trying to figure out which of my kidneys to sell so I can make rent."

"About that." This time he was the one sounding a little wheezy. "I have a... proposition."

"I'm not sleeping with you for grant money."

She grimaced as soon as the joke was out of her mouth, particularly when Leo's answering growl was so very forbidding. "Sorry, sorry, sorry," she said hastily. "It's just you said proposition, and it's kind of a funny word to use for..."

He was silent for so long that she worried he'd hung up on her. For all she knew he was about to retract whatever he'd called to offer her in the first place. But when he spoke again, it wasn't what she was expecting.

"What did you want me to apologize for, really? That day in my office."

His question took her by surprise, and her mouth went dry. "Wouldn't you like to know?"

"That's why I asked," he said impatiently. "Tell me what you wanted an apology for."

The old Leo wouldn't have pushed this hard, and he never would've used such a commanding tone.

A flash of what it would be like for adult Leo to issue those commands to her in bed hit her, and she squeezed her thighs together. Damn, he still did things to her vajean, especially this new version of him. He was a *man* now, and she was hyperaware of how attractive she found that, even while resentment curdled under her skin following every one of their interactions. Being near him was too damn complicated.

But she'd never shied away from a fight before, and she wasn't going to start now. "If you must know, Leonidas, you made me think you were going to kiss me that night at the Dairy Bar. And you did that on purpose to mess with me. Not cool."

"Not cool" was an understatement. She'd rather shave her own head than let Leo know the way she'd held her breath, waiting to feel his lips on hers again before he sucker-punched with his cruel words.

Thea's head slowly reappeared over the side of the bed, her eyes wide, but Faith waved a hand to get her to disappear again. For a second she'd forgotten someone else was in the room. Wonderful.

Another painful silence stretched on the line, and Faith wished like hell they were on a video call so she could see his expression right now. Their breakup had been devastating, although looking back on it now, she knew how unlikely it was for a pair of high school sweethearts to make it in the long run. But she still burned with regret over how things had ended, that her own immaturity and unchecked privilege had wounded him so badly. It made her stomach churn that they couldn't even have a single conversation as adults without clashing.

Leo was apparently having the same thoughts. "This is exactly why us working together is a bad idea," he finally said. He didn't even take the bait on "Leonidas"; in the past he'd always grumbled at her when she used his full name.

"Good thing we're not working together then," she said briskly to hide her swirl of emotions. "Because I don't appreciate being manipulated."

He cleared his throat, and she pictured him sitting in the middle of that office that didn't seem to fit him.

"I won't if you won't," he finally said.

"What, manipulate you? I never—" She started to remind him that she hadn't done a damn thing to him, but wasn't that at the heart of their decade-old pain? At least she'd gotten to apologize to him again for that fucking essay. It didn't erase how she'd treated him when she was eighteen, but she was glad she'd gotten to say it anyway. "Okay. Deal."

A pause, then, "Deal." He was gruff, but he sounded sincere—until he went and ruined it. "We're still not friends though."

Even though they'd gone all this time without speaking, the brutality of his statement was a punch in the gut.

Naturally, she punched back.

"Did you seriously call to remind me just how much we're not friends? Or did you call to gloat about me not getting the funding I desperately need?"

"I"—he broke off with another of those strangled growls—"I was *calling* with a proposition to get your funding, and don't you fucking dare make a sex reference this time."

A new source of funding. Her stomach swooped, but the pulse of optimism wasn't enough to keep her from joking. "Who, me?"

"Always you, Faith."

Her breath stuttered to a halt at his words, and in that

silence she heard the slightest creak, as if he was shifting in his chair. No way had he meant it in any romantic or possessive way. They weren't even *friends*, after all.

"Are you free tonight?" His voice was back to businesslike, the mood shift so sudden that she was grateful she was already sprawled on the ground. Leo left her unsteady.

"Y-yes."

"Olive Twist, seven o'clock. I'll give you the details then."

That no-nonsense tone again. None of it was making sense, but she didn't have any choices left. "Okay. Do I need to prepare anything specific? Bring any documentation?"

"No," he said. "But it's a nice after-work drinks place, so..."

She laughed at his unspoken audacity and at his assumption that she wouldn't be familiar with one of the fanciest drinks spot in town. "Are you about to tell me to wear something appropriate?"

Another Leo sigh. So far the constant sighing was the only unattractive part of adult Leo. Well, that and his immense dislike for her.

"I wouldn't dream of telling a grown woman how to dress," he said tersely. "See you tonight. And for God's sake, don't call me Leonidas." Then he hung up.

SIX

Leo was nervous, and it pissed him off.

He straightened his leather binder a fraction of an inch on the table in front of him, frowning at the Digham logo deeply embossed on the cover. He was pretty sure this folder cost more than his first car.

"Can I get you a drink, sir?"

He dragged his gaze up to see a cutely freckled waitress. On a different night, he might consider trying to charm her, but tonight was not the night for that. "Bourbon. Neat."

Her glossy lips curled into a smile as her eyes flicked from the folio to his suit jacket to the third finger of his left hand, ringless. "Top shelf?"

He hesitated. As always, his first instinct was to economize. But behind the waitress's halo of curly red hair, the sun hung low in the early August sky, glinting off the high-rise windows visible from the rooftop bar. He was sitting in a prime seat near the glass-paneled railing, and he didn't have to glance around at the tables dotting the concrete patio to know that he looked like he fit in among the other white-collar warriors.

"Sure."

The waitress gave him a wink before she headed to the bar, leaving Leo wondering yet again how the hell he'd gotten here.

Well, he knew *how,* of course. The son of Digham's CEO had spent his spring break tramping through a Peruvian forest under Leo's watchful eye. The kid had been flabbergasted that he shared a hometown with the Protect Our Rainforests liaison overseeing the reforestation project he was volunteering for and had returned to Beaucoeur, raving about Leo's leadership at POR. The very next week, Leo'd gotten a call he never in his life expected to receive. The Big Dig CEO himself—the man who called the shots at the helm of the global leader in development, manufacturing, and sales of large-machine engines—had an offer he couldn't refuse: move back home to head a new division designed to funnel Digham Foundation money into projects that would help people in Beaucoeur. As a bonus, he'd get paid an embarrassingly large salary to do it.

Speaking of. The waitress set a tulip-shaped glass in front of him, lingering as he took his first sip.

"Good?" she purred.

The liquid burned down his throat. It tasted expensive. "Good. Thank you."

She dimpled and sauntered off, leaving him to enjoy his pricey liquor. He'd loved working for POR, loved that he was making a difference every day with his sweat and his muscles and his labor. But the opportunity to make a difference in a new way was too tempting. He could put his nonprofit experience to work, helping the people he'd grown up with. He might even be in a better position to identify local needs that others at the foundation were blind to. But there was also a deep, dark corner of his heart that wanted to prove to people like Franklin Fox that he was good enough to sit at a desk in Big Dig HQ. At the very least, he was good enough to sit at this fancy bar drinking fancy booze.

The worst part of the deal might be trading his cargo shorts and sweat-stained T-shirts for a suit that suffocated him every day as he rubbed elbows with Vice President This and Corporate Counsel That. And right now his tightly buttoned collar was pressing into his neck.

Fuck it. With a vicious tug, he undid the knot on his tie and slid it off, popping the top button of his shirt. The conversation he was about to have was bound to be uncomfortable enough; he didn't need to feel strangled while he was having it.

Speaking of. The woman who'd occupied every one of his free thoughts for weeks appeared in the entryway to Olive Twist, her gaze sweeping across the space until she spotted him. Like usual, every molecule in Leo's body strained in her direction, as if his cells hadn't gotten the message that she wasn't for him.

She'd apparently gotten *his* message loud and clear; she was wearing that tweed suit again, and he almost regretted bringing it up on the phone with her. Even though she was dressed similarly to many of the women at the tables scattered across the concrete rooftop, she looked uncomfortable in the outfit, maybe even more uncomfortable than he was. Stiff in a way that didn't suit her body—a body that he was annoyingly interested in exploring.

Christ, this was a bad idea.

"Hi." She slid into the chair opposite his, barely

glancing at him as she set her purse on the floor and picked up the drinks menu, fidgeting with her hair. The blue streaks were gone, and Leo felt a pang at their loss. He'd kind of liked the rebellious look on her.

Within moments the redheaded waitress materialized, her eyes dropping to his newly exposed throat before she pivoted to take Faith's order. Once she'd given her order, Faith folded her hands in her lap and looked at him square in the eye.

"Why am I here, Leonidas?"

Heat crawled up the back of his neck. "I asked you not to—"

"Oh please, you practically dared me to." She waved an airy hand in his direction, and he bit back the unwelcome urge to laugh at her sass. "Besides, who's around to hear it?"

"That's not the point..." A noise at the entrance pulled his attention away from the gleam of her white-blond hair.

"What is it?" She twisted to peer behind her, where George Percival Voit III was slowly working his way across the deck, loudly greeting every person he knew as he made his circuit. When the CEO of Digham Corp. clapped eyes on Leo, he stopped midstride and made a beeline to their table.

Oh hell. This was happening. Leo rapped sharply on the table to get Faith's attention. "Whatever I say, I'm going to need you to agree with me, okay?" he said in a low tone.

She scoffed. "When have I ever done that?"

Holy Mary, Mother of God, grant him patience.

"Do you want the grant money or not?" Voit's rotund

figure was getting ever closer, and Leo was starting to sweat.

Her eyes narrowed. "How much are we talking?"

"Twice what you applied for."

Faith sucked in a soft breath. "Baby, I'll agree to anything you want for that kind of money."

His pulse jumped at her breathy tone, and he barely pulled himself together by the time his boss's boss's boss appeared at their table.

"Mr. Morales! And Miss Fox!" Voit beamed at them, looking from him to Faith, then back again. "Mind if I join you?"

What could he say but yes? "Please." Leo gestured at the empty chair to his left, and Voit settled into it with a comfortable sigh. The CEO's bald pink head barely cleared five foot five, but he dominated every room he entered with his basso voice and rafter-shaking laugh. This after-work bar was no exception.

Voit lifted a hand to beckon their waitress. "Miss Fox, I don't think I've seen you since your high school graduation party. How are your parents?"

His new boss had been at that goddamn party? Leo's stomach lurched at the memory, and Faith was rattled too, given the tightness at the corners of her eyes. Nobody else at the bar would've noticed, but he'd memorized every one of her expressions years ago. Yet her voice was light and friendly when she said, "They're well. They're leaving Friday for two weeks in Napa."

"Napa's wonderful this time of year," Voit said. "But not as wonderful as this new partnership, eh?"

Faith shot a glance Leo's way, and he swallowed a string of curses. He now had the head of an S&P 500 company observing him as he convinced Faith to move her nonprofit in a completely new direction. Yes, that was just fucking wonderful.

"It was fortunate," Leo began carefully, "that Faith had also applied for the environmental grant after the advisory board didn't select BUILD for the community grant."

Faith didn't even hesitate. She lifted her glass and said, "Here's to my good fortune."

When she knocked back a healthy sip, Leo followed suit. It couldn't make things worse at that point. The sun was disappearing behind the buildings on the horizon, taking Leo's hopes for a smooth meeting with it. Their waitress dropped off Voit's Malbec in time for him to raise his glass as well.

"Hear, hear! I didn't see it at first, but BUILD's the perfect choice for this new camping program."

"The... camping program. From the environmental grant. For my tutoring center." Slowly, ever so slowly, Faith turned her head in his direction, her blue eyes electric.

"Exactly." Voit paused to sip his wine. "Mr. Morales made such a compelling argument for why you should be picked as the first-ever recipient of the grant to fund the Dig Greener initiative."

Sweat prickled in Leo's hairline, and after another swallow of his bourbon, he launched into the explanation he'd been hoping to give Faith in a slightly more private setting.

"It was the last bullet point on your mission statement that sold me," he said, sending every bit of telepathy he didn't possess to urge her to act like she'd been on board all along.

Faith set her glass down and blotted her mouth with a napkin. "Promoting recreation and healthy lifestyles?"

Leo was momentarily distracted by the fact that her red lipstick was still perfect, but he pushed his wandering thoughts aside to focus on her puzzled expression. He couldn't blame her; the connection between BUILD and Dig Greener wasn't obvious. But he nodded encouragingly, willing her to play along. If she rejected this idea outright in front of Voit, God only knew what would happen.

"Exactly," he said. "And now you'll be connecting kids with environment-based educational programs with an emphasis on green initiatives that will make for a more sustainable Beaucoeur, like we agreed."

"Just like the last bullet point," she said faintly. "Just like we agreed." Thank God, she was catching on.

"It's brilliant!" Voit clapped his hands at them both. "When Mr. Morales asked us to create a grant to promote green initiatives in the area, I thought he might choose a recycling program or a campaign to promote the use of renewable energy. But a program to work with children... it was brilliant."

Thank God Voit had thought so; Leo had been spinning on the fly as he presented the proposal to the board.

"And then," Voit said, "he insisted that we vote immediately."

Shit damn hell. "I wouldn't say I *insisted*—"

Voit chuckled. "You said nothing but BUILD would do, and since Miss Fox was on board, there was no reason to delay the vote."

Leo's eyes cut to Faith, who had her wineglass in a stranglehold.

"If we hadn't voted then," he told her, "it would've

been another three months before the next board meeting."

Her lips parted in understanding. "And naturally Leo didn't want any delays since BUILD is the perfect... camping program."

"Hiking too," Voit said, and Leo could cheerfully have throttled him when Faith tilted her head in his direction, widening her eyes in horror. "Hiking?" she mouthed, and Leo replied with the tiniest of shrugs.

"I'm just glad Mr. Morales finally found an acceptable application for Dig Greener," Voit said. "Prior to yours, there wasn't a single one he wanted to take in front of the board."

"Lucky me," Faith murmured. Unlike before, he couldn't read her expression. His heart thundered in his chest. She was playing along the way he needed her to, but Voit had as good as told her that he'd gone above and way beyond to make this grant work for her.

You're not friends. You're not anything to each other.

"Lucky us." Voit swirled the remains of his wine in the glass. "Your personal statement moved me, Ms. Fox. Such strong motivation to do this work."

The topic shift froze Leo's blood in his veins. Faith's personal statement was the only document in the dozens of applications he'd reviewed that he hadn't actually read. He'd only gotten through the first sentence, and it had sounded so much like *her* that it hurt to have her voice echoing in his brain, so he'd set it aside. But if Voit was mentioning it now...

Buzzing kicked up at the base of his skull. Had she done it again? Used him to tell her own fucking story for her own fucking benefit? Twelve years ago, he'd been dressed in his brand-new graduation-day shirt and tie, hands shaking as he realized that Franklin Fox hadn't invited him into his study because he'd decided that Leo was worthy of dating his daughter. Instead Franklin had shoved the essay at him and thanked him for providing Faith with something of value during their relationship.

Something of value. Those words had haunted him for years. Had Faith managed to find value in him yet again to get what she needed for BUILD?

He dragged his eyes over to her, but she turned her head sharply toward the skyline, now purple in the twilight. Unaware of the tension crackling between the other two people at the table, Voit drained the rest of his glass and set it down on the metal table with a clang.

"I should run," he announced. "Nice seeing you, Ms. Fox. As soon as you sign the paperwork, we can transfer the funds to your account. Give my best to your parents."

"I will," Faith said faintly as Voit dropped a hundred-dollar bill on the table and strolled toward the exit, leaving the two of them alone again.

Leo didn't let the silence sit for long.

"Did you write about me?"

"Of course not!" Angry color flooded her cheeks. "I told you back then, I didn't even submit that essay. I felt terrible about it as soon as I finished it, so I wrote a new one that didn't involve you at all."

And her father had intentionally shown him the old one knowing exactly how he'd react. Leo's head throbbed.

"Read my statement if you don't believe me. I wrote about the importance of BUILD in a community like Beaucoeur." Faith's sigh sounded tired. "Speaking of. Am I correct that if I take a bunch of eleven-year-olds camping, I'll get the grant money I need to keep my other BUILD activities up and running?"

He finished his drink and set his glass down next to Voit's. They'd just lied to his new boss about how excited they were to work together. He was stuck with her now, so he might as well explain the thought process that had started this slow-moving train wreck in the first place.

"BUILD's a good fit because of your existing relationships with the local schools." Maybe if he focused on the work, the personal shit would take a backseat. "So Digham provides the funding, and you make connections with the students most likely to benefit from outdoor environmental education."

She nodded, sucking her lower lip into her mouth and releasing it with a pop. "Someone else would be doing the bulk of the outdoor work, right? Creating the lessons, leading the expeditions, working with the kids?" She gave a shudder. "Hiking?"

"Yes." He refused to be amused at her dramatic reaction. "Part of the grant is earmarked as salary for an outdoor education specialist who'll be the liaison with Big Dig."

Faith lifted her hands and let them fall, clearly frustrated, so he quickly added, "I have the name of someone who'd be perfect. We worked together for years in South America, and he's looking to move back to the States. He'll be free by the beginning of October."

"And until then, who's going to fill in?"

Here goes. "That would be me."

He thought her laughter had been unhinged before? The one she gave now was downright demonic. "Come on. How is that possibly going to work? Us together like that?"

"How the hell do I know?" he shot back, the insanity of their situation crashing down on him. When he'd hastily suggested Faith's program as the perfect fit for Dig Greener after the board rejected her community-development grant in favor of newer programs that needed more of a visibility boost, he'd thought he could handle it. He'd recalled the desperation on her face when she'd asked him for the extension, had been moved by her obvious dedication to her work. So he'd stretched the truth about Faith's buy-in to the program in order to get her the funding as soon as possible. And look where that had gotten him: he was a tool for Faith Fox to use. Again. But this time he'd willingly signed up for it.

"So we'll be working together," she said quietly.

He wasn't able to read her expression, but his heart lurched with a perverse burst of excitement. They were going to be thrown together. Hours in each other's company. He might not survive it, but at the same time, his heart pumped faster at the thought.

Her eyes were flat as she drained her glass.

"What a shame that we're not friends then. That would've made things a lot easier."

With that, she pushed away from the table and headed for the exit.

SEVEN

She was going to pass out. She was in a freaking open-air bar, but she couldn't draw enough air into her lungs.

Once she'd exited the patio, she paused in the dimly lit hallway, intending to collect her thoughts before riding the elevator down to her car. Instead, a strong hand closed around her elbow.

"We're not done talking about this."

Leo loomed over her, and she sucked in a trembly little breath at the sheer size of him. He was so much bigger than she remembered.

But that didn't mean he could get away with bossing her around. Yanking her arm out of his grip, she glared up at him. "Why? You know I need the money, so I'll agree to pretty much anything. Hell, things are so bad I moved back in with my parents, so I'm basically yours for the taking."

Her voice echoed along the concrete hallway, and Leo glanced around until he spotted a door marked STORAGE. He put a hand on the small of her back and steered her toward it. When he reached around her to twist the handle, it opened, and he pushed her inside, shutting the door behind them. They were plunged into darkness that had Faith's heart jumping to her throat until he flipped on the light switch.

Her whole life, when she was cornered, her first instinct was to attack. And she didn't think she'd ever felt more cornered than right now, trapped in a storage room with Leo. Most of the space was taken up by a few spare tables and a stack of chairs, and one wall was covered in shelves of folded tablecloths and other service settings. Her arm brushed against Leo's, and her lungs were full of his scent. She needed to get him to back off.

"You're loving this, aren't you?" The words emerged as poisonous darts that had him rocking back on his heels.

"Loving *what*?"

He glowered right back at her, not looking like he was enjoying anything at that moment.

But she was too worked up to pump the brakes. "Playing God with my life! Making me do things I didn't sign on for."

He dragged a hand down his face, rasping over the faint stubble on his jaw. "Forgive me. I thought I was giving you the funding you were desperate for."

"By making me *hike*," she spat out. "What about our history makes you think I'm in any way interested in that?"

"You don't have to hike!" He was clearly frustrated but was keeping his voice low, likely to avoid attracting attention from anyone in the hall. "I'll handle that part until William can move here!"

"You don't get to tell me who to hire!" she whisper-shouted back.

He threw his head back in aggravation, a growl rolling

through his throat, and for a moment the only sound in the small space was their loud breathing. Leo pulled himself back from the brink first, plunging his fingers into his thick hair. It was long enough on top that his curls made an appearance when he ruffled it, like he was doing now. And she fucking hated how appealing it made him.

"If you sign the contract tonight, I can get you your money first thing tomorrow," he said levelly. "Not three months from now."

Tomorrow. She could pay her employees, pay her office rent, pay *herself*.

"And you can just... give me this grant?"

"Again," he said impatiently, "*I* didn't. The board did. I just told them BUILD should be considered for the Dig Greener money."

"And that's okay?" Rules and audits and paperwork always made her nervous. "I only applied for the community grant."

He brushed her question aside. "All your paperwork's in order. The application materials for both are identical. I just added a check mark in the box for the environmental grant alongside the community one."

Feeling a little cheap and a little dizzy, she nodded. "Okay. Is there fine print in the agreement that's going to screw me over?"

He reached into his messenger bag, which he'd dropped next to her purse just inside the door, and pulled out a tablet. "No, but you're welcome to have your lawyer look it over first." He handed the device to her. "Here."

She accepted the tablet but didn't glance at the text as she considered how to ask the question that had been dogging her since she'd caught on to Leo's grand plan to fund her program.

"Just to be clear, this isn't special treatment for the girl who took your virginity, right?"

The look Leo gave her was molten, and when he answered, his voice was pure gravel. "I believe that was mutual virginity-taking."

Mistake. What an utter mistake to bring it up. Yes, she wanted his assurance that she'd gotten this grant through the merits of her program, just like she wanted to know that he truly didn't think she would've written about him in her personal statement for the grant. But that was the worst possible way to go about it. Talking about their history in his presence thickened her blood and turned her nerves into live wires.

Leo cleared his throat. "You're getting this grant because you're the best fit for what I need." He cleared his throat again, louder this time. "The best fit for what Dig Greener needs."

"Okay." She tapped on the document and scanned it quickly, taking in the boilerplate she'd grown used to after working with other grant-writing agencies over the years. The dollar amount was, as he promised, almost twice what she'd originally applied for, every year for three years, after a six-month probationary period and a satisfactory foundation report on progress up to that point. It was the answer to her prayers.

"Sign here?" She was almost whispering as she pointed to the blank at the bottom of the screen. Leo grunted in affirmation, but she hesitated, risking a look at his face. His lids were heavy as he studied her, his chin elevated, and she was briefly tempted to shove the tablet back at him, walk out of that room, and never look back. Working with Leo was such a colossally bad idea.

And then she remembered that she was sleeping in a

canopy bed with pink hearts printed on her sheets. She could do this.

With a flick of her index finger, she signed her name, but when she handed the tablet back to him, their fingers brushed, and she couldn't help her sharp inhale.

He dashed his own signature next to hers and locked the tablet screen, letting it fall back into his bag. But he didn't step away from her, and she was having a hard time breathing again.

"Did we just make the worst possible decision in the world?"

She didn't explain what she meant, but she didn't have to. His throat worked as he swallowed. "I don't know."

He shifted minutely closer to her, so close that she could feel the heat pouring off him.

"So it's not just me? You feel it too?" She whispered the words, terrified that he'd laugh at her, tell her she was imagining the tension that was making her nipples tight and the flesh between her legs pulse.

He was crowding her now, and although she could've taken a step to the side, she didn't. Instead, she held still while his body brushed against hers, grateful that the jacket sleeves hid her goose bumps.

"Do you think I want this?" His dark eyes bored into hers. "Believe me, I don't. I just need my dick to get with the program because this is never going to work otherwise."

Her knees wobbled, and she rested her hand on his abdomen to steady herself. In her defense, it was *right there*, so she really didn't have any other choice. But it probably would've been better if she'd just collapsed to the ground because what her fingers encountered was nothing but solid muscle and bone.

"I don't think I can do this knowing how much you hate me." She directed the words to his collarbones, not daring to meet his eyes.

"Is this hate?" The words sounded like he'd torn them from his throat, and *now* she looked at him. Heat lit his eyes as his gaze raked her face, and she curled her fingers into the smooth material of his suit coat, tugging him toward her until their chests were mashed together and her back was pressed against one of the iron tables. He was breathing as unevenly as she was, and triumph and horror tangled in her stomach at the knowledge that they were both experiencing the same helpless pull.

"I can't stop thinking about you." His face twisted almost as if he was in pain. "Ever since the restaurant, I can't stop thinking about touching you."

How could her body contain all these emotions? She was elated, furious, aroused. The arousal won out.

"Then touch me."

She slid onto the table, letting her legs fall open as she popped the button on her jacket. He stepped in front of her and, without breaking eye contact, ran his hands over her knees and under the hem of her skirt until he reached her hips. His fingers tightened, and he jerked her forward so the fabric rucked up and her throbbing core pressed against his erection. He made a guttural noise in the back of his throat at the contact.

"We both want this." It was a statement, not a question, and he punctuated it with a thrust of his cock against her clit that had her whimpering even though they were both still fully dressed.

"Yes," she gasped as pleasure rocketed to her brain. "I want this. I—"

He didn't let her finish, instead setting her on her feet and spinning her so her back was against his front. Then he pressed a hand between her shoulder blades and pushed her forward until she was bent over the table. The metal was cold against her cheek, and her fingers scrabbled for something to hold onto as he pushed her skirt all the way up to her waist and shoved his fingers past her underwear to stroke her.

His touch was impatient, possessive, and she got so wet, so quickly, she was almost embarrassed. "I've never... so fast..."

Her words were disjointed, but so were her thoughts. Not that it mattered; an almost-growl rumbled through him as he slid two long fingers into her, and she forgot what thoughts even were as he worked them in and out until she was shaking.

He pulled away abruptly, but before she could protest, she heard the rustle of fabric, the rip of a condom packet, and then his breath wasn't the only hot thing caressing her skin. Not being able to see him was delicious torture. She was at his mercy, unable to control what he did next. And what he did next was take his cock and trace it up and down the same path his fingers had just taken, circling her clit, then sliding up to tease her entrance, back and forth until she thought she'd explode.

"Fuck, Leo," she gasped. "Fill me up already."

He answered with a light slap to her ass, and then she felt the stretch of his cock sliding inside her body. God, she'd forgotten. How had she forgotten the way he fit her just right?

"That feels amaz—"

He cut her off with a hand over her mouth as he drove into her with hard strokes. He grunted with each thrust, and he kept her torso pinned to the black metal table. Shock danced along her skin when she realized what he was doing: No eye contact. No talking. No emotion. This wasn't Faith and Leo reconnecting; this was the collision of two bodies. She might as well be a stranger he was using to work out his lust.

She should be enraged. She should bite the hand covering her mouth, should stomp on his foot, should shake him off her. But in truth, the realization spiked her lust even higher. He wanted to use her body to work out all that anger coiling between them? Fine. She was on-fucking-board with that.

Arching her back, she thrust upward, straining up on her toes to grind against him each time his hips slammed into her, increasing the friction and meeting his determined silence with her own.

Leo broke first.

"Fai—fuck," he gasped, wrapping an arm around her chest and pulling her up against him. His fingers plunged under her tank, inside her bra, and he pinched her nipple, making her see stars. His other hand found her clit, and the stars became fireworks.

She was pinned to his body by his hands and his cock, and her mind short-circuited at the realization that they were still mostly dressed, their only skin-to-skin contact the places where his fingers tweaked and circled and teased and, of course, where he was thrusting and retreating and stoking the heat even higher.

She should feel cheap. She should feel used. Instead, she felt dirty and powerful and, oh hello, that was an orgasm shimmering on the horizon.

She pressed down on Leo's fingers where they circled her clit. "That's perfect. Stay right there," she gasped.

He did as instructed, chest heaving against her back as he worked her and worked her until she gasped and shuddered and sagged against him. Only then did he remove his hands from under her clothing to grasp her hips for his final frantic thrusts, ending in a muffled groan against her shoulder as he came.

They both slumped against the table afterward, his body hot against her back, the metal cool against her cheek.

When he finally pulled away from her, she felt the whisper of a touch against the nape of her neck. She almost wondered if he'd pressed his lips there but immediately dismissed the idea. This wasn't sex that ended with a kiss. This was desperation and pressure release, nothing more.

The thought brought her back to reality, and she immediately straightened, tugging her skirt back into place. Self-consciousness crept in at what had just happened, how she'd sounded, how she'd looked. What they'd just done.

He didn't seem bothered by anything though. He might still be in the room with her, but he'd clearly disappeared into his thoughts as he tossed the condom into the trash can in the corner, adjusted his pants, and pushed his hair back into place as best as he could. By the time he was dressed again, she was feeling awkward as hell, and when he opened his mouth to speak, she lifted her hand to stop him.

"Don't. Just don't."

His mouth snapped shut, and he watched her warily as she rebuttoned her jacket and felt behind her to confirm that yes, the safety pin holding her skirt together in lieu of the missing button hadn't gone anywhere.

"I don't need to hear it, okay?" She was suddenly bone-tired, and she didn't have anything left in her tank for another lecture from her sulky, hot-as-hell ex-boyfriend. "I get that we're not friends. I get that this was a mistake. You can skip the big speech."

He ran his thumb along a thick eyebrow before pressing it against his temple as if he had a headache. "I was just going to ask if you were okay to get home."

He sounded almost gentle. Almost like the boy she'd been crazy about in high school. But as she stared at him unspeaking, that hint of vulnerability vanished, and he became the iron-jawed asshole she'd been dealing with since he moved back to town.

"But you're obviously fine," he said tightly.

"Been taking care of myself for a while now." Back when she'd been a dumb kid, she'd dreamed that he'd be the one to do the taking-care-of someday, but she'd been wrong. And she hadn't made that mistake since.

There didn't seem to be much else to say after that, so she swooped her discarded purse off the floor and turned to leave. But something made her turn back. When she did, she found that he hadn't moved; his eyes were opaque, and the crooked collar of his shirt was the only sign of what they'd just done together.

"Um, thanks," she said. "For the grant. It means a lot."

His brows snapped together. "I didn't do it for you."

She inhaled hard through her nose, forcing herself to stay silent for a five count to keep herself from lashing back. Once she'd subdued her temper, she allowed herself to exhale.

"If you say so, Leo." Then she pushed the door open and left.

EIGHT

Leo knocked on the door and waited, jaw tight.

"Yes?" Carlisle Lockhart's eager voice fell several notches when Leo stepped into the office. "Oh, it's you. What do you need?"

You can quit treating me like someone who just shit in your cornflakes. But getting fired less than two months into this new job wasn't on Leo's vision board, so he bit back the sarcasm and said, "Press'll be here soon. Any advice?"

Carlisle's expression didn't shift. "On what?"

What did he think Leo meant? "I'm introducing the community grant recipients today."

His boss barely suppressed a yawn. "Oh that. I'm sure you can handle it."

Leo was absolutely sure he could not. It wasn't that talking to the media wasn't a strong suit of his. It was that he was an absolute train wreck when it came to talking to the media. He tended to growl out monosyllabic answers and scowl in a way that scared off the timid ones and looked terrifying on camera, or so he'd been told the handful of times POR had been featured on the news. But he wasn't about to give soft-handed Carlisle the satisfaction of admitting that. Still, this was his first public appearance as a foundation employee, and he wanted to get it right. He'd already had a meeting with Dale, a chipper guy from public relations, who'd prepped him for the kind of questions the press usually asked at these things. But he wanted to make sure he'd be delivering the proper messages on behalf of the foundation.

"Any specific talking points you think I should hit about the grants?"

"I'm sure I wouldn't know. You own"—he vaguely waved in Leo's direction—"all of this. You'll figure it out."

Naturally star-fucker Carlisle Lockhart thought *none* of this was important, "this" being helping the people who lived in his town. During their short time working together, the older man had made it clear that he found the community grant program to be at the bottom of his priority list, way behind dinners with celebrities and overseas jaunts to visit Big Dig's projects in China and India and Mexico. Why would he give a shit about providing mental health treatment for the unhoused in Beaucoeur when he could jet off to Bangladesh to visit the new medical clinics built with foundation money?

The hell of it was, every overseas program Carlisle bragged about was also life-changing, and Leo was proud to be part of the Big Dig team that was making it happen. But he was even prouder to be helping his neighbors. It just would've been nice to have a little more support from his boss.

"Okay then. Thanks," he muttered before retreating back to his office where he glowered at the note cards he was jotting important phrases onto as a safety net.

Carlisle was right; he'd been the driving force behind these programs, and he'd be able to talk about them without tripping himself up. Probably.

"Ready?"

He looked up to see Dale the PR guy standing in the doorway to accompany him to the press conference. Leo swooped up his note cards and followed him out of the office suite.

"We'll be in the smaller of the auditoriums today." The upbeat man grinned at him as they stepped on the elevator to take them to the second floor. His thick-framed glasses slid down his nose as he consulted a list on his phone. "And all the recipients are there waiting."

All the recipients. No one any more special than the others.

"Denise from the *Courier* is here, and we've got crews from the CBS and NBC affiliates and the local NPR station." His grin widened as if that was supposed to be good news. Then he waved his phone under Leo's nose. "Plus I'll be recording for the Digham website."

"Great." Not great. But it was part of his job now, and hadn't he mastered all kinds of new skills in his first year at POR? This was just another new one.

They reached the double doors of the amphitheater, and Leo hesitated before stepping through. He'd navigated the Amazon rainforest without a map after one of the POR volunteers used it as toilet paper. He could talk to a couple of local reporters.

He sucked a deep breath into his lungs and stepped through the door.

Right. A couple of local reporters—and Faith.

She was standing at the bottom of the tiered auditorium where he'd address the media, talking animatedly with someone he didn't recognize. And as nervous as he was, he couldn't help but notice that she looked... good. Comfortable. She was in dark jeans and a hot-pink blazer over a Beaucoeur BUILD T-shirt, and if he had to guess, he was seeing her in her normal work uniform. Not that damn tweed suit or those short-shorts that he'd been obsessing about for weeks.

This was the person she'd grown up to be: casual, laughing, gorgeous. And he was the idiot who'd thought he could fuck her out of his system.

"Ready?" Dale raised his brows expectantly over his glasses, gesturing at Leo to head to the front of the room.

"Of course." Time to forget about the temporary insanity that had him following Faith out of the rooftop bar and dragging her into that closet.

Once they reached where the group was clustered, Dale introduced him to the TV reporters in the audience —polished, glossy, white-toothed—and the decidedly less polished and glossy woman from the Beaucoeur newspaper. Leo shook all their hands but was too focused on the remarks he'd need to give to smile or do more than grunt a hello.

Greeting his grant recipients went fractionally better. He was acquainted with Isaac and Luna Hamoud, who ran Beaucoeur's new transitional housing facility, and he'd gone to school with the younger brother of Barrett Allen, the man in charge of the job retraining center. But he'd never met the woman who ran the fiber arts collective that provided jobs for those in the area who needed assistance.

"Char, this is Leo Morales," Dale said to the tall woman with the brown-and-gray braid and the clearly hand-knit sweater. "Leo, this is Char McDougall."

"Nice to meet you." Char grabbed his hand and squeezed it enthusiastically. "Hmm. Good grip. I could make a knitter out of you."

It was such an unexpected greeting that it pulled a small smile out of him. "I look forward to you trying."

And then there was no one left to greet but Faith. Her hands were tucked into the back pockets of her jeans as she listened to one of the reporters chattering away, but when Dale called her over, the animation on her face faded to artificial politeness. She definitely didn't look like someone who'd come on his cock in a dusty storage room twenty feet away from where white-collar Beaucoeur was sipping old-fashioneds.

"Leo, this is Faith Fox," Dale said. "Faith, this is—"

"Oh, Leo and I go way back." She lifted her chin in greeting, her demeanor cool compared to the smiles she'd shared with the rest of the room. Leo felt that chill to his marrow.

"Way back," he repeated stiffly. Fucking Faith in a closet was supposed to be something anonymous, something cheap. Something to clear his head and let him move on so they could work together.

It hadn't worked.

Dale's eyes zipped between the two of them—Leo's gaze hard and Faith's politely neutral—before he clapped his hands once. "Okay, let's... get this started." Raising his voice, he said, "If the press would take their seats?"

With a murmur, the half dozen members of the media settled themselves into the front row while the grant recipients sat on the chairs arranged behind the podium where he'd be speaking.

His guts churned as he approached the lectern and fished his note cards out of his pocket, dropping them on the surface and gripping the wooden sides. The action jostled the Digham logo placard attached to the front, which wobbled but held on. He heard one of the reporters exhale a relieved breath.

Going well so far, obviously.

"Thank you all for coming today." He knew he was scowling, knew his greeting sounded like a bark rather than a welcome, but hell, he was doing the best he could in front of even this small crowd. "I'm Leo Morales, and I'm Digham Foundation's new strategic grant manager. I'd like to introduce you to two new foundation grant programs, as well as the first round of recipients."

He gestured vaguely at the row of people behind him, feeling like the world's least enthusiastic game show host, before he shuffled to his next note card. This one was more a crutch than a necessity.

"The community-development grant program is designed to invest Digham money back into the Beaucoeur area, where I grew up. The people of Beaucoeur have been the lifeblood of Big Dig since its founding in"—the first trickle of sweat appeared on his neck as he struggled to make sense of the year written on the card in front of him—"since it was founded."

He glanced up to see all those eyes in the audience fixed on him, along with the red lights of the TV cameras. Clearing his throat, he shuffled to the next card.

"The foundation's advisory board has selected the recipients behind me for the inaugural grant that they believed to be the best community ambassadors for this mission."

As he spoke, he began to relax. He'd reviewed each of the applications, and he was comfortable talking about the merits of the recipients. One by one, he introduced the organizers in charge of the three funded programs, and they took turns stepping to the podium to give a short rundown of how they'd be using the money. Things were going smoothly, far more smoothly than he feared.

And then it was time to introduce Faith.

Before he began, he made the mistake of glancing over his shoulder. Faith was wearing her principal's-office smile as she sat with her ankles primly crossed under her chair, and he had another flash of unreality that he was involved in this. That he'd involved her in this. As his gaze lingered, she flicked her eyes away from him as if he was the least interesting person in the room. And maybe to her he was.

He glanced down at the cards and saw that he was gripping them tightly enough to crush the edges. He smoothed them flat and began speaking.

"The, uh, the next program is a passion project of mine." Shit, why did he use the word *passion*? It was the last thing he needed to be thinking about when it came to Faith.

Focus, fucker.

"I'm happy to say the Digham Foundation will partner with Beaucoeur BUILD to make the Dig Greener initiative a reality, and Faith Fox is here today to give an overview of the new programs her organization will be able to offer." He swallowed hard. He'd said it out loud, in front of cameras and everything. No going back now. They were in this together.

His pulse started to beat in his ears as he glanced at the next card. It was full of numbers, which immediately turned into a jumble of meaningless shapes. What the hell had he been thinking, including this in his talking points?

"Beaucoeur's, um, the city's environmental footprint isn't a small thing. The area produces carbon..."

He lifted the card up, hoping that bringing it closer would help him decipher what he'd painstakingly written out that morning.

"In terms of tons of carbon dioxide, Beaucoeur produces..."

The heavy black writing blurred into incomprehensible squiggle, and when he leaned forward to look more closely, he was so focused on the numbers marching across the paper that the center of his forehead smacked into the microphone with an aggressively audible *thunk*.

The reporters in the audience chuckled softly, and this time he outright crushed the cards in his fist. But indecipherable notes would just make things worse, so he forced his fingers to relax. Unfortunately he overcorrected, and the cards fluttered to the floor.

"Maldita sea la madre que te parió," he muttered. The curse landed directly in the microphone. Even if the reporters didn't understand the Spanish, his meaning was clear enough, and the polite chuckles turned into out-and-out laughs.

Embarrassment burned as he stooped to collect his fucking notes. He'd known he was risking it by including as many specific numbers as he had, but he'd wanted to do a thorough job, to make a case for the threat of climate change and the importance of education and activism. Instead, he'd succeeded in sweating and stammering and concussing himself with the microphone. Maybe if he just stayed crouched behind the podium, the room would clear out and he'd never have to face those reporters with their cameras again. Good plan.

Then a soft hand landed on his back, and a warm

body crouched next to him, swooping up the cards. Faith glanced at their contents, and when she looked up at him, the remoteness in her eyes had been replaced with an understanding that almost knocked him on his ass.

"I got this, okay?" Faith met his eyes, her blue gaze steady and calm, and he nodded curtly. Anything he tried to do at this point would undoubtedly make things worse.

After one more soft touch to his back, she rose and stepped to the podium. "Hi, everyone! Faith Fox from Beaucoeur BUILD. Oh, hey, Andy."

She waved at one of the TV guys, who gave a friendly salute back. Leo, meanwhile, loomed behind her like a big dolt.

"Thank you, Leo, for the introduction. I'm thrilled that BUILD's partnering with you and the Digham Foundation on a project I know is near and dear to your heart." She smiled over her shoulder at him, and the organ in question thumped hard as she did. Then she turned back to the audience and started to work her magic.

"Beaucoeur's environmental footprint is sizable, particularly for a town of our size." She spoke as if she'd practiced the speech and wasn't reading it cold off crumpled cards. "Although we're the twelfth-largest city in Illinois, our carbon footprint is the third largest in the state, producing almost one hundred tons of carbon dioxide annually."

The numbers flowed from her lips with a speed and dexterity that Leo could never have managed. As irritating as it was, he was grudgingly grateful that she'd taken this burden from him.

"So now you might be wondering," she continued with a wry grin, "how BUILD's getting involved. And that's pretty simple. At BUILD, we prioritize STEAM education—that's science, technology, engineering, arts, and math—but we haven't been as creative as we could've been in terms of hands-on application of those concepts, and we haven't focused nearly enough on protecting the world around us. So imagine how grateful I was to learn about Dig Greener."

At that point, Leo crossed his arms over his chest and surrendered complete control to Faith, who was funny and relaxed and informative in a way he'd never be able to manage. Resignation burned through him. They were back here again, with Faith swooping in to rescue him, but this time he was choosing to let it happen because it was the only way to keep this whole show on track.

When she finally reached the end of his cards, she thanked the reporters for their time and turned a questioning glance at him, but he just stepped past her to resume his place at the podium. His only focus now was on wrapping this up and getting away from all these watchful eyes.

The reporters had a few questions for him about specific plans for the various grant recipients, which he handled, but they mostly seemed eager to pack up after tossing out a half dozen queries or so. Within minutes of Dale thanking them all for coming and Leo shaking several hands, the room had cleared out except for him and Faith.

The auditorium that had seemed spacious moments ago was now too small for the two of them.

"I think that went well." She offered him a tentative smile, and he grunted in return. It was the only response he could manage as he struggled to keep his emotions in check.

She kept trying. "Nice job with that question about the Knit Nook—"

"It can't happen again," he bit out.

"A press conference?" She looked at him in confusion.

"Sex." He ground his molars in frustration. With her? Himself? He wasn't sure, so he punished them both. "I have no interest in a repeat of last week."

What a fucking lie. But it worked. She inhaled hard and turned abruptly to swoop up her bag. As she settled the strap over her shoulder with jerky motions, a small smile rippled across her face. "Figures my first orgasm from you would also be my last." Then she walked away, leaving him speechless for the second time that day.

NINE

Faith was in bed with her two favorite companions: a book and a bag of Twizzlers.

She really had intended to read some how-to manuals about camping, just to see what she'd signed on for with Dig Greener, but all the options had looked information-dense and dull, and the little bits she'd flipped through hadn't made the great outdoors seem all that great to her. Then at the suggestion of her librarian friend Darby, she'd checked out copies of *Wild* and *Last Child in the Woods*, but even those hadn't been able to hold her attention. So now she was reading a romance novel with a hot wilderness guide hero, which was much more her speed. Especially since she *would not be having sex with Leo again, full stop*. Might as well seek out fictional thrills.

She was on her stomach with her chin propped on the pillow, gnawing on a Twizzler while the bickering couple inched toward their first kiss, when her phone buzzed. She glanced at it and almost choked on her mouthful of licorice.

After that afternoon, there was no way Leo was

calling to say anything good. She'd annoyed him when all she'd been trying to do was help. And yes, like usual, her help had been a little steamroller-ish. But she understood how much he was struggling, and she *had* asked before stepping in. She'd been leading media Q&As for years with BUILD and could deal with reporters in her sleep, but just like always, it had jostled the Faith and Leo powder keg.

And now there he was, his number flashing on her screen, ready to screw up her day some more.

She sucked in a calming breath and hit Answer. "Hey."

"What did you mean your first and last orgasm?"

So much for him being too worked up to remember her parting shot.

"Hello to you," she shot back.

"What did you mean?" he growled.

Oh hell. That wasn't something she'd intended to share with him, but that's what he got for scowling and snapping and generally being a bag of dicks in her direction at every opportunity.

"I think it's pretty straightforward," she finally said. If she treated it like it wasn't a big deal, then it wouldn't be a big deal.

It was apparently a big deal to Leo. The silence on his end was so thick she could almost reach out and plunge her fingers into it. Finally he said, "So you're saying, all those times when—"

"No. Just forget I said anything." When would she learn that pettiness never paid? "We agreed that we weren't having sex again, so can you just drop it?"

"No, I can't just *drop it*."

Was he imitating her? Was that supposed to be *her*

prissy tone in those last two words? She started to tell him that dropping it was the only option, but she was talking to a dead line. He'd ended the call.

She collapsed and screamed into her pillow, venting her frustration into the mattress like a teenager throwing a tantrum. Leo was turning her into the brattiest version of herself.

Well, she wasn't that girl anymore. And adult Faith didn't care if adult Leo hung up on her a dozen times. His problems were his problems. She had a book to read and snacks to mainline.

Grimly determined not to let him ruin her night, she retrieved her e-reader and settled herself cross-legged against her headboard, turning her attention back to her book. She angrily chomped another Twizzler as she tried to force her scattered mind to pay attention to the sweet words of the hero on the page. Did any real man actually talk like that? Wilderness guide hottie was so clearly written by a woman. Every word coming from his mouth was charming and considerate and lovestruck and…

And kind of like Leo had sounded, once upon a time. Years ago.

Her phone buzzed again, and she dove for it. The bag of Twizzlers hit the floor.

LEO

Open your window.

Her heart slammed against her ribs. Surely he didn't mean…

She scrambled off the bed and bolted to her window, flicking the latch and hauling it up.

"What are you doing, Leonidas?"

"I told you," he said through gritted teeth as he

boosted himself from the first-story window sill to the porch roof adjacent to her room, "not to call me that."

After a paralyzed moment, her arms remembered how to work, and she popped the screen free and pulled it out of the frame just in time for the top of his head to appear over the ledge.

"Step back," he commanded. Then he was lifting himself through the opening and wriggling into her bedroom.

Leo Morales was in her bedroom.

He performed a graceful tuck and roll and glided to his feet as if gravity didn't actually work on him.

"That was easier when I was seventeen," he said.

She was too startled to censor herself. "Well, you've put on about forty pounds of muscles since then."

A rare smile slid across his face. "Noticed that, did you?" Then the smile was gone and the scowl was back. "What the fuck, Dutch? I never gave you an orgasm?"

She spun away and covered her face with her hands. "I told you I don't want to talk about this." Her words emerged muffled, and Leo circled to stand in front of her, arms folded and jaw tight.

"Well, I do. Because the thought that I never actually made you come in all the time we were together is..." He swallowed hard. "It's kind of destroying my whole concept of myself in a way that I really cannot deal with. So if you could just confirm or deny, that would be great."

She dropped her hands to glare at him. "The most words you've spoken to me since we started talking again, and it's about your sexual performance?" Her lip curled in an attempt to hide her pounding heart. "Typical man."

He jerked his hands up in exasperation. "Yes. Any

man would have his world rocked by the news that his girlfriend never enjoyed his touch."

"God, are we really doing this? Fine."

She crossed her arms, matching his combative body language. "It's not that I didn't enjoy it. I did. It made me happy. But I was also a teenager who had a strange relationship with her body and was pretty disconnected from some of those physical cues."

Was she going to tell him this next part? God, why not at this point? Cheeks burning, she continued.

"I thought I was feeling what I was supposed to be feeling because it felt good, but it wasn't until much later —with the help of an expensive vibrator that was a gift from a friend, by the way—that I realized what an orgasm actually felt like." She forced herself not to look away from him. "It wasn't you. It was me. Okay?"

His mouth dropped as she spilled the story of her sexual evolution, and it remained open as he stared at her in silence. Since it didn't look like he had anything to add, she said in a gentler tone, "I loved being with you back then." She wrapped her arms around her midsection, as if she could hug the memories close. "You made me feel special. And I loved making you..." Oh, now she was *really* blushing. Because she'd adored making him come back in the day, adored watching him lose himself in her hands and her mouth and her body.

Leo's burning gaze pinned her in place as he stepped closer. "So you had better sex with people after me?"

"Define better," she said with a weak laugh. "Actually, no. Not having this conversation with you. I don't owe you any explanations."

"But it sounds like I owe you orgasms." He was standing even closer to her now, and she could see his chest rise and fall with his accelerated breaths, could inhale his spicy, woodsy smell. Hair gel maybe? Some kind of manly body wash? Whatever it was made it impossible for her to think straight.

"You don't owe me anything." God, it was hot in her room. She should shut her window to keep the humid summer air out, but that would require stepping away from him, and she didn't have the strength.

"But you did come the other night?" he demanded.

"Y-yes."

He opened his mouth as if he wanted to ask more questions, but she put a hand on his chest before he could. And then she made the mistake of glancing down.

If she hadn't known the shape of Leo's cock before, she would now. Because he was in gray sweatpants. In her bedroom. In his hot adult body. And he was definitely, *definitely* into this conversation.

His gaze slid down, then back up, and he raised his brows but didn't make a move to touch her. In fact, the only person touching anybody here was her, her wayward fingers curling into the neckline of his shirt to brush against his skin.

With a start, she pulled her hand away and stepped back, right against the footboard of her bed. She sat down abruptly, her attempt to put some distance between them actually landing her in the worst possible place to ramp down the tension.

His eyes traveled over her shoulder, and his tongue swept across his lower lip. "Is that the same bed?" His tone was light, but a universe of meaning simmered under that simple question, and she sucked in a breath before answering.

"Same bed," she said. "Where the—"

"—magic happens. I remember."

She struggled to draw breath into her lungs as his eyes traced the cream-colored velvet headboard and tulle canopy overhead. This was where they'd had sex for the first time—the first time with each other and the first time ever for either of them—and he'd given her everything she'd dreamed of with her first love.

Of course now that she was an adult, she knew exactly what she needed in bed, just like she knew adult Leo could give it to her. And just like with those damn sweatpants, it was all she could think of.

Almost without meaning to, she leaned back on the mattress and propped her hands behind her, arching her back and popping her breasts. She was in a tank top and shorts, nothing sexy, but the hitch in Leo's breathing told her that he didn't care about that.

He bent forward and planted one hand on either side of her body, his fingers tense against the pink comforter. Leaning close, he whispered in her ear. "Are your parents home?"

She laughed, a little delighted and a little horrified by this game they were playing. She tilted her head so her cheek brushed his jaw, igniting a million sparks along her skin. "They're in California," she murmured. "We're all alone."

His hands moved from the mattress to her hips, and he trailed the pads of his fingers roughly down the outsides of her thighs, making her shiver. Hot intentions twisted behind his eyes, and she saw it, saw clearly the plans he was making for them. Ways he'd make her come. Ways he'd make *them* come. And oh, she wanted that. Wanted him to act out every dirty thought with her in this bed.

When his gaze locked on hers, they both froze. Because this wasn't anonymous. There was no way Leo could tell himself that this interaction was happening with a stranger, no way he could treat her like some nameless partner. Their hookup in the storage closet had been hot, but this time she wanted him to acknowledge that it was *her* he was touching.

And it worked. Until it didn't.

Awareness came back into his eyes first, the knowledge that there were a million reasons for them not to fall into bed together. Their history for one thing. Their present work situation for another. But still Leo didn't move. In the end she was the one who gently pushed him away. He complied immediately, straightening and clasping his hands behind his back. As he did, his eyes traveled around the room, and his disbelieving laugh snapped the tension.

"Good Lord, Dutch, nothing's changed."

A little thrill moved through her at the realization that he'd been too focused on her until now to pay attention to his surroundings.

"I guess my parents never bothered redecorating after I moved out."

Leo drifted to her wall of bookshelves, stuffed with her childhood books, knickknacks, and awards. He ran a finger over her mini T-Rex skeleton from a school trip to the Field Museum they'd gone on together, and he leaned close to look at her old high school speech trophies in the same place of pride after all these years. The main difference from twelve years ago was the absence of pictures of him. She'd shredded those immediately after their breakup when she'd been too incensed to think straight.

Her room wasn't entirely free of his ghost though. He

paused in front of her vanity where she'd placed the little glass serving bowl with the Dairy Bar logo etched on it. She'd overlooked it in her purge of Leo memorabilia and forgot all about it until she'd moved back in last month. She was using it to hold her jewelry now, perversely enjoying the bittersweet zing it gave her each time she touched it.

He picked it up and cradled it in his hands, and as he did, the weight of their history hit her all of a sudden. If she squinted she could almost see teenage Leo standing alongside today's version, holding the small box carefully wrapped in shiny red paper. The last gift he'd ever given her.

Today wasn't the first time he'd crawled through her window, and to pretend that they didn't share all those memories was ludicrous. She was hit with a sharp desire to stop fighting with him every time they were together.

"Hey, why don't we—" she began as he set the dish down and turned to her.

"Listen, what if—"

They both laughed softly, and then Leo spoke.

"It would probably be easier if we weren't..." He lifted a hand and let it fall.

"Constantly at each other's throats?"

"In any sense of the word." It was almost a joke.

"Yeah." She rubbed her hands over her thighs and offered the best olive branch she could think of. "So maybe not friends but friends-adjacent?"

His lips twitched into an almost smile. "Sure. Friends-adjacent."

How pathetic to feel such relief, but she did. She'd hated hating him.

"We need to set up a call with William," he said,

apparently ready to move on to the business side of their strange new relationship. "See if you think he'd be a good fit for BUILD." He paused, then added gruffly, "I do value your input, you know."

It was good to hear. "Sure. Let's get it scheduled."

With a nod, he turned toward the window, and Faith laughed.

"You can use the front door, you know."

He had one hand on the window frame and twisted to look back at her.

"Why start now?"

But the only thing that moved were his eyes drifting to her mouth, and she knew that all she had to do was stand up and press her lips against his, and he'd tumble her onto the bed and have her halfway to happy town in no time. And as tempting as that was, it would also open up a world of complications that neither of them needed right now. So she stayed perched on the bed, and Leo quirked one last tiny smile at her before he disappeared through her window, leaving her alone with a hollow ache in her stomach because goddamn, he'd looked good in those sweatpants.

THIRTEEN YEARS AGO

The first time Leo met Faith's parents was at the height of the summer before their senior year, which was unfortunate. His lifeguard job at the Beaucoeur public pool had left him tan as hell on top of his already brown skin, and he knew—he just *knew*—how much the WASPy couple were gritting their teeth as they shook his hand. When Faith's father had asked where he was from, he was pretty sure he didn't mean which side of town.

"See? That wasn't so bad." Faith grinned at him as she settled cross-legged onto her fussy pink bed.

He peeled his T-shirt away from his sweaty chest. "That was the most stressful five minutes of my life."

She tossed her head back with a shout of laughter that her parents could probably hear from downstairs, particularly since Faith's bedroom door was open. Even if her mother hadn't called a reminder at Faith as they'd climbed the stairs hand in hand, Leo would've insisted. He wanted Mr. and Mrs. Fox to like him, not wonder what he was doing to their only child under their roof.

Not that he'd hesitate to do anything Faith wanted. But he'd at least wait until her folks weren't home.

Even after months of dating, he was still a little overwhelmed to actually be here in the place where Faith ate and slept and studied. If she never invited him back in, he wanted to remember how it felt to be inside her inner sanctum. Unable to contain his curiosity, he ran his finger along the spines of the books in her bookcase. Hardbacks, all of them, their book jackets making a colorful pattern on her shelves.

"If it's so stressful, just sneak around the back and crawl through my window next time." She pointed, and he crossed the room to check it out.

"I bet I could." It looked possible to go from ground to sill to ledge to roof and then directly to the heaven of his girlfriend's arms without having to talk to her terrifying parents even once.

She beamed at him. "It's a plan. Now stop being weird. Come sit." When she patted the mattress, he walked across the plush cream carpet to perch gingerly on the edge, making sure to keep one foot on the floor, just like his mom always insisted Jessie do when she was hanging out with her girlfriend in her bedroom.

"So this is where the magic happens." He tilted his head back to look at the gauzy fabric draped above her bed.

She just laughed as she kicked off her sandals. "Where the mess happens, you mean."

She fell backward onto the bed while he took in the jumble of lipstick and hair ties and necklaces on her dresser, yesterday's flowery sundress draped over the arm of her desk chair, the framed photo on her bedside table of a much-younger Faith and Thea both dressed as Padmé Amidala for Halloween.

"Beautiful mess." He longed to stretch out next to her. "I see who'll be in charge of keeping our cabin clean."

Surprise danced across her face. "Our cabin?"

Shit. He'd spoken without thinking. He opened his mouth to backpedal, but after the initial furrowing of her brow, her expression turned dreamy. "Tell me about our cabin. Are we on a yacht?"

Her hand found his, and their fingers tangled on top of the pink comforter.

"No, it's the log cabin we buy after you graduate from college," he said. "In a forest somewhere. Just you and me and the trees."

"That sounds really nice."

Although she tugged on his hand to pull him down next to her, he stayed firmly upright. But the yearning on her face made him bold.

"Actually, forget that. Let's go to Vegas right now. Get hitched." He brought their joined hands to his mouth and pressed a kiss to her knuckles, the blood in his veins singing *her, her, her*. But her fingers tensed, and her eyes widened.

Shit. Now he *had* pushed too far. "Um, I was kidding. Of course," he said quickly.

She was looking at him in astonishment. "Most guys don't even, like, joke about that."

"What, getting married?"

She nodded, her hair slippery against the pillow.

He shrugged. "Most guys aren't dating you."

Most, hell. *He* was the guy dating her, and he wanted to be that guy forever. But she was probably going to tell him it was too much, too fast. He held his breath, waiting to be ejected from this pink paradise for wanting her too much. But when she finally spoke, her voice was full of joy.

"Okay. Let's go to Vegas. Get hitched. Live together in a cabin forever. Just you and me and the trees."

This time when she tugged on his hand, he didn't resist stretching out next to her. The door was open, and he could still kiss her with one foot on the floor.

TEN

"Did I ever tell you about the time I got bitten by an iguana?"

"An iguana?" Faith peeked around the stack of binders piled in front of her, nose adorably scrunched. "No. But we haven't exactly sat down to exchange our post high school life stories."

Leo nudged the binders over and held out his hand. "Nasty infection." He held his breath as she traced a finger along one of the pale half-moon scars bracketing the fleshy section under his pinky finger. "I had to leave the job site and head into Iquitos for antibiotics. For a minute there, I was scared I was going to lose the whole hand."

"Yikes. Did you bleed all over the place?"

Despite her gory question, the overall vibe between the two of them was relaxed. Agreeing to a cease-fire had put them both at ease during their first real workday together.

"Yep." He wiggled his fingers and ignored the way his hand still tingled from her touch. "Anyway, I bring it up only to say that almost bleeding to death in a jungle surrounded by biting iguanas was preferable to reading one more Beaucoeur BUILD annual report."

He scowled down at the hundreds of pages of metrics, assessments, and executive summaries dedicated to closing the loop, but Faith just widened her eyes in faux confusion.

"Geez, you'd think someone with a cushy office chair and a view of the city from the eighteenth floor would be used to pushing papers."

He laughed. "Never." In fact, BUILD's water-stained ceiling tiles and muddy orange carpet were much more his speed.

Faith patted his scarred hand. "There's more where that came from."

She stood and crossed the room to the battered bookcase running along the wall, stretching onto her tiptoes to reach another binder on the top shelf. And while his mother would scream bloody murder if she witnessed her only son not leaping up to help, Leo just couldn't make himself. Because today Faith was in a plain white T-shirt and a swingy red skirt that barely hit the tops of her knees. Every time she moved, that fluttery skirt would shift and give him a peek at her thighs, and when she lifted her arms above her head like that? Coño. He stopped breathing entirely.

The Faith he knew in high school had always been so solid in her convictions, so quick to voice her opinions. And her sturdy figure of today suited that no-fucks-given attitude so much better than the almost brittle thinness of her teenage years. Not that he'd say so out loud, of course; he knew better than to offer his opinion about things that weren't his business. His older sisters had knocked that lesson into his head early. But their not-so-gentle training didn't stop him from lacing his fingers behind his head and watching the material of the skirt pull against her nice plump ass or from almost falling out of his chair when she turned around and he had to abruptly avert his gaze so he wouldn't get busted checking her out.

"Can I ask you something?" she said as she resumed her seat.

Leo nodded absently, distracted with thoughts of shoving all the binders off the table to work off his orgasm debt to her.

"What did you really want to do with Dig Greener? I assume it wasn't supposed to be outdoor education."

Ah. She wanted an actual conversation. Not the time for inappropriate thoughts that they'd agreed not to have anymore.

Out of habit, he punted. "You mean environment-based educational programs with an emphasis on green initiatives?"

As he intended, Faith laughed. But then she looked at him expectantly, clearly prepared to wait him out until he provided her with an actual answer. That tactic had been his undoing when they'd met as kids, and it seemed to be working again today. Because when Faith's cheeks rounded into her small, private smile, the one that felt like it was just for him, he was putty. Always had been.

Complete honesty. Why not?

"Planting trees is important, but I wanted to do... *more*. Reach more people, develop more programs. Sustainability, community problem solving. That kind of thing. But it takes money and infrastructure to get something like that off the ground."

"So that's why you took a desk job." She nodded like

something had snapped into place for her. "Because you'd get resources you didn't have at Protect Our Rainforests."

Emotion lodged in his throat at her succinct explanation. Despite the years separating them, she understood his motivations almost as well as he did. Certainly better than his parents or his sisters, who still seemed a little confused about why he'd left POR to move back home. But Faith got that Digham was more than a simple desk job for him.

"Then a bossy blonde burst into my office, and here I am, getting ready to teach kids about conservation."

She worried at her lower lip. "I hope you're not too disappointed to be working with BUILD and not a recycling center or something."

"Are you kidding? It's perfect."

He almost didn't go on, but then he remembered standing in her bedroom the previous week and being bombarded with memories. They'd shared everything back then; who in the world would understand this better than Faith?

"I didn't really figure out how to learn until I got out of the classroom. My college classes that took me into the field were"—he smoothed a thumb over his eyebrow as he considered how to phrase it—"they were the first time I felt like I belonged somewhere. Like my brain worked right."

Her Cupid's bow mouth curved downward. "Your brain always worked right."

He snorted. "Not for algebra." Or for long division or remembering his phone code or figuring out how early he needed to leave to be on time for things.

"Anyway, when the idea popped into my head in that board meeting, I saw it in an instant: I can help the kids who do better with hands-on learning. And there's tons of research about the benefit of nature-based education programs. It's good for their brains."

Faith leaned forward, her moonlight hair falling around her face. "I don't want to make things weird, but it's truly an honor to get to help you do that."

Then she smiled at him, and it was like the sun hitting early-morning fog. He smiled back, helpless to do anything else, and for a moment they weren't exes or sort-of friends or even coworkers. They were Leo and Faith, Faith and Leo, as if they'd never been separated, never spent a moment apart, never broken each other's hearts.

An electric chime sounded, and Faith blinked and looked away.

"Oh damn, is it four already?" Faith grabbed her phone and checked the time. "Let's use my office to call William. Leave the binders; we can pick this back up when we're done."

He bit back a groan at the thought, and she gave a wicked laugh and ushered him through the door. The two of them were the only people in the BUILD suite today since most of her staff had taken other jobs to support themselves as the funds had dwindled, and it was taking time to hire them all back.

"Any last-minute things I need to know?" she asked as they headed down the hall.

"You're going to love him." He spoke without thinking, and she glanced at him curiously.

"Oh yeah?"

Why'd he have to go and say that out loud? He settled for grumbling, "All women do," aware as he did that he was just making things worse.

Faith pursed her lips, but before she could ask any

follow-up questions—probably something like, "Is that jealousy I hear?"—he pivoted. "You did review his résumé, right?"

His tone was accusatory, and it did its job of making her roll her eyes at him. "Of course. I was just wondering how you two met."

She led him into her shoebox office, which was so crammed with filing cabinets and stacks of papers that she could barely close the door. She gestured to her desk where a stackable metal chair was placed next to a slightly nicer one on wheels. Apparently they'd be chatting with William cheek to cheek in front of her laptop.

"On a POR job site near Manaus in Brazil about seven years ago. It was our first assignment together, and we hit it off. Worked together ever since. He took over as supervisor when I moved here."

For some reason he was reluctant to sing William's praises too much, so he limited his remarks to job-based observations. Besides, William would have no problems selling himself once he was on the line.

Faith settled into the chair next to him, her shoulder brushing his.

"Someday you're going to have to tell me how you ended up planting trees in South America for a living. You know, in the spirit of our new sort-of friendship."

"Boring story," he said. "A Protect Our Rainforests recruiter came to a campus job fair my senior year, and I said yes."

Faith twitched her ruby-red lips—the precise color of her skirt, not that he'd given it much thought—but the *ding* of William logging on interrupted any possible follow-up questions. The instant his friend's face appeared on-screen, Leo was treated to the sound of Faith's soft, involuntary gasp.

"Hey, y'all." William's drawl filled the room, and Faith lifted her hand in a dazed greeting.

"Hi!" She unfurled her brightest smile. "You must be William Cooper."

His answering smile was similarly radiant. "I am. And you must be Faith Fox."

"I am!" Simply being in William's virtual presence made her giggle.

Leo barely suppressed a sigh. "Looks like being the boss agrees with you."

He'd become something of an expert at the effect William had on women, and right now his friend was at sun-god level of tan and scruffy. No wonder Faith sounded a little breathless.

Then again, Leo'd been the one who had her panting not so long ago, hadn't he?

Faith jumped right into the conversation. "I'm not looking at this as an interview but more like a chance for us to get to know each other." She lowered her lids, glancing down at her list of questions, then smiled back up at William. "Since we'll be working so closely together."

Leo's smug satisfaction dimmed at her words and were extinguished entirely when William linked his fingers behind his head and grinned back. "Fire away."

She did, running through the list of things she wanted to grill William about, from his work history to his experience with kids to his philosophy on holiday office parties. Leo let his mind drift as their back-and-forth washed over him; he already knew his friend had the ideal background and personality to take the lead on Dig Greener. But his attention sharpened when Faith spoke his name.

"What?" His question came out most harshly than he intended, and Faith frowned.

"I was just asking William if he was there when you tangled with that iguana."

"I was," William said immediately. "Drove him to the hospital myself. I told him to be careful messing around in the jungle overgrowth."

Leo grunted. "I was searching for the canteen *you* dropped."

"Grandpa Leo, always making sure everyone in the group's safe and hydrated."

"Grandpa Leo?" Faith turned to him with a wide-open expression of glee, and he gave her his best glower in return.

"Don't get any ideas," he warned her. "And you"—he pointed to the screen—"I'll take back my recommendation."

Faith brushed him off. "Too late. The man's spent years on environmental education programs in South America. You were right; he's perfect."

A little *too* perfect. Leo watched sourly as William dialed up that golden-boy charm.

"Glad you think so," he said. "I loved working with those kids, but I'm excited to move back to the States. Plant some roots a little closer to home in my old age."

Faith leaned forward to prop her chin on her hand. "Oh yeah? Where are you from?"

"He's from Kentucky," Leo muttered. "And he's only thirty-four."

William's golden brows arched. "Well, *he's* a ball of sunshine, isn't he?"

"Oh, always." Faith smirked but didn't look away from the screen. "Just constant, unstoppable positivity. Was he like this when you worked together?"

"Every. Single. Day," William said.

What a delight, witnessing inside jokes spring up between his first love and his best friend. Leo swallowed his irritation and attempted to steer them back to actually important issues.

"Assuming you're still interested in the job, when could you start?" he asked.

William's teasing smile dropped. "I don't know if you heard, but Reggie's willing to take over as supervisor, so I can wrap pretty quickly."

Leo blinked. "Reggie didn't quit?"

"Nope. Decided to stick around," William said. "I was as surprised as you are."

Faith rolled ahead with the interview, blithely unaware of the actual conversation he and William were having beneath the surface.

"We'd like you here as soon as possible." She jerked her head toward Leo. "Until you're here, I'm stuck with this one."

"The horror." William refocused on her. "If I start wrapping things up now, I should be there by mid-September. Early October, tops—if I'm correct that this is a job offer, that is."

"An enthusiastic one," Faith said. "Leo vouches for you, and it seems like you and I will get along just fine."

"Better than fine." William's smugly happy tone had Leo wondering why he'd ever considered this guy a friend.

"Great!" She beamed. "I'll email an employment package for you to review."

"Great," William echoed. "Grandpa Leo, I assume you've already got a list of bars with the best tequila selection for me, yeah?"

Almost against his will, the corners of his mouth twitched upward. "On it."

"My man!" William gave them a double thumbs-up that should've looked ridiculous coming from a grown man but on William came off as self-assured. "See you both in Beaucoeur."

His box on the laptop went black, and Faith closed the program with a happy sigh.

"Wow. What a great guy!" she said, "It's exciting, right? Your friend's moving to town."

Leo's only answer was a grumble, which prompted Faith to huff in exasperation. "What's the problem now?"

"There's no problem," he said tersely. Just his unreasonable jealousy over the Faith/William energy flowing through the call. But it wasn't his business who she smiled at, and William was the missing piece of the puzzle to keep Dig Greener rolling forward. Leo's own wants were irrelevant.

Faith barreled ahead. "He's going to be great with the students. The teachers too. He seems patient, enthusiastic..."

"Like a golden retriever." He sounded childish, but he couldn't stop himself.

She just shrugged. "Everybody loves golden retrievers."

He was dying to ask if that's what *Faith* preferred these days, but her office phone rang, and he jumped at the chance to escape. He wandered back to the workroom as a text from his alleged friend appeared on his phone.

WILLIAM

That went well. Thanks again for recommending me.

LEO

Sure. So Reggie decided to stay?

WILLIAM

She did. You must be easy to get over.

LEO

There was nothing for her TO get over.

And there wasn't. Just a series of hookups over the years. Her threatening to quit POR if he left hadn't made sense to anybody, least of all him.

WILLIAM

By the way, you should've warned me about Faith.

LEO

??

WILLIAM

That she's hot, dude. Bombshell pinup-model hot.

Leo's fingers tightened around his phone as he pondered fast-acting poisons. Cut brake lines. Maybe a staged hiking accident. But he had no right getting pissed at William, especially since William had no idea about his history with Faith.

Still, he could try to throw some cold water on this.

LEO

You're going to be coworkers.

> **WILLIAM**
> Which is why I'm saying it to you one time before I drop it forever.

Right. William was a good guy.

> **WILLIAM**
> Just like you dropped it with Reggie.

Okay, maybe not such a good guy.

> **LEO**
> Fuck off, you know these are different situations.

> **WILLIAM**
> Just messing with you. Drinks on me once I get to town?

Leo tossed his phone down without bothering to respond. The sooner William got here, the sooner his friend would take over the day-to-day business with BUILD, freeing Leo from the frequent interactions with Faith. At that point whatever happened between his best friend and his ex-girlfriend wouldn't be any business of his.

He just needed to make it through the next few weeks, and then she'd be out of sight, out of mind.

ELEVEN

She'd almost made it out the front door when a voice from the dining room stopped her.

"Faithy? Is that you?"

Damn. So close. She blew out a breath and turned to face the parental music.

"Who else would it be?" Her tone was bright, but her pace was reluctant as she shuffled into the wood-paneled room. This early in the morning, it was awash in sunlight and smelled like bacon.

"Sit." Her mom patted the chair next to her. "It feels like we haven't seen you in weeks!"

That was eighty percent her backbreaking workload of getting BUILD up to speed and twenty percent intentional avoidance, but Faith wasn't a total asshole. She could sit and drink coffee with her parents for a few minutes before bolting.

"I've been so busy!" She chirped her response as she fetched a dainty china cup from the service tray and filled it from the carafe. "Now that kids are back in school, we're swamped getting all our programs rolled out."

Thanks to the grant, she was working long hours at BUILD, and Leo often joined her at the end of his workday at Digham, which she loved and hated in equal parts.

She settled into a chair across the table from her parents and snagged a muffin. Her mother frowned as she started to peel off the wrapper.

Kind. Calm. Collected.

"What's the rule?" Faith asked mildly.

Her mother sighed. "Apologies, sweetheart."

Faith had laid down the law against monitoring anyone else's food intake the first time she'd joined her parents for dinner after she moved in, and her mother had been surprisingly good about sticking to it. In fact, Betsy seemed so grateful to see her on a regular basis that Faith was pretty sure she could request a live orchestra to accompany every meal, and her mom would make it happen.

Her father, as always, was less demonstrative. Today he barely spared her a glance over the top of the *Beaucoeur Courier*. "Where are you off to so early on a Saturday?"

"BUILD has a table at the Gourd Olde Days Festival." Which she was going to be late to set up if she didn't finish her breakfast and leave. She gulped a scalding mouthful of coffee, immediately regretted it, and waved her hand like a maniac to fan away some of the heat.

"Isn't the Gourd festival just pumpkin crafts and beer tents?" Her mother's dainty nose wrinkled.

God, what a snob. "It's way more than that. There are tons of booths promoting local businesses." She kept her voice upbeat despite her irritation. "We're hoping to drive sign-ups to the new Dig Greener initiative. I'm really excited about it."

Both her parents hummed in response, but she'd already lost their attention. Although they'd never cared about the details of her work, it still stung to see her father so much more interested in the business section of the Saturday paper.

She knew one way to get him to notice her though.

"It's Leo Morales's baby, you know."

Yep, that did it. So much for kind, calm, *or* collected. The elder Foxes' heads snapped up in unison, their expressions uniformly aghast. Her mother's eyes even strayed to Faith's midsection.

"What did you say?" Betsy whispered.

Faith snorted and rubbed her stomach rolls. "Come on, that's pudge, not a pregnancy." Hadn't her parents made damn sure Leo wouldn't impregnate their daughter years ago? "What I mean is, Dig Greener is Leo's baby. It's his pet project at Digham."

Her mother smoothed a hand over her immaculate bob—a sure sign that she was ruffled—and her father dropped the paper onto his plate of scrambled eggs.

"Are you telling me that boy works for Big Dig?"

When she woke up this morning, she hadn't intended to choose violence, but there she was. Might as well have fun with it.

"*That man* is a grant manager for the Digham Foundation. He's the one who got me the money I needed to keep BUILD going." Franklin blinked at her as she casually twisted the knife. "In fact, we were having drinks last month when we ran into George. George Voit. He asked how you were doing."

His jaw dropped. "You and that boy had drinks with *George Voit?*"

"*That man,*" she said testily. "And yes, that's what I said. George is excited about the new program. And I'd love to tell you about it since you're both *so* interested in my work, but I'm already late. Thanks for the coffee."

She set her dainty little cup down with a clink, crammed the rest of her muffin into her mouth, wishing she'd ignored her mother's greeting and grabbed drive-through coffee the way she'd intended. Too many conversations with her parents ended like this one, with her intentionally pushing their buttons and them not knowing or caring about how to deal with their rebellious daughter. No mantra was strong enough to help her get through these encounters.

She really needed to set aside time to figure out her living situation, but she'd been going nonstop with the normal back-to-school craziness alongside rehiring her staff and getting Dig Greener up and running. Plus she felt a little uncomfortable giving herself a chunk of the grant to put down first and last on a new place. She'd worry about paying herself once everything at work had stabilized, but with her parents' travel schedule taking them out of town all the time and her own dawn-to-dusk work life, it was easier to just kind of coast along in her old canopy bed for the time being.

So she'd add apartment-hunting to her to-do list, but right now she needed to double-check that she'd loaded all the signage, brochures, and swag that she'd need into her old reliable car, then head to the Cavelier County fairgrounds where the Gourd Olde Days Festival was held every year. She'd just parked in the packed-earth lot closest to their assigned table, which was still quite the hike, when her phone dinged.

> LEO
>
> Here yet? I'll help you carry the stuff.

As far as texts went, it was about as practical as it got, but she still clasped her phone to her heart. Was it pathetic to swoon over a man who showed up and offered to be helpful? And did it increase or decrease the patheticness when the man in question was the love of her high school life who'd gotten even hotter since then?

> FAITH
>
> That would be great. Lot C, third row.

Ten minutes later, she was leaning against the passenger-side door, enjoying the sun on her face, when she discovered a sight she enjoyed even more: Leo weaving through the rows of parked vehicles on his way to her. When he was close enough, he shook his head.

"I still can't believe you drive the same car."

She patted the hood of her ancient Audi. "I never joke about my ride." And speaking of things she wouldn't mind riding. "Look at you, Mr. Corporate Casual."

She kept her tone light, but heat twisted in her belly. The fit of that Digham Foundation polo shirt ought to be illegal. It was just tight enough to show the ripple of his back muscles as he loaded the boxes of supplies onto her little dolly but not so tight that it looked like he was trying too hard.

And then there were his jeans. Lovingly broken in. Tight around thighs that had clearly been used for... she had no idea, actually. Digging? Hauling rocks? Cutting through the jungle with a machete? Some part of his do-gooder past life had given him leg muscles she wanted to wrap herself around.

"You ready?"

Flustered, she tore her eyes away and waved a hand in front of her burning cheeks. "The sun! It's so hot out here."

His tongue peeked out of the corner of his mouth as he smirked. "If you say so, Dutch," he said. "Let's do this."

TWO HOURS LATER, Faith had had enough.

"I need you to knock it off, Leonidas."

Their table at the Gourd Olde Days Festival was on a prime stretch of the fairgrounds, at the intersection of the rides and the concession tents where the festival-goers could buy every squash-based food item in existence. She'd interacted with a handful of families who'd been involved with Beaucoeur BUILD over the years and collected at least two dozen names of kids interested in Dig Greener. And she'd managed to do it all despite the storm cloud lurking behind her.

Leo folded his arms and scowled even harder. "Knock what off?"

"This"—she waved a hand—"this whole vaguely hostile vibe you've got going on. You look like you're ready to order a hit on the next person who takes a brochure."

He grunted. "Sorry you don't like my face."

She only hesitated for a moment before reaching up to rest her hands on his cheeks.

"I adore your face. I'd just adore it more if you were

using it to smile at the children who might sign up for Greener."

At her touch, his posture softened, and he leaned into her palm for the briefest of moments before pulling away. "Did you just tell me to smile more?"

"I believe I did," she said. "Are you going to listen?"

"No." He shifted his weight from foot to foot as he gazed around the crowded festival's main drag. "It's weird. Everything looks just the same."

Faith caught her lower lip in her teeth at the memory. She'd dragged him here when they'd been dating, pulling him from booth to booth and vendor to vendor while she exclaimed over the handmade jewelry and the painted gourds entered in the annual decorating contest. Although he'd claimed a town celebration devoted to produce wasn't his scene, he'd held her hand and eaten fried squash blossoms and given his opinion about which pair of pumpkin earrings he liked better. She was wearing them today, in fact, in the spirit of the festival.

"Come on, you loved it back in the day."

He glanced down at her, and although his face was stony, she could practically read his mind: it hadn't been the festival he'd loved. It had been her.

She blinked and looked away, unable to keep meeting his eyes with those thoughts rushing to the surface. Her gaze fixed on the booth across from BUILD's on the opposite side of the wide pedestrian path, and one of the booth's inhabitants shot her a cheery wave.

She brightened and waved back, grateful for the distraction. Her friend Mabel Bowen had apparently just started her shift behind the table for her radio station, 105.5 the Brick. Mabel mouthed an exaggerated "How are you?" then rolled her eyes and pointed at the guy in the booth with her. The station owner, Brandon Lowell, didn't notice a thing as he chatted up a pair of twenty-something women who'd stopped at the Brick's table.

Brandon stepped out of the booth with a T-shirt and stood way too close as he held it up to check the sizing on first one woman, then the other. Mabel silently pretended to gag, and Faith shot her a sympathetic grimace. Brandon was a wealthy sleaze who hadn't made a great impression on her when they'd met at the station a few months ago, and today wasn't doing much to improve that.

"Friends of yours?" Leo asked.

"Yeah," she said. "That's Mabel. She hates her boss so much it's almost funny."

"I know the feeling."

She assumed he was talking about that prick Carlisle Lockhart and couldn't disagree.

When his eyes strayed back to the Brick booth, she reluctantly asked, "Did you want me to introduce you?" It was on the tip of her tongue to tell him that Mabel was in a serious relationship, in case he was about to ruin her day by asking for an introduction to her hot friend. But he shook his head and rolled his shoulders restlessly.

"You just... how do you *know* everybody?"

"It's called living in your hometown. You should try it sometimes— Oh wait, that's literally what you're doing right now." She blinked up at him innocently, delighted when she caught the flicker of a smile. "Like I said, you should've walked in the parade. Burn off some of that broody energy."

"Me? Smiling and waving from a float?" He grimaced, but Faith had figured him out years ago; that was his "I'm secretly enjoying this conversation" grimace.

"It's okay; I'll just put you to work in front of the

table," she said. "You can attract all the moms who might be interested in your hiking program. Wait, sorry, your environment-based educational programs."

He smiled and shook his head. "Why me? Why not you?"

"I'm not the one who chose this shirt, buddy." She pinched the ultrasoft material where it stretched over his ribs, pulling it even tighter against his stomach.

The corners of his eyes crinkled as she flattened her hand against his side, starting a slow slide down his waist. And then a cheerful voice interrupted the moment.

"Hellooooo!"

Faith jumped away and turned to see two of her BUILD staff members headed in their direction.

"How'd it go?" Judging by their bright eyes and big smiles, the parade had been a success, but Faith always felt better hearing a full report.

"Fabulous," said Jonah, her language arts tutor and event planner. "We gave away all our candy, which means at least six hundred people have stickers with our logo and QR code."

"Excellent work!" Faith high-fived him, extra grateful to have him back on her staff full time thanks to the Digham Foundation money in the BUILD bank account. "How many of our tutoring kids showed up to walk with you?"

"Close to twenty," Elaine said, adjusting her oversized, rimless glasses. Then the retired calculus teacher shot Faith a sly glance. "Don't worry; we sent them home with their families instead of dropping them off with you to babysit."

She and Jonah laughed at Faith's groan, and Leo looked around in confusion.

"What am I missing?"

Jonah grinned. "The boss is scared of kids!"

"What boss?" Leo asked. When the other two pointed in her direction, he turned to her in surprise. "You? You're not scared of anything."

"It's not that I'm scared of them." She raised her voice to be heard above the laughter. "It's just that they outnumber us, and someday they're going to figure that out and use it to their advantage. Plus I never know how to, you know, *talk* to them."

Elaine leaned in to Leo and mouthed, "Terrified."

"If she doesn't deal with kids, why do you keep her around?" Leo's eye crinkles were back, and Faith's breath caught in her chest as he looked at her with the amused affection she'd only seen in her dreams for years.

"Oh, Faith knows more about pedagogical theory than some of my college professors," Jonah said. "Her lesson packets are things of beauty."

She shrugged modestly. "We all have our talents."

Like Leo, for example. His talent was looking at you like you were the only thing that mattered. It was a miracle to experience, and losing it was the coldest feeling imaginable. She should know.

She turned away from him, not wanting to dwell on the past any more today, and addressed her employees. "Jonah, did you say you're meeting Freddy for lunch?"

"Correct." He turned to Elaine. "Want to join me and the husband for pork tenderloin sandwiches? I assume these two have things under control here."

"Sure. Go," Faith said immediately. "Thanks again for parade duty!"

The pair left amid flurries of "see you on Monday," and then she was alone with Leo again.

"Nice people," he said.

"Yes. And they have jobs thanks to you."

He waved off her words. "Thanks to Big Dig and the work you already did on BUILD." He paused. "Even if you hate kids."

The eye crinkles. The only-person-in-the-universe look. It was all back, and she was in danger of drowning in it.

Or she was until a pack of shouting children descended on their table.

TWELVE

Nothing slammed the brakes on wayward sexual thoughts like the arrival of five of your blood relatives under the age of ten.

"Uncle Leo! Uncle Leo!"

The attack seemed to be coming from all sides, and when Leo stepped out from behind the table to intercept it, he was immediately swarmed by children. He swooped the youngest two into his arms while the other three clung to his legs and waist.

He was greeted with a chorus of "Uncle Leo!" and "Bendición!"

"Dios te bendiga," he replied automatically as he cuddled his twin nieces close and looked around. "Where is your mother?"

"Coming!"

Bearing down on him were not one, not two, but all three of his sisters, each one with an identically determined expression on her face. With a grim sense of foreboding, Leo realized why they were at the fairgrounds today, and it wasn't because they loved gourds.

His oldest sister Vanessa reached him first and pried one of her son's arms from around his waist. "Mom told us you'd be manning a booth today, so we wanted to come lend our support."

Her words were friendly, but Leo started to sweat when her glittering eyes swung over his shoulder to narrow on Faith.

The second oldest, Cecilia, reached his side and plucked first one and then the other twin out of his arms. "Some things you just have to see to believe." Like Vanessa, her gaze locked on the woman standing behind the table with a frozen smile on her face.

Jessie, only a year older than him and usually his ally, lifted her chin in his direction before folding her arms over her chest. "Like we'd miss the chance to come say hello."

"So nice of you," he said a touch desperately. "And it's great to see you, but why don't we just catch up at the house later?"

The nephews still clinging to his legs howled in disappointment, and he dropped a hand on each of their shoulders. "Lots of time to play at Abuelita's, right?"

"Mom said we could have pumpkin ice cream!" the deceptively angelic-looking Mateo wailed.

Leo crouched to rub his back. "And we can. Why don't we go do that now, in fact?" Like right now. Anything to move all this overly protective big sister energy away from the general area.

But it was too late. The trio were approaching the table in a mass of swinging hair, shiny earrings, and insincere smiles.

"Um, hi!" Faith's eyes bounced from one sister to the next. "It's so good to see all of you again!"

Vanessa tilted her head. "Mm-hmm. Mom said Leo's new job had him working with Fea, so we had to come see for ourselves."

"Vani," Leo said in warning, but none of his sisters paid him any notice.

"What?" Cecilia was all innocence. "It's been so long since we'd even thought about Fea, and now here she is."

He glanced at Faith to see if she understood the insult his sisters were throwing at her, but her brow was creased in confusion, not anger. Good. If she knew they were calling her ugly, he shuddered to think how things might escalate.

"*Fe*"—he hit the Spanish word for *faith* hard—"and I are getting students signed up for the program I started."

"Leo's been wonderful." Faith jumped in. "He's so passionate about outdoor education."

Vanessa bared her teeth in a grin. "That's our Leo. So passionate."

Faith's mouth snapped shut, but she didn't turn to him for help or shrink under their sisterly glares. Instead, she lifted her chin and said, "I've learned a lot from him about the importance of adding environmental concepts to a curriculum. It's going to be a life-changer for lots of kids in the area."

While she'd been effortlessly charming with everyone who'd stopped by their table prior to this, now she was stiff. His sisters would absorb her discomfort and use it to power up their aggressive but well-meaning defense of him.

He had to get them out of there.

"Pumpkin ice cream!" he shouted in desperation. "What do you say, Sammy? Mateo? Carlos?"

The kids whooped and swarmed their mother,

begging for treats, and to his vast relief, Vanessa relented. As a group, his sisters turned away from Faith with dismissive hair flips. "Coming?" Jessie called over her shoulder at him.

"Just a sec." He leaned over the table to peer at Faith. "You good?" he asked in an undertone.

She scrubbed her hands down the side of her jeans. "I'm not sure." She glanced down and exhaled slowly, and when she looked up, she was smiling. "No, it's fine. Go take them for ice cream. I'm good."

"You're sure?" He wanted to squeeze her shoulder—hell, he wanted to pull her into his arms and squeeze her whole body against his—but he didn't dare touch her. Not when they had an audience—or ever, come to think of it. Nothing good could come of hugging her.

"Of course." She waved him off, then did something equal parts stupid and brave. "Nice to see you all again," she called to his sisters. "I'd love it if your kids want to sign up for Leo's program!"

He snorted. "You're a glutton for punishment, aren't you?"

"Always." Her eyes danced with laughter, and she gave him a little shove. "Go, before there's gunplay."

"Back soon," he promised, then he hustled away to herd his family to a safe distance.

The concession area was pandemonium with lines snaking around the various food and drink booths. By the time everyone was seated with all the gourd-based food their hearts desired—butternut squash ravioli, gourd curry, pumpkin donuts and ice cream and beer—his wallet was significantly lighter and his patience was at an end.

"Care to tell me what the hell that was all about?" He

didn't want the kids to overhear, but he was too annoyed to put this conversation off any longer.

All three of his sisters turned wide, innocent eyes on him, as if this was just a regular Saturday outing.

"We just wanted to support you at your new job," Cecilia said.

"Bullshit."

Mateo's head whipped up. "Uncle Leo!"

"Sorry, kid," Leo called before turning back to his sisters. "But that's... *crap* and you know it."

Vanessa downed a spork full of whipped squash before answering, "Jessie, Cece, do you remember what Leo was like after that blanquita rica was done with him?"

Cecilia's lips pursed like she'd tasted something bad. "I sure do, Vani. The word *destroyed* comes to mind."

"Devastated," Jessie added. "The pits of despair."

"Come on, I wasn't—"

"Despair, Leo," Vanessa said firmly. "And we never, *ever* want you to have to go through that again. So when Mom told us you were working with that woman, we knew what we had to do."

Leo scrubbed his hands down his face. "Has it escaped your notice that I'm an adult man?"

"Never! You're our muñeco," Cece crooned as she pinched his cheek.

He batted her hand away. "I'm not your little doll."

His middle sister smiled and turned back to her squash, leaving his oldest sister to pick up the argument.

"We just wanted to remind Fea that you've got people looking out for you," Vanessa said.

Cece sniffed. "Fea? More like gordita."

"Hey." Leo's voice cracked above the cacophony of

the food tents, and everyone at the table froze. "None of that shit."

The tips of his ears burned at his outburst, but no way was he letting anyone in his family criticize Faith's appearance. Bad enough that they'd been calling her ugly without her realizing it. This, he wouldn't tolerate.

"She. Looks. Gorgeous." He enunciated every word with precision, glaring at each of them in turn as he did.

The kids quickly lost interest in the adult drama and turned back to their ice cream, but all three sisters were looking at him with a mix of concern and confusion on their faces.

Jessie was the first one to recover. "I hate to say it, but Leo's right. That girl is thick in the best possible way now."

Never had he been so grateful that he and Jessie had extremely similar taste in women.

"You know I liked her back in the day," she told him. "But I'll personally jab my heel into her neck if she hurts you again."

She calmly sipped her beer, leaving Leo to shake his head. "You guys got meaner while I was overseas."

"The world got meaner." Cece shrugged. "We adapted."

"Well, Faith didn't get meaner, so back off."

Vanessa leaned forward, eyes narrowed. "Wait, are you two back together?"

Did a rushed, fully clothed fuck in a semipublic place count?

"No," he snapped.

"Good," she snapped back. "Don't forget the way she used you."

As if he ever had. As if he could.

"This is temporary," he said. "William's moving to Beaucoeur to take over for me at BUILD, and I'll be back behind the desk at Digham. We'll barely see each other after that."

It hurt to picture it, but it's what needed to happen. Thankfully that unexpected flash of regret didn't register with anyone else because they'd latched onto a new topic.

"William?" Cece shrieked.

He winced. How had he forgotten his middle sister's infatuation with William? He'd brought his friend home with him for Thanksgiving a few years ago, and Cece had followed him around like a horny cartoon grandma the whole time. And now that she was divorced...

"Yes," he said reluctantly. "But I'm begging you not to—"

"Climb him like a tree? No deal," she said. "When did you say he's arriving?"

Just like that, Cece and Vani had their heads together, laughing and whispering about whatever diabolical plans they were hatching over poor William, who wasn't going to know what hit him once he got to Illinois. While that was happening, Jessie touched his elbow.

"Just a suggestion: I seduce Faith and break her heart. I'm willing to do that for you, out of revenge." She shot him a teasing grin, but it disappeared quickly when he answered with a growl. She pulled back in surprise. "Oh. I see."

"What?"

She cut her eyes across the table at their older sisters, then lowered her voice even more. "Tell me you're not still in love with her."

"Of course not." His answer was quick, automatic, and it was also true. He *wasn't* in love with her. But with every day that passed, he was remembering all the things he'd loved about being with her. He broke off a piece of his pumpkin donut and allowed one tiny confession to escape, for Jessie's ears only. "It'll be good for William to get here though."

Jessie shot him a sympathetic smile. "Both my offers still stand: seduction and neck-stabbing."

"Thanks," he said. "I'll let you know."

By now, everyone had finished with their gourd-based meals, and the kids were squirming in their seats. Leo excused himself to return to the BUILD tent but only after his sisters made him promise he'd be at their parents's for Sunday dinner the following day. Like he'd miss it. Being closer to family was part of the reason he'd moved back home, and he hadn't regretted that decision until today.

As he headed back to their booth, Faith's words about living in his hometown floated to the front of his brain, and he forced himself to make eye contact with the people he was passing, even smiling and nodding when it seemed appropriate. It wasn't necessarily a huge moment of personal growth, but he didn't burst into flames either, not even when his old second-grade teacher called him by name and pulled him aside for a chat.

And that's the reason he was so glad to be back by Faith's side. It was a desire to let her take the lead in chatting with the public and not at all pleasure at being in her presence again.

"Here." He thrust a napkin-wrapped donut into her hand. "I brought you this."

She blinked at him in surprise. "Thanks! My favorite."

"I remember," he said gruffly, trying not to watch too

closely as she took a bite and chased the stray icing flecks from her lower lip with her tongue.

"So do we need to talk about what just happened?" she asked around a full mouth.

"God no. They're just..."

"Overprotective," she said.

"Pains in my ass."

She laughed softly, then fell into a thoughtful silence. "Do they know why we broke up?"

"The whole story."

"Ah. So I guess that explains all of that." She exhaled hard. "I'm lucky I didn't end up in traction." She wadded up the now-empty napkin and shoved it into the trash bag under the table.

The day slid to a quick close after that, and Leo found that chatting with the people who stopped wasn't overly painful as long as he stuck to the Dig Greener highlights. Faith was right; he believed in the program, and the more he talked about it, the more names they added to their list of interested kids. It was all she could talk about as they loaded the remaining supplies into her car.

"I can't believe how many sign-ups we got! If that many kids want to get involved, we may need to hire another outdoorsy person or two." She settled the last box into her trunk and turned to face him. The sun was hitting the horizon behind her, its dying rays coating her in brilliant orange light. She was so bright he had to squint to look at her.

"Maybe we could recruit some Rayman students. Offer college credit," he said. Then, almost without meaning to, he added, "And I can help out occasionally, if you'd like."

Her eyes slid over him, and he was sure they both

understood that this directly contradicted the William escape plan. But neither of them acknowledged it.

Instead, he said, "I'll follow you to BUILD and help you unload."

Faith straightened. "That's okay. It's not that many boxes."

"I'll see you there." He turned and jogged to the lot where he'd parked before she could contradict him. But despite his hustle, Faith got to the BUILD office before he did, and she'd carried in almost everything by the time he slid into the staff parking in the alley.

"You really do take care of yourself, don't you?" he said as he pulled the final box from her hands.

She slammed the trunk. "Yes. I do."

She held the BUILD door open for him, and he carried the box into the workroom to stack with the others. "Do you want to unpack things tonight?" he asked.

Instead of answering, she gave a jaw-cracking yawn.

"Guess tomorrow works too," he said.

"Sorry." She gave a rueful little laugh. "Long day."

"No kidding."

She flipped off the lights as they walked down the hall to the exit, and once they reached the alley, she turned and fitted her key in the lock, jiggling the handle for good measure.

Leo looked around with a frown. "Is it always this dark?"

She glanced up. "Yeah. That typically happens after the sun goes down."

"This isn't safe. You leave out this door every night?" He realized that he'd only visited the office during the day, and he'd always parked in the lot in front.

"It's fine," she said dismissively. "My car's right by the door."

Leo glanced up and down the dim alley, which was empty save a dumpster at one end. In fact, this whole neighborhood wasn't what he'd call desirable once the sun was down. The block was all businesses that kept nine-to-five hours, so no one would be around if Faith ran into trouble in the inky blackness of the alley. Faith or any of the BUILD employees, of course.

"Aren't you usually the last one here at night?" he asked. "And don't you usually stay pretty late? This neighborhood isn't—"

"Hey." She rested her hand against his chest. "I've been coming and going for six years now without any trouble. You don't need to worry about me."

But he would. He'd be thinking about her leaving work after dark from now on. Worrying, exactly as she said.

"Besides," she added. "William gets here soon. I'll have an escort."

"Right." He rocked back on his heels, teeth clenched. "William."

Like he'd told his sisters, William moving to town meant that his time working this closely with Faith was coming to an end and he could focus on the job he'd actually been hired for.

That also meant he wouldn't be around when Faith and William started working together. William, who made her laugh over Zoom. William, who charmed every woman in his orbit.

Leo would be on the outside of their little circle at BUILD, which was for the best.

It was all for the best.

THIRTEEN

The list of places Leo would rather be was short: anywhere but here.

He was trapped in a windowless conference room on a Tuesday afternoon while one of the Digham attorneys specializing in compliance droned on about action items related to the upcoming project reviews the foundation would be undertaking.

Action items might be what finally drove Leo right over the edge.

To make matters worse, those action items involved numbers—grant amounts, expenditures, debt-to-asset ratios—that made him shut down even faster than usual when faced with a task that involved sitting at a table and taking notes. Thankfully he wouldn't be responsible for any of the program reviews under discussion today, but he'd eventually have to run them for the programs he oversaw, so Carlisle had asked him to sit in on the meeting.

Maybe it wasn't action items that would drive him

over the edge but the ever-present fluorescent lighting in this damn boardroom.

His first instinct, still, was defensive insecurity at sitting around a table full of people with advanced degrees and soft hands, but that gut reaction was getting weaker the longer he spent around his coworkers. Most of them weren't so bad, even if he didn't quite think of himself as one of them yet. At least it was getting easier to carry on the small-talk that everyone around him seemed to have mastered.

"Shall we take a quick break?" the attorney running the meeting asked. At the murmurs of assent, the silver-haired man glanced his chunky gold watch. "Back in fifteen, folks."

The room filled with chatter and electronic dings as people checked their email and chatted with their neighbors—including the woman on his left.

"So how are you enjoying your first compliance meeting?" Savannah Goldbaum, the foundation's grant manager and his direct report, grinned at him. He returned the woman's question with a look of horror.

"Are we supposed to be *enjoying* this?"

"Oh no. Not at all." But her round face was all smiles as she said it. "It gets less scary the longer you're here."

When he'd started at Digham, he'd found Savannah's life-coach vibe overbearing. But he soon realized that she was subtly nudging him onto the corporate path, and the more she helped walk him through the ins and outs of life at Big Dig, the more he'd appreciated her unflappable good cheer.

"It's a lot," he said. "All these numbers..."

His throat threatened to close at the thought of being

responsible for any kind of audit of his programs, but Savannah waved it off.

"That's what I'm for, along with the Digham accounting department. They do our audits, Legal reviews our contracts, and Communications does our PR. If we need help, we just have to ask for it."

"Good to know," Leo said evenly while everything inside him unclenched. Intellectually he'd known somebody somewhere would be doing oversight, but it hadn't occurred to him that he might get called on to talk numbers. Stated goals, he could meet and achieve. Program outcomes, he could assess. But budgets? Those he could turn over to the people with calculators without a backward glance.

"Oh! I need to catch Mark while he's on the eighteenth floor." Savannah waved at a middle-aged man sitting several seats down, checking his phone. "Mark! Can we talk about the Digham holiday gala for a second?"

The man glanced up and returned Savannah's wave, tucking his phone into his suit pocket as he rose.

"One of the Big Dig lawyers?" Leo asked in an undertone as the man approached.

"Divorced, two kids, loves golf," she said equally quietly. "Is absolutely going to ask you to play a round with him."

"Fantastic," he said with a groan as Mark made it to their side of the table.

"Hello to the foundation staff." He gave a friendly little salute and adjusted his belted pants up over his belly. "Leo Morales, right? The man who stopped saving the world to join us in Beaucoeur."

"I like to think I'm saving the world in a different way

now," Leo said. What an embarrassingly earnest answer. It was also mostly true, although days like today were tough.

Mark's face split into a smile, revealing flawless white veneers. "Do you ever hit the links? It's the perfect cure for a desk job."

The tips of his ears got hot, and he answered more curtly than he intended. "Not my game."

Golf was a sore spot. Not only had it been ridiculously out of reach when he was a kid in Beaucoeur, but golf courses were insanely bad for the environment. Its popularity with his new coworkers both appalled him and left him with that outsider feeling that he'd resented in high school.

His short response didn't deter the ruddy-faced Mark though. The man clapped him on the back with a fleshy hand.

"We'll teach you to love it." He chortled. "Wait until you get your first set of clubs. It'll change your life. How're your new Callaways treating you, Savannah?"

Her reply kicked off a debate about the merits of the various local courses that Leo felt free to ignore. Everyone at Digham seemed to be equally comfortable in stifling boardrooms and well-manicured greens. Were none of them screaming to be out in the autumn sun using their bodies to work, along with their brains?

Apparently not; the compliance lawyer reentered the room and called the meeting back to order, and everyone settled in for another two hours that stuffed Leo's head with rules and left him wanting to run laps around the building just to put his muscles to use. It was almost enough to make him consider giving golf a try despite all the pesticides and fertilizer and excessive water usage. It wouldn't be the same as ending each workday covered in sweat and dirt, but at least he'd be able to stretch his legs.

As it was, he was coming home at night full of jittery, unspent energy. For that reason alone he'd be glad when William was in Beaucoeur; he'd have someone to go for a jog or hit the gym with. Then again, it would also mean William was working with Faith every day, side by side.

Fucking hell. He was jealous of his friend over things his friend hadn't even done yet, in a job he'd recommended him for. And it was all because of *her*.

Things had been easier when Faith had lived in his mind as a villain, his biggest regret and his shameful fantasy rolled into one. But the more time he spent with her, the more he realized that he'd been holding on to his decade-old anger out of habit. Letting go of it was like setting a burden down. It allowed him to see Faith for who she was today: stubborn and sarcastic, sure, but also funny and driven and interesting and caring.

Hot as hell too. Couldn't forget that.

While he'd been obsessing over his ex-girlfriend, the meeting had finally dragged to an end, and Leo grabbed his binder and practically sprinted from the room. Back at his office, he stashed his notes and yanked off his jacket and tie. The jacket got tossed over his office chair, and the tie got shoved into his top desk drawer. He'd just popped his top button and was considering doing a set of pushups just to burn off some of his tension when Darla knocked on his door.

"Hi there. Did you want me to get you the rundown on the employee United Way campaign you'll be heading up next month?"

He bit back a groan. "Can it wait? I barely survived the compliance meeting."

The older woman smiled sympathetically. "Those really are terrible, aren't they?"

He shook his head, still a bit numb from sitting for so long. "*Terrible*. I need to do something outside this building."

"I don't suppose you need to visit the Knit Nook?" she asked hopefully. "Char's holding some variegated sock yarn for me to pick up."

Did he *need* to visit the Knit Nook? No. But at the same time, yes. A resounding yes.

"I haven't seen how their new space is shaping up," he said slowly.

"Perfect!" Darla turned to exit, then pivoted back immediately, a thoughtful look on her face. "You know, the overseas grant managers spend plenty of time in the field, working with people on the funded projects."

"Oh yeah?" He paused in the act of shrugging on his jacket. The tie could stay in the drawer.

"It seems to me that you can justify spending this afternoon with Char's people." She raised her brows. "In fact, when she called this morning to tell me my order was ready, she said they had a huge stash of yarn that needed to be boxed and organized for shipping. They could probably use some help."

The first real smile of the day touched his lips. "You're a lifesaver."

"Just doing my job," she replied before she bustled out of the office.

He was breathing a little easier by the time he reached his car in the parking garage, but he still cranked his windows down to let the brisk autumn air rush in as he drove toward the converted downtown warehouse where Char had set up her yarn shop. The nearest on-street parking he could find was two blocks over, and he took his time walking to the entrance, enjoying the sun on his face and the business of the street. He passed a coffeehouse, an arcade, and a CrossFit gym, all buzzing with customers. Beaucoeur had grown in the decade he'd been gone, and he was excited to help it develop in sustainable ways.

When he pushed open the door to the Knit Nook, Char gave a happy shout and hustled around the counter to pull him into a soft, squishy hug.

"Our hero!" she cheered. "Look what you made possible!"

Ignoring his protests that the advisory board had been the ones to make the decision, she proudly swept her arm out to show off the dozens of display cases with yarn and supplies and pattern books along the old brick walls. A cluster of people in comfortable armchairs were knitting and chatting, and in the center of the space, eight women were turning puffy mounds of yellow-white wool into strands of yarn using complicated-looking spinning machines that they operated with their feet.

She introduced them one by one, and although she gave their names and not their circumstances, Leo knew that each of them had struggled with poverty, unemployment, and unsafe living situations before Char had put them to work making hand-spun, small-batch yarn that she sold online to crafters around the country. Others she tasked with knitting sweaters, scarves, hats, and afghans. She sold some of them on Etsy, and others she donated to shelters that needed supplies. Any profits she made were funneled back into the shop so it could serve more people in need of work, a purpose, a community.

"This all looks incredible." He spun on his heel to

take it all in again. "Darla tells me you might need some help with a yarn shipment?"

The tall woman flipped her graying braid over her shoulder. "If you have the time, yes. We've been finishing up a huge order that came in last week, and we're behind."

"Point the way," he said. And he spent the next hour getting a crash course in all things fiber: weights and colors and dye lots. He now knew what both variegated *and* sock meant when it came to yarn, and he quickly mastered wrapping each skein in a label, stamping it with the dye lot number, and boxing it for shipment while the women in the shop kept their spinning wheels turning.

When he'd finished packing the boxes, Char pointed him to a stash of worsted weight yarn—look at him using the lingo—that needed to be shelved for sale. As he piled the soft skeins into the square shelves, he learned the soothing magic of rainbow-colored sorting.

When there was no merchandise left for him to arrange, he returned to the counter. "What else have you got for me?"

Char cast him a sly look. "Do you want to try?" She gestured to the spinning machines.

Leo immediately held up his hands. "Oh, I don't think so. I don't want to ruin your merchandise."

But the women laughingly encouraged him, and he started to weaken. A new skill, something to occupy his hands...

"Let's do it," he said, rolling up his sleeves.

Char grabbed an extra stool for him, and he watched intently as one by one each woman demonstrated her technique for feeding the raw wool into the spinning wheel. He guessed the youngest in the group to be in her twenties, a painfully thin woman with mousy-brown hair and blotchy skin. Her fingers were a blur as she plucked and spun and twisted. When the woman with the salt-and-pepper bob took her turn at showing him the ropes, her movements were slower and more deliberate as she pinched and slid the wool while working the treadle. Each woman had a slightly different technique, but they all had the same basic motions at the heart of their work.

After observing all of them, he was ready to try, and the young woman stood to let him take her place. His motions were tentative as he did his best to copy their steps, and they all laughed gently when his first efforts emerged lumpy.

"No, mijo. Mírame," the oldest woman in the group commanded, and he immediately straightened. His DNA was coded to respect abuelitas the world over, and he concentrated on the woman's fingers, the knuckles swollen and knobby with arthritis, as she dipped and twisted the wool to produce a perfect strand of yarn. He painstakingly attempted to re-create her motions, his tongue caught between his teeth as he struggled to maintain a steady speed and tension.

By the end of the hour, he'd managed to produce a few measly yards of almost passable yarn, and Char held it up for display the way you'd present a favorite toddler's crayon drawing. The women all cheered, and he experienced a spurt of pride at having *done that*.

"Next time, we'll see what you can do with a pair of needles," she called after him as he made his goodbyes and headed out the door.

His whole body felt looser as he strolled back to his car. Working with his hands always did that for him. In fact he was feeling so good that he considered driving straight to BUILD, where he'd get to see Faith's face light up when he walked in.

But that was exactly the reason he should point his car back to the office. There was no temptation there, no ruby-red lips tipping up at the corners to welcome him. And he'd been playing with fire enough these days.

FOURTEEN

Faith put her car in park and pulled up her text history to double-check the address. William couldn't possibly have intended to send her to a McMansion in the bougiest part of Beaucoeur for their introductory dinner. But the address matched the numbers on the all-brick mailbox in front of the lush expanse of lawn, so she grabbed her tray of brownies and six-pack of beer and trotted up the curved sidewalk to the two-story entryway.

For a house built in the past decade or two, it wasn't bad-looking, with a gray stone exterior and white columns flanking the front door. The windows in the front gave a clear view through the open floor plan to the sprawling yard in the back. None of it was what she expected given the little she knew about William—and the lot that she knew about his salary—but she seemed to be in the right place.

She pressed the doorbell, and the chime echoed through the house for a long moment before footsteps approached and the door flew open to reveal the last person she expected to see.

"Leo?"

"Faith! Hi!" His surprised delight sizzled through her blood to lodge somewhere in the vicinity of her heart.

"What are *you* doing here?" she blurted.

He reached out to grab the brownies that were in danger of slipping out of her suddenly nerveless fingers. "I live here."

She took a step back to glance at the house number again, as if it had somehow changed in the past ten seconds. "I thought William lived here," she said, like that was any kind of explanation.

When she looked back, that dazzling smile was gone. "You're here for William?"

As if he'd been summoned, the tall blond man appeared over Leo's shoulder.

"There she is!" he said. "Just in time."

Leo swung his head around. "What's she doing here?"

And that's about when Faith started contemplating getting back in her car and driving until she reached the ocean. A solid three days on the road ought to do it, and then she could wade out into the water and let the current take her.

William stepped in before she could make good on her plans. "I told you I wanted to talk about work stuff tonight before I officially start next week."

"Yes. And?" Leo asked impatiently.

"And she's part of the team." William's tone made it clear that this should be obvious to everyone involved. "So I asked her to come for dinner."

"William said he was having a cookout." The bottles clinked gently as she lifted the cardboard case of beer. As far as conversational gambits went, it was up there with "I carried a watermelon," but it was the best she could come up with at the moment.

"And Leo clearly didn't tell you that I'm staying with him until I find my own place." While Leo had reverted to an even more severe scowl than usual, William tucked his hands into his pockets as he grinned at her, all loose limbs and good cheer.

"He did not," she said. In fact, she hadn't heard much from Leo at all in the past week.

"So are you going to let her in or...?" William looked expectantly at Leo, whose flint-hard gaze traveled from her to William and back again before he finally stepped aside. She took a cautious step over the threshold, afraid that there might be a second wave of attack waiting for her, but William simply took the brownies from Leo's hands and the beer from hers and disappeared into the house, leaving the two of them alone.

"I had no idea you lived—"

"So you're already talking with William." Leo kicked the door shut, then turned and leaned against it, arms crossed. "That's great. Great that you're getting along."

His voice sounded off, but she answered anyway. "I think so, yes. Why do you look like you want to punch something?"

"I don't—" He ran a hand through his thick hair, ruffling the curls. "Honestly, I don't know. It's good that you two get along."

"He seems nice so far," she said. "And you two are friends, so it tracks that I'd like him too."

"Yeah. William's incredibly likable."

He spoke through clenched teeth, and she took a moment to consider his words. Did he think she was *interested* in William? Sure, he was even cuter in person, his hair sandy and tousled, his jaw covered in the golden glint of a beard. But he didn't do a damn thing for her.

"Hey, I'm not—" she began, but a call from farther into the house cut her off.

"Grandpa Leo! Time to put the meat on the grill."

Leo pushed himself off the door but didn't meet her eyes. "Let's get this over with."

"Well, when you put it like that," she muttered as she followed him through the house.

As they moved through the living room, she tried not to pay too much attention to their surroundings—for some reason it felt intrusive to scour Leo's living space for clues about the man he'd become—but the old-world Tuscan decorating scheme was too much to ignore.

"Gotta say, this isn't how I pictured your house."

The look he tossed over his shoulder as he pulled open the sliding door was incredulous. "This stuff isn't mine." *You idiot*, his tone implied.

He was clearly waiting for her to step through first, so she did.

"Then you're going to have to explain how you ended up living in this part of town with furniture that even my grandmother would've rejected as a bit stuffy."

His pained expression didn't budge as he pulled the door shut and joined her on the stone patio where William stood in front of a massive grill built into a stone structure that looked more likely to withstand a tornado than her last house.

"I'm renting from a Digham engineer who's working overseas for three years," he said curtly. "She and her husband didn't want to bother selling, then buying something new when they moved back, so I get cheap rent and they get somebody making sure their pipes don't freeze."

"Ahhhh." That made so much more sense. "So those aren't your wrought-iron rooster statues?"

William tossed his head back with a roar of laughter. "Does this poor girl not understand how you lived before you went corporate?"

She sat down on a patio chair, grateful she'd worn her favorite cardigan. It was getting chilly as the sun began to set and long shadows stretched across the backyard.

"Nope. Leo hasn't shared many personal details," she said. Or any details, really.

William adjusted a knob on the grill, then placed three massive steaks on to cook. "Weird. He's usually so talkative."

"A natural-born storyteller," she agreed. "Just cannot get that guy to shut up once he starts sharing."

Leo sighed and flipped a switch on the table in the center of a circle of patio chairs, and flames fired to life. "I cannot tell you how fun this is for me."

"What, me and Faith ganging up on you?" William asked.

"Yes," he grumbled, pulling his chair closer to the fire. The flames provided a blast of much-needed heat, and Faith followed suit as William grabbed a beer for each of them, passing them around before joining them around the low table.

"Since Leo isn't chatty, let me tell you all about life at Protect Our Rainforests," William said. "We're headquartered in Iquitos, Peru. That's where we run most of our community programs and stage our work trips. Picture the crappiest college dorm you've ever seen, and then add unstable Wi-Fi and a revolving roster of youthful volunteers with questionable hygiene and you've got the idea."

"No log cabin?" Faith asked Leo.

He almost smiled. "Nope. Lots of tents though. During the dry months, we'd usually camp at our job sites so we could work uninterrupted."

"We stayed in town during the rainy season," William added. "Worked jobs in the nearby villages."

"What kind of jobs?" Faith was almost embarrassed by how excited she was to learn more about Leo's life while they'd been apart.

"Planting trees that the villagers can use for fruit or building materials," Leo said. "Monitoring what we planted in years past to be sure they're developing properly and helping the native wildlife thrive."

William picked up the thread. "We ran educational programs and worked with the locals to build up their economies or stop logging and deforestation. We also had biologists and erosion specialists and that kind of thing consult for us," he said. "Reggie coordinated our visiting experts before I handed over the reins to the whole operation."

"Wow." Such an underwhelming sentiment as she considered the organization and sweat that must've gone into every aspect of their jobs.

"I know we made it sound glamorous, but don't forget the insects." Leo rubbed his thumb along his unshaven jaw, his hair a tumble across his forehead. "You've never seen bugs that big."

William took a long pull of beer. "At least the dorms didn't have bullet ants."

Both men shuddered, clearly lost in some past ant-based trauma, before William ambled to the grill to fuss with the food.

"I tell you all this," he said, "to explain that neither of

us any sense of style beyond 'is it clean enough to wear in the jungle?'"

"Not true. Nothing we owned was ever truly clean," Leo said, and they both laughed.

Faith drank in the sight of them before murmuring, "Oh my God, the women of Beaucoeur are going to eat you both up."

Her comment had William laughing even harder, but it brought Leo's scowl back. That, she realized, was on brand for each of them: William laughing, Leo brooding. A flavor for every craving. Almost against her will, her eyes drifted to her right, where Leo's throat worked as he took a long pull from his bottle. She gripped the arm of the chair to keep from flinging herself onto his lap to press her lips against that bit of skin. William was attractive, sure, but she only had eyes for one person here.

She was on the brink of completely spiraling when William changed the subject.

"So what pop culture did we miss over the past decade?"

She leaped on the topic. "Let's see... about a dozen new *Star Wars* projects and at least three *Barbarian Time Brigand* movies."

William chuckled as he flipped the steaks. "Oh, that one made sure we saw every new *BTB* movie as soon as they hit Brazil." He jerked his head toward Leo, and Faith laughed.

"Still a fanboy, huh?"

He gave a *sorry, not sorry* shrug. "It's not like you ever stop loving Griff the time-traveling dragon."

"Nerd," William coughed out. But it was an affectionate roast, and the three of them debated the merits of the biggest sci-fi franchises until William pulled the meat off the grill and served them up with baked potatoes and asparagus he'd charred over the flames. They ate around the fire, which the men assured her was normal for them, and even though she was much more of an indoor cat, it was a fun vibe.

Once they'd finished their meals and dug into her brownies, Faith remembered that she was actually there for a reason beyond dinner with two good-looking guys. She set her empty plate aside, wiped her mouth on a napkin, and summoned her most professional tone. "William."

"Faith," he said immediately.

"You wanted to make some plans. Should we start talking about that now?" she asked.

"You bet." He leaned forward to rest his elbows on his knees, his half-full bottle of beer dangling from his fingers. "I'm thinking I could adapt a few of the educational programs I ran in South America. Lots of emphasis on sustainable practices and preserving native plants. The importance of biodiversity. Things like that but tailored to Beaucoeur's specific demands."

"Sounds great," she said. "How can I help?"

"Pedagogy. Make sure my lesson plans are appropriate for each of the ages I'm working with." The laid-back guy from earlier in the day was nowhere in sight now. "I also need time to get up to speed on the needs of the area. The landscape, the physical resources. I'd love to start a mentoring program for kids who'd like careers with park districts, national forests, that kind of thing. And I need to know what hands-on programs would be most beneficial."

"I can help with that." Leo was sprawled in his chair, a relaxed counterpoint to William's all-business body language. "I majored in Forestry at SIUC. Did my capstone project on conservation needs in the state park system."

Faith blinked at him in surprise. "You went to Southern? That's not what we..."

Her throat tightened as the memories rushed in.

"Lots of things you don't know, Dutch." His eyes locked on hers and didn't budge.

The plan had been for him to find a job so he could move to Evanston with her. She'd study business at Northwestern while he figured out what he wanted to do with his life. And after she graduated, they'd move to that cabin in the woods he always talked about. That part had been hazier for her, but Leo wanted it so badly that her high school self had believed they'd make it work.

They hadn't, of course. That plan had imploded when their relationship did, and he'd reentered her life again a few months ago as a fully formed adult with a history she wasn't privy to. It broke her heart a little.

"Sorry," William said. "What am I missing here?"

She and Leo both jolted as if his words had broken the spell locking them into place. William looked from his friend to her as he waited for someone to provide an explanation, but Faith had no idea what to say. Had Leo not told him anything about their history? And if not, why not? The two of them seemed so close.

Leo was apparently too busy locking his jaw shut to clarify anything, but somebody had to say *something*, so she finally mumbled, "Um, Leo and I knew each other in high school."

William's confused expression didn't clear up at her halting explanation—until it did.

"Oh, you two *knew* each other in high school," he said. "Got it."

He raised his bottle in a toast, which jostled Leo to life, although he barely glanced up from the flames dancing in front of him. "That was a long time ago. It's no big deal."

Faith tried like hell not to react, but his words hit her like a slap, and she surged to her feet.

"Hey, I should go," she said with a shaky laugh. "I've been here way longer than I intended."

She suddenly became aware of the cold night air pressing in around their cozy fire circle, and she wrapped her cardigan tighter around her midsection. "Thanks so much for dinner, William. It was fantastic."

He and Leo both stood too, but William was the one who moved first, slinging a casual arm around her shoulders. "Thrilled you could make it. I can't wait to see what we can do together."

She jumped a little at the unexpected contact but relaxed just as quickly. He smelled like wood smoke and citrus, and honestly the extra warmth was welcome now that she was farther from the fire.

"Will you guys eat the brownies if I leave them?" Dumb question, but she needed to get out of there as quickly as possible.

"Absolutely," William said. And then he was steering her toward the door as he ran down his plans to hit the ground running next week at BUILD.

When they reached the sliding door into the house, Faith paused and looked back. Leo was standing motionless; his face was obscured by darkness and his silhouette outlined by the fire. But she could see that his hands were jammed into his pockets.

"Good night, Leo," she called, then slipped into the house without waiting for him to respond.

TWELVE YEARS AGO

When he heard her Audi grind to a halt and her car door slam, he stopped pacing around his bedroom and stepped onto the porch, leaning against the rusty metal railing with as much disinterest as he could muster.

"Making a charity call, *duchess*?"

The word was poisonous on his lips, and he could see when she registered that this wasn't the same pet name he usually used.

"No." Her face was splotchy as she approached, stepping over the cracked concrete where only weeds flourished. She was still in her white ruffled dress. Hell, her graduation party was probably still in full swing. He bet her parents were popping another bottle of champagne right now and wondering where their little darling was. "You've got it all wrong. You were never, ever—"

"Never supposed to see that? Yeah, I bet not." He sneered the words, and she stopped short on the sidewalk. "Poor, pathetic Leo, too dumb to know just how dumb he is. Thank God you were there to fix me."

She was near tears. He was too, but he kept it locked down.

"Never. Not once did I think that about you." She climbed the steps and tried to put her hands on his chest, but he flinched backward, and her arms dropped to her sides.

He wanted to believe her. God, he did. But he'd read the college admissions essay her father had shown him, seen in her own words the way she took credit for working with him on his math homework, for introducing him to the study skills she'd researched online.

"You diagnosed me," he spat out. "Are you a fucking doctor now?"

She didn't answer, so he asked again, louder. "You gave it a name. What's wrong with me, Faith?"

She dropped her head and whispered, "Dyscalculia." Then she looked up, eyes glistening. "But it was just a suggestion I read! And yes, I *did* look up ways to help you learn. I helped you pass algebra, didn't I? You graduated because of me. You're welcome, by the way."

She hurled the last words at him. Good. He wanted to have this fight.

"You made me some... some *project* to help get you into college." He slashed a hand through the air. "You wrote about me. About how you bought me lunch and helped me study. About how stupid I am, and how *befriending me* was such a growth experience for you."

"Never stupid, Leo. Never. It's just, my father thought..."

Her words trailed off when she glimpsed his furious expression.

"Your fucking father." He actually might puke. "Glad

he found some way to make all the time you spent with me worthwhile."

"I didn't even end up submitting that stupid essay! Quit being an asshole and listen!" she shouted. "It felt wrong to talk about you like that, so I changed it to what I learned on my mission trip to the Appalachians."

His laugh was cruel and exactly what she deserved. "So you wrote about some other poor kids. Great."

"It's totally different!" She stamped her foot, just a rich girl throwing a tantrum. "I don't even know why my dad showed you the old one!"

"Don't you?" He tossed the accusation at her, and her mouth snapped shut like she hadn't considered that until right now. "I think we both know why he wanted me to read that."

She sucked in a hard breath as the wheels turned in her brain. "I'll kill him."

"It's not all his fault. *You're* the one who wrote it." He yelled the words, helpless to control his fury and embarrassment and betrayal. "*You* thought those things, put them down on paper."

A tear tracked down her cheek, and then another. Before long, she was crying, sobbing in great bursts that tore at his heart. Part of him wanted to soothe her, to wipe away her tears and suck the salt off his fingers. Another part of him wanted to join in. Wanted to cry about how small she'd made him feel.

"Why'd you do it?" His voice cracked as he pleaded with her. That's how badly he wanted to understand what made her think this was okay.

"I..." She took a shuddery breath and swiped angrily at her cheeks. "I was panicked. I didn't have a good hook for my essay. What have I ever done in my life that's interesting?" When she looked at him now, her eyes were wet but sharp. She was ready to defend herself. "And I really did work hard to figure out ways to make numbers easier for you. I read so much about different learning styles. I even talked to Mrs. Davies about it."

"The *special ed* teacher? You talked to her about me?" He clutched the railing so hard the metal groaned.

"I didn't think you'd find out! Not about any of this!" she cried. "Mrs. Davies would never say anything! I did it to help you."

"You did it to help *you*! You Foxes." He sneered. "Doing whatever you want to whoever you want, just to get what you think you deserve."

She was reaching for him again, and this time he grabbed her by the wrist to ward off her touch.

"I love you, Leo!" Her voice shook, and he dropped her hand as if it burned him.

"That's not love. That's pity. You've been taking notes and thinking about what a great little story I'll be for your roommate when you're off at Northwestern, just like Daddy wants." He dug the heels of his hands into his eyes. "I thought I actually meant something to you. God, I really am stupid."

That last bit he said more to himself than to her. Before she could respond, he reached into his back pocket and pulled out a piece of paper. His great triumph. His grand plan to keep them together forever. Crumpling the paper, he flung it at her. It bounced off her chest and landed on the ground between them.

"I got accepted into Oakten so I could move to Evanston with you. I was going to tell you tonight."

"Th-the community college?"

She blinked up at him, eyelashes clumped together with tears, and this time he couldn't hold back a sob.

"I would've gone anywhere for you. I would've figured out a way to build us a house on the sun if that's where you wanted to go."

She was crying again, heaving great silent sobs as she bent to pick up the paper. "Just let me explain! I wasn't—"

But he'd heard enough. He kicked open the door and let it slam shut behind him, barricading himself in his bedroom and jamming his pillow over his head so he wouldn't be able to hear her.

It didn't work. Not for the eternity she stood on his front stoop calling his name and not when she decided to stop.

"Fine!" she finally shouted. "Go to hell, Leo."

That fucking pillow didn't stop a damn thing. He heard the exact moment she gave up on him, walked down the crumbling sidewalk, and drove out of his life forever.

FIFTEEN

"Okay, team. Who's ready?"

Faith bounced like a cheerleader and madly wiggled her fingers, an enormous grin on her face. Being this upbeat was exhausting, but after that cookout at Leo's, she was working overtime to keep the Dig Greener dynamic... not weird, for lack of a better term. So what if William didn't know about her history with Leo? And so what if Leo aggressively didn't want to talk about it? She'd just have to muscle through and make sure their awkward little trio kept running smoothly. If she was laying it on a little thick, well, there was too much at stake for her not to at least try.

Thankfully William played along, slapping her a high five. "Hell yes. Let's do this."

Leo grunted.

She looked down to hide her smile when William shot her an amused glance. Leo'd been extra grumbly since William had started full time at BUILD two weeks ago, and she didn't want to make it worse by openly laughing with his friend. But she also needed Leo to get over himself for the next thirty minutes because they were cooling their heels outside the on-air studio at the Brick, waiting to pitch Dig Greener on the morning show. Her friend Mabel was one of the show's cohosts, and she waved at them through the booth window, enormous headphones covering her ears. Faith waved back cheerfully. She'd met Mabel through Thea, and even though it was a little weird when your best friend made other friends, Faith was a big enough person to admit that Mabel was a lot of fun.

"Who's the blonde?" William's gaze locked on Mabel, and Faith gave his shoulder a sympathetic pat.

"Taken," she said. "Super taken."

The on-air lights over the door snapped off, and two seconds later Mabel opened it and gestured them inside. The booth was a tight fit for five people, but they made it work. Mabel sat across the board from her cohost Dave, and the rest of them crowded along the cluttered desktop between the two radio people. Faith ended up sandwiched between William and Leo. Grumpy on the right, golden on the left.

Dave's lean face twisted in concentration as he fiddled with a knob. "All right, children, who's been on the radio before? Other than Faith. She's a repeat offender."

She dramatically tossed her hair. "I shill for BUILD."

"We've both done a lot of press," William said. "*CBS News Sunday Morning* actually did a segment on us once."

Faith looked at Leo in surprise. "For real?"

Predictably, his brows snapped together. "It was a few years ago."

"Wow!" Faith nudged his shoulder. "You're, like, famous!"

Mabel clapped excitedly. "I had no idea we were interviewing celebrities today!"

Faith joined Mabel in an excited squeal as William struck a triumphant pose and Leo rolled his eyes.

"Two minutes." Dave had his eyes on the screen in front of him that counted down the time left in the Mountain Goats song currently playing. "I'll introduce you all, and then one of you needs to take the lead on answering questions."

William snapped to attention. It's one of the things Faith liked the most about him. He could joke around and be the biggest goof in the room, but the instant it was time to work, he was nothing but focused.

"I will. Faith can jump in whenever, and Leo can talk about the Digham Foundation."

Dave nodded absently as he swung a microphone in their direction. "Go Team Save-the-Planet!"

William leaned an elbow on the desktop, casual and ready to chat. Leo scrubbed his palms down the sides of his pants and exhaled hard.

"You good?" she asked quietly.

He grimaced. "It's part of the job."

"Just talk to them like you talked to me that day in the office. Explain why it's important to you."

He shifted uncomfortably, and she bumped him with her shoulder. "Come on, I'm *much* scarier to talk to than the entire Beaucoeur community."

He snorted softly. "Dutch, you are *terrifying*."

"So then this'll be a piece of cake." She grinned and gave his knee a quick squeeze, and as she turned back to the main group, she caught Mabel watching her with a thoughtful expression.

Girl telepathy activated. *Be cool. Don't comment about me touching my ex-boyfriend/current colleague/object of my nighttime vibrator fantasies.*

Apparently it worked because Mabel just pasted on a bright smile and adjusted her headphones as Dave took them out of the song and introduced her, William, and Leo.

William jumped right in with his golden retriever energy, introducing Dig Greener with cheerful enthusiasm that the parents of Beaucoeur were going to eat up and concluding with an invitation to an informational meeting a week from Thursday.

When he stopped talking and nudged the mic in her direction, she picked up the ball.

"At Beaucoeur BUILD, we're thrilled to add Dig Greener to our offerings. There's so much research out there on the benefits of outdoor education on children's brains and social development, and William's definitely the guy you want with you when you're heading into the forest."

The group all laughed politely, then Dave asked, "Leo, what made the Digham Foundation decide to get into environmental work?"

Faith nudged the mic in Leo's direction as all eyes in the room fell on him. Although he looked like he was facing down a firing squad, he leaned forward to speak.

"It's actually a big reason that I took the job," he said, his voice low and serious. "I grew up in Beaucoeur, but I spent the first eight years of my career working in South America, and I saw what a difference these programs could make to the communities there."

Faith melted a little. She couldn't help it. His commitment to this work was attractive as hell.

"I figured the Digham Foundation would have the resources to build a strong, hands-on program," he continued. "How could I pass up the chance to make a difference in the town where I grew up?"

Melt. Melty melty melt.

"And what made Digham want to get into bed with BUILD for this project?" Dave asked.

The question made her eyes pop. He didn't mean it literally. No way did Dave literally mean *in bed*. But she still had to bite her lip to control a wildly inappropriate laugh. And Leo, who hadn't exactly been relaxed at the start of this process, was now rigid as a tree trunk.

She bit the bullet and answered that one.

"BUILD has experience working with so many of the schools in the area that we were able to get Dig Greener up and running much faster than if they were starting from scratch."

Mabel's lips were pursed in amusement. "I'll admit, I was surprised at first when I heard BUILD was involved, but it makes sense when you think about it. Plus it seems like there's great chemistry between the foundation and BUILD."

Okay, that *had* to be intentional. Although she and Mabel were friends, she definitely hadn't opened up about her history with Leo. But maybe Thea had?

While she was shooting Mabel a *what the hell* glare, Leo surprised her by stepping in to answer.

"It's been a pleasure to work with BUILD," he said evenly. "We've been able to build on a strong foundation, and I hope that relationship will deepen and grow as the years pass."

Somehow while he'd been speaking, he'd shifted so his whole body was facing her, his hand resting on the back of her chair, his thumb brushing against her back. When she risked a glance at him, he was looking right at her, his expression unreadable. And why would she see anything remarkable on his face? He'd answered a simple question with a simple answer, and she was the weirdo looking for deeper meanings.

"There you have it," Dave said to conclude their segment. "Two Thursdays from now, get all the details from the trio out to save their little corner of the world. Next up, new music by the Sleepwalkers, so don't go anywhere."

Once the mics were off, Leo was up and out the door. William just shook his head and watched him go. "It was like that after the CBS interview too. He'll talk about the work, but he sprints into his cave afterward. I'll take him for an early lunch or something."

William followed Leo out the door, leaving Faith to look between Mabel and Dave.

"You two," she said suspiciously. "Was that intentional?"

"What?" Mabel was all innocence.

"Oh, the part where we messed with you a little because you were practically sitting on your ex-boyfriend's lap?" Dave asked.

Faith's mouth dropped open. "First of all, how dare?"

"How dare?" Mabel pressed a hand to her heart in mock outrage.

"How. Dare."

The deejay grinned and flicked her fingers. "You're a pro. I knew nothing would rattle you."

Wrong. Leo rattled her all the time with his dark looks and tiny moments of sweetness.

"You two are so lucky that I'm cool under pressure," she said. "And how did you even *know* about us?"

"Please," Mabel scoffed. "I was in the same room as the two of you just now. It wouldn't have been hard to guess even if Thea hadn't mentioned something."

Faith gestured to Leo's empty chair. "He was nervous! I was calming him down."

"By massaging his leg?" Mabel asked.

"Whatever," she grumbled. "Thanks for the publicity anyway."

"Anytime!" Mabel chirped. "Join us for yoga next weekend?"

Yoga actually meant donuts, and Faith promised to check her schedule, then said goodbye and headed for the exit. She was rummaging through her purse in search of her keys as she crossed the station parking lot when a sports car came tearing down the aisle. She lurched out of the way, heart pounding at the near miss, and when the black Porsche rocketed to a stop in a nearby spot, she charged at it.

"What the hell?" she shouted as the driver swung the door open.

A tall man stepped out. Expensive suit, expensive haircut, expensive shades. Brandon Lowell, rich asshole radio station owner.

"You were walking where I was trying to drive," he said.

She made a disgusted sound in her throat and moved to brush past him, but he stepped into her path, not bothering to remove his shades as he studied her. After a moment, he snapped his fingers. "Thea's friend."

"Mabel's boss," she spat back.

"God, I love how much she hates me." His smirk matched his patrician features. Although he was blond, he wasn't a friendly breed like William. He was an Afghan hound, all sleek and arrogant and pointy-nosed.

"Faith Fox," he said, clearly pleased with himself for remembering. "You grew up rich, right?"

Faith's demand for an apology died on her lips at his non sequitur, and she glanced down at herself. Nothing about her said rich, from the frayed hem of her jeans to her BUILD T-shirt and marigold cardigan.

"Rich? Me?"

Brandon shrugged. "I can smell it on you. You grew up with money." He raised a lazy hand, pointing from her head down to her toes. "You take care of your skin. Your hair's shiny. Your accessories cost more than the rest of your outfit."

She glanced down at her Chloé ballet flats and Louis Vuitton Neverfull tote, grudgingly impressed that he'd recognized the most expensive items on her body. Some lessons from childhood had stuck with her, including the durability of quality leather goods, so she'd become an expert thrift-store hunter and outlet-mall gatherer.

"Also," Brandon continued, "my dick seems interested in getting to know you, and it always sniffs out women of quality."

"Ugh." She wrinkled her nose. "Does talking about your dick sniffing things generally work for you?"

"You'd be surprised." Then his smirk disappeared, all his amused arrogance draining away. "Your father."

His whiplash shift to serious left her unbalanced, and when he removed his sunglasses to reveal piercing blue eyes, she studied them to see if this was more bored rich-guy bullshit.

"What about my father?" she asked cautiously.

"Do you get along?"

Faith had a meeting to get to, but something about his tone kept her feet rooted in place. "No."

That pulled a small smile from him. "So maybe that's just how it is with rich daddies." Tears suddenly collected along his lower eyelids, and he sucked in a ragged breath.

"Um, everything okay?" She edged closer, still uncertain what she was dealing with. Just in case, she extended her hand to pat him on the arm or catch him if he was about to topple over.

"Mine's dead."

Faith sucked in a breath, her hand falling to her side. "I'm... God, I'm so sorry."

"Last week." He scrubbed a hand down his face. "I wasn't there. He didn't want me there."

He said the last part mostly to himself, and Faith didn't have *any* response to that, although she was suddenly close to tears herself. Because she understood. God, how she understood.

They were strangers, yet grief was grief, and she only hesitated a moment before stepping forward, intending to hug him. But he stiffened as she drew near, as if everything in him rejected her attempt at sympathy, so she stayed put. The only sound was his harsh breathing and the rustle of the orange and yellow leaves on the trees at the edge of the parking lot.

Although she wasn't a natural with the kids who came into BUILD, she did know that a well-placed question could sometimes unlock words that needed to get out in the open. "Did you spend your life disappointing him?"

she asked gently. "Or did you spend your life succeeding in ways he didn't appreciate?"

"Both." The word was bitter. "I hated him." His voice cracked. "I loved him."

Then almost as quickly as his walls had crumbled, he exhaled shakily and slipped back behind his arrogant mask. His nostrils flared as he pantomimed raising a glass. "Here's to us poor little rich kids."

She followed his lead and clinked his pretend drink against hers, feeling a little guilty at being so relieved that he'd pulled himself back from the brink. Vulnerability didn't sit well on those elegant features.

"So can I buy you a real drink sometime?" He smirked at her, and she scoffed.

"Oh, I'm *so* not sleeping with you."

He raised his brows. "I don't recall asking you to."

"Good. And don't forget I'm not rich anymore. In fact I've got a meeting to get to." But she didn't want to just leave him alone in the parking lot. "Are you going to be okay?"

His finely sculpted lips tightened. "No. And yes." Then he grudgingly added, "Thank you."

He seemed so lost standing next to his flashy Porsche with his hands in his pockets that she almost offered up her number if he ever needed to talk. But that might give him the wrong idea, and Lord knew she didn't need the complication right now.

"You're welcome. And again, I'm so sorry," she said with a sad little smile before turning and heading to her car. She hoped putting a few miles between them would shake her melancholy mood, but Brandon's simmering grief was still on her mind as she pulled into the alley behind BUILD to discover a man standing on a ladder next to the building's rear entrance. The back of his gray coveralls read River Town Security.

"Can I help you?" she called up after she'd parked.

"Just finishing my installation." He lifted the brim of his hat with his screwdriver, then used it to tap the small white floodlight unit above the door.

Faith stepped closer and squinted up at it. "I didn't order this."

He shrugged and turned back to his work. "Somebody did. This was the address for the job."

She frowned up at him, wondering which of her staff might've authorized a purchase like this without running it past her. Elaine, maybe? As she was considering who to talk to about it, the man in the overalls flew down the ladder and landed lightly on the ground next to her.

"This baby's start of the art," he said. "Motion sensors linked to a terminal inside the office and an app on your phone so you can always see who's coming and going. And it'll light up the whole alley after dark."

Her heart gave a little flip as realization dawned, and after the security guy headed inside to make sure the monitor was hooked up properly, she grabbed her phone and tapped a number.

"Hey."

Was it her imagination, or did Leo's voice sound a tiny bit warmer than normal?

"Hey yourself. Did you send someone to install a security camera at BUILD?"

"Of course," he said promptly. "I told you, it's too dark when you come and go at night."

Her heart flipped again. So many chest calisthenics over this man. "You didn't need to do that." She tried to sound disapproving and missed by a mile.

"I absolutely did."

"Th-thank you." She wasn't sure why she stumbled over the simple words. All he'd done was notice her surroundings, get concerned for her safety, and proactively do something about it. No big deal.

"You're welcome, Dutch." And then he hung up, leaving her grinning in the alley.

SIXTEEN

"Headed out?"

Savannah's cheerful voice stopped Leo in his tracks as he was walking through the main office toward the exit.

"Uh, yeah." He was suddenly grateful that he hadn't pulled off his tie and rolled up his sleeves yet. "Jobs Inc. and then maybe BUILD too."

Definitely BUILD too, but he didn't need to sound too eager. His whole approach to the job had changed after that transformative day at the Knit Nook. If his overseas colleagues spent their time working directly with the people involved in their grants, then so would he. For every three hours he spent in a meeting, he was trying to spend three hours with the people those meetings were intended to help. He'd visited Char again on Monday to box up another big shipment, and the Hamouds always needed volunteers to help with laundry, cleaning, cooking, and serving meals at their facility, so he tried to swing by at least twice a week.

He'd actually been at Jobs Inc. the day before, helping

rearrange the computer lab to get it ready for a training workshop on spreadsheet software, and he'd promised to swing by today to move all the equipment back into place. As for BUILD, he hadn't been by since William had started working there, but he had an actual idea he wanted to float past his friend. It was a decent excuse for him to pay a visit, as opposed to his usual low-grade longing to just stop in.

"Can I say that I love how much time you're spending with your projects?" Savannah glanced over her shoulder, confirming that their boss's office door was shut and Darla was busy on a call. Still, she lowered her voice. "It's so great to have the foundation be a little more visible in all parts of Beaucoeur instead of just the..."

"The country-club set?" he suggested.

"Yep. We're good for more than just the open bar at the foundation gala." She snapped her fingers as a thought struck her. "Speaking of, don't forget to invite your grant recipients. The gala's for all Digham employees who've supported our programs throughout the year, and it's a great opportunity for them to see how they could get involved next year."

Leo had received and promptly ignored the informational email about the November black-tie event. A fancy hotel ballroom party was about as far away from his POR experience as he could imagine, so he hadn't wasted any time trying to imagine it. But he'd apparently have to navigate it with Faith in attendance, probably in some kind of dress that would drive him to distraction all night.

But of course his response to Savannah was a quick, "Sure thing."

She smiled wryly. "As you can imagine, it's the only Beaucoeur-based event that Carlisle enjoys."

His eyes drifted to their boss's closed door.

"It's so strange," he said in an undertone. "He's so proud of the work we're doing overseas, but point him a few blocks west of Big Dig HQ, and *nothing*."

Savannah shrugged. "There's no chance that he'll bump into a celebrity looking for job retraining in Beaucoeur." Her lips quirked. "Oh, did you hear? Ashton Kutcher's giving the keynote speech at the foundation director conference in Chicago next month."

"Seriously? What does Ashton Kutcher know about running a 501(c)(3)?"

"No idea." She wrinkled her nose. "Anyway, Carlisle is from a different time. He doesn't quite get the potential impact of the grants you're working on."

"And that's why it's good that I'm here."

To his surprise, he meant every word of that. He'd been concerned that corporate life would bury him in red tape, swallow him whole, maybe even exposure him as a fraud who couldn't hack it in a suit and tie. But those worries had receded to the background as he'd settled in and found a groove. Met people. Discovered that his new coworkers—most of them anyway—were welcoming and curious about his previous work experience and what he was building in the community. And now that he was getting out from behind his desk more often, he could almost describe himself as... fulfilled.

"My advice?" Savannah leaned closer and dropped her voice even more. "Don't worry about what Carlisle's saying about your programs. They're just as important as everything else this office handles. He'll come around."

She smiled at him encouragingly before ducking back into her office, leaving Leo's contentment to curdle around the edges. Who the fuck was Carlisle talking to about his grants? It must be bad enough if Savannah was mentioning it, although it wasn't bad enough for their boss to actually sit down with him to address how to fix it.

His eyes narrowed on Carlisle's shut door, and he considered barging in and getting it all out in the open, starting with how the guy had hated him on sight. But that would likely make things worse, so Leo did what he did best: he left the building.

Getting out of the office helped. He focused better in those interminable meetings if he knew he'd be able to use his body on a project later that day. And fuck Carlisle if he didn't consider that an important part of the job. It was. It was meaningful work, and it made a difference. He knew that in his bones.

Like today, for instance. At Jobs Inc. he spent an hour shuffling desks around with Barrett, trading Beaucoeur High School memories the whole time. After that, he was free to visit BUILD.

The drive was short since the office sat at the outskirts of the warehouse district where the developers' efforts to rehab old buildings stopped and the cheap strip malls and generic office buildings began. But it was within reasonable walking distance of two grade schools and a junior high, so the location made sense. And with the security cameras he'd had installed, he felt infinitely better about Faith coming and going at night.

About the whole staff coming and going at night, that was.

He pulled around back and clocked William's 4Runner but not Faith's battered Audi. He swallowed a pang of disappointment and reminded himself it was for the best. William hadn't brought up his history with Faith since the cookout, but Leo knew his friend's curiosity hadn't been met, just like he knew he couldn't possibly explain the snarl of emotions that being near her created. He didn't hate her anymore, he'd never stopped wanting her, and he clammed up every time he had to watch her laughing with his friend. So it was good that she wasn't there today because he had actual business to discuss.

Inside the BUILD office, half a dozen kids were sitting at the long worktables with books and notepads spread in front of them. Elaine and Jonah floated from student to student, pausing to point at something on a paper or to answer a question. A wave of emotion built in his chest. Faith did this, and he'd helped her keep it going. One of those kids might even be getting the math help he hadn't known he needed at that age.

Leo waved to the two tutors he'd met at the gourd festival before tracking William down in his new office.

"Well, well, well, if it isn't Grandpa Leo, come to check up on me."

Leo grunted. "You're older than I am, asshole."

"You're grouchier in Beaucoeur," William said with a mournful shake of his head.

That wasn't true; Leo was actually less stressed now than he'd been at POR where he'd juggled constantly shifting rosters of volunteer and inventory and travel schedules. But he'd been wearing hard-soled shoes and a tie all day while William was in a BUILD polo and hiking boots, and he probably knew what Faith was wearing, what she'd had for lunch. It was enough to make him a little growlier than usual, yes, but he chose to ignore William's cheerful dig and jump into why he'd stopped by.

"I had a thought," Leo said. "You're nervous about running those overnight camping programs, so why don't we do a dry run?"

"Hey, I'm never nervous." William straightened indignantly. "But say more things about the dry run."

Leo sat down and crossed one ankle over the other, linking his fingers over his stomach. "We do a two-day trek at Starved Rock with a couple of hand-selected kids to see how the planned activities go. Iron out the wrinkles before we throw it open to the students signing up for the program."

"I like it," William said. "Where do we find available kids?"

Leo held up a "one second" finger as he pulled out his phone and tapped out a text message. Within twenty seconds he had his answer. "We can take my nephews. You moved here with all your camping gear, right?"

"I did." They grinned at each other. "So which of us is doing grocery shopping for five?"

"Six."

They both turned to see Faith leaning against the doorframe.

"What's that?" William asked.

"Grocery shopping for six." She walked into the room. "I'm coming too."

Leo's whole body tensed up. "No. No way."

"What, is this a no-girls-allowed thing?" she asked with a scoff.

"Yes," Leo said, overlapping with William's definitive, "No."

She straightened to glare at him. "BUILD's my baby, and Greener is technically a BUILD program. I want to go."

William glanced over at him. "She's got a point."

"She doesn't even hike!" he objected.

"Ahem." She snapped her fingers to get their attention. "*She's* standing right here."

"You're right." William ducked his head in apology. "It would be good for you to see the lessons in action. Also, you need a break. You're working too much, boss."

William winked, Faith laughed, and Leo knew he'd never survive an overnight hiking trip with those two. He wanted to be near her all the time, but not like this. Watching her and William joking on the trail while his nephews watched their every move? His stomach revolted at the thought.

Faith narrowed her eyes as she looked at him. "Why don't you want me to go?"

"You're..." He gestured at her, struggling to put it into words.

She was room service and aged whiskey, leopard-print skirts and high-heeled boots. She was the opposite of nature. What if she hated it, this pastime that he loved? Worse, what if she loved it and became even harder for him to resist?

His silence stretched long enough that a flash of temper crossed her face. "If you think I can't handle it, just say so," she snapped.

"It's not that," he said reluctantly. "But would you even enjoy it?"

It wasn't the strongest rebuttal, and she grinned a shark's smile at him, all teeth and menace. "A walk in the woods with you, Leonidas? What could be more fun?"

"You could get hurt," he gritted out. Just the thought of her tripping over a root or a rock, scraping that soft skin, maybe even breaking a bone... He couldn't bear seeing her injured on his watch.

William laughed, then unsuccessfully tried to turn it into a cough. "Starved Rock isn't challenging terrain, right? And we'll have kids with us, so we'll be taking it easy."

Faith pretended to buff her nails against her shirt. "I don't mean to brag, but I do fifty minutes on my mom's elliptical every morning."

"You're a natural." William extended his hand, and he and Faith executed some kind of elaborate handshake ritual that involved clapping and snapping and finger-wiggling. It screamed ease and familiarity and hours together, and Leo was the asshole seething with envy over it when he should be relieved the program was in such good hands.

His jaw tight, he pulled out another excuse. "You don't have any supplies. Overnight in the woods requires all kinds of equipment."

"I've got plenty of extras," William said immediately. "And so does Leo."

Leo didn't even try to hide his annoyance. "Dude!"

"It's settled then." Faith's lips curled into a smug smile. "When do we leave?"

ONE WEEK before their camping trip, Leo found Faith and William in her office. She was sitting, and he had his hand on the back of her chair, leaning over her shoulder to point at something on her laptop screen. The casual intimacy of it created a hollow feeling in his stomach.

Faith glanced up before he had a chance to school his

expression, and her own expression shifted from welcoming to questioning. Did she sense the jealousy dripping off him? Possibly. Her greeting was more reserved than usual.

"Hey." She leaned away from William the slightest bit.

"Hey!" William's greeting was effusive as always.

Leo didn't bother to hide his scowl. "Hi."

William gestured to the laptop. "We were just working out supplies. I'll carry the big tent for us and the boys. And you've got a two-person one for Faith, right?"

"Yes." Faith sleeping in his tent would be fine. Nothing that should occupy his thoughts for the next seven days.

"Earth to Leo." William snapped his fingers to get his attention. "I asked if the boys have sleeping bags."

Right. The trip. "They do."

Faith raised a hand like a kid in class. "I don't."

"No worries," William said with a grin. "You're welcome to one of mine."

Leo also had extras, but competing with William over who got to provide Faith with a place to sleep seemed childish even though he really, really wanted to.

"I also don't know what to wear," she said. "Any suggestions?"

"Wool socks," Leo and William replied in unison.

"Ooookay. Anything else? And telling me not to come isn't an option." She jabbed a finger in Leo's direction.

"I've already lost that fight," he said, resigned to helping her figure out what to put on that body he couldn't stop thinking about. "You're going to want moisture-wicking fabrics and plenty of layers. A T-shirt, a flannel, a raincoat just in case. Good boots."

"Boots? My Adidas won't cut it?"

Leo shuddered at the memories that question unlocked, and William took one look at his face and guffawed.

"Do you know how many college girls Grandpa Leo had to educate about proper footwear?"

Faith cocked her head and blinked at him, all big doe eyes and innocent curiosity. "No. How many college girls did you educate, Leo?"

"Christ." He dragged a hand through his hair and changed the subject. "I'm actually here for a reason. We've got a complication."

Faith smirked. "Don't tell me. There's some new reason that I can't go." She leaned back in her chair and pressed a finger to her lips as if she was deep in thought. "All hikers must now be certified EMTs."

William jumped into the game. "An uptick in wolf attacks means everyone needs to carry a crossbow at all times?"

"I know!" Faith snapped her fingers. "No women allowed. Their periods attract bears."

For the millionth time he reminded himself how great it was that those two were getting along. Faith was opinionated and bossy, and William didn't like to take orders from anyone. Yet somehow they did nothing but laugh and high-five every time they were together.

Leo had to raise his voice to be heard over their chuckling.

"No, actually, it's a scheduling thing." He hated how peevish he sounded, but watching them constantly act like they were posing for a BUILD brochure about the benefits of a congenial work environment was wearing on him. "The ranger who was going to hike with us has a conflict on Saturday afternoon. He needs one of us to get there that morning so he can prep us on which trails have the best examples of erosion."

"Okay. So we just leave earlier," William said.

"Nope." Faith had already spotted the problem. "We can't pick the kids up until one."

"God forbid Mateo misses a Saturday soccer game," Leo grumbled.

"Reschedule?" William asked.

"Or split up," Faith said. "One group meets the ranger, and the other collects the kids. Then we hike together."

"I like that idea," William said. "So Faith and I meet the ranger, and Leo brings the kids."

He held up his hand for another fucking high five, which Faith happily provided. "Ranger buddies!"

"No." Leo almost shouted the word, then fumbled for a reasonable objection to an equally reasonable plan. "William's going to be head of the outdoor education programs. He should get used to dealing with kids."

William shrugged. "Sure. So Faith and I get the kids while you get the lessons set up."

This time it was Faith who balked. "Which sister would we be picking them up from?"

"Vanessa."

She barely hid her wince. "Maybe William should get the kids solo," she said slowly, "which I guess means Leo and I could meet the ranger?"

"Makes sense to me." The tension in his chest eased. "William's on kid duty, and Faith's with me."

"I'm with you," she repeated a little faintly.

She wasn't really with him, but at least for a few hours next Saturday, he could pretend she was.

"Sorry," she murmured, gesturing to an incoming call on her cell phone. Once she'd ducked out of the office, William turned back to the laptop.

"That's not going to be a problem, right?" His tone was casual, but his question wasn't.

Leo immediately bristled. "Meaning?"

"Meaning I'm not an idiot." William crossed his arms and leveled that don't-bullshit-me look that he had seen millions of times over the years, although it was usually directed at POR volunteers who thought they'd arrived in Brazil for a week of vacation. "You want me to believe that you two had a no-big-deal thing in high school that doesn't matter to either of you anymore?"

He didn't want to lie to his best friend, but he also didn't want any extra drama.

"I hadn't seen her since graduation day until I moved back home." That was true at least.

"So it wasn't serious?" William raised his hands in a defensive gesture before Leo could object to the question. "I'm just trying to figure out what you pulled me into the middle of."

"You're not in the middle of anything." He chose to ignore the first part of the question, and for a blissful second it looked like his friend had dropped it.

"If you say so." William stood, pocketed his phone, and headed for the door. "I've got a meeting at the park district in twenty. Quick question though. When did you get that tattoo that you always told me had no significance whatsoever?"

Leo froze, his eyes darting down to the black outline of the fox visible under his rolled-up shirtsleeve. "High school."

"Mm-hmm." William tilted his head. "And remind me what Faith's last name is?"

"It's Fox," he gritted out.

"Well, *that* is an interesting coincidence." William's mouth twisted into a devilish smile. "See you back at the house tonight."

SEVENTEEN

Faith bit into her strawberry fritter and tried to ignore her friends. Unfortunately her friends refused to ignore her.

"Stop staring," she mumbled around her mouthful of delicious pastry.

Thea eyed her over the rim of her coffee cup. "We will when you start spilling."

"Or do I need to ambush you on-air again?" Mabel added.

Faith stalled for time with another bite of fritter.

"You two are way too happy in your relationships to be messing with your single friend."

Thea reached across the table to rest her hand on Faith's. "It's because we're happy that we're messing with you."

Easy for her to say. They were meeting for Sunday-morning coffee in Thea's sun-soaked kitchen, and Faith couldn't possibly be happier that her friend had landed her dream house and her dream man and her dream life. But it was also a reminder that she wasn't at that stage. Like, at all.

"I need to find a new place to live," she said gloomily.

"Not what we wanted to talk about, but yeah, what's up with that?" Thea asked.

"Inertia," she said. "Crazy work schedule. A little bit of laziness. Generally distracted. The usual."

"Oh!" Thea's face lit up. "Babe!" she called, and almost instantly Aiden popped his head into the kitchen.

"I thought it was no boys allowed." He hovered in the doorway like he might get zapped if he set foot on the ceramic tile.

"Boy? You're all man, baby," she purred before turning to business. "You're almost done with that flip on Fort Road, right?"

"Yep." He propped his shoulder against the doorframe, and Faith was reminded yet again that Thea had landed an incredibly attractive guy. "Should be ready to list in the next month or so."

"Three bedrooms, two baths, nice backyard?" she asked.

At his nod, she turned toward Faith with an excited wriggle. "Well? You know Murdoch Construction does quality work."

"And the seller might cut you a deal," Aiden added with a wink that had Thea blushing.

"Agree to look at it," Mabel whispered loudly. "They're two seconds away from trying to sell you a timeshare."

Faith stood to refill her coffee, nodding at Aiden as she passed by. "Fine. Let me know when it's ready for a walkthrough."

Thea nodded, apparently satisfied at her successful real estate bullying, and shooed Aiden back out of the kitchen. "Okay, no boys starts now."

Before he disappeared again, he braved the kitchen to kiss his girlfriend, then ambled off to do whatever reformed playboys did on a Sunday morning.

Once he was gone, two pairs of eyes turned to Faith again.

"What?" she asked. "What can you possibly want to know so badly?"

"Um, everything about Leo," Thea said.

"He told me I have to go to the Digham Foundation gala in November, so I guess I need to find a dress." She grabbed a spoon and swirled it through the cream in her coffee until it was the color of a toasted marshmallow. "Other than that, there's nothing to talk about."

"Lies!" Mabel gasped. "You forget, I've been in the unique position to observe you not once but twice in the past month. First was at ye old gourd fest where I seem to recall some face touching and a few yearning looks. Maybe a little bit of leaning from both of you."

"There was no leaning," Faith insisted hotly.

Had there been leaning though?

"And let's revisit the second time Mabel was in a position to observe you," Thea said. "Which is two more times than I've been able to, by the way. Rude."

Faith tossed her hands in the air. "Hello? Busy, lazy, inertia, remember? Of course I've been a bad friend! I can barely manage to dress myself these days."

Faith gestured down her body, but the skepticism on the two faces looking back at her made her reconsider. "Okay, fine. I look adorable most days." Like today. Why wear plain leggings when you could wear leggings with a sequined stripe down each leg? "But you're right. Work's cutting into friend time."

"I forgive you," Thea said graciously. "Anyway, back

to that time Mabel interviewed you on her morning show and I heard a man basically announce that he wanted to build a lasting relationship with the hottie sitting next to him. Is that about right?"

Mabel primly patted her lips with a napkin. "That's what I heard."

"Come on." Faith clunked her mug down on the table. "That's not what it was. He practically bites my head off every time he comes around BUILD these days. And he clearly would rather saw off his own arm than have me go along on this overnight camping trip next weekend."

Mabel's eyes popped wide. "Camping? *You?*"

"Yes, me!" Then she caught sight of the sequins again. Okay, maybe Mabel had a point. "I'll admit, I was opposed to the whole hiking situation when Leo first brought it up, but the idea's grown on me."

Actually, *Leo* had grown on her, as had his quiet enthusiasm for the general concept of being outside. When she'd heard the guys planning that practice trip, her yearning to be part of it had caught her off guard. So she'd acted on impulse, and now apparently she had to go buy a bunch of survival gear. But it would be worth it to see Leo doing something he loved that much.

Probably. Hiking sounded dusty.

"I think it's great," said Thea, ever the loyal friend. "And you're actually going to the gala together?"

"We talked about him picking me up, yes." As she expected, this information tidbit made the other two squeal.

"See?" Thea shrieked. "I bet you're already halfway to rekindling something."

"We rekindled already," Faith said without thinking. "And we agreed not to let it happen again."

"Wait." Thea dropped her jelly-filled donut. "Rekindled? Do you mean *rekindled*?"

Mabel leaned forward and cupped a hand around her ear. "I'm sorry, did you just say that you banged your hot, growly ex?"

Faith could've denied it, but what was the point? "Once." She bared her teeth in a comical grimace. "In a storage room at Olive Twist."

"Oh my God!" Mabel hollered while Thea gave an outraged gasp.

"You didn't tell me!"

True, and Faith had been feeling bad about that.

"Sorry, babes. I should've. It's just... I wasn't sure how to talk about it." Or if she even wanted to talk about this new relationship with Leo, if that's even what it was. He was friendly, then he growled. He opened up the slightest bit, then he retreated behind that frowny exterior. And it all felt too deeply personal and frustrating and exciting to share even with Thea, who was already overprotective about Faith's well-being when it came to Leo. "It wasn't exactly a hookup, but it didn't start anything long-term either. It was..."

"Hot?" Mabel waggled her brows.

"God yes," she breathed, drifting back to those frantic few moments among the tablecloths before snapping back to the present. "But it's not something we can do again. We work together. We have all that history. And I think he still kind of hates me."

"I doubt that." Mabel crumpled up a napkin and tossed it onto her empty plate. "In any case, you're hanging out all the time with the extremely charismatic William. Bet he hates that more than he hates you."

"William? Nah, they're friends," she said immediately. "And he's not my type."

Then again, hadn't she told Leo weeks ago that William was everybody's type? And hadn't Leo completely iced over when she'd shown up at his house, looking for William? But that couldn't be it. Not when they still had a decade-old fight standing between them that neither of them seemed interested in revisiting. Leo was already coming around BUILD less now that William was there full time. After their overnight hike this weekend, his visits would probably dry up altogether, and they'd go back to being strangers again. And wasn't that depressing as hell?

Speaking of depressing.

"Is your boss doing okay?" she asked Mabel. She hadn't been able to fully shake the memory of Brandon Lowell's grief and hoped he'd found somebody to talk to about it.

Mabel was the wrong person to ask. "How should I know? With any luck, he's dead." She scoffed so hard her blond ponytail twitched.

Oh. Awkward. "It's actually his dad who's dead," she said quietly.

Mabel's mouth dropped open, then snapped shut. It was Thea who surprised her.

"*Good*," her normally kindhearted friend hissed. "Brandon's dad was an *asshole*."

She stood and whisked their empty plates off the table, stomping her little feet toward the sink. Faith and Mabel exchanged a confused glance.

"When did you meet him?" Mabel asked.

Thea rinsed each dish and slammed them into the dishwasher one by one. "I didn't. I caught the tail end of a phone conversation Brandon was having with him earlier this year. It was one of the worst things I've ever heard. Brandon's a jerk, but nobody deserves *that*." She angrily dried her hands and tossed the towel on the countertop. "You"—she pointed at Mabel—"better be nice to him the next time you see him. Rich people have parent problems too."

Mabel held up her hands. "Okay."

"I mean it," Thea insisted. "Be. Nice."

"I will!"

Faith hadn't intended to turn the conversational spotlight quite so forcefully away from herself, but it had done the trick, and they all settled back into Thea's sunny breakfast nook with fresh coffee and a new focus.

An hour later, as she and Mabel were headed for the door, Thea grabbed her hand.

"I'm here any time you want to talk about Leo," she said. "I know this must be a lot for you."

Faith pulled her friend into a hug, squeezing her tight. "Thanks. When I need a sounding board, you know you're my person."

AS SHE DROVE BACK HOME, she tried to start a mental list of all the things she'd need to do that week: look over that new algebra tutoring packet, figure out what the hell to wear on a camping trip, maybe visit that house Aiden was finishing up. But her brain kept returning to what Thea had said about Brandon's father.

Thea knew about the problems Faith had had with

her parents over the years, including that massive blowup over Leo. But she'd never sounded half as upset about it as she did about Brandon's father.

Rich people have parent problems too. Wasn't that the truth?

She turned in to her parents' driveway and put the car into park in the third stall of the garage. But she sat in the driver's seat after she'd turned off the engine. Was she really going to do this? Try to have a pleasant conversation with them? One where she didn't leap to take offense or intentionally provoke a fight?

Brandon's devastated face swam through her memory again. All that anger, all that hurt, and nowhere to put it.

Some bridges weren't mendable, but maybe she could see if hers was. She should at least try while she still had the chance. Taking a deep breath, she popped open her door and headed into the house.

"Mom? Dad?"

"In here."

Franklin called to her from his study. Her resolve wavered. When was the last time she'd had a solo conversation with him? Oh yeah, during her high school graduation party that had ended early when she'd stormed out.

She almost bolted for the safety of her bedroom, but that was cowardly. She was a lot of things, but she wasn't a coward.

She dragged her feet in the direction of the study off the main floor landing.

"Hi." She hesitated in the doorway, looking around for any signs that her dad was a different guy than he'd been twelve years ago. Like her bedroom, nothing much in the stuffy room had changed. Big heavy desk, stiff damask curtains, blocky bookshelves full of brass nautical equipment and unread hardbacks.

"Can I help you with something?" Franklin asked, peering at her over his reading glasses.

"Um." She didn't have a real plan for this, so she blurted out the first thing she could grab on to. "Do you have any camping supplies?"

He pulled off his glasses. "Your mother bought a hammock and some solar lights for a garden party a few years ago. Is that what you have in mind?"

"No." She took a hesitant step into the office. This was the room where they'd had that final, terrible fight. Being surrounded by this much heavy oak furniture apparently encouraged her to make rash decisions, like telling her parents that she'd never set foot in their house again. "I meant actual camping. Tents and sleeping bags. I'm going for an overnight trip next weekend."

Her father's face went slack. "You? *Camping?*"

"God, why does everybody say that?" She threw her hands in the air and turned to go. "Whatever. Sorry for bothering you."

So much for repairing bridges. Nobody could say she hadn't tried.

"This camping trip. Is it part of your new program?"

She paused, turning slowly in surprise. Her father was asking a follow-up question? One that involved her *job*?

"Yes," she said. "It's kind of a trial run to see how a few of the Dig Greener lessons work with different age groups before we start taking more kids."

"That's good. Smart to do a soft launch." He folded his glasses and tapped them on his palm. Was he... was he nervous? Her larger-than-life, both-his-bark-*and*-his-bite-are-bad father was *nervous*?

She moved a little farther into the study. "You should see some of the studies they've done on how getting out into nature helps kids in the classroom. It's really cool how it's all linked in their brains."

This pulled a small smile to his lips. "I don't know if you remember this, but I was an Eagle Scout."

"That's right! I'd completely forgotten." She sat down on the chair in front of his desk and folded her hands in her lap, trying to shake the unreality of reminiscing with her father in his study after years of frosty communication.

"Got my merit badge in camping," he said proudly. "So I actually do know a thing or two about the outdoors."

"But not enough to have a tent." Her question was a gentle tease, and her father responded in kind.

"On your mother's watch? Never." He hesitated, turning his glasses around and around in his hand. "I ran into George Voit at the club last week. He told me what a fine concept the outdoor education program is. He sounded excited that the foundation is in business with you."

His last words were stiff, and although he'd probably meant it as a compliment, they heated Faith's blood.

"Oh, so George Voit says what I'm doing is important, and you suddenly think it's worth talking to me about?" She shot to her feet.

Her father stood too, thick gray brows slamming together to meet over his nose. He drew a breath to fire back, starting the fight she'd halfway been expecting when she walked in here. But after a moment he deflated.

"I guess so." He leaned forward to rest his hands on his desk. "I guess that's a good point."

She dropped into the chair like a sack of potatoes. Her dad had just admitted that she was *right*?

He sat too, sighing heavily as he did. "I was so disappointed that you didn't want to come work at Fox Industries. And that was selfish of me." He gazed at her levelly. "I'm still disappointed, but I won't apologize for being pleased when the most powerful CEO in town tells me what a good job you've done." He pointed at her, some of his fire returning. "I do wish you were doing something *for* profit. But this nonprofit business seems to be important too. Sort of like Boy Scouts were for me."

His words left her speechless. She hadn't expected praise from him. Not today and maybe not ever.

"Thanks," she said, her throat tight. Maybe it didn't matter why her father had finally accepted her calling. Maybe it was just important that he *had*?

Their gazes locked, and they slowly exchanged smiles. Apparently they were able to survive a conversation if they both kept their tempers in check for long enough to do it. Wild.

Her father leaned back in his chair. "And then there's Leo Morales."

The name hit her like an electrical prod. "What about him?"

"Voit says he's an outstanding addition to the foundation. Moving them in new directions. Bringing energy to the whole group." He shook his head. "And after everything we did to keep you away from that boy."

"That man." He'd shocked her so much by bringing that up that she responded on autopilot. Yet his tone wasn't malicious, just regretful. She pressed her hands flat against the tops of her thighs and asked the question that had dogged her for twelve years. "Why did you hate him so much?"

"We never hated him."

Her mother's voice came from behind her, and Faith whipped around to see Betsy standing in the doorway. "But we saw the way you used to look at him."

"How did I look at him?" She whispered the question, almost afraid of the answer.

"Like he was your whole world." Betsy smoothed a hand over her bob as she crossed the room to sit in the chair across from her. "We were terrified that you'd get pregnant or that you'd put off college. That because you loved him, we'd lose you."

"And then we lost you anyway," her father said gruffly.

She sucked in a deep breath, trying to control the tears burning behind her eyes. She'd been so young and so angry. So unwilling to listen to anybody. Her parents. Leo. All those people who'd cared about her.

"You didn't lose me," she managed. "I'm here now."

Her mother pressed her lips together, and the room was silent for a moment before her father spoke.

"I'm so sorry. I've been sorry every day since then." His lips curved down, deepening the grooves on either side of his mouth. "I shouldn't have interfered. You were right to be furious."

They were good words. Words she didn't know how much she'd needed to hear until right now. They couldn't undo years of anger and separation, but they were a good start.

And she supposed she ought to own up to her part in all of it too.

"I'm sorry I wouldn't listen to your apology until now." It didn't seem like enough, but it drew a smile to her father's face.

"Would you... like to have dinner with us tonight?" her mom asked. "I'm making a roast and potatoes."

Faith sniffled. Her mom was offering to serve carbs? How could she say no?

"Sure thing, Emily Gilmore."

Betsy patted her hair one more time. "Please. I'm much nicer to my maids."

EIGHTEEN

"I don't know about you two, but I'm blown away."

She was flanked by Leo and William as they left the informational meeting about Dig Greener, and each of the men had his arms full.

"Way more interest than I was expecting," William agreed, turning sideways so the stand-up display case would fit through the exit of the Beaucoeur Public Library. He was carrying that and the table banner while Leo had the laptop and the box of pamphlets—printed on recycled paper of course. She'd hauled that equipment in and out of so many schools on her own over the years that she didn't even feel bad about letting them do the heavy lifting this time.

"Not me. I figured this would be a big draw." Leo was smiling as he said it, about as thrilled as she'd ever seen him. "This is great."

It was only two months until December and the end of Dig Greener's probationary period. She was guessing the fifty people who'd shown up today would be a strong argument in favor of full-funding approval.

"Good thing Saturday's our practice hike. Sounds like we need to get things moving sooner rather than later." William stashed the supplies in his car and turned to her. "You have everything you need, boss?"

She winced. "Um. I've still got some shopping to do."

"What kind of shopping?" Leo's body language shifted from pleased to wary so fast it almost gave her whiplash.

"Well," she hedged, "you said moisture-wicking?"

"If you want some help, I can—" William started to offer, but Leo beat him to it.

"I got this," Leo barked. "You and me, Dutch. Let's go."

With zero discussion, he steered her away from William's Toyota and loaded her into his own passenger seat.

"Let me guess," she said once he was settled into the driver's seat. "This is a rental from a Big Dig employee stationed on the moon for the month?"

She tried not to scour the interior for any details about his life, but her resolve broke immediately, although nothing about his disappointingly generic Subaru Outback revealed anything of interest.

"Funny." His voice was flat, but she saw crinkles around his eyes and took it as a win. "I do own a couple of personal items."

"So it's this and the tiny tent?"

"Yep. The sum total of my possessions."

Given what he and William had described about their lives with POR, he might not actually be kidding.

As they headed toward the biggest outdoor outfitter in town, she risked a question that had been bothering her for two weeks. "Since you're taking me, does that mean you're finally okay with me coming?"

She was aiming for breezy, but in truth she wanted to know why he had a bug up his butt about her going camping. She thought they were getting along fine—better than fine, sometimes—but he seemed determined to keep her away from his precious woods.

His gaze flicked over to her while they waited at a stoplight near the outdoor mall. "What Faith Fox wants, Faith Fox gets. I learned that a long time ago."

The eye crinkles again. His words might say one thing, but his body language said another. He was teasing her, like he used to. She wanted more of it.

"Apparently what I want is wool socks and moisture-wicking pants."

He smiled, as she hoped he would, and then they were parked and walking up to Hiking HQ. Although she'd lived in Beaucoeur her whole life and liked to shop local, she'd never set foot on the premises until today. Its massive exterior was covered in redwood planks arranged at sharp angles, and an oversized fiberglass moose stood next to the entrance, a pumpkin at its huge feet, marking the fact that Halloween was a week away.

"Hey, we should get a shot with the moose." Then, in case that sounded like a naked attempt to take a selfie with him, she quickly added, "For the BUILD socials."

"Sure." He stood next to her while she held her camera at arm's length. The end result had her grinning and him frowning and the moose looming over them, its nostrils bigger than either of their heads.

"Perfect." She tapped out a quick caption for the BUILD Instagram account and posted it, her heart giving a tiny squeeze. They still looked good together.

"Let's do this." He stepped forward and held the door open for her. Once they were inside, he gestured to the left. "Clothes first."

She obediently followed him to the apparel section, which contained rack after rack of clothes made out of impenetrable-looking, space-age material.

"Pants," he said, pointing to the first rack. She dutifully thumbed through the offerings, sending a silent thank-you to the universe that Hiking HQ actually carried plus sizes.

"Pants!" She held up two pairs to try on, and he moved her to the shirts.

"These are not cute," she complained as she slid her fingers over hanger after hanger of solid colors and earth tones.

"Nature's not always cute, Dutch. Bloody in fang and claw and all that."

"I didn't agree to blood or fangs." She shuddered and got back to picking out options, at which point she dumped her armful of clothes into a dressing room and started trying on her new gear. Both pairs of pants worked, along with a few of the magical moisture-wicking shirts.

"Do you have a waterproof jacket?" he asked when she emerged from the dressing room.

"Does faux leopard count?"

He lifted his eyes to the heavens and beckoned her to follow him to outerwear, where she found an acceptably cute hot-pink number.

"You're turning into Richard Gere from *Pretty Woman*," she announced as she draped the jacket over the pile of clothes in his arms. He rewarded her with a smile, and she hoped he was remembering how they'd spent hours watching classic rom-coms on her bedroom TV in high school.

"Okay, Vivian. Let's do shoes next."

"Shoes," she crooned as she followed him to the next part of the store.

"Sit." He pointed to a bench, then flagged down a Hiking HQ employee. "What's your shoe size, Dutch?"

"Nine and a half wide."

He turned to Sheila the shoe department worker. "Can you help me pick some options?"

The two of them disappeared into the wilds of the footwear section, and he returned with half a dozen pairs of socks and three shoeboxes.

"Start with these," he said. "They're the brightest colors they have."

She picked up the first pair of socks and ran her fingers over the pink, yellow, and aqua stripes. He'd picked out socks he thought she'd like. "That was thoughtful," she managed to say through the lump in her throat. He eye-crinkled at her, and she forced herself to tear her gaze away as she kicked off her flats. When she pulled on the socks, she wiggled her toes in delight at the thick material.

"I will never get cold in these," she declared.

"You will if they get wet. That's why you pack multiple pairs." He shoved the first box over to her. "Here."

She pulled out a pair of disappointingly practical tan boots, which she slid on and laced up. Leo knelt and pinched his thumb against the tip of the boot. "Too big. Next pair."

"Okay," she said a little breathlessly. She hadn't been physically, spiritually, or emotionally prepared for Leo to fall to his knees at her feet. *That* man in *that* dress shirt with *those* rolled-up sleeves, kneeling in front of her with his head of unruly curls? A girl needed a warning and some electrolytes first.

Then he handed the next box to her, and its contents managed to distract her from the Leo show. "I love them!" she gasped, holding up a pair of boots with a bright teal body.

His lips twitched. "Then let's hope they fit."

She shoved her feet into them and hastily tied the laces so Leo could repeat his toe-pinching action. He nodded in approval, but when she made a move to stand, he pressed his palm against her knee.

"Hang on."

He slid his hand down to wrap his fingers around the back of her calf, holding her steady as he tightened each of the laces on one boot with a finger. His brow furrowed in concentration as he worked, and when he glanced up at her, his gaze was far hotter than it had any right to be given his task.

She might've whimpered out loud. She wasn't quite sure. All she knew was that his hand on her leg seemed to have a direct line to her vagina, which gave a little pulse when he stroked his thumb gently along the outside of her calf.

Thank the sweet baby Jesus she'd worn a skirt today—and that she'd shaved that morning.

After an eternity of tightening and squeezing, he released her left leg and moved on to the right one, repeating the whole delicious process. Oh God, she needed to get a grip. This wasn't seduction, it was trying on shoes. Still, her knees were trembling when he finally stood and held out his hands to pull her to her feet.

"Walk up and down the aisle for me," he commanded.

She swallowed hard and did as he instructed, striding down the space and back, feeling self-conscious the whole time that Leo was watching her.

"How do they feel?"

She looked down at the tips of the blue boots. "Good, I think." Her voice sounded thready, and she did a little spin to try to find her equilibrium.

"No pinching? No rubbing? They should have a little give to accommodate your feet swelling by the end of the day."

"I don't think so." She turned away from him to take another stroll, swinging her hips a bit as she walked, trying to get the shoes to move with her. When she glanced over her shoulder, Leo wasn't watching her feet. His narrowed eyes were pinned to her butt, the expression on his face almost pained.

She suddenly wasn't so grateful for this pencil skirt. It always made her feel confident, which was why she'd worn it for the big informational meeting, but the way Leo was staring at her right now, it didn't look like he appreciated every curve and bump of her ass on display under the tight green material.

She whipped around and walked double time back to the bench. "I like them." She started yanking at the laces to get them off, determined to joke herself into a better mood. "So what's next? Wedges with rhinestones? Maybe something with a chunky heel and a strap?"

He snorted. "Now you *do* sound like one of those college kids."

"Why do I get a sense that that isn't a compliment?" She tucked the shoes back into the box and set it on her lap.

"Because it isn't," he said shortly.

There was another topic she'd like to know a little more about.

"So when William said you 'educated them,' he really did just mean about footwear?" She was playing with fire even bringing it up, but that remark had annoyingly lodged itself in her brain.

Leo snorted. "Definitely. Even if they all hadn't been too young for me, Reggie would've had my balls."

The name rang a bell. "Reggie. The guy who took over for William?" she asked. "Why would he care what you did with the volunteers?"

"Reggie's a woman." His eyes didn't quite meet hers as he said it, and just like William figuring out that she and Leo had history, she swiftly put some things together about Reggie.

"Oh," she said inanely.

Reggie, who'd surprised Leo by not quitting POR after he left.

Reggie, who undoubtedly didn't need help picking out clothes for hiking.

Reggie, who probably didn't breathe a sigh of relief that the store carried extended sizes.

Faith was comfortable in her body most days, but it smarted like hell to jump to the highly reasonable conclusion that Leo's last girlfriend, the one who was leading groups of hikers through the Amazonian rainforest right now, was physically everything she wasn't—at least, not anymore. And she'd bet Leo's face didn't contort when he looked at Reggie in a tight skirt.

He'd been quiet while she was having her existential freak-out, and he ducked his head now to peer at her. "Everything good?"

She pasted a big, bright smile onto her face and chirped, "Of course!" because setting fire to every wretched piece of tan-colored clothing in this store would be preferable to letting a single drop of insecurity show right now. "Is this all then?"

"Backpack next," he said, towing her to a different section of the store where he made her slide frightening complicated packs on and off, then left her all flustered as he clipped and tightened straps around her chest and hips. Unlike their shoe encounter, his touch was impersonal and businesslike, and she was left with the sense that this was how he'd have handled those college girls. Reggie though... she bet he wasn't nearly as brisk with her.

"Now are we done?" If her voice sounded a little desperate, it was. God, she needed to move past that. But the whole excursion was turning into a reminder that she and Leo lived in different worlds. She was an idiot for trying to force herself into his.

"One more thing." He led her one aisle over to where a bunch of ski pole-looking things lined the racks.

"What are those?"

"Hiking poles." He tucked the clothes and boots into the backpack he'd selected for her and set them aside, then scanned the rows before choosing three different poles and handing one to her. "This might work for someone your height. Plus it's purple. You like purple, right?"

"I don't understand." She held the pole limply in one hand. "Why do I need this?"

"Stability. A little extra support as you hike."

"I know how to walk, Leo."

"Of course you do. But it's different in the forest." His

voice was calm, and it just made her more uncomfortable. "It would be easy for you to fall and hurt yourself. It'll support your ankles. Help you balance."

Her face heated as she stared at the sticks in her hand. "Are you saying I need extra help because... because..."

She shoved the pole out in front of her, unable to bring herself to finish. She never apologized for her body, for taking up more space than the world often wanted her to, but something about standing in front of Leo and asking if he thought she needed help walking through the woods made her burn with humiliation.

"These are really common," he said, apparently unaware that she was a cauldron about to boil over. "Lots of the volunteers we got at POR use them if they don't have much hiking experience. But especially for you on your first hike, I want to be sure..."

He finally noticed the look on her face and stopped talking, but her emotions were getting too big to control. As pissed as she was at herself for letting all this bother her, she had some anger left over for Leo even though what he was saying made sense.

Kind. Calm. Collected.

Fuck it.

"Does *Reggie* use them too?" Acid churned in her gut as she said it.

"Not usually." Leo shoved his hair off his forehead in frustration. "I'm just trying to keep you safe since you're new to hiking. If you could not assume the worst of me, that would be great."

She stared at him as a whole new anger twisted through her. He was accusing *her* of thinking the worst of *him*? That was fucking rich.

"You. Want me. Not to assume the worst." She could barely hear herself over the blood pounding in her ears.

"Yes," he spat out.

Her laugh was shrill. "You do see the irony, right? Because you've always been so good about not assuming the worst of *me*."

She saw the instant her meaning washed over him; his jaw hardened so fast that the muscles bunched under his skin. Their staring contest ended when he shook his head and took a step back, the fight draining from his body.

"Do what you want, duchess," he said, not meeting her eyes. "You always do."

This time the words weren't playful, and he turned on his heel and left the aisle with her supplies in his arms. When she joined him minutes later at the checkout, he didn't say a word about her leaving the poles behind in that fucking aisle.

NINETEEN

For the millionth time that morning, Leo considered knocking on William's bedroom door and asking him to switch.

And for the millionth time that morning, he nailed his feet to the floor and continued making final adjustments to his backpack. It would undoubtedly be smarter for him to pick up Vani's kids by himself while Faith went with William to meet the ranger, but he just couldn't bring himself to make the ask. William would be way too delighted for one thing. And for another thing... well, Faith might be way too delighted too. Why'd he recommend William for the job in the first place?

This was going to be a long two days.

At six on the dot, the early-morning quiet was interrupted by a knock on the door, followed by Faith's voice calling, "Hello?"

"In the kitchen," he called back, mentally preparing himself for battle after the disastrous end of their shopping trip two days ago. But Faith just breezed into the room and dramatically dropped her backpack onto the tiled floor.

"Does all camping have to start so *early?*" she demanded.

He momentarily lost the power of speech. After bracing himself for a continuation of their standoff at Hiking HQ, he was instead met with a different kind of torture.

She looked fucking adorable. He was always low-key turned on by her work outfits at BUILD. That tight skirt she'd been wearing when he took her shopping, for example? They'd barely been speaking when he dropped her off at the car, but that hadn't kept him from fantasizing about stripping her out of it and fucking her at least six different ways. But the woman standing in his kitchen with a crooked smile on her face was a fantasy he didn't even know he'd been harboring.

She'd topped her new merino wool T-shirt with a purple plaid flannel that she'd knotted at the waist, and her brand-new khaki pants and garish boots were crying out for some trail dirt. But that wasn't the only thing that pulled a smile to his lips.

The blue was back in her hair. She'd done it up in two long braids, the streaks of color twisting playfully through the loops. The shade was slightly different this time, closer in color to her new shoes, and he'd bet cash money that it was intentional.

Trail Faith was absolutely. Fucking. Adorable.

He cleared his throat and pushed that thought far, far down, still unsure what her mood was like. "Six *is* late. I let you sleep in."

"You outdoor types are exhausting." But she smiled as she shook her head, and thank the Blessed Virgin Mary that he hadn't asked William to swap. If she was willing to ignore the out-of-nowhere disagreement that had exposed the black hole at the heart of their relationship, so was he. It was the only way to survive the weekend and possibly this whole damn partnership.

"I made coffee." He gestured at the empty mug next to the pot on the counter.

"Yes! Thank yo— What are you doing?"

He'd set her bag on the kitchen island and was unzipping the top compartment.

"I figured you'd need some help packing. There's an art to it."

But when he flipped the top open, he saw her sunscreen, bandanna, first aid kit, and trail mix settled in neat as a pin, exactly as it should be.

"This looks good," he said in surprise.

"It should." She didn't look up from the coffee as she poured. "William packed it for me."

He let go of the bag as if it had burned him. "What? When?"

"Yesterday. He came by my place after work to help me get it all sorted."

"He..." The question was strangely hard to push out. "William went to your parents' house?"

She flicked a smile at him. "Used the front door and everything."

Golden-boy William had parked in the driveway, had rung the bell, had shaken her father's hand maybe.

He pivoted and crossed to the refrigerator, yanking the door open and letting the air cool the blood pulsing in his temples. Once he was fractionally back under control, he grabbed the milk and walked to the island with it.

Faith waved him off, so he poured some into his mug and returned it to the rack in the door.

So what if William had helped her pack? So what if he'd seen her bedroom? So what if he'd sat on the magic bed? It was Faith's business, not his. All they did when they were together was trip over the land mines of their past and wound each other with the shrapnel. For God's sake, he should *want* her to pair up with William if only to shut down this miserable push-pull he felt every time they were together.

While he was spinning out, Faith was excitedly poking through the contents of her bag. "I can't believe how much stuff he fit in here. And it's not as uncomfortable as I expected."

"That's physics for you." He refocused on the actual conversation. "What did he pack?"

Not only did he need to know what supplies William had equipped her with, but he was perversely curious about whether William had handled the clothes that *he'd* chosen for her at Hiking HQ. The ones he'd imagined helping her pack properly before they left today.

Hot jealousy surged yet again, and he choked it back as Faith started pointing to the various compartments.

"Extra clothes, including socks. Raincoat. Spare water. Sleeping pad and bag. Oh, and he put the stove and cookware in the middle part. He said since he's carrying the big tent and you're carrying the food, I could handle that stuff."

He nodded, running down his mental checklist. Their food supply didn't have any tree nuts for Mateo's allergy or any strawberries for Faith's, so they were good there. But he wanted to know what else William had put in her backpack.

"Did he pack you a reflective blanket? Lighter? Compass?"

She shook her head. "Yes, yes, no. I wouldn't know what to do with a compass if I had one."

"No problem. Just stick with me." For more reasons than she knew, he wanted that. But he didn't say so out loud and simply rezipped her bag and nudged it closer to her. "Any questions before we go?"

"One, maybe." She fiddled with the end of one of the braids, looking uncomfortable for the first time that morning. "Which Leo am I going to get over the next couple of days?"

"What do you mean?"

"Come on." Her eyes lingered on his face. "Are you going to be the short-tempered guy who grunts one-syllable answers? Or are you going to be the guy who helps carry heavy boxes from my car and has an unnecessary security system installed at work?"

"It was necessary," he said.

She rolled her eyes. "I told you that—"

"I need you to be safe."

His words stopped her complaint, and for a beat the only sound in the kitchen was the hum of the fridge.

"And then there's the third guy," Faith said slowly. "Do you know the one I'm talking about?"

He was helpless to look away from her. "Tell me."

"Well, one time he had sex with me in a closet." She flushed as if she couldn't believe she'd just said that out loud.

"Oh. That guy." He had to shift his weight as his dick twitched to life. "The one who tried to protect you from his sisters?"

"That's the one." She took a tiny step closer to him. "He also laughs at my jokes sometimes."

"And occasionally forgets that it isn't his job to take care of you." He leaned closer, inhaling her sweet shampoo and bitter coffee smell.

But her expression clouded. "He also might suggest I get some hiking poles, and I might get offended for reasons that are entirely my own deal and not at all about him."

"I'm sorry," he said immediately, although he still wasn't quite sure what happened there. "I didn't mean to upset you."

"I know. I'm sorry too."

They were standing face-to-face now, so close he could slip a finger into her belt loop and pull her against him. He resisted the urge, but it was hard.

"So which guy do you want on the trip this weekend?" he murmured.

"I don't know." She rested her hand on the island between them. "Sometimes when that third guy looks at me, it feels like..."

"Like nothing's changed?" He was almost scared to say the words out loud, but she nodded, so he did maybe the bravest thing he'd ever done and rested his hand on top of hers. "Faith—"

And then his motherfucking roommate ruined everything.

"Good morning!"

She jerked her hand away as William shuffled into the kitchen, blinking sleepily. Leo had never wanted to kick his friend in the balls more than he did at that moment.

"Morning!" Faith spun away and busied herself

checking the zippers on her pack. "Leo and I were just getting ready to head off."

"Oh, about that." William pushed a hand through his sleep-wild hair as he headed for the coffee. "I've got her carrying the stove and the fuel, so—"

"Yeah, she said." Leo narrowed his eyes on William as he selected a mug. "So nice of you to help her pack."

"I'm a very nice guy." He poured and leaned against the sink, crossing one ankle over the other. "How's the forecast?"

"Small chance of rain toward midnight," he said. "I'm willing to risk it."

"Yep." William glanced at the clock on the microwave. "If you're meeting the ranger at the lodge at nine and you leave now, you'll have plenty of buffer."

"Thanks," Leo said. For years, William had helped him work out travel times and when to leave for appointments, so it was nice to have their system carry on in Beaucoeur.

"Cool." His friend yawned into a stretch, and that's when he realized that William was only wearing boxers, and Faith was *right there*.

He was suddenly motivated to get on the road regardless of buffer time.

"Ready?" He sidled over to stand between Faith and William.

She nodded and picked up her bag, slinging it over first one shoulder, then the other, securing it around her waist and grabbing onto the straps.

"Well? Will I do?"

His eyes went a little unfocused as he looked at her, luminous in the middle of his kitchen. He had to swallow before he could speak.

"You're perfect." He cleared his throat. "Let's go."

IN THE CAR, neither of them said much as they headed toward the interstate. Leo was caught in the moment of their near miss, and given her silence, that might be where Faith was living too. The drive to Starved Rock State Park would take about an hour, and right now it seemed like the only conversation was going to come from the radio, where a woman chattered away before launching into the music. Faith laughed softly a few notes in.

"What are the odds?" She whipped out her phone and tapped furiously. "That's Mabel. I'm sure she'll get a kick out of hearing that she made things awkward on a road trip with my hot ex-boyfriend."

"What?" He shot her a confused glance.

"Pssht, stop it with the fake modesty." She wrinkled her nose at him. "All you've done since high school is level up your hotness, you dork."

"That's not..."

But her words obliterated his initial question. She thought he'd gotten better-looking? He'd filled out since high school, sure. Had put on some muscle. But all that time in the Brazilian sun had left him harder too. His skin felt tougher, his hair coarser. He had lines around his eyes that didn't go away when he stopped smiling, and his hands were a mess of scars and calluses. Still, he puffed out his chest just a bit at learning that the prettiest girl he'd ever known still thought he was attractive.

Shit. No. That wasn't helpful. This trip was about the kids, about Dig Greener. He shook his head and focused on the actual source of his confusion. "What I mean is, why is that song awkward?"

Faith looked at him as if he were especially dim. "It's the song that was playing during our first kiss."

"No, it's not."

She turned in her seat, adjusting the seatbelt strap so she could face him. "Are you maybe thinking about some *other* girl you kissed under the bleachers at halftime of a basketball game while the pom squad danced to Katy Perry?"

"That wasn't our first kiss." He didn't pull his eyes from the road, but his peripheral vision picked up on her surprised flail.

"No? Please educate me. When was our first kiss?"

"The first time I kissed my *one and only high school girlfriend*," he said, "was in the hallway in front of her locker. Right before advanced bio, if I recall."

He flicked his gaze over to her. Still adorable even though her mouth was open in shock.

"What, that? That was just a peck. Kisses without tongue don't count."

"Oh yes they fucking do." He sank into the memory. "You were freaking out about a test, and you were so damn cute that I forgot how nervous I was to even be holding your hand and just went for it." He lifted a shoulder and let it fall. "The hallway was our first kiss."

She stared at him for a long moment before straightening to sit forward. "You're wrong, but in the interest of not picking stupid fights, I'll stop arguing."

"As long as you acknowledge that our song isn't Katy Perry."

"No deal, Leonidas."

She glanced at him with laughter dancing in her eyes,

and he groaned. "I beg you, stop. Nobody other than my mother's called me that since…"

His hands tightened around the steering wheel. Faith was the last nonblood relative to call him by his full name. His mind drifted back to New Year's Eve of their senior year when he'd climbed into her bedroom window while her parents were hosting a fancy crystal glasses-and-tuxedoes party downstairs. She'd yelped and called him Leonidas when he'd slipped his cold hands under her shirt.

His chest tightened at the memory. His first sex. His first love. His first… everything.

This was ridiculous. He was a grown man who'd had plenty of female company since they'd broken up. Girlfriends even. Women who'd kept the memory of his greatest regret tucked safely away.

But now here he was, alone in a car with that very regret, who was probably wondering why he'd gone silent. Or maybe she was remembering the same night. His lips on her skin, his fingers in her hair, his mouth on her…

He cleared his throat and refocused on the conversation. "I haven't heard that since they called my name at graduation."

"Right," she said. "SIUC, huh?"

Now she was the one changing the subject. He rolled with it. "It's no Northwestern, but my parents were proud." He thought for a bit and opted for total honestly. Faith was one of the few people who'd truly understand, after all. "Hell, I was proud."

"You should be. I'm proud too." The quiet intensity of her voice told him that she really did grasp the work it had taken him to accomplish. The humility to ask for the help he needed.

She leaned over and squeezed his knee. The brief contact burned through him even though she removed her hand as quickly as she'd placed it there.

"Also," she said briskly, "I didn't go to Northwestern. Too expensive after I told my parents to go to hell. I took out loans and went to UIC."

The news caught him by surprise. "For real? After all that legacy talk?"

"My dad was *pissed*." She shrugged. "But so was I. He knew exactly what he was doing when he showed you that essay. And our relationship hasn't ever recovered from that."

Leo didn't know what to say, but hearing that she'd burned down her relationship with the man who'd caused him so much pain didn't bring the satisfaction it once might have. Instead, he just felt sorrow. For her, for himself. For her parents even. He was sure they never intended to drive a wedge between them and their only child.

They lapsed into silence. The radio station dissolved into static as they traveled out of the Beaucoeur area, and he reached forward to turn it down.

"Do we need to talk about the shopping trip?" he asked.

The worst moments of their relationship kept resurfacing, and despite her cheerful attitude today, he wasn't quite sure how to move forward without addressing it.

"Nope." Her voice was firm, shutting down any future conversation.

If that's what she wanted, that's how he'd play it. Maybe it was better to just let it stay in the past with the rest of the messes they'd made.

She gave a little smirk. "I will say, William laughed

and laughed when I told him about the poles. Said Grandpa Leo was at it again."

He grunted at hearing that stupid nickname on her lips, but she blithely continued. "He said using poles on a hike in Starved Rock was beyond overkill. Like wrapping a basketball in bubble wrap to roll it across the floor."

An unwilling laugh escaped him. William wasn't wrong, but at least he hadn't figured out what was behind Leo's sudden obsession with safety. Or if he had, at least he had the decency to keep his mouth shut to Faith.

"So *do* you want to wrap me in bubble wrap?" she asked.

Yes. But he stuck with a half-truth.

"I trust you when you say you can handle it." There. That was accurate without confessing how much the thought of her getting hurt made his insides tangle up into knots.

Before she could press the issue, he pointed up through the windshield at the overcast sky. "Looks like we might get rain sooner than we thought."

She ducked her head to look. "Yikes. Am I going to get wet?" Her hands flew to her newly blue braids.

"That's why Dig Greener bought you the pinkest jacket in history."

"My precious," she crooned, and he laughed again. He hadn't laughed this much since...

Since he'd been her boyfriend all those years ago. He was lighter when he was around her. Sometimes anyway. Other times, he saw her turning those open, sunny smiles on William, and he had to pull himself from a black hole of jealousy that he wasn't entitled to feel.

But William wasn't here right now, was he?

TWENTY

"Okay, I'll admit it. This is kind of fun."

Leo glanced over his shoulder at her, a big, heart-stopping smile on his lips. "Yeah?"

Her breath caught in her chest—and not just because she was tromping through the woods like some sort of mountaineer. His delight at her enjoyment left her feeling a little giddy. And she *was* enjoying herself. Despite the fact that she had the contents of a small apartment strapped to her back and the clouds were gathering ominously above their heads. Despite the fact that she was that weird combination of chilled but sweating that turned everything clammy. And despite the fact that her thigh muscles were sore and she was thirsty and had to pee.

Despite it all, she was enjoying herself, and it had everything to do with Leo. Specifically, it had to do with the fourth version of Leo that she'd discovered once they'd set foot on the hard-packed Starved Rock trail. She was used to seeing him in suits by now, and she'd spent most of her free time at the Gourd Olde Days Festival sneaking glances at the whole torso situation happening under his shirt. But she wasn't prepared for this plaid-wearing, scruff-sporting, ruggedly masculine man who'd apparently been born with a compass for a brain and Illinois river water running through his veins.

When they'd met Ranger Steve a few hours ago, he'd dragged them to a million different spots to point out a million different rocks and plants, and Leo had asked all kinds of questions that she couldn't even begin to follow about sediment layers and erosion patterns and conservation efforts. They'd parted ways with Steve about an hour ago, and she was beginning to realize that she'd never actually seen Leo in his natural habitat until today. And this relaxed, confident outdoorsy man was giving her a serious competency boner.

The guy in question stopped walking to consult his GPS, which was a crying shame; she couldn't watch the muscles shift under his shirt if he was standing still.

"There." He pointed, and hey, those muscles were back.

"That's the spot you reserved for the night?" She dragged her eyes away from his ridiculously attractive shoulders. The camping spot didn't look particularly special, although the ground was mostly flat, and there were stumps in a semicircle, presumably designed for sitting around a fire.

"Yep. It's close to the water, but it's on high enough ground to keep us safe."

"Safe?" That sounded alarming, but he slanted her one of those cocky grins he had in abundance when he wasn't trapped inside four walls.

"From flash floods, Bigfoot, that kind of thing," he said.

"Ha." Being in nature even made him funnier somehow. Looser. God, what would he have been like in charge of his own team in Brazil? Calling the shots, making plans...

"Faith? Did you hear me?"

His amused question snapped her out of her trance, and his tongue darted out to stroke along the corner of his mouth as he watched her watching him.

"What? No, I..." Could she blame her flushed face on exertion? Probably not. Outdoors Leo was giving her pants feelings, and the gleam in his eyes told her he knew it.

"I asked if you were interested in a quick detour before we set up camp," he said. "If we head a little south, I can show you something you'll love."

"Oh. Yeah, sure. Definitely!"

But instead of setting them in motion, Leo tilted his head to study her face.

"When's the last time you put on sunblock?"

She touched her cheeks. Could he possibly think she was sunburned and not singed by lust? "The parking lot," she managed.

"We're both overdue. Turn around." He made a circular motion with his finger, and she did as he asked, holding still while he opened the top compartment of her bag to grab the sunblock. He made quick work of his face, neck, and hands. "One of my worst-ever sunburns happened on an overcast day like this. You've got to be careful."

When he was done, he handed the bottle over to her, and she smeared a fair amount onto her own face and neck before capping the bottle.

"Rookie." He gave a laughing shake of his head. "You're not even half-done."

She looked at him in surprise. "What?"

He plucked the bottle from her fingers and flipped open the cap to squeeze a healthy amount into his palm, then grabbed her left hand. She jumped a little at his touch but forced herself to hold still as he rubbed the sunblock up her arms under the rolled cuffs of her flannel shirt. She shivered when he moved back down to work the lotion in between her fingers. Even though there was nothing sexual about it, his fingers sliding between each of hers had her struggling to breathe.

"Am I good?" she managed to ask.

He shook his head and stepped closer after adding a little more sunblock to his palm. He rubbed his hands together and then set them on either side of her neck. Her whole body tensed as he rubbed the cool lotion down to the vee of her chest exposed by her shirt. His palms were rough, and as they scraped lightly against her skin, the sensation traveled straight to her nipples.

His eyes darted down, then back up, and when he spoke, his voice was hoarse.

"It's easy to miss spots when you do it yourself." His eyes locked on hers, he slid his hands around to the back of her neck, spreading the lotion from her hairline to inside the shirt collar. Her head felt like a balloon connected to her body with a string, and when he gently squeezed the base of her neck after he was done, she almost drifted away.

"You didn't get the back of your neck either," she murmured, reaching for the bottle almost in a trance.

He held perfectly still as she slid her palms around the

sides of his neck, his muscles and tendons tense. But she took her time smoothing in the lotion, working her fingers up into his hairline, tickling the back of his neck and pulling goose bumps to the surface of his skin as he gradually relaxed under her touch. She lingered when she shouldn't have, enjoying the texture of his hair, thick and a little damp with sweat. Somehow her fingers ended up locked behind his neck, and she stepped closer as he dropped his hands to her hips.

A breeze kicked up, and she involuntarily shivered. Her movements snapped the spell they were under, and she stepped away with a nervous little laugh.

"So much for sunscreen time." Leo reached behind her to return the bottle to her pack. "Shall we?"

She pushed away her longing to ignore reality and wrap her arms around him again, instead falling into step as Leo led them toward what she was assuming was south. Her thoughts raced as they walked. Obviously they were attracted to each other. That had been the case a decade ago, so it wasn't a surprise that this was unchanged. Over the past few months, they'd managed to wallpaper over all the cracks in their relationship, but this weird circling pattern they were in wasn't going to last forever.

When she rang his doorbell that morning, she'd had to fight back an almost nauseating attack of nerves. What she's said to him at the store... she was embarrassed that she'd let her body-image issues run riot like that. And yes, she'd overreacted—she'd happily acknowledge that now, especially in light of William's amusement over those damn hiking poles—but her response to Leo's words was a problem. They had so much shit between them that they'd never sorted out. If they didn't stay away from each other, that dam was going to crumble and their past would come rushing in.

But that was tomorrow's problem. Today Leo wanted to show her something, and she wanted to see it.

Within twenty minutes, her trust paid off as the trees lining the trail thinned out before falling away entirely to reveal a sandstone canyon stretching in front of them. Trees and mossy patches clung to the smooth light-brown sides made of layers of stone that were so round in places that they almost looked like pancakes stacked on top of one another and rising fifty feet into the air. As they moved closer, Faith became aware of a rushing sound.

"Is that...?" She walked a few more steps into the canyon and gasped.

Water flowed in a broad line down the curved lip of one side of the smooth walls, tossing spray into the air and creating a rainbow mist that hung over the canyon. She blindly reached for Leo's hand, gripping it as she sucked in air.

"This has been here the whole time?" she asked in wonder.

He laughed softly, his fingers tightening around hers. "The whole time, Dutch."

She wasn't sure how long they stood in that place, watching the endless spill of water, but it was long enough for her to feel inconsequentially small in terms of the space she occupied on the planet while at the same time the churn of the water over the weather-worn stone soothed some of the restlessness in her blood and made her feel like she was standing with the only other person in the universe.

"Is hiking always like this?"

He glanced down at her before answering. "Not always." He looked back to the waterfall. "But yeah, lots of times it is."

And that's when the heavens opened up. A torrent of rain drenched them immediately, and although Faith's first instinct was to shriek and curl into a ball, Leo pulled her into motion to run toward the nearest canyon wall where a stone overhang provided a bit of protection from the downpour.

"Rain jacket!" he shouted over the racket.

Teeth chattering, she fumbled to unstrap her pack and opened the outermost compartment to fish out her new coat. She pulled it on and zipped it to her chin. "It got c-cold so fast!"

"I know!" He'd pulled his jacket on too, and they huddled together under the narrow ledge, watching the water fall in sheets inches away. "This wasn't in the forecast."

She shivered. "Do you think William and the kids are out in this too?"

"Hope not." He groped in his pocket to pull out his phone and tapped a saved number. "Hey, how's it going there?"

He had to shout over the pounding of the rain, then listened to a mostly one-sided conversation that ended with his terse "Good plan" before he hung up.

"He and the boys are sitting in a car in the parking lot, but he's going to drive them back home once this lets up. We'll try again another weekend."

Lightning cracked across the canyon. "Smart," she said. "But won't they be disappointed?"

"Nah. He's going to pull through McDonald's on the way."

Just like that, her stomach rumbled. It was almost Pavlovian. "Lucky kids," she muttered.

He smiled down at her. "Once we hike out of here, I'll take you to the Dairy Bar."

"Okay." Another bolt of lightning flashed overhead, followed closely by a thunderclap that had her shrinking back against the sandstone wall. "Not liking this part of nature," she announced, which made Leo toss his head back with a laugh.

"You have to take the good with the bad."

He pulled her down to sit, and once they were arranged with their backs against the stone, he wrapped an arm around her shoulders and tucked her against his side. It didn't really warm her up, but it did ignite a spark in her chest that had nothing to do with the temperature.

"There are eighteen of these canyons in the park." His voice tickled her ear over the clatter of the rain all around them. "They were formed when the glaciers covering the area started to retreat."

"How recently?" She rested her head against his shoulder, relieved to stretch out her tired legs.

"Thousands and thousands and thousands of years ago." He ran a hand down one of her wet braids. "*Retreat* sounds dramatic, but that actually means they all melted. This is what they left behind."

"Good job, glaciers."

She felt his chest quake with a small laugh, and then he talked on, telling her about the history of the park, the wildlife in it, the nonnative plants that had invaded over the years and how the rangers had tried to battle them back. Her eyes drooped as his low voice mixed with the sound of the rain.

When she opened them again, everything was quiet. She was stiff and disoriented, the rain had stopped, and she was alone. Both packs were on the ground next to her, but there was no sign of Leo.

She scrambled to her feet, fear clutching her by the throat. What animals had he been talking about as she drifted off? Were there bears around? Or mountain lions? Oh God, what if he'd been eaten by a wild boar or fallen off a cliff? Or finally decided she wasn't worth the trouble and just vanished into the trees?

"Leo?" Then, louder, she called, "*Leo?*"

Almost immediately, his voice floated back. "Coming!" Twenty seconds later, he jogged into view, his boots splashing through the puddles covering the canyon floor. "So there's—"

She launched herself at him, and he caught her immediately, wrapping his strong, not-devoured-by-wild-animals arms around her.

"I thought you left me." Her words were muffled as she pressed her face into his chest.

"Hey, shhh." He stroked down her back. "Shhh. I would never."

She clung to him while her heart settled back to a normal rate, and when she finally pulled away, she felt like an idiot.

"Sorry." She swiped at her nose with the sleeve of her jacket. "It's just that if I was alone out here, I would die. Like literally some poor hiker would find my bones come the spring thaw."

He guided her back to their discarded packs. "I'm sorry. I wanted to see how the main trail looked after the rain. It's just at the mouth of the canyon, so I figured I didn't need to wake you."

"And?" She leaned against the rock, her knees still a little shaky.

"And there's good news and bad news," he said. "The bad news is, the trail's washed out, so you're not going to get that twist cone quite yet."

"Damn. What's the good news?"

"The good news is, we won't have to sleep on the ground tonight because we have a tent."

Her eyes widened. "No."

"Afraid so," he said cheerfully. "Let's go make camp."

TWENTY-ONE

Leo stood next to Faith, looking at the tiny red dome in front of them. There was really only one thing to be done.

"I'll just sleep outside."

"You will not," she replied immediately.

He glanced at the ground adjacent to the tent, then back at the entrance. "I think I have to."

She didn't answer right away, presumably too busy calculating the space inside the canvas structure he'd set up.

"In my defense," he said, "it would've been fine for just you."

"Barely." She cocked her head. "This can seriously fit two people?"

She wasn't going to like this next part. "Yeah, when it's, ah, a couple."

Again, she paused before speaking.

"Like you and Reggie?"

Before he could respond, she walked to the tent and knelt to crawl inside. As far as shutting down any possible reply went, it was pretty effective.

"Shoes!" he called.

"Sorry!" She froze half in and half out of the entrance before wriggling around so she was sitting in the opening facing him, her muddy boots resting on the flap of canvas he'd pegged down at the entrance like a doormat. She crossed her ankles and pulled her legs into her chest. "I had no idea how nice sitting down was until right now."

"You were a champ today."

She snorted, but he crouched so they were eye level. "I mean it. Good job."

"Turns out hiking is just walking but a tiny bit harder." She rested her cheek against her knee. "You were very patient. Thanks for making today fun."

He spoke without thinking. "Making you happy makes me happy."

He heard her soft intake of breath, and something close to panic seized him. The ease that had kept him aloft all day was nowhere to be found as Faith sat in his tent, looking up at him with that soft look on her face. The only thing he could feel right now was *want*, which meant he needed to retreat.

When they'd agreed to work together in August, he'd sworn to himself that he'd keep his distance from her. He wouldn't let himself forget that she was a Fox, which meant she was entirely capable of destroying him all over again. Collaborating on the grant was one thing, but sharing unguarded emotion like that was absolutely not allowed. Or at least it shouldn't be. He knew it, and so did she.

"Anyway, I'm sleeping outside."

Although his words were almost defiant, her only reaction was a tightening of her lips. The universe though? The universe wasted no time in punishing him for thinking he'd be able to keep away from this woman. They'd had a few hours of clear weather after the deluge, but thunder rolled across the sky the instant the words were out of his mouth, and fat drops of rain began to patter against the trees overhead.

"Give it up, Morales." She uncrossed her legs and started unlacing her boots. "Even you can't prefer the wet ground to my company."

His shoulders dropped in defeat. Whatever the opposite of a cockblock was, that's what was happening here. Every single thing leading up to this moment had maneuvered him into that tiny tent with her. And goddammit, part of him was elated.

Faith had shucked her boots and climbed all the way inside, giving him room to duck into the tent before it started raining in earnest. He kept his back to her as he unlaced and tugged off his own boots, setting them next to hers under the tent's small awning. Then he took a deep breath and turned to meet his fate. His Faith.

She was sitting cross-legged on the ground, with her hands folded in her lap. "What now?"

A million ways he could answer that, but the safest one was to treat this like any other overnight in the woods. Which it was, or it would be if he could just keep his shit together.

"Now we feed ourselves and get ready for bed."

"It's, what, five o'clock?" But she yawned as she said it, giggling as her mouth snapped shut. "Okay, yeah, food and bed."

Leo started the settling-in process, grabbing a lightweight LED lantern from his backpack and hanging it from a hook at the top of the tent, flipping it on to illuminate everything under the red dome.

"You did get too much sun." He resisted the urge to touch the tip of her pink nose.

Faith shrugged and continued pulling off her flannel. "It was inevitable. You'll just have to slather me up before we head out tomorrow."

He swallowed hard. "Okay."

He grabbed their boots and placed them in a waterproof bag in the corner of the tent, safe from the rain. Then he zipped up the entrance, shutting out the rest of the world. Shutting him inside, with her.

He worked in silence to pull out the jerky and applesauce packets and trail mix, things they could eat without messing with the camping stove.

"Keep hydrated." He handed her a bottle, and she obediently drank. A little too enthusiastically though; some of it trickled down her chin to wet the neck of her shirt.

"Damn." She patted at it as she handed back the bottle. "Actually, do you mind if I change? It's cold, and I'm dying to get out of this b-bra."

She stumbled over the word. They both heard it. They both ignored it. "Sure. I'll just..." He pivoted so his back was to her and he was facing the tent wall. He occupied himself with unpacking his sleeping pad and bag, hoping like hell that the noise he was making would drown out the sound of Faith undressing.

It did not. He was excruciatingly aware of the slide of fabric against skin, the hiss of a zipper, fabric hitting the ground, a soft exhale.

He wasn't going to survive the night.

Determined to stick with the plan to treat this like any other sleepover, he shifted to unfurl the pad that would keep him from sleeping directly on the hard ground, but when he started to unroll the sleeping bag that would go on top, his heart sank.

"Dammit!"

"Oh God, what?"

"I…" His back still facing her, he gestured helplessly at the bag he'd tossed to the corner of the tent. "It's wet. A corner must've been sitting in a puddle during the rain."

He let his head fall forward. Of course there'd be one more thing. Laughter built in his chest until he couldn't keep it inside.

"What's so funny?" she asked. "And you can turn around."

He did, and his laughter came even harder when he did. She looked perfect. The lantern made her white-blond hair glow like silver, and she'd changed into leggings and a soft pink shirt that made his mouth water. But her face fell at his delight, and she crossed her arms over her chest defensively.

"It's not you. You're beautiful." He clamped down on the laughter. "It's…" He pointed at his sleeping bag again. "It's that. It's this." He pointed overhead where rain spattered cozily against the roof. "It's out there." He pointed beyond them to the washed-out section of trail separating them from their car.

"I'm sorry you're having such a bad time." She shrank into herself a tiny bit, and he shook his head.

"No, you don't get it. I'm having a really, really good time." His heart was at war with his brain, and he was so tired of fighting it.

Her head lifted, and she nodded slowly. "Ah. Yeah, I get it." Her eyes dropped, then bounced back up to his. "So what would you normally do if you were down a sleeping bag?"

He'd led countless groups on countless overnight excursions. He could be a professional. "It's already cold, and it'll get colder. I'd need to find someone willing to unzip their bag so we could both use it like a quilt."

Her control barely held as she said, "Well, good thing I'm here to volunteer."

"Good thing," he said a little hoarsely.

They were quiet again as she turned around so he could change into flannel pants and his favorite Elizabeth Warren sweatshirt, and when she turned back around, they arranged their sleeping pads side by side and inflated their pillows. Then he unzipped the bag that William had loaned her.

"Huh."

"What?" She looked up from where she was pawing through her supplies.

"William gave you his best sleeping bag."

She located a pair of the colorful striped socks he'd picked out for her at the store and settled onto the pad to pull them on. "That was nice of him."

"Yeah. Nice." He unfurled the open bag with a snap of his wrists. "I knew you were going to love him."

She straightened her legs out in front of her, pointing her newly covered toes. "Come on, I don't love William. I like working with him." She reached for her side of the blanket and pulled it up to her waist. "Here's my question: Do *you* like me working with him?"

"Obviously." He stretched up to snap off the lantern, realizing as he did how cold it had gotten in the tent. "I suggested him."

They were plunged into darkness. The rain had started to let up as they finished their nighttime preparation, but clouds still covered the moon, blotting out the ambient light. He only knew Faith had lain down when she pulled the blanket up, so he followed suit, lying on his back inches away from her.

"Then why do you end up biting my head off every time the three of us are together?" She fidgeted in the dark next to him. "I know it's not jealousy. Hell, when we actually had sex, you didn't even acknowledge it was me."

His eyes fluttered shut at the memory. "I knew it was you. The whole fucking time, Dutch."

For a moment, the only sound was their breathing. Even in the dark, he could tell when she rolled to face him. Her voice was closer, the heat from her body more immediate.

"I need you to understand that using you wasn't ever... I loved you so much, Leo."

He immediately knew that she wasn't talking about sex at a rooftop bar. She was talking about that day twelve years ago when they'd shouted terrible things at each other and blown up each other's worlds.

"I'm so sorry," she said hoarsely. "So many times, I wished I could go back. Tell myself not to write any of that. Tell my dad I didn't need a killer essay to get into college. Tell him not to mess with my life. But mostly I've wanted to tell you how sorry I am that I ever wrote it. It wasn't my place to use your story like that, and I've been ashamed ever since."

In the past, any reminder of their old fight would've hit like a baseball to the solar plexus, but not tonight. Not after seeing her at her job, witnessing her commitment to her work. Not after spending enough time around her that forgiveness and understanding had seeped into those old places where hurt and resentment used to fester.

"Thank you for saying that." He turned so he was

facing her too, even if all he could see was the faintest outline of the curve of her cheek. Maybe that was for the best; this conversation was easier in the dark. "I appreciate you saying that to me."

She shifted, her knee grazing his under the sleeping bag. "I did think of you as different from me when we first met. I knew you didn't have any money, and I liked being able to help you." Another shift, and that contact disappeared. He missed it. "And then I had to build my own life without my parents's money, and I realized how fucked up that was. I'm sorry for ever thinking I was some kind of savior to you." She gave a bitter little laugh. "All the privilege in the world, and I was trying to do good for selfish reasons."

He let her words wash over him, surprised at how good it felt to hear her say all that out loud. Then again, they'd had a bit of a reversal recently. He understood that part of her now more than he ever had. "It's so easy to get caught up in the logistics of your work and forget the actual humans involved," he said. "Why do you think I started getting out of the office to work directly with the people in town?"

"I thought it was because sitting behind a desk makes you stir crazy."

He snorted softly. "Okay, that's the other reason." God, she knew him so well, just like he knew her. The truth was, he'd never loved anyone the way he'd loved her: with his whole, open heart and all the trust a child has that the world couldn't touch them. But it had. And then it had tossed them back together years later and given them both the chance to apologize.

"I'm sorry too." For everything. For all of it. For shutting her down, for being too full of wounded pride, for refusing to forgive the girl he'd loved. "I should've listened to you that day. Let you explain." He hesitated before saying the rest of it. "You actually did help me, you know? I still use some of the stuff you suggested."

"Really?" Her voice was a little shaky.

He nodded even though she couldn't see him.

"Smartphones help a lot. I don't have to memorize phone numbers. And my passcode, I just remember the pattern, not the numbers, like you said." What else? How else had she helped him figure out ways to navigate a world of numbers? "I can't tell you how many centimeters deep you should dig a hole for a tree, but when I used a ruler, I could actually *see* it. And I can plant a hundred trees an hour now because my hands know how deep to dig after all those years."

Her fingers brushed against his, and it took all his strength not to grab them and hang on forever.

"William understands a little. He helps me keep track of how early I need to leave for meetings and things, kind of like you used to."

"I got so mad when you were late to pick me up until I figured out that something else might be going on." Her voice was thick with memories. Memories of him that she'd hung onto.

"At least directions have never been a problem for me, thank God." Little mercies that the points of the compass made sense to him.

"Good thing for me." She shifted a little closer, robbing him of his breath. "I'd have been screwed without you today."

He inched closer too, sliding his hands along her jaw and into her hair. He held on to her as if she might disappear now that they'd both shared those enormous truths, and when his thumbs brushed her cheeks, they came away wet.

Tears. She'd been crying.

"Don't." He leaned forward in the dark to press his lips again the damp tracks.

She gave a little sob-laugh. "Okay." And then she kissed him. Just a soft press of her lips against his. And he was undone.

"Faith," he breathed, tightening his hands in her hair before kissing her back.

Never dreamed. He never *dreamed* he'd be here again with her. She tasted the same, smelled the same. She'd always smelled good to him but not because of any particular scent. It was like the chemical makeup of her skin called to him. And her lips still fit against his like they'd been created just for that purpose. He pressed kiss after kiss against her mouth, along her jaw, down her neck. They were sweet kisses, almost chaste, but she made a noise deep in her throat and pressed up against him, returning those soft brushes of his mouth with her own.

He trailed his lips over to her ear. "I'm kissing you, duchess."

"Yes." She rolled her hips against his, the contact electric. "Keep going."

"I will." He kissed her hairline. He kissed her chin. He kissed her mouth again. "But only if you agree that the hallway was our first kiss."

"What do you...?" She fell back against her pillow with a disbelieving laugh. "No tongue. You have me this hot for you, and you haven't used your tongue."

"Not yet anyway."

"If I agree to the hallway"—her fingers crept under the hem of his sweatshirt—"will you?"

He bit back a groan as her touch swept over his ribs. "Yes."

"Okay. Hallway was our first kiss."

Her last word ended in a squeak when he grabbed her hands and lifted them over her head, pinning her to the ground as he rolled on top of her and plunged his tongue into her mouth, seeking her heat, her sweetness. He nudged her knee open so he could rock against her core, and she tangled her fingers with his and kissed him back.

Leo lost track of how long they stayed locked together like that, open mouths, hot breaths, small moans. But it wasn't enough. He wanted her begging. He wanted her as mindless as he was right now.

He broke their kiss and shifted to the side so he could trail his hand down her stomach before dipping his fingers below the waistband of her pants. "Can I?"

"Yes. Anything." She shifted restlessly against him, and he wasted no time sliding his hand under her layers.

His touch was light at first, a gentle up and down stroke, but after a few passes, his fingers were as wet and slippery as her pussy.

"Tell me what feels best." He circled her clit with the tip of one finger, and she jolted.

"That. A little slower." She grabbed a handful of his hair and kissed him into compliance, not that he wasn't already willing to do anything she said. He circled and teased and lived and died with every soft gasp that spilled from her lips, but it still wasn't enough.

He propped himself up on one arm and shifted slightly downward so he could slide two fingers inside her while he pressed circles onto her clit with his thumb. "Good?" He bit down semi-gently on one of the diamond-hard nipples poking through her shirt.

"Fuck. Yes," she said in a tight voice.

So he pumped his fingers into her and grazed his teeth back and forth over her nipple, applying pressure to her clit until her back arched off the ground and she clenched and pulsed and cried out his name.

He slowed his motions as the tension drained from her body, resting his hand almost protectively over her sweet pussy. He was rock hard and aching, but he didn't want to move, not when his cheek rested between her breasts and he could feel her heartbeat pounding away.

Slowly, ever so slowly, her hands drifted up his back to rest on his shoulders, and for the first time in a long, long time, everything inside him settled into a peaceful place.

TWENTY-TWO

"Camping. Is. Awesome."

She was still in the grips of a ridiculously good afterglow as she said it, and Leo dropped a kiss to her sternum that seared through her shirt before he rolled over to flop onto his back.

"Agreed."

The clouds had started to break up while he was playing her body like a fiddle, and traces of silvery moonlight trickled through the nylon overhead, which meant she could clearly see his cock tenting the front of his sweats. With zero self-consciousness, he squeezed it once before releasing it and tucking his arm behind his head. His eyes were shut, and she could just make out the lush curve of his bottom lip.

It was too much for her to resist.

"Can I?" She repeated the words he'd said to her earlier and trailed her hand downward, but he caught it and brought it to his lips, brushing a kiss over her knuckles.

"Not tonight."

Everything inside her turned to ice. In her experience, a guy turning you down for sex wasn't the best sign. But when she tried to pull away, he held tight to her hand, refusing to let go.

"The things I want to do to you, Dutch," he said in a low voice. "There's not enough room in this tent."

Everything that was frozen melted. "Oh." She gulped. "Okay."

"Plus," he said, releasing her hand, "I didn't pack condoms for this trip. Obviously."

Her discomfort eased even more. "That's actually a mark in your favor, given that it was supposed to be an all-ages outing."

"Thanks." He grinned over at her. "But maybe when we're back in town—"

"Sex?"

His smile turned teasing. "I was thinking dinner. Maybe a movie."

"And then sex?" She scooched closer and did the extremely brave thing of resting her head on his chest.

He immediately slid an arm under her and hugged her close. "One-track mind." He rested his cheek against the top of her head, his stubble catching on the loose strands of her hair. "But yes, if you insist, we can have all the sex you want. Whenever you want it." He paused, then muttered, "Especially where William can hear."

She tried to pinch the negative amount of fat she found on his torso.

"Hey!" he objected.

"I've changed a lot since high school, but I haven't picked up an exhibitionist streak."

"You really haven't changed that much." At her disbelieving snort, he ran a hand down her back. "Still smart. Still mouthy. Still the hottest girl I know."

"Mmmpf." She nestled closer to him, intending to launch into all kinds of counterarguments about how she'd only gotten more stubborn over the years, more argumentative. Bigger and louder in every way. Instead, the day caught up with her, and rather than debating with him, she fell hard into sleep, only to return to consciousness with sunshine and birdsong surrounding her.

Sunshine and birdsong and Leo. They'd shifted in their sleep into big spoon/little spoon position, and his arm around her waist was maybe the nicest way she'd ever woken up.

He stirred as she grew more alert.

"Morning."

His voice was sleep husky. It did things to all the parts of her that he'd had his hands on last night.

"Morning," she said with a yawn. "I can't believe we never actually spent a night together until now."

He dropped a kiss behind her ear. "I was well-behaved in high school."

"Ha." Her sarcasm was a first instinct, but she reconsidered. "Actually, you really were."

"My parents raised me right." He fiddled with a lock of her hair. "Blue, huh?"

She wiggled around to face him. "It makes me feel brave."

He twined a strand around his finger. "You needed to be brave to go camping?"

"I needed to be brave to be around you."

He dropped her hair and pulled back immediately. "Not because I scare you, right?"

He looked ready to bolt out of the tent if she said yes. God, he was cute when he was flustered.

"No," she said. "But also kind of."

His brows jumped in alarm, and she slid a foot down his leg, drawing their lower bodies closer together in what she hoped was a comforting gesture.

"Not *you* you. But, like, this. Us." Falling again. Maybe even loving him again. And always the fear of hurting again.

She didn't say it, but he pursed his lips like he was thinking similar thoughts. And why wouldn't he be? They'd both been through it. It had probably sucked just as much for him.

If it had, that memory didn't keep him from wrapping his arms around her and pulling her into his body to rest his chin on her head on the pillow. They lay like that for a long time. A good, long time. And it was nice and comforting and felt like coming home.

But at the same time, she needed to *know*.

"So we're good?" Her heart lodged in her throat as she added, "You forgive me?"

After a moment, his head moved against hers in a nod, and all the blood in her veins thawed.

"Yes." He shifted to rub his cheek against her hair. "I wish you hadn't written what you did. And I wish I hadn't reacted the way I did. If we'd been a little older, maybe it would've gone differently."

"Or maybe not," Faith said, thinking about their fight in the hiking store.

He laughed softly. "Or maybe not. But it happened, and we built our lives, and now we're here."

"Now we're here."

"Nowhere else I'd rather be," he added a little gruffly.

"Nowhere." She pressed herself close, shivering a little as her body started to register that she was lying on the ground outside in late October. "Okay, maybe in an actual bed."

A groan rumbled through his chest. "If we were in an actual bed..."

Heat fired through her despite the chilly air, and she poked a finger into his side. "Time to check the trail situation?"

"Definitely." He unwound himself from around her and crawled to the opening, unzipping it to let in more cold and light. "Want to come with me?"

She waved him off. "You go ahead. I'm going to pee behind a tree, and I'm going to curse your name the whole time I do it."

He glanced over his shoulder as he tugged on his boots. "I thought you loved hiking now?"

The carefree look on his face made her buoyant.

"Fine. You make outdoor bathrooms worth it. Happy?"

He twisted around and tugged her toward him, planting a quick kiss on her mouth.

"I really, really am, Dutch."

AS MUCH FUN as camping had turned out to be, Faith was damn glad when the car came into view.

"Yes!" She jogged the last few feet and threw herself against the passenger door. "Take me back to central heat and Netflix and couches!"

Leo was still strolling through the parking lot as she struggled out of her pack, groaning and stretching out her spine once the backpack was on the ground. When he joined her at the car, he didn't rush to unburden himself. Instead, he turned and looked back at the start of the trail that had carried them into and then out of the forest.

"What's up?" Maybe this was some kind of end-of-hike tradition she didn't know about.

"Just taking a second to lock it all in." He flashed her a smile as he unbuckled his straps. "This was a good trip."

She blushed, but she didn't look away. It was clear that she was the reason he was storing this all in his memory, and she loved it.

He grabbed both their bags and stashed them in the back, and she tried to wipe as much of the trail mud off her boots as she could before climbing into his pristine car. Once they were buckled in and on the way, she nibbled on her lip before saying, "Confession time?"

He glanced at her apprehensively. "Okay."

"I think walking back through all that mud would've been easier if I'd had hiking poles."

As she'd hoped, he gave a shout of laughter. Then he reached over and took her hand. They rode like that all the way back to Beaucoeur.

When they made it to his house, he fetched both their bags and carried hers to her car for her. After an easy, companionable morning, she was suddenly nervous. Leo too, maybe. He hooked his thumbs through his belt loops and rocked back on his heels before asking, "Do you want to come in?" He jerked his head toward that huge stone house that didn't fit him at all.

She was tempted. But she was also a little gross.

"Rain check? I want to go home and shower."

His expression didn't change when she gestured

down at herself, but she didn't want to leave anything to chance.

"I mean it on the rain check." She stepped closer to him and wrapped her arms around his waist. "You promised me dinner. Dinner *and* a movie actually."

"That I did." He walked her backward a step and pinned her against the car. "Also sex."

He kissed her soundly. Her heart was hammering in her chest when he finally pulled away, and she was starting to wonder how much she actually needed to go home and shower when a voice intruded on their moment.

"Morning, lovebirds!"

They turned to find a barefoot, shorts-clad William standing on the doorstep with a steaming mug of coffee in his hand and a shit-eating grin on his face.

Her instinct was to pull away—this was her new employee after all—but Leo simply slung a casual arm around her shoulder.

"Wish I could say I'm sorry you didn't make it yesterday, but I'm not."

"Evidently." William raised his mug in salute and headed back into the house, pausing only to say, "I'm about to scramble some eggs if you want to stay for breakfast, Fox."

"Tempting," she called as he stepped inside.

"Come in. Stay." Leo dropped his hands to her hips, but she just bit her lip.

"It's too awkward. And I'm too covered in trail mud." His mouth twitched downward, so she pressed her lips against his to sweeten the sting of her answer. "And we actually already have a date scheduled. You're taking me to the foundation gala next Saturday, remember?"

"Like I'd forget." He kissed her one more time, and when he pulled away, his smile was so bright and open that her breath caught in her chest. She hadn't seen *this* Leo in so long. God, she'd missed him.

He shouldered his backpack and waited until she got into her car and backed out of the driveway before he turned and loped up the steps to his house, disappearing inside.

She made it as far as the street leading out of his subdivision before she finally gave in to the voice screaming at her that she'd be the biggest dummy on Earth if she didn't turn around *right fucking now*.

And so she did, zooming back through the sleepy Sunday-morning neighborhood and rocketing to a halt in Leo's driveway. She raced up the steps and then hesitated, unsure if she should ring the bell or just open the door and walk inside. But a moment later the door flung itself open to reveal a grinning Leo.

"I heard your car door," he said. "You came back for scrambled eggs, right?"

She stepped over the threshold.

"Yep," she said. "For the eggs."

He pushed the door shut behind her. "Okay. Want to head to the kitchen?" His eyes danced, and she grabbed on to his shoulders. Such good, muscly shoulders.

"I don't actually." She tilted her face up and kissed him, and unlike last night in the tent, he didn't hold back for a second. He backed her against the door and licked greedily at the seam of her lips until she opened for him so he could invade her mouth with his tongue. He overwhelmed her, the taste of him, the scent of him, and she kissed him back just as hungrily, wanting more than he could possibly give her in the hallway.

But he seemed determined to try. He grabbed the back of her knee with an impatient growl and lifted her leg to his waist so he could grind against her. Both fully clothed, both standing, both breathing hard from just a few minutes of kissing. His body was the only thing keeping her from collapsing into a heap of neediness on the floor. And his cock... She could feel every inch of him through her magical waterproof hiking pants, and when she tilted her hips just the tiniest bit forward, all that hardness hit a spot that made her whimper.

She tugged at his hair and deepened the kiss, wondering how to get him naked without breaking contact with that mouth of his that was soft and firm and hungry and gentle all at the same time.

In the end it was the jingle of keys that cut through the haze of lust wrapping around the two of them.

"I'm thinking I might do breakfast out today," William announced loudly from the entrance to the living room.

Leo tore his mouth away from hers, looking at her in dazed wonder for a second before they both turned their heads toward the third person in the room. William grinned sunnily at them.

"Then I'll do some programming work at the office. Maybe hit the gym afterward." He flipped the key ring into the air and caught it with a flourish. "You two'll have the place to yourselves for hours, so be as loud as you want."

He winked and disappeared, and the garage door whirred open moments later.

She and Leo were alone.

TWENTY-THREE

She came back.

Those three words had been humming through Leo's blood since Faith had roared down his street and landed on his doorstep. She turned her car around, and she came back.

They'd been staring at each other since William left. Now that the house was theirs, the frantic need to claim her had receded and been replaced by the desire to savor her. His gaze moved from her lips, untouched by her usual bold lipstick, to her eyes, clear and trusting, to her hair, a wavy mess of corn silk and blue. He needed to wrap his fists around it as he pounded into her.

Okay, maybe the time for savoring was over.

"Tell me what you want." He pressed his thumb against the center of her lower lip and dragged it to the corner of her mouth. "What did you come back for?"

"You." Her tongue darted out to stroke the tip of his thumb. "I came back for you."

He groaned and rested his forehead against hers. Those words on her lips were a benediction.

"I'm yours." It was a confession. A promise. "Whatever you want."

It was as true now as it had been all those years ago. They'd grown into the adults they might not have become if they'd stayed together, but Faith had never fully left him. The tune he couldn't quite get out of his head. The cold lake water at the end of a strenuous day. The homemade coconut ice cream from his childhood, the one he could never find a perfect match for in any store. He'd spent a long time hating her, but he could admit it now: he'd spent even longer missing her.

But she was here now. And she was smiling at him.

Then her expression changed, and she sank her perfect teeth into that plump lower lip, denting the tender flesh as she gazed up at him.

"Do you know what I want?"

He leaned close, drawn in by that breathy voice and those big blue eyes.

"I want to wash the rainwater out of my hair and the mud out from under my fingernails." She dragged those very nails diagonally across his chest, all five points of contact burning through his shirt, as she leaned up to whisper in his ear. "And then when I'm scrubbed and clean and sweet-smelling, I want you to show me what the tent was too small to handle last night."

Her cheeks rounded in a devilish smile, and he actually felt every drop of blood drain from his head and straight to his dick.

"Upstairs," he barked, grabbing her hand and pulling her after him. Her laughter drifted behind them as they rushed to his bedroom.

"Shower's through there. Can I—" He stopped short

of asking to join her, and she glanced over her shoulder with a wry little smile.

"Maybe next time?" Another flash of white teeth on that pink lower lip, and she shut the door behind her with a click. Moments later, water started to hiss from the shower.

"Clean towels in the cabinet," he called through the door, only moving away at her shout of affirmation. He grabbed clean sweats from his dresser and headed to the bathroom William was using, running himself through the world's fastest shower, briskly patting himself dry, and pulling on the sweats. He made it back to his room just in time to hear the spray snap off and the glass shower door swing open.

She was naked in his bathroom. She was about to be naked with him.

Emotion swelled under his rib cage, and he wasn't sure whether to shove it down or run at it head-on. Loving her had been ecstasy, and losing her had fucked him up. Sex with her was never going to be easy or casual, but he didn't care. She might be dangerous, but she also felt like the answer to a question he'd been asking for years.

The door swung open, and Faith emerged in a cloud of hot steam. As she'd promised, she was flushed and pink from the heat of the water, her hair sleek and damp down her back. And she was wearing his ridiculous satin robe. He braced himself for her to give him shit about it, but she just fiddled with the belt. The perfect opportunity to roast him, and Faith Fox took a pass?

"Everything good?" he asked.

She shrugged and crossed her arms. "Yeah."

He took a step back, confused about the shift in her

mood. Her shoulders were tense, and her mouth was a flat line.

"Do you want to slow things down? Stop?" he asked. "That's fine. Just say the word."

It wasn't fine. A howl of disappointment crawled up his throat, but something had changed for her while she was showering, so he slammed on the brakes. He just hoped like hell she wasn't upset about something he'd done.

A hand crept up to hold the robe closed at the base of her throat. "No, I..."

Then he saw it in her expression: apprehension. She was nervous. Her eyes flicked to where her toes dug into the carpet, and her lip bites this time weren't coy and playful. Where the hell had that come from?

He took a step toward her, ready to stop the instant she gave him any kind of sign that this wasn't welcome. But she let him approach, let him kiss her gently.

"What's happening right now, Dutch?" he asked against her mouth. "Did you suddenly realize it's me? Did you remember that you actually hate me?"

Even joking about it ripped at something inside him, and that panicky pain got worse when she didn't correct him right away.

"The problem is..." She sighed. "The problem is, it's *you*."

The day suddenly wasn't as glorious as it had been thirty seconds ago.

"I thought we were okay now," he managed to say. "Forgiveness-wise."

"We are." Her smile was brief, but her face settled back into that anxious expression that was twisting him all up. "It's just that..."

She swallowed hard before speaking again, and when she did, her words came out in a rush. "The last time we were together, I was a teenager with some fucked-up eating habits. Now..."

"Now?" he prompted gently, still not quite sure what was clouding her blue eyes.

"Now look at me!" She flung her arms wide and gestured down her body.

He frowned. "Still not seeing the problem."

She gave a little growl.

"I'm not a teenager anymore, Leo! And I'm definitely not surviving on a fraction of a hamburger every day." She closed her eyes and gritted out, "I'm bigger than I was before. You're going to notice. Fully dressed is one thing, but naked... I don't look the same anymore. Not like what you remember from before. And I'm worried you won't... like it."

She barely managed to choke out the last few words, leaving him too stunned to respond. Then he scoffed.

She opened her eyes in outrage. "Don't you *dare* laugh."

"I swear I'm not."

Every cell in her body was vibrating with insecurity, and it killed him. He'd just have to make her see what he saw.

He approached cautiously and reached for her hand, leading her a few steps closer to the bed. "Dutch, you're a *woman*. You're luscious." He sat on the bed and pulled her in front of him. "You're *ripe*." He ran his hands up her forearms, pushing under the sleeves of his ridiculous robe. He reached her elbows, ran his thumbs across the bend there, and kept going until he gripped the softness of her upper arms.

"These arms? I want them wrapped around me."

The crease in her brow hadn't gone away yet, but at least she was listening to him, so he trailed his hands down her sides and hooked them under the belt of the robe.

Slowly, ever so slowly, he loosened the knot, watching her face the whole time in case she wanted him to stop. But her eyes were pinned to his hands loosening the strip of satin keeping the robe closed. Once it was undone, he let the green fabric slip through his fingers, and the robe parted at the center. He sucked in a hard breath at the vertical strip of pale skin it revealed.

"This waist?" His hands crept under the material, resting briefly on her body's natural curves before sliding downward. "These hips?"

He tightened his grip, and she inhaled shakily.

"I want to hold on to them while I pound into you." He looked up at her, caught her gaze. Held it. "I want to press so hard I leave bruises on your skin."

He parted the robe just a bit more and placed a kiss on the soft swell of her stomach above her belly button.

"Duchess skin, touched by an unworthy man."

She gasped his name, and lightning quick, he stood, spun her around, and sat her on the bed where he'd just been. This time when she looked at him he saw desire in her eyes, the first sparks of heat.

He took that as an okay to slide the robe over one shoulder. She helped him by slipping her arm free, and when he moved to peel the satin from her other shoulder, she was already in motion. The robe slid off her torso to pool on the mattress, leaving her naked from the waist up.

He had to squeeze his eyes shut to get control of

himself. Pouncing on her wasn't the next step, unfortunately. Instead, he knelt in front of her and reached out with infinite slowness, again giving her every chance to stop him. But the only change was an increase in her breathing.

"These breasts?" He glanced up at her as he filled his palms and rubbed his thumbs over the pink tips of her nipples, back and forth until they both moaned. "God, these breasts are what men dream of holding. Of licking."

So he did, first one, then the other, until she whimpered and buried her fingers in his hair, pressing him harder against her.

He reluctantly pulled away, but he had one more point to make.

"And Faith, these thighs?" He was kissing down her body now, shifting the green satin out of the way as he moved over her stomach, her hip, down, down, down. "These soft thighs? A man could lay his head here and never want to leave."

He nudged his body between her knees and nestled his cheek into the crease of her leg where it met her body. He breathed her in for a second, her sweetness, her arousal.

"Shift up," he murmured, crawling onto the bed. "Let me show you."

She wriggled backward to make room for him, and for the first time since she'd emerged from the bathroom, she smiled. It was tentative and a little hopeful, and his heart clenched at the sight of it. Ten minutes ago, he'd been anticipating pleasure. Now he was focused on *her*. Proving to her that she was as attractive to him as she'd ever been. As she'd always be.

He started by leaning up to kiss her. Slow, deep, a little messy. He invaded her mouth with his tongue and worked his fingers into the still-wet strands of her hair, tilting her head back to give him access to her neck.

"You always had the softest skin"—he brushed his mouth over the curve of her throat—"right here." He let his hot breath fan over the patch of skin he'd just moistened with his tongue, and she shivered. "You still do."

The first time he'd ever touched her, he'd done it with a mixture of enthusiasm and gratitude that this beautiful girl was letting him kiss her, unhook her bra, lift up her skirt. All these years later, his enthusiasm and gratitude were still very much in place. But this time they were joined by a third element, and an important one at that: experience.

He moved downward, kissing and touching as he went. Her collarbones, her sternum. The sides of her breast. She sucked in a gasp when he ran his teeth across one of her nipples, her hands grabbing at the comforter as a flush traveled down her neck and chest.

"There's a plant that grows in the rain forest. Heliconia." He spoke between long, slow sweeps of his tongue over her breasts, swirling around and around to the straining tips of each. "Their leaves are bright pink, almost red." Another lick. A pause to suck a patch of skin into his mouth. A scrape of his teeth until her back arched. "Your nipples, Dutch. When you're turned on, they're that same color." He wrapped his lips around one and sucked, then released it with a pop. "No wonder I could never get you out of my head."

He moved faster down her body now, desperate to see if every part of her was as he remembered.

"Fuck, Dutch. Your pussy too." He glanced up at her,

but she'd tossed her head back at the first stroke of his middle finger from her slit to her clit. "Pink and pretty as a Heliconia."

Then he settled between her legs to keep convincing her that as far as he was concerned, every part of her was perfect.

TWENTY-FOUR

Faith was convinced.

She'd let that critical voice in her head intrude and had a tiny little freak-out in Leo's Tuscan country bathroom. She usually had no problem ignoring that bitch on the rare occasions that it popped up, but in that moment, looking at her waterlogged self in the mirror post-shower, being with Leo felt different from being with any of the people who'd come before. Well, before *and* after. The people who'd come between. None of them knew her the way he did, knew the ins and outs of her teenage body. And the thought that she might not live up to a memory or an expectation that he'd been carrying with him had made her want to bolt.

Not anymore though. He'd worked some kind of magic in the past twenty minutes with his words, his touch. Comparing her to a jungle plant had been good too. Very good.

Almost as good as the orgasm he'd just given her.

"That," she gasped, "was incredible." She almost asked where he'd learned that fluttery thing with his tongue but realized she didn't actually want to know. Him having it in his bag of tricks was good enough for her.

"That was just the start." He swiped at his mouth with his forearm and grinned as he kissed his way back up her body. Unlike yesterday, he didn't stop her when she reached for his cock, and it only took a couple of strokes before she knew she was going to need him naked, right now.

"Off." She tugged at his waistband, and he immediately pulled his sweatpants down and tossed them aside. When he did, the muscles in his stomach and arms flexed, and she gave an appreciative sigh. He wasn't gym-pretty with machine-built muscles. He was work-hardened, all lean and sinewy. "How do you do it? Haven't you been sitting behind a desk for months?"

"Rock-climbing wall," he said absently as he twisted again, the muscles along his back shifting as he rummaged through his bedside table drawer. "Running. Jacking off to thoughts of you."

His unselfconscious admission made everything inside her throb. "Oh my God, fuck me already, Morales," she groaned.

"Yes, ma'am." He rolled on the condom and knelt between her legs with his cock in his hand, notching himself into place. Finally. And of all the frowns he'd sent her way over the past five months, this was her absolute favorite. His brow was creased in concentration, his eyes narrowed as he watched himself disappear slowly into her body, torturously slowly. The burn, the stretch. She didn't think she'd ever get enough.

Once he was fully seated, his pelvis tight against her, he let his head fall back with a groan. "Christ, Faith, you feel so good." He pulled out just as slowly as he entered, then surged forward again. "My favorite. Always."

Favorite. Always. She clung to the words as he reached for her hips and did exactly what he'd promised to do: he grabbed. Squeezed. He manhandled her, lifting her ass up to rest on his thighs so he could penetrate her at a different angle. He went so deep that it left her gasping, her inner walls gripping him tight as he moved.

"Do you know how long I've wanted to do this?" His voice was gravel, and he kept his gaze locked on her as he moved. "Dreamed about licking your pretty breasts, fucking you with my tongue and then my cock until you come? It's so much fucking better than I remembered, Dutch."

She moaned at his string of dirty talk. His words earlier had been the sweetness that she needed, but this... this made her absolutely feral.

"Harder," she demanded. "I wanna feel you in the back of my throat."

"*Fuuuuck.*" He drew the word out and bit off the *K*, his fingers digging into her hips so hard that he probably would leave those bruises he'd talked about. He pulled out, but before she could object, he flipped her onto her stomach, smacked her ass, and said, "On your knees."

She complied, aware as she did that this put them in a similar position to their storage closet sex. But this time couldn't have been more different. Leo covered her body with his as he drove deep, inching them both forward along the mattress with the force of his thrusts. He grabbed her hair and forced her head back so he could kiss her, an uncoordinated clash of tongue and teeth and lips as he moved inside her. Then he dropped her hair to cup her breast, pinch her nipple, stroke her stomach, wrap a hand around her forearm to brace himself for an especially frantic thrust. It was like he wanted to touch all of her at once, and she wanted that too. Wanted him in her, on top of her, underneath her.

That familiar tension started to coil between her legs, telling her that she could come again without much trouble at all.

"Leo. Here." She shoved his hand down, unable to form complete sentences but still wanting him to give her what she needed. He rolled them both to the side, hitching her leg up and over his hip so he could reach her clit.

"God, look at you." He dropped his sweat-damp forehead against her shoulder and gazed down her body. "Perfect. Heliconia. Pink."

He punctuated each word with a thrust of his cock, a slap of his fingers against her clit, and she groaned as she came. And then he was coming too, his cock pulsing as he emptied himself into her still-throbbing passage.

Afterward, he eased her leg down and wrapped himself tightly around her. She shivered from an aftershock that sent tingles through her, and he huffed into her ear as he pulled out. But he didn't roll away. He held her tight, sweaty skin and straggly hair and all. And she was scared to open her mouth, scared that if she spoke right now, she might fumble toward something all too truthful. But it was too soon for that. They'd just found each other again. Their apologies were still too fresh for this feeling growing in her heart. So she tipped her chin back and planted a kiss on the section of his jaw she could reach.

"I have to confess something." He spoke the words quietly. "Because I know you, Dutch. Smart girls like you always Google these things."

"Oh God." Some of her languor leaked away. "What? Do I need to put on pants for this?"

He swatted her lightly on the ass. "No pants allowed. But I do need you to know. Heliconia?"

"Mmm," she said. "My new favorite plant."

"Heliconia is its genus name." He kissed the spot right behind her ear. "It's more commonly known as the lobster-claw plant."

"Leo!" She wriggled out of his arms and pulled herself up to sit cross-legged, her nakedness forgotten. "Are you telling me that you compared all my pink bits to *lobster claws*?"

She giggled over the last two words, too blissed-out on sex pheromones to be actually mad. Besides, she didn't much care what the plant was called if it had made him think of her over the years.

"I compared my *favorite* pink bits to lobster claws." He grabbed for her hand and kissed the back of it.

Favorite. Again, that word. She didn't know exactly what he meant by it, but it thrilled her to hear it on his lips.

"My girl's all hard exoskeleton and pinchy parts," he said smugly as he let her go and stretched out on the bed, his hands linked behind his head. God, he was hot. That long, lean body, that pretty face, that gorgeous cock.

Still, she couldn't just let this new information go without a response. Turning her fingers into a claw shape, she pinched his side, then rolled off the bed when he yelped and grabbed for her.

"I'm gonna go prevent a UTI." She jerked a thumb toward the bathroom, grabbed the robe that had gotten kicked to the foot of the bed, and skipped off. Once her bladder was empty and she was washing her hands, she caught a glimpse of herself in the mirror. She was grinning. Glowing.

And she must've still been riding some kind of orgasm high because as she stood there, she eased the robe open and examined herself in the same mirror that had sent her spiraling earlier, trying to see what Leo saw. Her nipples were stiff and pink, her labia still swollen and flushed too. Not just from arousal either; she was pretty sure she had whisker burn from Leo's weekend stubble.

She'd never felt sexier.

She grinned at her reflection as she belted the robe, shaking her fingers through the roots of her hair to fluff it up. There was no way she could look any more thoroughly fucked by the man she...

By the man she was feeling perfectly ordinary feelings for. Nothing unusual. Nothing scary or rushed. Nope, nothing to see here at all.

She swiftly retied the robe and pressed the backs of her hands against her cheeks, willing her flush to subside and her lips to lose the dopey grin. Leo was waiting for her on the other side of the door, and she had no idea what *he* was thinking. So she tossed the door open with a flourish, determined to push that postsex rush of feelings aside.

"Care to tell me when you started hanging out at the Playboy Mansion?"

She struck a dramatic pose in his poison-apple-green robe, and he groaned.

"It was a gift." He gestured helplessly at scorpions embroidered top to bottom on the satin. "Jessie thought it was hilarious a few Christmases ago."

She did a little twirl, the ends of the robe fluttering around her calves. "It's giving me '70s rock star on quaaludes. It's giving me Mrs. Havisham. It's giving me—"

She cut off with a squeak when he rolled off the bed and grabbed her midtwirl, pulling her against his lovely bare chest. "It's giving me ideas about untying that belt and pulling it off you." He ended the threat with a nip to her ear.

She dropped her head against his shoulder. "I can't wait to see it on you," she said, teasing him.

"Take it off again and you can."

She smirked. "Okay." She loosened the belt and let it fall to the floor, but it would be a few more hours before either of them was in a position to put any clothes back on.

"SO THIS IS where you really live."

"What do you mean?" Leo stacked his empty plate on top of hers and set them both on his nightstand, then brushed the sandwich crumbs from the sheets, tucked her under his arm, and snuggled them against the pillows.

"I mean that outside of this room, no part of this house feels like you," she said. "But in here, I see you."

She hadn't noticed right away—she'd had lots of other things on her mind initially—but once she'd been able to take a breather and examine her surroundings, she'd discovered little bits of Leo everywhere.

"I hate to break it to you, but none of this furniture is mine." He reached over his head to grip the massive wooden headboard behind them.

"Wait, this old-world walnut bedroom set isn't *yours*?"

She slapped her hands to her cheeks in faux chagrin. "My mistake."

Since she was already sitting up, she slid off the mattress to do a circuit around the room. It was huge, like most primary suites in places like this tended to be, and the walls and floor were beige and brown.

"The rest of the house is this"—she flicked a finger at the elaborately carved footboard—"but this stands out."

She stroked the edge of a colorful woven blanket that he was using as his comforter. If she had to guess, he'd bought it locally during his time at POR.

"These, of course." She walked to the dresser, which held a handful of framed photos: Leo and his sisters. Leo and his parents. Leo midconversation with an indigenous family she assumed lived in one of the villages he'd worked with in Brazil. Leo grinning with a group of POR workers in front of a lush green jungle background.

On the opposite wall was a framed photo of a kind of squarish mountain. She'd never seen anything like it before, but she could guess who in this room had. "Yours?"

He crossed the room to join her. "That's Monte Roraima. It's a tabletop mountain. That's why the sides are flat like that."

"Cool," she said, meaning it. Since when did she care this much about nature?

He reached for her hand. "It's on the border of Brazil, Venezuela, and Guyana. Some people say it took a billion years to form. Billion with a *B*." He shook his head. "I'm shit at math, but even I know that's a long time."

They stared in silence at the cliff walls of the mountain before Faith spotted something out of the corner of her eye.

"Oh my God." She darted over and snatched up the little stuffed dragon. "Is this Griff? What's he wearing?"

She brought it closer to her nose, but Leo plucked it from her fingers with a sigh.

"It's a jersey for the Puerto Rico national fútbol team," he said as he returned Griff to the shelf he occupied along with a decorative floral plaque that clearly belonged to the actual owners of the home.

"A tiny jersey!" She squealed and pressed her hands over her heart. "You're so cute."

"It's just the stuff I had in my room at POR," he grumbled, but he was smiling a little as he said it. "That's why it all fits in here."

"I love it." She spun in a circle, looking for any more Leo touches, and made a beeline when she spotted a small basket in the corner of the room. She reached inside and pulled out a set of needles with about eight inches of flat blue knitting on them.

"Um. That's also mine," he said.

"You knit?" Her mouth dropped.

"Learning." He shrugged. "Char's teaching me."

"Oh!" Well, that made sense. More than sense actually. It made her heart pitter-patter to know that he'd been spending that much time at the Knit Nook. "So what are you making?"

"It's a scarf," he said a little reluctantly.

She rubbed the finished section against her cheek. "I didn't think you could get cuter than Griff in a soccer jersey, but you went and did it, you old softy."

"Okay, that's enough," he said with another one of those not-scowl scowls. "I thought the blue would look good with your eyes. Your hair." He twined one of her blue strands around his finger.

"Leo." She pressed her lips together, almost scared to ask. "Are you knitting me a scarf?"

He shrugged again, color touching his cheeks. "Maybe. I mean, it might not be very good by the time I'm done with it. The pattern doesn't take much counting. Just back and forth across the row, so..."

For a second, she couldn't speak. She just hugged the bundle of yarn to her chest and blinked at the tears that inexplicably appeared at the corner of her eyes. He thought about her. Her eyes, her hair. And he was learning something new from one of the programs he'd helped to fund.

She was very close to being swept off her feet. Time to ground herself before she got bowled over entirely.

She set the knitting back in the basket and walked to his framed photos, picking up the one with the dozen or so POR volunteers posing in front of the Amazon. Leo's arm was slung around a thin, tan woman with effortlessly cool, short, tousled hair.

"This is Reggie, isn't it?"

She turned the picture to face him, and Leo answered reluctantly. "Yes?"

"Oh God, she's everything I was afraid of." She swung it back for a closer look. "She's the anti-me."

He pulled the frame out of her hand and set it back on the dresser without a second glance. "What do you mean?"

She pointed. "Tiny. Looks good in khaki. Probably graceful as a little gazelle."

He canted his head to the side. "Dutch, are you jealous?"

"No! I'm just saying, take every single thing that she is, and I am the opposite."

Not tiny. Not a gazelle. Okay, maybe she was jealous. But Leo's eyes burned into hers as he slid a hand behind her neck and pulled her close.

"It's always been you, Faith." The words fanned across her lips as he bent to kiss her, a velvety brush of his mouth against hers.

The struggle. The struggle not to fall. She trailed her fingers up his ribs and made one final effort to joke her way out of these dangerous emotional waters. "See? Such a softy."

It worked. Leo started walking backward toward the bed, arms outstretched. "Nothing soft on me, Dutch."

"Oh yeah? Does that mean you've got something *hard* for me?" She didn't have to fake much of the breathiness in her voice.

He raised his brows in an invitation. "Guess you'll have to come over here and find out."

So she did.

TWENTY-FIVE

Leo was standing on Faith's doorstep. He was ringing the bell. He was walking through her front door.

Not her window. Her front door.

"Leo!" Faith's mother greeted him from the entryway. "My goodness, you did grow up, didn't you?"

She smiled at him, and although his fight-or-flight reflexes were engaged, he managed to return a pleasant enough greeting.

"It's good to see you again, Mrs. Fox." She'd barely changed since he'd seen her last, and although her hair was more white-silver than blond-silver now, her eyes were still the same shade as her daughter's.

"Call me Betsy. You're not seventeen anymore. And don't you look nice?" Her eyes swept down his tuxedo, which sure as hell better look nice. He'd actually bought the damn thing two weeks ago, reasoning that Digham threw fancy parties left and right, so he might as well be prepared.

Betsy smiled approvingly at him one more time. "I'll tell Faithy you're here. She's just finishing getting ready."

"Thank you," he called after her as she started to climb one of the two staircases curving along opposite walls of the circular foyer.

Like Betsy, the white marble entryway hadn't changed much since his last visit either, with footsteps and voices still echoing off every single hard surface. He paced in a slow circle, hoping to settle his racing pulse. When he'd asked Faith weeks ago if she wanted to come with him to the gala, he hadn't expected their relationship to change quite so much in the meantime. And now they were sleeping together with no real conversation about what any of it meant. They'd agreed to act like colleagues tonight, but he was still jumpy as hell about being here now and going somewhere so fancy on her arm.

"Hello, son."

Franklin appeared in a doorway to his left, and hoo boy, he thought his fight-or-flight was dialed up before? Now he was balanced on the balls of his feet and ready to run.

"Hello, sir," he replied as neutrally as he could. Unlike her mother, Faith's dad looked twelve years older than the night of her graduation party. He was heavier, and the hair left on his head was white and cottony. His soft face reflected a soft life, and he barely resembled the man who'd loomed so large in Leo's memory for years.

"Join me for a drink?" He gestured Leo to follow him, so he joined Franklin at the wet bar in the corner of the sitting room. "Whiskey okay?"

"Please," Leo said. "Just one though. I'm driving your daughter tonight."

Franklin bobbed his head in approval and poured them both two fingers of amber liquid from a cut-crystal decanter. He handed Leo one of the glasses, and they sipped in silence. It was cold out, but this room was overheated. Or maybe his nerves were working overtime. Those same nerves were likely to blame for the words that came tumbling out of his mouth almost unbidden.

"I dreamed about punching you in the face for so long."

He froze in horror as his blurted confession hung in the air between them, but after a stunned moment, Franklin barked a laugh.

"I felt exactly the same." He raised his glass in a toast that Leo was eventually able to return once all his muscles unlocked. They both swallowed mouthfuls of the smoky drink before Franklin spoke again.

"If you ever have a daughter who announces that she's found the love of her life at sixteen, you'll feel the same." He stared into his glass. "I realized too late that I should've let her make her own decisions."

The older man's forehead creased, his broad face shifting into a serious, almost pained expression as he met Leo's eyes. "I'm sorry for not respecting you both enough to do that."

Franklin shifted his glass to his left hand and stuck out his right, and it took Leo a long moment to realize that he was offering to shake his hand.

For a split second every single past grievance rushed back. How long had he dreamed of telling this old man that he could fuck right off for ruining his life? But the moment passed just as quickly. The truth was, Franklin hadn't ruined Leo's life, or Faith's. They'd both gotten their educations and built their careers. Lived separate lives and grown into the people they were meant to be. Hell, Leo lived in a nicer house than he ever could've dreamed of as a kid because of the choices he'd made after high school, and he was in a tuxedo ready to take a spectacular woman to a black-tie event. He doubted any of that would've happened if he'd followed Faith to Evanston without any goals of his own.

Franklin had been a villain, but it sounded like he'd lost Faith for as many years as Leo himself had. If that wasn't enough punishment, he didn't know what was.

He swallowed the last of his misgivings and clasped Franklin's hand with his own. The man's shoulders relaxed, and at the end of the handshake, he clapped Leo on the back. "So tell me how you're liking life at Digham."

Twenty minutes later, two pairs of footsteps tapped their way into the room, and when Leo turned to the doorway, time seemed to stop.

Faith was *everything*. Her hair was curled and piled on top of her head, all blond tonight. She'd explained that she used temporary dye, but the way it could go from bright blue to moonlight blond still seemed like magic to him. Her lips were natural too, a soft pink rather than the scarlet he'd been expecting. Not that it mattered; she had the most gorgeous mouth he'd ever seen no matter the shade.

And then there was her dress. The black fabric swooped dramatically over one shoulder, exposing her round arms and shoulders and curving over her breasts. It gathered at her waist, and the skirt...

He audibly gulped. The skirt had a slit that ran all the way up one side of the front, exposing a sliver of leg up to her thigh.

He was dazzled. And then he was alarmed when Faith's expression twisted into a grimace.

"No!" She stalked forward, pointing accusatorially.

"No no no no *no*. You will not ruin this for me again, Dad."

As she charged toward them, the slit parted to show more of her leg than Leo was comfortable with in her parents' living room.

"What are you two talking about?" she asked suspiciously, stepping between him and Franklin.

Leo rested a hand on her waist, slightly nervous to touch her in front of her father but unable to keep his hands off her for another second.

"We were discussing whiskey." Franklin raised his glass in proof. "Your young man is trying to convince me to try it mixed with coconut water."

"Because it's delicious. You won't regret it," Leo said, circling his thumb against Faith's back in an attempt to assure her that things were going fine.

Franklin bobbed his head. "All right. The next time you're over."

The next time.

Leo nodded, a little dazed, then turned to Faith's mom. "I can also ask my mother to set aside a little extra coquito when she and my aunts start making it for Christmas. It's a Puerto Rican tradition, kind of like eggnog. Plenty of rum."

"Oh." Betsy blinked, then smiled. "That would be lovely. Thank you."

When he looked at Faith, her eyes were wide as they darted from her mother to her father and back to him, like she was an audience member at a play.

He gave her waist a squeeze and leaned close to murmur, "You look incredible."

As he hoped, she blushed.

"And you should always wear a tux." She stepped in

front of him and brushed her hands over the shoulders of his black jacket, then adjusted his bow tie a fraction of an inch.

"Even when we're hiking?"

She tossed her head back in a laugh. "Especially when we're hiking."

"Done." They grinned at each other, and if they'd been alone, he'd have kissed her until they were both breathless. "We should get moving, right?" William had shoved him out the door in plenty of time to pick Faith up, but it didn't hurt to check.

"Yep." She patted his lapels one last time and scooped up a tiny black purse and furry wrap that she'd dropped on a table near the door. "Bye, Mom! Bye, Dad! Don't wait up," she called as she headed out, her heels clicking over the marble tile in the entryway.

Leo hesitated, wanting to say *something* to celebrate surviving an encounter with Franklin and Betsy Fox. But he heard the front door open and didn't want to keep Faith waiting in the cold.

"I should..." He pointed over his shoulder. "Thank you."

Oh hell, what was he thanking them for? But the elder Foxes had moved to stand side by side and were smiling at him.

Smiling. At him.

"Thank *you*," Franklin said gruffly. "Have a good time tonight."

"We will."

Then he turned and followed Faith out the door, his feelings about her family shifting and tumbling like flakes in a snow globe.

THE INSTANT they'd driven out of sight of her parents' house, Faith said, "Pull over."

"Why?" He steered to the curb and put the car in park. "Did you forget something?"

He glanced into the back seat as if the answer was lying on the floor mats, then whipped back around when she unbuckled her seat belt and reached over to undo his.

"I didn't want to put on my lipstick until I had a chance to greet you properly."

He understood immediately and met her halfway as she leaned across the console, unable to wait another second to touch her. He rested his hands on the sides of her neck so he wouldn't disturb her hair, but there was nothing careful about his kiss. It was hot, hungry, his tongue sweeping into her mouth to tangle with hers. She smelled like hairspray and expensive perfume, and it went straight to his head.

"Let's skip this thing," he growled when they broke apart. "Go back to my place. Nobody'll notice we're not there."

"Don't tempt me." She ran her hand down his arm. "You in a tux is making me crazy."

His hand dropped to her leg, exposed when her skirt had shifted as they kissed. His fingers traveled upward, and she shivered. But before things could get really interesting, a car approached from the other direction, slowing as it passed them. He reluctantly removed his hand and put the car back in drive.

"You're too hot for a front-seat make-out anyway," he said. "That dress is back seat material at the very least."

She primly patted her hair, then reached into her

purse and pulled out a tube of lipstick and a mirror. "Damn straight. Let's get this over with so we can go have formal-wear sex."

But getting it over with proved to be difficult once they arrived in the ballroom. Digham employees were packed in elbow to elbow, a few of whom he knew but the majority of whom he didn't. Faith though? She knew everyone.

"Sure! I'll make a call!" she chirped at the end of a conversation with an older couple, both of whom were lifetime Big Dig employees. It was the sixth interaction of the night that ended with her promising to follow up with a grandchild's school or to see about adding some new subject to the tutoring roster. His head spun at the names she recalled and details she was able to dredge up about their family members, professions, hobbies. They'd agreed to attend the event as colleagues only, but it was hard not to look at her with hearts in his eyes when she was kicking ass and taking names all the way around the room.

"Doing okay?" He gave in to temptation and traced his fingers over the curve of her shoulder. "Can I get you a drink?"

She tilted her head toward him. "That would be amazing. Something with gin?"

"For you, anything." He needed to actually leave her side to fetch it for her, but his body didn't want to be separated from her quite yet. Not when she was smiling up at him, all red-lipped and radiant. His eyes swept over her hair. "I notice there's no blue tonight."

She pursed her lips in a smile. "Please. I don't need courage to face down this crowd."

"I do," he said, glancing around at the tuxedoes and

glittering gowns surrounding him. "I almost asked if I could borrow some of your dye for myself."

She laughed and brushed her fingers along one of his curls. "Anytime."

"There you are. I've been looking for you."

At the sound of his boss's voice, Faith yanked her hand away, and Leo took a small step away.

"Carlisle. Hi." The moment with Faith had been punctured by a man who sounded annoyed that Leo hadn't read his mind and somehow presented himself without a search. He barely controlled his scowl as he asked, "Can I help you with something?"

Carlisle Lockhart didn't even glance Faith's way as he said, "A few people were curious about my newest employee. Are you free for some introductions?"

No. He wanted to bring Faith drinks and watch her work the room for the rest of the night. But he also knew that it was important to meet more of his Digham coworkers, so he nodded. "Of course."

Carlisle looked even less pleased to be dealing with Leo at a party than he usually did when they had to interact at the office, which was saying something. But as the man started to pivot away, even Leo, with his minimal experience in corporate life and events where everyone wore tuxedoes, knew that doing so without acknowledging the woman standing next to him was beyond rude.

"Carlisle, have you met Faith Fox? She runs Beaucoeur BUILD, the Dig Greener grant recipient."

His boss's eyebrows jumped, then lowered immediately as he looked from Leo to Faith and then back again. Faith jumped right in.

"Hi again!" She extended her hand, and Carlisle gripped it with the tips of his fingers in a half-hearted shake. "We met at Digham HQ in July. You helped me find the foundation office."

His frown deepened. "Oh, that was you. You look"—he blinked—"different."

Leo remembered that day vividly. Faith had been vibrating with anxiety and combativeness and passion for her work, and even in her grungy moving clothes, she'd been gorgeous. If that's not how Carlisle remembered her, his opinion wasn't worth considering.

Faith apparently felt so too because her smile was razor-tipped. "So good to see you again too." She smiled up at Leo. "I promised my parents I'd say hello to George Voit when I saw him tonight, so I'd better go make the rounds."

Damn she was good, casually mentioning the Big Dig CEO in front of his name-dropping boss. She rested a hand on his arm for the briefest moment. "Leo, thanks for the invitation tonight. I love chatting with new people about BUILD."

With that, she turned and was swallowed up in the crowd while his bicep burned from her fleeting touch. Carlisle gave an impatient huff and moved in the other direction, clearly expecting Leo to follow him.

He spent the rest of the night meeting a dizzying number of new people, all of whom smiled and shook his hand and congratulated him on the work he was doing with the foundation while Carlisle hovered on the edges like a turd in a punch bowl. He bumped into his other grant recipients as the night wore on and was delighted to introduce Char McDougall and Barrett Allen and Isaac and Luna Hamoud to Big Dig employees eager to learn about the work the company was helping to fund in Beaucoeur. He even managed to get Faith that gin and tonic she'd requested, letting his finger trail along the back of her hand oh so briefly as she accepted it from him. Then they were pulled in different directions, and the night spun on.

When the event finally started to draw to a close, Faith signaled him from near the ballroom exit. His cheeks ached from the uncharacteristic amount of smiling he'd been doing, so he gratefully made his excuses and slipped out after her. They drove straight to his house, and she introduced him to the wonders of formal-wear sex, which was a lot like regular sex but probably had a bigger dry-cleaning bill.

Afterward, their limbs tangled together on top of his sheets, she pressed soft kisses over his heart and said, "I didn't get enough time with you tonight. Can we hang tomorrow?"

"Love to." Then he groaned. "Can't."

She pulled away. "Making excuses already?"

"No. But there's a big family thing at my parents' house. My cousins are in town from New Jersey, so we're all getting together."

"Mmm." She rested her head against his shoulder and ran her nails gently over his chest. "You can't miss that."

"Come with me."

Her fingers stopped moving. "Really?"

"Of course." The invitation had been spontaneous, but it settled right in his heart.

"Will your sisters be nicer to me?" Her chest rose and pressed against his side as she sucked in a steadying breath. "Because I can handle myself around them if I have to, but I'd rather not have to."

"I'll take care of it." He kissed the top of her head. "Tell them they're not allowed to hassle my girlfriend."

She stopped breathing entirely. So did he. He'd tossed the word out there because he was tired of keeping his feelings inside, and he braced himself for however she'd respond.

Moonlight poured through the window, turning the room silver. When she looked up at him again, her eyes shimmered with the same unearthly glow.

"Okay. I'd love to come."

TWENTY-SIX

"Not too late to back out, Dutch."

Faith dug her elbow into his ribs, or at least she tried to. He was too muscly to get much traction. "That's not helping! You being nervous makes *me* nervous!"

She'd met his parents years ago, but she guessed whatever was waiting for her behind that bright red door was going to be more intense than that. Hence the nerves. But Leo had asked her to come, which meant more to her than she could put into words, and for that reason alone she was here. Hell, if he asked, she'd probably swim with piranhas or use a Greyhound bus bathroom. Meeting all his aunts should be a piece of cake. So here she was in her nicest jeans and her cutest sweater, and she'd made the brownies that never failed to win every potluck.

She was still nervous as hell.

"I'm not worried. You'll be great," Leo said. "I've never seen a person you couldn't charm if you wanted to." Then he pressed his forehead against hers and lowered his voice. "I just wish we were still naked in my bed."

Was it bad form to make out with the baby of the

family on his parents' doorstep? It probably was. The question was how much she cared.

"Oh my God. What are those?"

Faith jumped away from Leo to see his sister Jessie staring at the plate in her hand.

"Um, brownies?"

Jessie rolled her eyes, done up with the most perfect winged eyeliner Faith had ever seen. "You're seriously letting her walk in there with brownies?" she asked her brother. *"Brownies?"*

Leo shrugged. "She wanted to bring something."

Jessie scoffed and yanked the plate out of Faith's hand. "Absolutely not. Here." She pushed a bottle of rum into Faith's fingers. "Give them this."

"But everyone loves my brownies," Faith objected.

"Trust me."

And weirdly enough, Faith did. Even though Jessie'd been kind of a bitch at the Gourd Olde Days Festival, Leo's sister had actually been a good friend in high school. Jessie was a year ahead of them, so Faith had gotten to spend time with her when she came over to study. Jessie had even been Faith's cafeteria buddy one semester when her lunch period didn't overlap with Leo's or Thea's. She'd been shocked by his sisters's hostility at the fairgrounds, but especially Jessie. Of course, she also understood. She didn't have siblings, but she did almost rip Aiden limb from limb after he and Thea had their falling out. If she'd felt that protective over her best friend's broken heart, she couldn't even imagine how three older sisters had reacted after her breakup with Leo.

"It's true." Leo nodded gravely. "Rum is the way to every Puerto Rican's heart."

Faith tilted her head. "And you're just telling me this

now? I've been wasting time being nice to you and..." She let her eyes drift down to the front of his jeans as she nibbled on a thumbnail.

Leo's eyes flared as Jessie wailed, "No! Stop!"

"I'm sorry!" Faith clapped a hand over her mouth, her cheeks heating. "I'm so nervous. It makes me inappropriate."

Jessie ran her assessing gaze from Faith's head down to her toes before nodding. "You'll do fine. Leo prepared everybody well."

What the hell did that mean? Faith desperately wanted to ask, but it was too late. Jessie flung open the front door and shouted, "We're here! And Leo brought a white girl!"

Faith stepped into the living room that was wall-to-wall people and sound. At least four different conversations were happening at once while a Pixar movie played for a group of children sprawled in front of the television in the corner. Loud dance music poured from the kitchen, along with the clatter of spoons against pots and the most amazing cooking smells Faith had ever inhaled. The dozen or so people in attendance all turned to welcome the newcomers, and she hung back while Leo and Jessie moved around the room, greeting their relatives and exchanging the greeting that she'd heard Leo give his nephews at the fairgrounds.

Once everyone in the room had been hugged and kissed, their eyes all fell on her.

"Hi!" She gave her best *you're gonna love me* smile. "I'm Faith Fox. I, um, brought rum?" She held up the bottle, and a cheer went around the room. Then she, too, was wrapped in countless pairs of arms welcoming her to the house.

"Ben-di-she-own," she said tentatively to an older man with an epic white mustache. She tried to sound it out as best as she could, and he grinned and pinched her cheek, replying in Spanish with the phrase everyone had just said to Leo and Jessie.

After the man moved away, Leo wrapped his arm around her waist. "Bendición is how we greet older folks in our family, and then they give us their blessing." He smiled down at her, his eyes warm. "You did good."

"Thanks." She grinned right back up at him, feeling warm and welcome all over. Then she tensed up again when his mother speed-walked from the kitchen directly over to them, and Leo stepped forward to hug her.

"Mijo!" Luisa wrapped her arms around Leo and squeezed. She was tiny, at least a foot shorter than all her children, but she hugged him so hard that he could barely do the call-and-response greeting. Then she turned to Faith, surprising her by pulling her into a slightly less intense hug. Apparently Luisa didn't hold as many grudges as her daughters did.

"It's wonderful to see you again." Luisa stepped back but kept her arms on Faith's elbows. "Leo tells me he is enjoying working with you."

"I'm enjoying working with him too." Had Leo not told his family about their relationship? Maybe not. Even though he'd dropped the "girlfriend" word the day before, *she* barely knew what he was thinking, so it might be safest to assume nobody knew anything about anybody. She kept it breezy. "I love your new home. When did you move?"

Visiting the Morales family in high school had always felt like taking a trip to Oppositesville. Their house had been small and shabby and bursting with warmth and welcome, while her own was big and sterile and cold.

Luisa was all smiles as she gestured at the yellow living room walls, the overstuffed bookshelves, the framed family photos. This new house was larger, the furniture nicer, but the warmth remained. "About ten years ago. It's a much better neighborhood, and I have room for my grandchildren when they want to stay."

"She couldn't resist slipping in the grandkids line," Jessie whispered.

Leo grunted. "The first of many."

Vanessa, Leo's terrifying older sister, joined their group. "Careful. We might have company, but Mom *will* break out the chancla."

The three Morales siblings laughed, then Vanessa caught sight of the plate in Jessie's hands and shrieked. "Girl, what is that? Did you bring *dessert*?"

Jessie gritted her teeth in a smile. "Yeah, I thought I'd try something new. Everybody loves brownies, right?"

Luisa took the plate, holding it out in front of her as if it might be radioactive. "Mya made her flan, and Sofia brought pineapple rum cake, but we'll... we'll find a place for these on the table." She shoved the plate into the hands of a passing woman who was headed to the kitchen, then turned to Faith, all smiles. "And you brought rum! What a thoughtful girl."

Luisa plucked the bottle from her fingers, and moments later, one of the out-of-town cousins she'd been introduced to earlier slid a glass into her hand. "Drink up!" he said cheerfully.

Faith glanced around to see that the siblings all had their own glasses, so she shrugged and joined in. It was rum, and it was delicious, and it made the general conversation go down easily as everyone gravitated toward the couches in the living room. Faith sat and sipped and enjoyed the sibling interplay happening over one of the *Toy Story* installments on the TV, particularly when Cecilia joined them and all four of them started giving each other nonstop shit. As an only child, she found it fascinating to observe.

She was having such a good time that she didn't even object when Leo excused himself to make the rounds with some of the family that he hadn't seen in a few years. His spot next to her on the couch was swiftly claimed by yet another cousin from New Jersey.

"Hi," the woman said. "I'm Rachel. Do you mind holding her while I eat?"

Without warning, Rachel plopped an infant on Faith's lap.

"Um…" She looked around for some place to set her Solo cup and settled on gripping it in her teeth so she could wrap both hands around the wriggly creature.

Jessie laughed. "Look at that. A natural."

Faith tried to smile around the cup, but she didn't take her eyes off the baby for long. The tiny human was objectively adorable in her ruffled dress, but she also felt extremely breakable, and Faith wanted to hand her back as soon as possible.

After the longest six minutes in history, Rachel finished her plate and set it aside, reclaiming her child. As soon as her hands were free, Faith took a long gulp of her drink and thanked her child-free stars.

"Sorry," Rachel said as she adjusted the baby on her lap, "I didn't catch your name."

She sat up straight. "Faith, but I think you can also call me Fea?" She offered up the name she'd heard Leo's sisters use at the fairgrounds, hoping to show how well she could fit in with his family.

What she got instead was a moment of shocked silence and then an explosion of laughter from everyone on the couches.

"Oh no!" Jessie wailed as Cecilia slowly slid down the couch and onto the floor in a human puddle.

"What?" Faith looked around in confusion. "That's what you guys said at the fairgrounds, right? Fea?"

The word prompted another gale of laughter that left her bewildered until finally Rachel took pity on her. Wiping her streaming eyes, she gasped out, "Oh my God, blanquita. Fea means ugly."

"What?" she shrieked, mouth stretching wide in shock.

"We couldn't help it!" Vanessa hooted. "It was too good to pass up!"

Faith raised her hands in confusion, unsure just how offended she should be. This time Jessie was the one who stepped in.

"Fe means faith," she said. "And with fea sounding so close..."

Faith gasped as she finally got the joke. "You absolute *bitches*!" she howled. Then she was struck by a horrible, hilarious realization. "That's how I introduced myself to your grandma just now!"

That just made everyone in the room shriek some more. Cecilia in particular lay twitching on the floor, too overcome with laughter to stand.

"What did I miss?" Leo came strolling back over and wedged himself next to her on the couch.

"Your sisters"—she swung a finger over all three of them—"have been calling me ugly!"

Leo closed his eyes with a groan. "I begged you guys not to!"

"We didn't!" Vanessa said. "She brought it up!"

Faith was doubled over with laughter now too. "I just wanted to fit in!" And somehow being the butt of the joke accomplished that.

"Good Lord, duchess. You do know how to make friends, don't you?" Leo slid his arm along the couch behind her, and she leaned into him, still giggling. After this sisterly harassment, she deserved to cuddle up against his nice, solid chest.

Once the laughter died down, Rachel shifted the baby to her other knee and turned to Leo.

"So tell me all about your new job," she said. "It's all your mom talks to my mom about. 'Leo's off saving the world, Leo's teaching college kids how to save the world, Leo's moving back home to save the world some more.'" Her tone was exasperated, and Leo chuckled.

"It's not quite that dramatic, but I did a lot of projects around the Amazon that I hope will be helpful to the people living there for years to come." He relaxed against the arm of the couch with a drink in one hand, wrapping his other hand around Faith's shoulder.

"So modest." Faith smiled up at him, and he gave her hair a playful tug before continuing.

"As for the college kids, yeah, some of them were amazing volunteers." He shrugged, sipped his drink, gave her hair another pet. "But way too many were just there to spend daddy's money on a résumé builder. It's part of the reason I wanted to move here and work in the community. So many worthwhile projects I can tackle locally."

All the people listening on the couches murmured approvingly, but not Faith. She was frozen. Stabbed in the heart by his offhanded comment. *Daddy's money.* The same words he'd thrown in her face back in June. She leaned away from him, swallowing thickly. He probably didn't mean anything by it, but to think that he'd lump her in with those spoiled kids who'd complained about footwear and made him and William roll their eyes...

She inhaled hard and willed herself not to spiral out of control. He might not have meant anything personal. He was just talking to his family. It wasn't about her, right?

He must've noticed her shifting uncomfortably because he turned to look at her. "You okay?"

She stared at him with a furrowed brow, wanting to ask but scared to find out.

When she didn't speak, he frowned and bent forward to sniff her drink. "What's in this?" He grabbed the cup from her and took a drink. "Is this strawberries?"

Vanessa waved a casual hand toward the kitchen. "Probably. Dad wanted us to try some new rum fruit drink."

"*What?*" Leo stood and dropped to his knees in front of Faith, his eyes intent on hers. "Are you okay? Your throat? Your breathing?" He turned his head to yell over his shoulder, "I told you guys, no strawberries! She's allergic."

That killed the conversation, and his sisters watched anxiously as he swung those amazing dark eyes back onto her, his hands moving to the side of her neck. "Any swelling? Do I need to get you to a hospital?"

His frantic gaze bored into her, leaving her too surprised to move. But his careful touch combined with the actual fear on his face quickly broke her paralysis.

"No! No. I'm fine." She wrapped her fingers around his. "I outgrew that allergy years ago. It's fine."

His thumbs stroked her jawline. "Christ, Dutch, are you sure?"

"I think I know my own allergies," she murmured. Then she repeated his action from the front porch a few hours ago and pressed her forehead against his, a little overwhelmed at the intensity of his response. Even if it was thoroughly misplaced, it lit a glow inside of her. "I'm fine. I swear."

He exhaled hard and kissed her forehead. "Coño. Don't scare me like that again." He rose and resumed his place next to her, and when they turned back to the group, everyone was staring at them with various degrees of speculation and understanding on their faces.

Faith, too, felt a little more clarity. He *did* care about her again. He had to, right? This wasn't just sex, wasn't just the memory of their old affection for one another. He might have opinions about how she'd been raised, but he'd taken her camping, he'd called her his girlfriend, and he'd been ready to carry her out the door to the hospital from the looks of things.

It was good. Things were good. And that knowledge let her turn to his sisters and wiggle her fingers in a "bring it on" gesture.

"Okay, hit me. I want the meanest Spanish names to call your brother when he gets out of line."

As she'd hoped, that pulled everybody in the group back into the fun, and she left his parents' house with a number of wicked things she planned to use in bed with him later.

TWENTY-SEVEN

Leo was leaning against the kitchen island, chugging a bottle of Gatorade when the garage door rumbled open and then shut again. Moments later, his roommate loped into view, a smirk on his face as he flopped his gym bag on the floor.

"I didn't see a sock on the front door handle, so I figured it was safe to come in."

Leo didn't have enough strength left to control his grin. Not only was he physically spent, but this was the third straight weekend that he'd had Faith in his bedroom, and he was basically existing on joy and sex pheromones at this point.

"Yeah, she said she wanted to be able to walk straight tomorrow at work so she headed home to get ready for the week."

Smug? Him? Absolutely, especially when William eyed the empty Gatorade bottle next to the half-full one he'd just set on the island.

"So it's just sex? I'm actually starting to get hurt that

you're not braiding my hair and sharing your relationship secrets."

Leo grabbed the empty bottle and tossed it into the recycling bin. It was a stall, but really why hold back any details at this point?

"I'm guessing you've got most of it figured out," he said. "We were together in high school. The fox tattoo was for her. We had a bad breakup that sent me running to Southern Illinois for college and then to the Amazon after that."

William nodded, clearly not hearing anything that surprised him. "Is she why you moved home?"

"No." He spun the remaining bottle between his palms, eyes fixed on the neon-yellow liquid sloshing inside. "I didn't even know she still lived in town. We just bumped into each other and..."

"And bumped *into* each other," William finished for him.

Leo shook his head. "No. It's bigger than that."

His friend immediately dropped his amused grin. "Oh shit. Like *bigger* bigger?"

Yes. If it was up to him, yes. He didn't say it out loud, but his body language must've been screaming it because William gave a low whistle.

"So it's like that. No wonder Reggie never stood a chance."

"I never—"

William waved him off. "Yeah, yeah, you never promised her anything, she knew the score, it was never serious. I've heard it all before. And maybe I finally get it. Faith's the one who got away."

No point in denying it anymore, to William or to himself. "She is."

But he had her again, or at least he thought he did. All the parts of their lives were tangling together, and he loved it: work, home, meals, families. And he was damn sure not letting her down in the orgasm department this time around. She knew what she needed and communicated it forcefully. God, it was hot how forcefully she communicated what she needed.

"Oh buddy, your face right now." William shook his head, then his expression turned serious. "Just don't blow up my life, okay?"

That pulled him up short. "What do you mean?"

"I mean," William said patiently, "that I quit my old job to come work for her. Please don't fuck that up for me."

A little tingle of unease washed over him. "I won't." But he leaned against the kitchen counter and forced himself to consider the worst-case scenarios. They hadn't intended to hurt each other last time, and look what had happened. If they tried again and then broke up, would it blow back on him? On William? On her? Hell, he didn't even know if she was willing to take that risk once she'd had some time to really think about it.

His postsex glow was fading. Fucking William. He'd just gotten her back into his life. Into his bed. And now he wanted to rewind to sixty seconds ago before William had introduced this whisper of doubt. "It's not going to be a problem."

"If you say so."

The skepticism in his friend's voice burrowed under his skin. "I said it'll be fine."

"I was just asking." William raised his hands in surrender. "You're awfully grumpy for someone who's regularly getting laid."

Getting laid. What an enormous understatement.

"Oh my God. I've never seen you like this. You're really in it with her."

"I am." He wasn't sure he'd ever been out of it. All that time he spent hating her was time spent *feeling* for her.

"So this time around, is it as good as you remembered?"

Leo wasn't a fuck-and-tell kind of guy, but he couldn't control the endorphins rioting through him. "Even better, man," he said quietly. It was the truest thing he could think of and as much detail as he was willing to share.

"Seeing you with her." William shook his head. "You're happy in a way I've never seen you happy before. So yeah, figure out how to make it work."

"I will." Because he wanted it all. The job. Dig Greener. And Faith. He'd lost her once, and every attempt to guard himself from her again had failed. He'd just have to find a way to keep her this time.

William sighed. "If it really is like that, I guess I ought to start thinking about finding my own place."

A good friend would tell him not to hurry, that he was welcome to stay as long as he needed. But that same good friend had plans to get Faith naked in every room in his house.

"No big rush. But I'll help you move your three boxes of belongings into that new place soon as you're ready," Leo offered.

He tried to ignore Faith's absence in his house for the rest of the afternoon as he did laundry and incorporated Savannah's notes into his United Way campaign materials and played some *Mario Kart* with William. By the time the sun was setting, he couldn't take it anymore.

"I'm going to her house." He needed to see her again. His whole body missed her.

"Should I expect to see you back tonight?" William asked.

"Hope not."

His friend's guffaw followed him out the door as he got in his car to drive to Faith's. Well, to drive a block over from Faith's so he could hoof it to her house, cutting through backyards once he reached the house next door. Good thing these lots were massive enough that nobody bothered with fences around here.

He should probably feel more ridiculous than he did sneaking around, yet there was something sort of thrilling about climbing in through her window even though she was an enthusiastically consenting adult. Once he was standing under her window, he grabbed his phone to text her, but something made him pause. The light was on in her room, its familiar yellow glow catching in his chest. That warmth grew to fill every inch of space until his rib cage couldn't contain it anymore.

He'd felt this way years ago, standing in the grass and looking up at the magical portal that would usher him into the secret world of the girl he loved. And here he was again. Same girl. Same feelings too, he was starting to realize.

He turned that thought over and found no fear in it, only rightness. Like this was inevitable. They'd set this into motion when they'd run into each other at the country club, despite the insults and the dredged-up hurt. Despite the sex that he'd tried to keep dirty and anonymous, hoping to push her out of his system. Through all of that, he was always destined to end up here with his shoes getting wet in the damp grass because the Foxes still ran their goddamn sprinklers in the evening.

Unable to wait any longer, he tapped out a text:

LEO
Open your window.

She appeared almost instantly, sliding open the glass and popping the screen. She blew a kiss, then hooked a thumb in the neckline of her T-shirt, pulling it down to expose a fair amount of cleavage, and all of his cautious thoughts blew right out of his head. Fuck, he wanted to do a lot of dirty things to her tonight, but he wanted to start by resting his head right there in the space between her breasts.

Apparently he'd been standing there staring for too long because she rolled her eyes, grabbed her phone, and typed furiously. A moment later, the text popped up:

FAITH
Should I get started without you?

His eyes zipped up to the window just in time to catch her pulling her shirt over her head and tossing it to the ground. It landed at his feet, and she gave him the briefest glimpse of those soft, amazing tits before she disappeared.

Leo had never made that trip up to her room faster. By the time he crawled through the window and shut it after him, she was on the bed naked. One knee was bent, and she was swirling a finger around one nipple, already flushed that perfect shade of pink that had haunted him for years.

"What took you so long?"

He held up her shirt. "A duchess in a tower threw this at me, and I had to rescue it."

"My hero," she crooned, but the playfulness on her face turned molten when he moved to stand at the foot of the bed.

"How quiet do we need to be?" He reached down and grabbed her foot, running his thumb over the curve of her instep and digging into the pressure point she loved.

His touch made her moan, and she clapped a hand over her mouth. "Quieter than that," she whispered. "I suppose it's polite to respect the rules of the house."

He pulled off his shirt. "Is one of those rules 'no audible fucking'?"

She sucked her bottom lip into her mouth, her bright eyes following his hands as he yanked off his pants. "Maybe a little audible."

That, he could work with. He stretched out next to her and did exactly what had propelled him up the side of her house so quickly: he buried his face between her breasts and just breathed for a moment, content to be surrounded by the softest, sweetest skin on earth.

He turned slightly to place a kiss on the side of one ivory swell. "Just a little?"

Another kiss, this one closer to her nipple, but he was holding his breath, waiting for her answer.

"Just"—she gasped when his lips closed over the pink tip—"a little."

He sucked harder and bracketed two fingers around her other nipple and squeezed until she was thrashing underneath him, making soft little sounds, exactly as she'd requested.

She groped around her nightstand until she grabbed a condom, which she all but flung at him. He was no dummy. He rolled it on immediately and was inside her in even less time than it took him to climb through her window.

His first stroke into her made them both gasp, and for a long moment they just looked at each other. Her gaze traveled from his eyes to his mouth, his hair, his chin, like she was committing every part of him to memory. And he would've done the same if he hadn't already cataloged every one of her expressions, every minor shift in muscle and mood that made her face so endlessly fascinating to him. Hell, he'd devour every part of her if he could, consume her so he never had to be without her again.

He slid his hands into her hair and held her in place so he could kiss her as he thrust into her wet heat, his heart throbbing in his chest every time his cock slid home. It had been such a long drought, and touching her was like drinking from the coolest, freshest water source imaginable.

"I don't think I'll ever get tired of kissing you." She stroked a hand down his back, and his rhythm stuttered at hearing her speaking a version of his own thoughts out loud.

What else could he do but kiss her and kiss her and kiss her some more? When he was finally able to tear his mouth away, he pushed himself up to lean back on his knees. He wanted to watch her face when she came.

He slowed his thrusts, making them methodical. Not too slow, not too fast. His thumb found her clit and circled it until her back arched. The sight of her unraveling was too much.

"The way your tits move when I'm fucking you," he growled. "Fuck, Dutch. It's killing me."

He slammed into her, making her breasts bounce one

more time before he fell forward to press them together, biting and licking and sucking her until he felt her start to clench around him.

"Give it to me." He slid his hand down to her clit one more time, and all it took was another sweep of his fingers before she cried out and he surged upward to catch the noise in his mouth, to swallow her ecstasy as he emptied himself inside her.

Afterward, they lay side by side as their breathing returned to normal, and she gave a shaky laugh. "That might have been too loud."

He laughed too, gripped by fierce joy. "No regrets."

"None," she agreed. When she shivered again, he shifted to the side to pull the covers over them.

"Something's been driving me crazy," he said as she burrowed her head into his neck. "I'm dying to know."

"Anything," she asked sleepily.

"What does the BUILD stand for in Beaucoeur BUILD?"

Her yawn ended in a seal bark of a laugh that had her clapping a hand over her mouth. And in that moment he toppled back into love with her. Fully, no holding back in love. That undignified laugh was all it took to make him completely hers again.

"Would you believe that nobody's ever asked me that?" she asked.

"Nope," he said, nuzzling her neck and drowning in his love for her.

"They haven't, and I'm glad because"—her voice dropped to a low, conspiratorial tone—"it doesn't stand for a damn thing."

"No way." Her confession cut through his surging emotions, and he pulled back in surprise.

She giggled. "I just liked the sound of it but never could come up with a good acronym. So if anybody asks, just tell them it's proprietary information and you legally can't share it."

He smoothed a lock of her hair, and she lifted a hand to trace the fox tattoo. It was her favorite postsex pastime, and he was addicted to the way her fingers on his inner arm summoned goose bumps to his skin.

"For you, Dutch, anything." And then he held her close and watched her fall asleep.

TWENTY-EIGHT

"You really brought me back to the scene of the crime, huh?"

Faith sipped her gin fizz and glanced around the crowded rooftop bar. The unseasonably mild November weather had lured all of white-collar Beaucoeur out to Olive Twist tonight, and the strategically placed heat lamps were keeping the space warm enough for everyone to enjoy their drinks outside, possibly for the last time that year.

Leo's eyes were even warmer than the lamps when they landed on her. "I have recently been accused of being soft."

"Who would say that?" She gasped and rested a hand at the base of her throat. "You're a big strong man. Nothing soft about you. There's even a storage closet nearby where you could prove it to me."

He growled and grabbed her hand. "Don't tempt me." He pressed a quick kiss to her knuckles before releasing her.

She bit her lip as she studied him, not sure how she'd

gotten lucky enough to call this man hers not once, but twice.

"Closets aren't really my preference, especially when I can sex you up in a nice soft bed in front of Griff the dragon."

The corners of his eyes crinkled, and her heart took flight. She'd always loved being the person who made him laugh, and this time around, his lightness felt even harder won. He was serious about work, about his grant recipients, about hiking, about his family and friends. He was even serious when he was fucking her, all focused determination and mind-blowing stamina. But her favorite parts of their time together were moments like yesterday morning when he'd collapsed on top of her in a sweaty heap and laughed as they came down from their shared orgasm high. She wanted those carefree smiles for herself, and she wanted them forever.

The crinkles deepened as he twined his fingers through hers on top of the snowy-white tablecloth. "Faith, I'd like—"

An outraged gasp interrupted their moment of happiness, and her head whipped up to see Leo's boss glaring down at them.

"So it's true," he sneered. "You *are* involved with one of your grant recipients."

Carlisle Lockhart was puffed up like a fleshy pink frog, his neck folds quivering above his tightly buttoned collar. She yanked her hand away, and when Leo cast her a panicky glance, she saw it. Saw in his eyes what he was going to do before he did it.

"No!" He shot to his feet. "It's not like that. This isn't..."

"Isn't what?" Carlisle snapped.

Sweat appeared at Leo's hairline. "It's nothing inappropriate. It's just—"

"This is a clear violation of foundation policy." Carlisle's nose twitched as if he smelled something bad. "I knew there was something off when I saw you together at the gala, and when Darla told me where you'd gone after our meeting this afternoon, I guessed what I'd find."

Leo took a step away from their table. A step away from her.

"I haven't violated policy. This"—he gestured over his shoulder to Faith—"isn't any kind of conflict."

"This shouldn't be happening at all," the older man said crisply.

"This?" Faith wasn't about to be talked about like an inanimate object. She stood too, but her optimistic heart compressed when Leo shifted away as her shoulder brushed his.

"Nothing happened until after the grant paperwork was signed," she insisted.

Carlisle's eyes snapped to her, his assessing gaze cataloging her body just as it had at the foundation office all those months ago. And even though she was dressed in business casual this time, he obviously still found her wanting.

"How soon after?" he asked politely.

Leo's jaw clenched, and guilt poured off him in waves. Their silence was enough of an indictment for the man in front of them.

"Pull the grant," Carlisle barked, clearly unconcerned that their little scene was starting to attract attention from nearby tables. "The Digham Foundation has rules for a reason, and I won't let some pushy new employee trample all over them."

Faith slowly sank into her chair.

The grant. She was going to lose everything because she'd fallen back in love with the one person she shouldn't have. She risked a glance at Leo, but he was locked in place, fists clenched and expression furious. He looked ready to explode, but Carlisle carried on with his casual evisceration of their lives.

"Or you could resign. Then the grant stays in place, and it doesn't matter what you do in your personal life." His smile was triumphant. A master chess player moving into checkmate.

The men locked eyes, and Faith was scared to even fidget for fear they'd point those flinty stares at her and she'd be turned into stone.

Finally Carlisle gave a jovial smile and waved at someone over Leo's shoulder. "I need to get back to the foundation. So much paperwork to review, you know, and a six-month probationary review just around the corner. I'm sure it's all on the up-and-up, but if it's not..."

God, the probationary review. So many ways BUILD could lose its funding. A quick glance at Leo wasn't any help; his chest rose and fell as he took in great gulps of air, but he still said nothing.

Carlisle dropped any pretense of a smile as he leaned forward to get right in Leo's face. "Be in my office first thing tomorrow with your resignation letter or with paperwork terminating the grant. Your choice."

He pulled back and straightened his shirt cuff. "I warned George Voit you were a bad choice." He sniffed, then he turned and walked away.

After a stunned moment, Faith was the first to speak.

"Fuck that guy. We didn't do anything wrong."

Leo looked queasy. "I pushed the board to approve

you for a grant you didn't apply for." His voice creaked from his throat. "I told them you were on board before you'd agreed. We had sex in a closet two seconds after you signed the paperwork."

Faith's heart sank. "Yes, but—"

"We've been sleeping together for almost a month. It doesn't look good, Faith."

Sleeping together? Was that all they'd been doing? She'd thought they were building something real, something permanent. And she'd thought he felt the same, but now he was reducing it to a just month of sex? She pressed her fingers to her mouth and was surprised to find them trembling. "Okay." She exhaled a steady stream of air, groping for calm. "Okay. But nothing started between us until after I signed—"

"It doesn't matter." He was looking everywhere but at her. "He's a thirty-year veteran, and I've been here for barely six months. He's got all the power here. I'm just..."

He swallowed but didn't finish the thought, and Faith gestured wildly around the room.

"So we'll network. We'll find you another job."

Another thick silence enveloped him as he rotated ever so slowly to face her.

"What?"

His surprise shocked her, and she lurched to her feet.

"What do you mean *what*? I assumed..."

"You assumed I'd *quit*?"

She blinked at his outrage. "Well, yes." She held up a hand when he started to growl. "You're good at everything I've seen you do! Digham, POR, hiking and camping, Dig Greener. You'd land on your feet!"

"And you wouldn't?" he snapped.

"Probably," she snapped back. "But it's not just me, is

it? It's William and Jonah and my other employees. It's all those kids, Leo. Big Dig will be fine without you, and you can find another community organization to work for. But without that grant, BUILD goes away, and those kids lose all those programs. Do you want that?"

"No!" He plunged his hands into his hair, ruining his careful wave. "Of course not. But..."

Her breaths were starting to come faster. "Without the grant, I can't keep BUILD going. God knows I never would've worked with you in the first place if I'd had any other options."

He turned liquid eyes on her, hurt and anger rolling off him, and she shook her head sharply. "I don't mean it like that, but Leo, *come on*. You know I was desperate."

A gust of wind caught a strand of her hair, whipping it across her cheek. She impatiently batted it back, noticing as she did that people were openly staring. Leo noticed too, and a dull flush crept over his cheeks. He wrapped a hand around her elbow and started to pull her toward the exit, but she yanked free, grabbing her purse and clutching it to her chest with a glare. He stepped back and gestured for her to lead the way out, which she did with a lift of her chin. Once they were in the hallway, he glanced up and down until he spotted that same storage room door.

"Don't even think about it," she snapped, digging in her heels when he tried to guide her toward it with a hand on the small of her back.

Her chest ached. What if she'd said no to being manhandled into that closet all those months ago? If they'd never had that anonymous-yet-not encounter, maybe they could've avoided this moment. The feelings and the fallout. Then again, maybe this moment was always inevitable once they were back in each other's worlds.

"You want to talk in the hallway, fine," Leo said.

"Fine," she spat back.

"I know how you feel about BUILD. Of course I do, and I'll do everything I can to protect it." He reached for her hand, and in a moment of weakness she let him take it. Let herself enjoy his warm, strong fingers wrapped around hers. "But Faith, my job's important too."

His touch turned from comforting to restrictive. "Your job? You said it yourself, you've barely been there for six months!" She pulled her hand back to stare at him incredulously.

"Which means if I quit now, I failed. And they were right. Everybody who..." He clenched his jaw as he fell silent.

"Everybody who *what?*" Her voice was sharp, but she wasn't feeling particularly soft-hearted at the moment.

"Everybody who told me I'd never survive in an office. Who didn't think I was... smart enough."

He mumbled the last two words, and her anger dropped. "No." She rested her hand on his arm. "You've always been smart enough. You're great at your job. It's just—"

"Just nothing." He shook her hand off, engaged in the fight again. "Didn't you once say you were the reason I graduated from high school? Don't tell me I don't have anything to prove. To you. To people like your dad. I'm not quitting."

All she could do was stare at him, her heart pumping like she was running a race.

"Besides," he added, "I'm the only one of us who's paying rent at the moment, aren't I, duchess?"

He was going there? He was goddamn going there?

Kind. Calm. Motherfucking enraged.

Any trace of sympathy fled as she accepted that he was never going to forgive her for her upbringing. That daddy's money shit was going to come up over and over and over until his resentment poisoned everything. For a moment, all she wanted to do was collapse onto the polished concrete floor and weep at the unfairness of it all. Instead, she lifted herself to her full height and pushed all the ice in her veins into her voice so she'd cut him the way he'd just cut her.

"Fine. Don't worry about me or my grant. You can keep your precious job." She watched with satisfaction as the blood drained from his face.

She turned and made it two steps before he called after her. "Dutch, wait."

Hope leaped in her chest. He was reconsidering. He was willing to save her life's work. But she almost crumbled when she saw his bleak expression.

"Let me at least drive you home." He lifted his hand, then let it fall when she stared at it in disgust.

He wasn't going to change his mind. She was on her own.

"No, thanks." A bitter taste coated her tongue. "I'll figure something out. I always do."

He didn't stop her when she walked away this time, which was just as well because she couldn't hold back the tears anymore. She strode down the hall toward the elevator, digging through her purse to pull out her phone to call a Lyft, when she collided with a man in a suit.

"Hey! Careful."

A pair of hands steadied her, and she whipped her head up to see a blurry blond face. She dashed the tears out of her eyes and groaned. "How are you always where I don't want you to be?"

Brandon Lowell smirked at her. "Great to know I've made an impression."

She opened her mouth to snap something back at him. She was Faith Fox. She had a retort for every circumstance. But to her horror, all that came out was a watery sob.

His expression immediately shifted to discomfort. "Hey." He patted her shoulder awkwardly. "It's okay."

She shook her head as she rooted around in her bag for a tissue. "It's not." Dammit, of course she didn't have anything to blot with when she really needed it.

"Stay." Having commanded her like a dog, Brandon disappeared into the bar area only to reappear with a handful of cocktail napkins. "Here."

"Thanks." She miserably wiped at her eyes, and the napkin came away mascara-smeared. "Oh my God, I have to get out of here."

"I wasn't in the mood to have networking drinks anyway. Shall we?" He gestured toward the elevator, and she nodded.

"Why not? You're cheaper than a Lyft."

"I'm lots of things, but I'm not cheap." He pressed the Call button and followed her in after the doors rumbled open.

She snuck a glance at him on their way down to the attached parking garage. She'd spent next to no time with him, but even through her own haze of misery she could see that he was still struggling. His features were still sharply elegant under the harsh lighting, but his eyes were shadowed and the lines around his mouth were deeper than they'd been the last time she'd seen him. Even his normally razor-neat hair was looking untrimmed. He was still the picture of privileged upper-class beauty, but the seams on his normally immaculate facade were showing.

He opened the passenger-side door of his low-slung black Porsche that he'd almost run her down with a few weeks ago, and she set aside her own heartache to ask, "How are things going?"

Brandon said nothing, just shut her door and walked around to his side. Only after he was settled in did he respond.

"Worse."

She exhaled in sympathy but didn't press for details, and he didn't seem inclined to share, instead asking, "Where am I taking you?"

She rattled off the address, and he entered it into the nav system. Before he pulled away from the curb, his eyes slid over to her legs, visible in her favorite swingy skirt.

"I'm still not sleeping with you," she muttered, adjusting the red fabric to cover as much of her knees as she could.

"I'm still not asking." His response was unruffled. "Then again"—his eyes returned to her legs—"you're not leaving here with tall, dark, and angry, are you?"

She turned to glower at him, but with that smirk back on his face, he at least looked a little less sad.

"My life may have collapsed," he said with a shrug as he backed out of the parking spot, "but I still keep tabs on every hot woman in the room."

"Wow. I'm flattered," she said flatly.

"You should be." Arrogant was actually a pretty good look for him. If only she was in the market. "Want to tell me about the fight with the boyfriend?"

"Nope."

"Okay." He inserted his ticket into the parking garage machine, and the mechanical arm lifted to turn them loose on the streets of Beaucoeur. "Ride in silence, listen to the radio, or carry on inconsequential conversation so neither of us have to think about how empty we both are inside?"

"Um. Inconsequential conversation over the radio?"

He flipped it on, and low music filled the car. "Can you believe this weather?"

For the rest of the ride they chatted away like two kids who'd grown up surrounded by preoccupied adults, which is exactly what they were. It kept her brain busy enough that she didn't dwell on her bruised heart.

When he pulled into her parents' massive drive, Brandon gave a whistle. "I changed my mind. Sleep with me. Make me your kept man."

She snorted. "This belongs to my parents, but if you're patient, I'll probably inherit it someday."

The playfulness fell from his face, and he sagged like she'd shot him in the gut. "Don't be so sure about that."

Oh, she recognized that mixture of fear and anger in his voice. Once upon a time she too went from having everything to having nothing. It wasn't her business, and she should just thank him and head inside. But instead, she turned so her back was against the car door and she could see his profile as he leaned against the headrest. His mouth was pulled taut, his eyes shut.

"You don't have to tell me the details, but is this is a money thing? As in you suddenly don't have what you used to?" She glanced at the house where she'd grown up, with its rows of windows and four sets of columns and the fountain in the center of the circular drive. She didn't know a single other person in Beaucoeur whose house had a fountain. "It sucks, but you'll be okay in the end. You've still got *you*, after all."

His eyes snapped open, and his fingers tightened around the steering wheel.

"I'm not sure that's much to work with." Then his nostrils flared, and he released his grip, turning something almost like his usual self-assured smile her way. "I appreciate it though. Good luck with your boyfriend."

"Thanks." She popped the door open and climbed out, holding her skirt against her thigh so she wouldn't flash her vajean as she climbed out of the low vehicle. "Good luck with your life."

Before she could shut the door, he leaned across the seat. "Hey, if things don't work out with you two, track me down. I'm sure I'll be back in the saddle in a few weeks."

She rolled her eyes and slammed the door, and he peeled out, leaving her on her parents' doorstep. All the lights were off, which meant they were out for the night.

An unexpected swell of sorrow hit her. Had she actually been hoping to tell them what had happened? Let her mom hug her and her dad promise everything would be okay? God, nothing in her life made sense anymore. The only thing she could think to do was change into her pajamas, crawl into bed, and hope that she'd eventually wake up in Leo's bed to discover that the past few hours had all been a bad dream.

TWENTY-NINE

Leo had been staring at the laptop screen for so long that the words had started to blur. Conflict of interest. Violation of policies. Recusal. Termination.

The Digham Foundation bylaws made it clear: he was fucked. Everything good in his life was going to slip away because no matter what he chose, he had to give up something he loved.

The slam of the door to the garage and the stampeding of multiple feet pulled him away from his doomscrolling. William found him in the dining room, took one look at his expression, and said, "Jesus, who died?"

"Oh my God, is Mom okay? Dad?"

That got his attention. He blinked. Blinked again. Yep, that was his middle sister Cece standing in the kitchen while their nephews shrieked and ran laps around the island, shouting "Bendición, Uncle Leo!" Because why not? Why not make this shitty day even more chaotic?

"Dios te bendiga," he called back, still trying to make sense of this invasion of family.

"Oye! Muñeco!" Cece got in his face, snapping her fingers at him. "I asked if our parents are okay. And Abuela?"

"They're fine," he said hastily. "Everybody's fine."

Cece let out a breath, while William sucked one in. "It's Faith, isn't it?"

He nodded miserably, his stomach sinking even more when his sister's eyes narrowed.

She turned to William. "You guys have video games, right?"

"Nintendo Switch."

"Sammy! Carlos! Mateo!" The boys stopped shrieking and gathered around their aunt. "William's going to get you set up to play *Super Smash Brothers*. Go. Play. Be quiet. Your uncle and I need to have a talk."

They shrieked and followed William to the TV room. Once the decibel level had dropped, Leo was able to think straight enough to ask, "What's happening right now?"

Cece slumped into a dining room chair with a groan. "Ranger Rick wanted to do a make-up hike after your trip got rained out. Vani had to work, so I volunteered to pick up the boys and be the second adult."

"Bet you hated that." His world might be ending, but he could still give his sister shit for her obvious crush on William.

She swished her hair over her shoulder. "It was a sacrifice." Her face lit up when the man in question reentered the room, and she artfully positioned herself on the edge of the seat with another toss of her hair.

"What happened?" William sat down in the chair opposite Cece, not wasting time on niceties.

His sister's flirty face dropped, and she folded her

arms over her chest with a fierce scowl. "What did the blanquita rica do now?"

"It wasn't her. Mostly." He scrubbed a thumb over his eyebrow. "My boss caught us together at Olive Twist. Gave me an ultimatum: I quit, or she loses her funding. Or maybe both if he finds anything off about her paperwork."

Which he very well could. Fuck.

"Fuck." William said out loud, face slack. And didn't that just make Leo feel even shittier?

"I'm sorry," he said. "You warned me."

"I did. But I'm sorry too." William tilted his head toward the ceiling, the cogs in his brain already at work. "So the problem isn't any self-dealing."

"No," Leo said immediately. That was the one thing he was sure of. The IRS rules against foundations enriching themselves didn't apply here since they were talking about grant money instead of property or leases or goods and services. "There's no private benefit, no disqualified people. The problem's the foundation bylaws."

He shoved his laptop toward William, who skimmed the same document Leo'd been staring at for two hours.

"So your boss is pissed that you gave money to your girlfriend?" Cece drummed her nails against the tabletop, the tap-tap-tap burrowing directly into his skull where a headache was brewing.

"I don't"—God, he was already exhausted by the excuses he'd been making to himself and everyone else for way too long—"I don't vote on the grants. That's the board of directors. I just vet them, then oversee them once they're paid out."

William gestured to the screen. "The foundation

rules state that Leo needed to disclose his relationship with Faith and recuse himself from all involvement with her grant."

He plunged his fingers into his hair. "Relationship... I mean, how do you define that? *She and I* have barely defined it. It's only been a couple of weeks."

His eyes snapped up at Williams' scoff. "You two have been sniffing around each other since the day I got here."

"Before that," Cece said. "Vani and Jessie and I saw this coming from a mile away. He's always been hopeless when it comes to the blanquita."

Hopeful. He'd been *hopeful*. Until today, anyway.

"She expected me to quit," he muttered. "Didn't even ask me about it. Just assumed." He pressed his lips together, but it wasn't enough to keep the next part in. "And she got a ride home from the bar with someone else. Some blond guy. I saw them leave together."

The only sound in the room was the scrape of Cece's chair over the wood planks of the dining room floor. She calmly unhooked one of her earrings, then the other, as she stood. "What's her address?"

"Not necessary." But Leo's muttered words weren't enough to cut through the sisterly rage.

"What. Is her. Address?" Cece was trembling now, and she had her phone out. Fuck, if she was texting Vani and Jess, there might actually be a murder tonight.

William shot him an alarmed glance, but Leo made a quick motion from under the table for his friend to stand down. He'd been dealing with sister drama from birth.

"Cece. Cecilia." He spoke her name calmly, hoping it would get her attention. "Nobody's going to anybody's house. I said some things too, okay? Neither of us was at our best in the moment. And Faith's a lot of things, but she's not out looking for revenge sex right now."

He hoped not, anyway. *Coño.*

His sister met his eyes for a brief stare-down before she huffed and dropped into her chair, shoving her phone back in her purse. "Okay. *For now.*"

That was one crisis averted. Now to the looming disaster.

"I don't want her to lose her funding. But I don't want to lose my job. Her dad..."

He breathed in hard, and Cece's face softened. "What about her dad?"

"He was so nice to me." He was almost embarrassed to admit how good that had felt. "We talked about Digham, about what I was doing there. It felt like I was finally good enough. Like this job is how I make myself good enough for her."

"Fuck that." This time the anger came from the opposite side of the table, and William's hands fisted as he spoke. "You don't have to prove anything to anybody."

William didn't know the whole story of their first breakup. But Cece did.

"I get it," she said, her voice gentler than he'd maybe ever heard it. "Billy's right. You're the best guy I know, and you don't have anything to prove. But I get why that job's important to you. We weren't exactly supportive when you told us about it."

He shrugged, although the memory of his family's skepticism still stung.

"We were wrong," she said. "And we all said so."

That was news to him. "You did? When?"

"Not to your face, obviously." She waved a dismissive hand, then looped her earrings back into her ears. "But all of us hear things. Mom and Dad. The aunties. People tell them when they see you out volunteering, or when you talk at their kids' school. Titi Marie loves that yarn you helped make."

"Cece," he began, but his throat closed up, the words dying on his lips. Her expression told him that she understood enough.

"What you're doing is important." She reached out and squeezed his hand. "But you're important too, with or without that job."

They exchanged smiles, and no matter what happened, he'd made the right decision in moving back home. He'd missed his family.

"So you don't want to quit." William had no problem interrupting their sibling moment. "But I'd like to keep my job too."

Right. The issue at hand. "Now you see my problem." Leo threw himself back against his chair.

"Lawyer?" William asked.

"Maybe. I mean, she and I weren't involved when I recommended her for the grant, and I haven't done any program review activities since we started, you know..."

"Fucking?" Cece suggested.

He sucked in a deep breath. Exhaled. Spoke.

"I love her."

There. It was out, and now everyone was looking at him with pity. Yes, the sex was great. But it was also love, or at least it was for him. Faith, though... she'd walked away from him today. It was their graduation-day breakup all over again. Him standing still while she stormed out of his life.

"Oh." He snapped his fingers as one of the pieces from that afternoon fell into place. "That radio station asshole. That's who she left with." He knew he'd seen that weaselly face somewhere before.

"Maybe she was looking for new funding?" Cece suggested, and he was grateful that she was trying to put a positive spin on things for his sake.

"Yeah. Maybe." He sighed. "Anybody got any rich friends who want to fund an educational nonprofit with a strong emphasis on environmental issues?"

His sister laughed, but William tapped a finger to his lips in thought. "We did work with a lot of wealthy volunteers over the years, and POR has a few guardian angel donors. Maybe one of them wants to help with a domestic program. I could make some calls."

It was something. If they could replace the Foundation money with some other source, then Faith could keep her doors open, and he and William could both keep their jobs.

"But do you want to work at Digham if it means dealing with that asshole for the rest of your life?" Cece curled her lip.

"Oh, I refuse to give him the satisfaction of quitting," he said immediately. That's the one thing he knew to be true from the bottom of his heart. He'd never give Carlisle *that*. "Besides, the work I'm doing is important. I'd report to Satan himself if it meant I could make sure local programs get funding."

"Okay," Cece said. "So Billy shakes down some rich donors, and I prepare to kick Fea's ass at a moment's notice."

"Fe." His lips twitched. "She's onto you now."

Cece stuck out her chin. "I'll call her what I call her, and she'll take it."

William tipped his head to study her, expression

thoughtful. "I genuinely don't know which of you would win in a fight."

"Me," she preened. "I fight dirty."

Leo knew better than to count Faith out, but encouraging more speculation about the topic seemed unwise. Plus he didn't like the way William was eyeing his sister. Also, had Cece called him *Billy*?

God, now wasn't the time to worry about that. "Okay, let's focus. None of that can happen by tomorrow morning, so what can we do now?"

"I should probably feed the boys," Cece said.

William held up his phone. "I can order pizza."

Leo was too agitated to even think about food, but his nephews shrieked in delight thirty minutes later when the doorbell rang. After the adults settled them down with loaded plates and instructions not to wipe their greasy fingers anywhere but on a napkin, he accepted a slice of pineapple pepperoni, but it sat untouched in front of him as he considered the other tangle in this knot he'd created for himself.

"There's one more thing," he said reluctantly.

William and Cece both froze mid-chew, and William gestured with his free hand for Leo to continue.

"Faith only applied for the community grant." He shoved his plate away and rested his elbows on the table. "When the board voted her down, I told them she should also be considered for the Dig Greener money. Told them she'd also applied for that one too. And after they voted yes, I went back to my office and checked the box on her application and *then* called to see if that was okay."

William swiped at his mouth with a napkin. "Okay. So how bad is that?"

"Fuck if I know." He ruffled his hair, not caring that

he probably looked like a mad scientist by now. "But it's not gonna look great if anybody finds out, especially with the..." He circled his hand in the air, vaguely indicating sex.

The worried look that William and Cece exchanged wasn't helpful.

"I just wanted to help her," he said tiredly. "All anybody wants to do is make a difference, right? And help where they can?"

"Damn straight," his sister said. "So you tell the truth tomorrow. You suggested a worthwhile organization for funding, and after the grant was officially in place, you and the head of the organization got closer. Skip the details unless they press you."

William picked up the narrative from there. "You were in the process of asking her if it had gotten serious enough for you do the disclosure and recusal process when your boss found you and gave you the ultimatum."

"I was literally opening my mouth to ask if she was okay with me talking to Savannah today when Carlisle ambushed us." What a cluster.

"Shit. I need to go." Cece stood and picked up her plate. "Vani will cut me if I mess up the boys's bedtime routines."

She walked behind his chair, resting her hand on his shoulder as she kissed the top of his head. "Keep me updated?"

He squeezed her fingers. "I will. Thanks."

In a blink she collected the boys and their dirty dishes, stacked the mess in the kitchen, and had them all marching toward the door. She leveled a finger at him before she left.

"First dibs on kicking Fe's ass if it comes to that."

"You got it." At least she'd called her Fe. That was progress.

The house fell silent once his family had cleared out, and William ambled to the fridge to fetch them both beers. Leo accepted the bottle with a muttered "thanks" and popped the top. But instead of drinking, he stared at the label and relived all his mistakes. The ones from today, from a few months ago, from that last day of high school. So many fucking mistakes that brought him here.

"If she showed up at the front door right now," William asked, "what would you do?"

Leo's answer was immediate.

"Beg her for forgiveness. Tell her I know she's not some spoiled rich girl. That I respect the hell out of her. That I love her."

"But not enough to quit your job for her?"

His head snapped up. "Are you kidding me?"

"Sorry," William said. "But if you love her..."

"I do." Another sweep of his fingers through his hair, this time accompanied by a sigh that he pulled from the soles of his feet. As satisfying as he found his job, the truth was that he could find another if he had to. But in his whole life he'd never found someone he could love as much as he loved Faith. Not even close.

"I might," he said slowly. "Be willing to quit, that is. But fuck, I wish she loved me enough not to ask me to."

If she'd just held off on making assumptions, they could be sitting side by side at the table, making a plan together. But she'd put herself first. A Fox at heart. And yet he still loved her.

"Maybe she's reconsidered. Boss has a bit of a temper, yeah? Maybe she needed time to cool down." William pointed at Leo's cell phone, sitting on the table next to the laptop. "Doesn't hurt to call."

It'd hurt like hell if he did and she told him to go to hell. Knowing Faith, there was at least a twenty percent chance of that.

"No." He shook his head. "I won't let it go another twelve years, but I want to handle things myself tomorrow. It's my responsibility to fix it. She didn't do anything wrong. I did."

And if Carlisle found the digital copy of her original grant application, figured out what he'd done to make sure Faith got a board vote for the Dig Greener funds... well that was a different sin than falling back in love with her over the past six months, wasn't it? That was an intentional act on his part, and if there was a possibility that he could get fired for it, then maybe it was better to make a deal. Resign quietly to guarantee that her funding stayed in place. Carlisle might even go for it because if he went quietly, there'd be no scandal to attach to the foundation's name because of his paperwork tricks.

He looked up to see William's steady gaze on him. Supportive, no matter what.

Leo lifted his bottle in a resigned toast. "There are other jobs out there if it comes to that, right?"

"Buddy, if you can survive sharing a tiny tent with me for half a decade, you can do anything. We'll figure it out."

They tapped their bottles together and drank. Whatever happened tomorrow, he wasn't alone. And he'd fight like hell to hold on to everything he loved.

THIRTY

Faith sat in the dark and stared at her phone.

She should call him. She should call him, she should call him, she should call him.

But her fingers didn't move. She was huddled on her parents' TV room couch at seven in the morning with the lights off, too scared to even send a text.

What could she possibly say? She'd panicked. She'd screwed up. She'd made assumptions about what he wanted, what he'd prioritize. She'd been careless with him yesterday, just like she'd been careless with him years before.

She loved him.

Any of those things would be good, but her fingers refused to move.

Because she was scared. He'd pushed back yesterday, and if she called him, she might find out that he really did think she was just another spoiled rich kid who hadn't learned from her mistakes. And she wasn't sure she could recover from that.

The lights in the den flipped on without warning, and both she and her mother shrieked.

"Faith! Why are you sitting in the dark?"

Her mother's hands flew to the neck of her floral-print, quilted robe, exactly like the one she always wore in the mornings when Faith was a kid. Seeing her like that tugged something inside her to the surface, and rather than make excuses or slide out to hide in her room, Faith rushed forward and wrapped her arms around her in a hug.

Betsy hugged her back immediately, and as she guided Faith to the couch, she called, "Franklin!"

Her father appeared in the doorway a moment later, blinking at the two women. "What happened?"

"I... We..." Then to her horror, Faith burst into tears. The next thing she knew, both her parents were there bookending her on the couch, rubbing her back and murmuring soft words. Her dad handed her tissues, and her mom grabbed a throw pillow to put on Faith's lap so she could fold in on herself to weep.

She relayed the Olive Twist confrontation between sobs, and when she was done, she was greeted with parental silence.

"Well?" She scrubbed at her eyes. "Can you believe he'd do that? That he'd pull my funding without a second thought?"

Franklin and Betsy exchanged glances over her head, which vaulted the whole morning into bonkers-land. "Wait, you're taking his side?"

"We're always on your side, kiddo," her dad said. "But..."

She gaped at him, and her mom laughed softly.

"What's so funny?" She turned her shocked glare on her mother.

"You haven't cared what we thought for years," Betsy said carefully.

She twisted to lay her head in her mother's lap, pillow and all, and Betsy immediately started stroking her hair. She hadn't experienced this familiar comforting touch in so long that she couldn't speak for a moment.

"Well, I'm asking now," she finally said through a tight throat. "What should I do?"

Her father hesitated before answering, "We want what you want."

A year ago—hell, a month ago—she would've blown this off as her father not caring enough about her life to have an opinion, but something had shifted in the past few weeks. She'd changed, or they had, and she actually believed him. But that didn't mean she had an answer for him.

"I don't know what I want anymore," she confessed.

"Don't you?" Her mother brushed a lock of hair off her forehead and looked down at her in gentle surprise. "You've always gone after what you wanted no matter what anyone else tried to tell you."

"That's a nice way of saying stubborn."

Her dad laughed softly. "And we know who you got that from. But look what you've built. That took a strong will."

"And I'm going to lose it." Reality crashed in again, and she had to bite her tongue to keep from letting loose with another sob. "I know you guys don't care what happens to BUILD, but *I* do."

Her mother's hand stilled before she started stroking her hair again. "I'll admit we didn't understand it at first, but with you living here, we've seen more of what you do. We're so proud of you, honey."

"And not just because people like George Voit are too." Her dad gently patted her ankle, which was poking off the couch at an awkward angle, and Faith was so overcome with emotion that she didn't dare lift her face from the pillow. She was probably smearing epic levels of snot onto her mother's decor, but all her emotions seemed to be streaming out of her face right now.

"Whatever you want to do, we'll support you," he concluded.

What did she want?

"I want BUILD. I want the outdoor program. And I want Leo," she said. "I love him." Again. Still. She wasn't sure she'd ever stopped.

"Does he feel the same?" her mother asked with another stroke of her hair.

She shrugged helplessly.

"Well, it won't take much for him to start again, I would guess," her mom said. "Don't forget, we also saw the way he used to look at *you*."

"How did he look at me?" She pulled herself upright to whisper the question.

Her mom sighed. "Like he couldn't believe his luck. When you came downstairs in that prom dress your senior year..." She shook her head with a soft laugh. "The way his whole body surged toward you. No wonder we worried we'd end up extremely young grandparents."

"It's the same way he looked at you the night of the gala," her father added gruffly.

She pressed the pillow to her chest, where joy was tangling with sorrow. Her dad handed her another tissue, and she mopped her face and swiped at her nose.

"It's impossible." She crushed the soggy Kleenex in her fist. "I can't lose my funding, but it's not fair of me to ask him to quit. Making it work at Digham is really important to him." She glanced at her dad. "I think he thinks a corporate job will make you like him."

"All he has to do is love my daughter and treat her with respect," he said, eyes glistening. "The rest isn't important as long as you're happy."

So what *was* important? Continuing to rebuild her relationship with her parents was becoming a priority. And she wanted Leo in her life too, but she also wanted BUILD, and Dig Greener. Something had to give.

Then she remembered what she'd told Brandon last night when he dropped her off: she still had *herself*. She'd created BUILD out of nothing. She'd set aside her completely rational fear of children to tutor them in junior high gyms that smelled like moldy cottage cheese, and she'd turned up at countless school board meetings to advocate for whatever tiny line items they could spare in their annual budgets. She'd celebrated when she'd hired people to work directly with students, freeing her up for curricular design and administrative tasks. She didn't want to do it all from scratch again, but she would. If she lost the funding but she got to keep Leo, it'd be survivable. She could go back to working out of her car while she built BUILD back up again.

Then she remembered her other responsibilities. Elaine and Jonah and William, along with the BUILD part-timers. If she returned the money, they'd be jobless until she could figure something out.

She was back to square one. "This is about more than just me and him. I can't return the grant without letting down everyone on my payroll."

Her father cleared his throat. "You know, we do still have the money we set aside for your trust fund."

Her whole body jolted, a knee-jerk reaction to twelve years of independence, and she opened her mouth to turn him down. But Leo's job was on the line. So was hers and all her employees. And her father was offering a solution.

She exhaled hard and let go of the last shreds of her stubborn pride. "I'd like to try to fix this on my own. But if I can't, I'd be so grateful if I could use that money to keep BUILD running for a little longer."

Another look passed between her parents before her father spoke again. "What if Fox Industries set up its own foundation and made BUILD the first recipient? I don't know what your annual budget looks like, but between your trust and a Fox grant, it might at least cover payroll while you fundraise elsewhere."

She wasn't going to cry again. She didn't have enough moisture left in her body for more tears. Yet her cheeks were wet again.

"That would be incredible." She dashed away the tears so she could see her father's hopeful face more clearly. "And if I do manage to save Leo's job *and* my grant, I'd love it if you'd put that trust money into the Fox foundation for some other organization that needs it."

Her mom's face lit up. "And if your young man ends up without a job, we could use someone with experience to get things up and running."

Faith gave a laugh-sob, and her father gave her a solid pat on the back.

"Go talk to him," he said. "We're here for you, whatever happens."

"Thanks," she said, throat tight. Then she added, "I love you both."

Suddenly she wasn't the only one with tears in their eyes as her parents wrapped her in a two-sided hug that only ended when Faith reluctantly disentangled herself.

"I should probably call him," she said. "He's supposed to meet with his boss soon."

She scooped her phone off the floor, and her heart gave a little jump at the text on her lock screen. But it wasn't from Leo.

"Oh my God." She jumped off the couch. "I have to go. I love you both! I have to go!"

She bolted from the room without a backward glance, her parents's shouts of "We love you too" ringing in her ears.

Shoving her feet in the first pair of shoes she could find—her mom's gardening clogs—she launched herself into her car, dialing a number and fumbling for her headphones as she pulled out of the garage.

She read the text from William one more time as she waited for him to pick up.

"What the hell do you mean, he's *quitting*?" she barked when he answered.

"Exactly what I texted. When he left this morning, he was prepared to quit to make sure BUILD kept its funding."

William's voice had none of its usual warmth, and Faith winced at the damage she'd probably need to undo in that relationship. But not until she'd fixed things with Leo. "And why'd he leave his phone with you?"

"I'm not sure. His sisters were blowing it up this morning, so he shut it down, and then he left it in the kitchen."

"And he's already at Digham?"

"He didn't want to be late, so I made sure he left half an hour ago."

She cursed and glanced at the clock in her car. She had eighteen minutes before the meeting was supposed to start, which wasn't enough time for morning traffic and downtown stoplights and finding parking and haggling with security.

"Shit. Shit!"

She hit the gas and passed a car going fifteen below the speed limit on a residential street.

"I'll be honest," William said, "I'm not sure who to root for here. Because whatever happens today, somebody's out of a job."

She laid on the horn when the idiot in front of her didn't speed through the yellow light, catching them both at a red on the slowest stoplight in town.

"I'm going to take care of you," she promised. "I'll figure something out. Dig Greener's part of BUILD now, and I take care of my people. You'll have a job as long as I'm in charge. Go, go, go!"

The last bit was directed at the absolute knob in the left turn lane, who was backing traffic up on both sides of the intersection.

"I'm so relieved," he said drily. "The broke woman's making promises. At least Leo and I can both go back to POR if we have to."

She groaned. "Are you fucking with me right now?"

"Is that directed at me or some driver?"

"You! You're seriously suggesting that I just wave goodbye as Leo skips off to join *goddamn Reggie* in the sexy jungle?"

William's brief silence came to an end with a snort of laughter. "Well, I guess that answers that."

"What?" Finally a green light. She pressed the pedal all the way to the floor and shot through the intersection.

"How you feel about him."

Ah. That. "I love him so much that I'm willing to risk all our jobs to prove it to him."

"That's great!" William said. "I'm so— Wait, I thought you said you were going to take care of all of us."

"Gah! I will! Don't worry. I have to go." She disconnected and tossed her phone down on the seat next to her as she neared the series of badly timed stoplights stationed at every one-way downtown street. She could see the damn Digham building blocks in the distance, but the stupid traffic laws were keeping her from the love of her life.

Her phone chirped again. Thea. She scooped it up.

"*Leo's* going to *quit?*"

Her friend's agitated voice punched her eardrums, and Faith was almost too surprised to respond. "How on earth do you know about that?"

"One of Leo's sisters is a paralegal for Reynolds and Routh, and apparently one of the junior associates was at Olive Twist and saw the whole thing go down."

Faith accelerated, then had to stop immediately at another red. "Still not clear how you found out that he decided to quit. *I* just found out."

A burst of male laughter crackled over the line, which meant Thea was at the front desk of Murdoch Construction as the guys all drank coffee and gossiped and got ready for the day. She raised her voice to be heard over the noise.

"Aiden's redoing the kitchen at their firm. He's there taking measurements right now and overheard the lawyer asking Vanessa about it. She said when she called Leo this morning, he told her that the safest thing to do was resign to make sure your funding stayed put."

"No," Faith moaned, both because she'd hit yet another light and because she didn't want him to make this sacrifice for her.

"So yeah, I just wanted to let you know."

"I appreciate it, babes. I'm gonna go get my man back and make sure we both have jobs by the end of the day."

"If anybody can it's you," Thea said. "Love you. Call me when it's done."

She hung up as she reached the Big Dig parking garage, thank God. She whipped the car into the entrance, snatched the ticket from the machine, and wound her way up the structure until she found a spot. She tossed herself out of the car and jogged for the elevator, groaning when she looked down at herself.

Again. She was braving Big Dig HQ in the worst possible outfit *again*. If nothing else, maybe he'd see that her love for him was bigger than her vanity. She just had to make it to the eighteenth floor before he did something he couldn't take back.

THIRTY-ONE

Leo was already sweating, and the meeting hadn't even started.

Carlisle's door was shut, but he was in there. Enjoying making him wait, no doubt.

Darla met his eyes for the five hundredth time since he'd arrived, but this time she actually said something.

"I am so, so sorry," she said softly. "When he asked me where you'd gone, I had no idea he'd do *that*."

She pressed her lips together, the groove between her brows deepening. She was wearing her usual pale pink lipstick, and her hair was styled into its usual hard hat, but she looked pale and upset.

"It's okay. This was inevitable." His attempt to be reassuring missed the mark, and instead he sounded tired. Sleep hadn't come at all last night, and he was the kind of exhausted that coffee couldn't touch.

"Well, for what it's worth, I—"

Whatever Darla was about to say was lost when Carlisle threw his door open. He didn't say a word, just stared Leo down before turning and walking back into his office.

He sucked in a deep breath and stood. Was today the last day he'd put on a suit and tie to go into the office? Weird; he might actually miss that daily ritual of suiting up.

Darla leaned to the right as he walked by so she was close enough to whisper, "Good luck."

He smiled wanly. "Thanks." At least he had a friendly face to send him off. Nobody else was in yet this morning, but maybe that was for the best. Nobody'd be around to witness whatever was about to go down.

"Shut the door," Carlisle said crisply when he entered the room. "Have a seat."

Leo did as instructed. The back of his neck was hot, but his hands were cold. Carlisle was unruffled though, sitting across his enormous desk with a pleased look on his Spam-colored face.

"Sir, I—"

Carlisle raised an authoritative hand to cut him off, and Leo snapped his mouth shut, tension coiling in his stomach.

"I know I said yesterday that you had a choice between resigning or pulling your girlfriend's funding, but certain things have come to light since then that I'd like you to explain to me."

His stubby-fingered hand rested on top of a file marked Beaucoeur BUILD, and Leo immediately knew what was in there. Faith's original application and probably a copy of the one he'd submitted for final approval. The difference in the checkboxes. Fuck.

"Are you able to explain some discrepancies in—"

The door burst open. "Wait!"

Leo spun in his chair to see the most beautiful sight imaginable: Faith, wild-eyed, wild-haired, wearing Crocs and the rattiest Fall Out Boy sweatshirt he'd ever seen. She didn't spare a glance at Carlisle as she slammed the door behind her and walked straight over to him. "Don't quit for me."

His heart leaped, and that sick tension fled. She was *here*.

"I think I have to." He stood and took her hands.

"What is she doing here?" Carlisle said sharply.

Leo shrugged. "You'll have to ask her. She does what she wants."

"Yes, she does," Faith said. She turned her most disdainful gaze on Carlisle, her regal posture completely at odds with the sushi print on her pajama pants. "You thought you could bully the man I love into making a choice between his job and me, but I'm here to tell you that—"

The door flew open again.

"Carlisle, how could you?"

Both he and Faith turned to see Savannah slam the door shut and charge forward, cheeks flushed.

"We discussed this. No matter what you think about Leo personally, he's doing an outstanding job with the community grants. And if there's some kind of conflict with one of the recipients, I'll just take over that particular case."

She glanced at Faith and lost the rhythm of her speech as she absorbed the details of her outfit, but she quickly refocused. "I'll have all oversight with BUILD. Leo's recused, and we're able to keep a valuable new employee. There's no conflict here."

She folded her arms and glared at Carlisle, who

glared back. "There was a conflict from the beginning," he snapped. "The whole grant is tainted."

"Says who?" Faith asked hotly. "We weren't involved when the board voted and when I signed."

Skepticism twisted Carlisle's face, and Leo bit back a growl. At this point he wanted it all out in the open so this man had nothing over him.

"We got *involved* about three minutes after she signed," Leo said. When Faith turned to him with a *shut the fuck up* expression, he just shrugged. "I want to be honest about everything."

"Okay, but we didn't actually get into a real relationship until a month ago," Faith said.

For a second, they were the only people in the room. "So it's serious for you too?" he asked, heart in his throat as he waited for her to answer the question he'd intended to ask at Olive Twist the day before.

Her mouth softened. "Of course." She reached for his hand again, and he brought it to his mouth to press a kiss to her knuckles. Then he remembered their audience and glanced guiltily at Savannah.

Savannah beamed at him, then turned her hard stare back on Carlisle. "He just said the vote and her signature happened before they started dating. He can still recuse without conflict."

"I disagree," Carlisle snapped. "And he also needs to explain this." He reached for the folder, but before he could pull out the paperwork, the door slammed open again.

"Stop!"

"Char?" Leo was starting to wonder if he was having a fever dream. But no, his subconscious wouldn't be able to conjure up that lumpy brown hand-knit sweater on its own.

The tall woman advanced on Carlisle with an outstretched finger. "Are you the person who's destroying the best thing to ever happen to the Knit Nook?"

Carlisle shrank away from her angry point. "I have no idea what you're talking about."

Faith scoffed. "Take a guess."

"Him, of course!" Char flung her arm in Leo's direction. "He's kind. He's thoughtful. He works hard. I've got a shop full of people sobbing right now because they heard he's being forced to quit."

"How does everybody know about this?" Leo muttered, and Faith slipped an arm around his waist.

"The whole town's talking about it apparently." She squeezed him close. "My man's got community support."

He gazed down at her, lost in love for a second, when a knock sounded on the open door.

"While people are offering evidence," Darla said, stepping into the room with a stack of notes and papers, "I'd like to say that since the community grants rolled out, I've gotten more phone calls and thank-yous than I've ever seen. They're not all directly about Leo, but people in town are seeing the work that Digham's doing, and they're responding."

Savannah clapped in delight. "That's wonderful! See, Carlisle? All that important work we've always done overseas, but it's happening here now too."

Carlisle turned his furious gaze on Leo. "Is that everyone? Or should we expect more people off the street to join us?"

Was it wrong to enjoy his boss's discomfort as much as he did? He tugged one of his shirt cuffs a little straighter and said, "I had to beg my mother and sisters to stay away. If you think *this* is a scene, just know that it could be even louder."

Faith snorted, Char guffawed, and Carlisle slammed his hand on his desk.

"If everyone would please! Shut! Up!" he bellowed. "I've been trying to get him"—he pointed at Leo—"to explain inconsistencies in her"—the finger moved to Faith—"application."

Next to him, Faith's body tensed. "What's he talking about?" she asked quietly.

Leo squeezed his eyes shut briefly, then forced them open. This was it. No amount of defenders could explain this away.

He stepped forward, wanting to distance himself from Faith as Carlisle pulled two pieces of paper from the folder and held them up triumphantly.

"This is the original Beaucoeur BUILD application, time-stamped for a few minutes after the deadline." He glared at Leo and sniffed. "Already making exceptions."

Everyone in the room gave varying degrees of muttering and eye-rolling as Carlisle continued. "But you'll see that this original application cover sheet only has the community grant box checked and not the Dig Greener grant. But *here*"—he pointed to the second sheet with a flourish, like a prime-time defense attorney—"we see a different application cover sheet, time-stamped half an hour after the July meeting of the board. And what do we have?"

He brandished the sheet and got dead silence in return, so he answered his own question. "It's a check mark next to the Dig Greener box." He slammed the paper down on his desk in triumph. "That woman didn't apply for the environmental grant on her original application. It doesn't take a genius to wonder who changed her paperwork after the vote."

All eyes fell on Leo, but in that moment all the turmoil he'd been feeling for hours was gone. This was ludicrous. If Carlisle wanted him gone so badly, he could trust Savannah to carry on his work.

"I amended her application," Leo said in a clear, carrying voice. "Her program was a good fit, and I believed that it deserved full consideration by the board."

"It's not your place," Carlisle hissed, folding his arms over his chest.

"Actually, it is."

Every single head swiveled to look at the doorway as George Voit, the Big Dig CEO himself, strode into the room. The crowd parted so the small man could walk directly up to Carlisle, who'd fallen into a trembling silence.

"Mr. Lockhart, you know as well as I do that we hire our strategic grant managers to vet these applications and make sure the funding is going to the best possible sources," Voit said in a chiding tone.

As if they were watching a tennis match, everyone in the room turned to see Carlisle's response. His pink face reddened. "Yes, but he had no right—"

"Mr. Morales had every right," Voit said. "It's precisely why I hired him. He brings a unique perspective. I want him to be hands-on in all aspects of this job. The question is why *you* wouldn't want that."

Carlisle's mouth flopped like a fish. "Well, I... I mean, there's this inappropriate relationship."

Voit turned to Leo, who reached for Faith's hand.

"Inappropriate?" Voit laughed. "I saw these two

together at Ms. Fox's high school graduation party years ago, and I'm glad to see them together again."

Leo slid his eyes to Faith, who looked as poleaxed as he felt. This leader of industry had enough space in his brain to recall a relationship between two random teenagers from years ago and to then champion them now? Faith's eyes got even rounder as she apparently came to the same realization. All Leo could do was shake his head and wonder what surreal twist would come next.

It came from Darla, who delicately cleared her throat.

"Carlisle, wasn't your son-in-law the author of one of the Dig Greener grants that wasn't approved?"

Carlisle harrumphed as he studiously avoided meeting the eyes of anyone in the room. "That's not quite how I'd put it," he muttered as he straightened a paper on the desk.

Char gave a loud "Mm-hmm," and the room fell silent until Voit spoke again.

"I have a solution, if anyone would like to hear it." He didn't wait for any encouragement to share it, which was probably how he ended up in charge of a *Fortune* 100 company. "Mr. Morales will report to Ms. Goldbaum, and Ms. Goldbaum will report to me. Mr. Lockhart, you'll remain the public face of the foundation, attending all events and conferences and workshops, and you'll report to me. But Ms. Goldbaum will have complete oversight of all grants. Is this amenable to everyone?"

A smile spread across Savannah's face. "Yes. I'd like to take that on very much, sir."

Carlisle sputtered some more, but in the end, he nodded. "I accept. Although I want to see this all written up and *properly documented.*" He shot a poisonous glance at Leo, but it rolled right off his back.

He had his job. He had the respect of the community and the CEO. He had a direct report he enjoyed working with. And he had Faith's hand in his. God, he was glad to have her by his side for all this. His touchstone. His foundation.

"Darla, can you get started typing up that new workflow for review?" Savannah asked.

The silver-haired woman nodded and hustled out the door. Char quickly followed, stopping only to give Leo a bone-crushing hug. "Another yarn shipment's ready to go out if you have any time to help this week."

"Wouldn't miss it," he said after he'd wrestled his emotions back under control enough to speak.

George Voit tucked his hands in his pockets and rocked back on his heels to study him and Faith.

"I hear nothing but good things about Dig Greener," he said jovially. "Keep up the good work, you two." Then he, too, was gone, leaving them with Savannah and a visibly fuming Carlisle.

"I think the two of us need to have a conversation about the new workflow breakdown." Savannah gestured to the door. "Leo, if you wouldn't mind continuing your conversation with Faith in your own office?"

"Gladly."

He grabbed his girl by the hand and pulled her out of Carlisle's office. Darla waved her arms in a silent cheer as he hustled Faith through the main office, and he returned her gesture with an exuberant fist pump of his own. Then he ushered Faith into his office and shut the door behind them.

They were alone, and he didn't know where to start.

"Dutch." He pulled her into his arms. "Faith."

She smiled up at him, joy rolling off her. "Oh my God, we did it. And I'm so sorry for—"

He crushed his mouth against hers. They had time for the rest of it. The apologies. The explanations. And it probably wouldn't be the last time that her stubbornness and his pride got in the way, but as long as their fights ended in a kiss this hot and all-consuming, they'd be fine.

He pulled away far sooner than he wanted to, but they *were* at his place of work. And he had a question burning in his chest. "Dutch, you said something just now."

A blush touched her cheeks. "I said a few things."

"I'm most interested in you saying something about the man you love."

Her lips pursed as she pretended to search her memory. "Did I?"

"Do you?" He loosened his arms and stepped back, wanting to give her space to answer. His heart plummeted when she hesitated.

"Daddy's money." Her lips tightened, and she looked nervous for the first time all morning. "You've mentioned it a few times, and I have to know. Is that going to be a thing with you forever? Because I can't change how I grew up."

"I wouldn't change anything about you." He spoke firmly, anxious to banish the nerves on her face. "Our past is our past. I just know that I need you in my future."

"Okay. In that case." She stepped back into his arms and buried her face in his neck. "I love you so much, Leo." She lifted her chin to meet his eyes with hers, steady and shining. "And not the way I did when we were kids. That's still there. That never went away. But on top of that is…"

She shrugged, at a rare loss for words. So he offered some.

"Everything. On top of that is everything you are today. And I love every part of you."

And then he slid his fingers into her moonlight hair, but he paused before he kissed her.

"No blue today?"

She tilted her face up and brushed her lips gently against his. Joy trickled through his veins at the realization that those light, teasing touches would be his for the rest of his life.

"Nope," she said. "I don't need courage. I've got you."

EPILOGUE

ONE MONTH LATER

Faith gave one last glance at her reflection in her compact, nodded in approval, and stepped out of the Lyft. The rumble of Las Vegas Boulevard fell away as her eyes landed on the best-looking man she'd ever seen.

Leo stalked up to her, brows furrowed. "You look..." He swallowed hard, and his hands moved everywhere: over her shoulders, down her back, around her waist. "You look incredible. Is this...?"

"A white version of the dress I wore to the foundation gala?" Lucky her, it came in two colors. She grabbed his hand and used it to steady herself as she spun. "You seemed to like it, so I thought I'd surprise you." The skirt flared, giving him what she hoped was an appropriately scandalous glimpse of her leg. When she was facing him again, he looked like he'd swallowed his own tongue. Mission accomplished.

"Marry me." He pulled her close and growled the words into her ear, and she laughed and rested her hands on the lapels of his tuxedo.

"I believe that's the reason we caught a redeye last night."

They might not be starting their life together in a log cabin in the woods, but the Little Church of the West was the closest thing she could find with its redwood exterior and pioneer town vibes. And life was long; maybe someday they'd achieve Leo's childhood goal. For now, she was elated that the rest of their long-ago dreams were coming true.

"You got everything set up?" she asked. He'd gone ahead to make the arrangements while she finished getting ready. And if she were being honest, she'd wanted the big arrival moment, had wanted to see his face when he saw her in her dress on their wedding day. He hadn't disappointed her.

"All set," he said. "But are you sure you don't want our families here? Our friends?"

She wanted to celebrate with them, of course, but that's what their big, splashy Beaucoeur reception was for. Today was about the two of them.

"All I want is you, Leonidas. Let's get hitched."

His eyes blazed. "Let's get hitched." He traced a thumb down the line of her neck, but he didn't kiss her yet. She was familiar with every part of this man's romantic heart and knew he was waiting until he'd be kissing her as her husband.

"Leo and Faith?" An assistant with a clipboard called their names from the doorway into the church and beckoned them forward.

"Ready?" He held out his hand.

She took it. "Ready."

*Want to drop in on Leo and Faith's wedding reception?
Click here for this sweet, swoony bonus epilogue:*
www.sarawhitney.com/fate

A FREE hot-cook-next door romance? Yes, chef!
www.sarawhitney.com/vibes

You can also scan the QR codes to grab these bonus reads on your phone:

 The bonus epilogue

 The free novella

ACKNOWLEDGMENTS

Writing this book was not without its challenges. (Snicker, snort, understatement.) Heartfelt gratitude goes to Tanya, who let me pick her brain about all things Boricua. Leo and his family wouldn't be here without you. Thank you for all the fraaaaanch toast. Then there's Natalie, who said, "Just make it an outdoor education grant" and saved the whole book, and Erin, who sent me that clip of Will Bailey talking to Toby Ziegler and honestly saved *me* a little bit. Nat and Erin also patiently answered my ridiculous outdoorsy questions; I now know that the answer is always wool socks. I love all three of you so much. Thanks for putting up with me.

I also owe a debt of gratitude to authors Genevieve Jack and Jordan Bloom, who made immensely helpful suggestions in the book's final stages, as did Holly and Spooky and Jenny and Colleen. And author Skye Malone: thanks, always. The more hotter is for you. Bottomless thanks goes to Amy from my real-world Beaucoeur for sharing her foundation knowledge and to Brigid from the Heaving Bosoms writers' group for answering my panicky question about whether the ending of this book held together legally.

Any mistakes about tents, grants, camping, coquito, Starved Rock, and Ashton Kutcher are entirely mine.

ALSO BY SARA WHITNEY

Cinnamon Roll Alphas

Tempting Heat

Tempting Taste

Tempting Talk

Tempting Lies

Tempting Fate

Hot Under The Mistletoe

My Fake Bad Boyfriend

My Holiday Hookup Road Trip

My Not-So-Secret Santa

My Wicked Winter War

Standalone Novellas

Game On

Ghosted

Bold Vibes Only

PRAISE FOR SARA WHITNEY

Tempting Heat

"Perfectly written, hits all the beats... It was a real pleasure to read." *Jen Prokop, the Fated Mates podcast*

Tempting Taste

"Sara Whitney pulled together the most fun you'll have in a bakery with this one! Hello to my new book boyfriend." *Christina Hovland, author of the Mile High Matched series*

Tempting Lies

"The right blend of sass and steam. Sara Whitney's smooth, upbeat prose is a delight to read. I devoured it fast. Too fast." *Elle Greco, author of the LA Rock Star Romance series"*

Tempting Fate

"It balanced sweet, spicy, emotional and hilarious so incredibly well." *Sarah, Book Obsession Confessions*

My Holiday Hookup Road Trip

"Steamy and funny and just a damn good time." *Beth, B and her Books*

My Fake Bad Boyfriend

"This story had me laughing out loud from start to finish, and I completely adored it... One of my favorites of 2021." *Laurie, Laurie Reads Romance*

ABOUT THE AUTHOR

Sara Whitney worked as a journalist and film critic before she earned her Ph.D. and entered academia. She divides her time between professoring, authoring, and entertainment journalism, and she almost certainly has an opinion about your favorite TV show.

Sara writes her sexy, sunny romance novels in Illinois, where she's surrounded by books, cats, half-full coffee cups, and practically empty bags of Swedish Fish.

Keep up with the latest news (and snag a copy of enemies-to-lovers romp *Game On* for free!) by subscribing to Sara's mailing list at **www.SaraWhitney.com/VIP** or use your phone's camera to scan the code below:

www.ingramcontent.com/pod-product-compliance
Lightning Source LLC
LaVergne TN
LVHW030240250326
834688LV00047B/1727